Treasured: A Higher Realms Novel

Treasured: A Higher Realms Novel

* * *

Patricia J Ricks

Patricia J Ricks
patriciajricks.author@gmail.com

www.patriciajricks.com

Cover by Fiona Jayde Media
www.fionajaydemedia.com

Special thanks to the editor, Lindsey of Eschler Editing
www.eschlerediting.com

Interior book design © 2013, BookDesignTemplates.com

Colorado Springs / Patricia J Ricks — First Edition

ISBN 978-0-578-46889-1

Printed in the United States of America

Dedicated to my family and friends

1

The Beemer

Tara MacInnes slammed her book closed as a crack of thunder and lightning lit up the car.

"They're just stories," She told herself, setting the book aside on the leather seat next to her. Tara loved getting lost in stories and letting her imagination run wild, especially ones about fairies, trolls, giants and so on. She loved them all.

Tara sat back in the driver's seat of the Beemer and watched as big drops of rain hit the windshield and then slid down, making little rivers. She had been sitting in the car in the big circular drive of her parents' estate for over an hour and had hoped the rain would have stopped by now. No such luck.

Tara thought about the story she had been reading – a prince who falls in love with the wrong girl when he was supposed to marry the princess.

The princess's father, the king, was a tyrant, and her mother – well let's just say Tara was glad her mother was nothing like that. As Tara grabbed her book and shoved it in her bag along with the keys, her phone let her know she had a message. She eagerly grabbed her phone, hoping it was from Mark. It was from her Dad. They had landed in Scotland. Another message came in, and this time it was Mark. She quickly opened up the message. He was back from his trip and wanted to see her. Mark had been Tara's good friend since fifth grade, although she wanted him to be more. He had never asked her out, which for Tara was positively unacceptable. However, she was too shy to ask him, that was part of her problem; she was not assertive enough, nothing like every other girl he had dated.

"He wants to see me!" She practically screamed as she put her phone in her bag. Tara took a deep breath she then opened the car door. The rain fell down harder. "Seriously?" She yelled as she slammed the door and ran for the house. Tara quickly ran up the steps and as she opened the door another loud crack of thunder made her yell. She briskly stepped into the large foyer and slammed the door. She never liked thunder or lightning when it was so close, although she liked to watch and listen to it when it was far away.

"Alana! I'm home!" she yelled as she kicked off her soaking wet sneakers. Her wet bare feet felt cold against the smooth marble flooring. Tara shivered as she felt the water run down her head, her long dark hair a stringy mess like a seeping wet mop. The wetness soaked through her clothes and clung to her skin. The late spring rains in Connecticut could still be fairly cold. Alana was the head maid at the estate, and Tara's nanny, even though she was too old for a nanny now. She still relied on Alana more than she should at her age.

"Ah! Tara! Tis guid tae hae ye hame lass!" Alana exclaimed in her thick Scottish brogue accent as she kissed Tara's cheek. Alana was from Scotland like Tara's father, although not the same area.

"Och! Look at ye, drooched tae th'bane." She handed Tara the towel she had in her hand.

"Thanks." Tara wiped off her face, then bent down to wipe off her feet and she started cleaning up the puddles she had made.

"Never ye mind that now lass, I'll clean it up later." Alana grabbed the towel as Tara stood up.

"Hae ye heard fae yer parents?"

"Yeah, they landed safely." Alana nodded her head.

"It's not fair, Alana!" Tara blurted out as she pulled her bag back up on her shoulder, which had slipped down her arm. "I didn't mean to wreck Dad's old car, I was just so mad that my luggage went to Boston instead of here. Now instead of going with my parents they are making me get a job for the summer to help pay for the damages." She let out a deep sigh. Alana stood their hands on her hips. She smiled and nodded her head, which is what she would usually do if there was something she wanted to say but thought better of it.

Tara continued. "I didn't mean to run that stop sign, and now my summer is ruined!"

Alana made a clicking sound with her tongue, as she often did when her patience was being tried.

✳ 4 ✳

"I can't even be in the summer riding program at school. I worked hard to get into that program, too." Tara's parents had sent her to attend an all-girls school, with no boys to distract her from her studies. Oh, but there were plenty of distractions, like the boys' school up the road. She had been attending The Ethel Walker School, which had the best equestrian program in the country – another distraction, though not at first. Her parents thought it would be a good school for her to attend to try to get over her fear of horses, and it had helped, however the fear was still there.

"Ye better gang change yer drookit claes afore ye catch a cauld."

Tara, who had made it a few steps up the staircase, turned around. "Yes, I am going to change my clothes right now, and no, I am not going to catch a cold." She went up a few more steps then turned around again.

"You know what I was thinking, Alana? All those stories you told me growing up, and the ones I have read, mostly about fairies. Well, what if they were real? Fairies, I mean. Well then, I could just sprinkle fairy dust on that stupid wrecked car, and Bam! Good as new." Alana let out a chuckle as Tara let out a big sigh.

"Ah will bring ye up some het cuppa 'n' scones. Och 'n' yer luggage is in yer room."

"Yes, my luggage, oh and tea and scones would be great. Thanks Alana!" Tara got another message on her phone, so she ran up the rest of the stairs, flung open her door, slammed it shut and quickly found some cozy jammies to change into. She saw her suitcases strewn on the floor, however decided to unpack them later. She opened up the message on her phone, hoping it was from Mark, which it was. Tara grabbed a towel and plopped on her bed, drying her hair as she read the message. He wanted to see her tomorrow! She told him she could stop by his work close to when his shift was over. He also told her he had broken up with Arlene.

"Wow," Tara thought as she read that. It surprised her to hear it, since they had been dating for over a year. Arlene was tall, athletic, and very, well, gorgeous. Like the girls you would see in the Sports Illustrated swimsuit magazines. Tara felt plain near her. Tara did not consider herself to be very athletic, though she did enjoy hiking, fishing, yoga, swimming, canoeing, and riding – none of which she really did competitively. Reading, however, she did anytime she could.

She put the wet towel in her laundry basket and realized the room felt a bit stuffy, so she went over to the window and opened it. The rain was coming straight down softly now, and there was no thunder or lightning, much to her relief. She watched as the gentle breeze coming in made her curtains blow into her room, rippling as if they were waves on water. She breathed in the fresh, cool air that had a hint of the sea.

"Ah," Tara said contentedly as she leaned on the windowsill. She turned around and grabbed the book her Grandparents had given her. She had just gotten comfortable when there was a knock on her door.

"Come in," Tara said and Alana came in with a tray. Tara set her book down. "Oh good, tea and scones." Alana set the tray down on her bedside table. Tara's phone rang, and she saw that it was her mother calling.

"Hi, Mum," she said, and then just listened. After a moment, she said, "Gran fell and broke her hip? Is she going to be okay?" Then she nodded as she listened, and relayed what her Mum was saying so Alana could hear.

"Grandpa took her to the hospital because she needs surgery, so Mum and Dad are driving there now." Alana nodded her lips pierced tight, as she poured some tea for Tara. "Okay, love you too. Okay, Dad, bye." Her father of course had joined in on the conversation, like he usually did. Tara hung up the phone.

"Dinna fash yirsel Tara, a'm sure yer Gran wull be braw." Alana patted Tara's shoulder.

"I know she will be fine, I just wish I was there too."

Alana sat down on the edge of the bed. "Ah ken that ye wish ye cuid be there, a'm sorry ye aren't."

"Yeah," Tara said taking a sip of her tea. "That's so good, just what I needed."

Alana nodded, then stood and went to the window.

"Shuid ah claise yer windae? Tis getting mirk?"

Tara looked out her window. It was getting dark and she could see short bursts of lightning off in the distance. The rain still came down steadily. "Ah, no Alana, keep it open."

Alana nodded and turned to walk towards the door. "Is there anythin'nelse yi'll need afore ah gang tae kip?"

Tara looked up and smiled. "Oh, you're going to bed? No, I do not need anything else. Thanks, Alana."

"Aricht goodnight then." Alana closed the door.

Tara ate her scone and drank her tea as she read her book. She noticed some heart-shaped pieces of tablet and a glass of milk by her bed.

"Where those there before?" She asked herself. Tablet was a sugary concoction from Scotland, almost like fudge–one of Tara's favorite treats. Alana would make it for Tara on special occasions, like coming home from school when she was away for months. She grabbed a piece of the buttery treat and let it melt in her mouth. Once her tea and snack were gone, Tara snuggled down into the soft warm covers of her bed. She continued reading her book, and as on most nights, she fell asleep without turning off her light.

$$* \atop * \; * $$

2

The Banshee

A crack of thunder woke Tara from her dream. She was in a meadow with a bear – a friendly bear, she thought. The bear was odd, how it stood and walked it seemed intelligent. She sat up as the book she had been reading earlier fell onto the floor with a thud. She left it were it fell. She felt drained, like she had not slept in weeks. She had left her window open and the wind and rain had picked up, her now sopping wet curtains had made a huge puddle on the wooden floor, they hung heavily and continued to dripped onto the floor. She looked at her clock. Twelve-thirty. She still felt the pull of sleep on her eyelids as she yawned and stretched. She grabbed her book and set it on her night stand. Her phone buzzed to life, she saw that it was the hospital in Galway. She picked it up and heard her grandfather's voice speak on the other side of the line.

"Hello Tara, wanted to let you know your Gran is out of surgery she is resting now."

A wave of relief washed over her as she sighed and fell back onto her pillows. "Have you heard from your parents?" her grandfather asked. "I can't seem to get ahold of them" There was static on the line, and Tara was having a hard time hearing him.

"No Grandpa, I haven't. I will try to get ahold of them," she told him. There was more static.

"What did you say Tara?" he asked.

"I will call them." More static, then he said he had to go and the line went dead. Tara sighed with frustration. She called her father, and it went straight to voicemail. Her mother also, voicemail. "Strange," she thought. They always picked up when she called. She sent them a text message instead, and hoped they would get it. She closed the window till it was open just a crack. She had been looking for a towel as she tried getting ahold of her parents, finding one she started cleaning up the water on the floor. Tossing it in her dirty clothes basket she then grabbed her book and again, laid down on the many pillows that decorated her bed, and began to read. She had been reading for a while when she heard the rain start to fall hard. A crack of thunder made her jump. The rain poured straight down.

She got up and went to her window. A flash of lightning lit up the estate. Tara saw a figure walking along the edge of the forest near the pond, another crack of thunder made Tara jump and a bolt of lightning lit up the dark so she could see that it was a woman dressed in a long white nightgown. The woman was drenched; her long black hair fell in wet strands down her back and shoulders. Another crack of thunder. Then she heard it, or her. The woman was crying. Tara opened her window wider, and leaned out into the night as the rain came in, getting her arms and clothes wet.

"Hello!" Tara called out. "Can I help you?" The woman's white dress was blowing in all different directions as the wind picked up, her bare feet covered in mud. Her hair blew in every direction as well and she turned and looked up at Tara. Her dark eyes widened and her mouth seemed to stretch out sideways and down, making her cheeks and chin look wider, and longer than normal, so that her mouth looked like a black deepening chasm. All while a piercing loud wail came from her lips, causing Tara to cover her ears with her hands. It rang out through her head, causing it to throb. The hair on Tara's arms stood on end and chills ran throughout her whole body. The woman still wailed on.

"Alana! Alana!" Tara yelled, still covering her ears as she pulled herself back into her room. After a few minutes Alana came running into the bedroom, her hair in curlers.

"Whit's it, bairn?" She then gasped and said something in Scottish Gaelic that Tara could not understand, as she too covered her ears. Tara uncovered her ears just long enough to point out the window. Alana approached the window. She was still covering her ears as she looked in the direction Tara was pointing toward the woman.

"There!" Tara said impatiently, just as the woman faded into the trees. Her wails had now turned into quieter sobs that could barely be heard over the storm. The wind had died down now too, but the rain came down in sheets. Alana stared silently, her eyes wide.

"Where is she going? I think she needs help." Tara was terrified by the whole scene.

"Do not wish her back, child," Alana said, pushing Tara aside and quickly closing the window and curtains.

"But Alana! I think she needs help." Tara was confused.

"No one ever wishes to see a Banshee." She shooed Tara away from the window.

"A Banshee? Tara laughed nervously as she looked back out the window, not being able to make out much as the rain covered the glass.

"Oh, come on, Alana," Tara said as she turned to sit on the edge of her bed. "She needs help, I think. What if her car broke down or something? I would wail like that too, on a night like this, if that happened to me."

"No! That wis a Banshee." Alana pulled open the curtains, looking out again. The woman had disappeared.

Alana closed the curtains, and turned to look at Tara. Tara shook her head as if to clear the images from her mind.

"Come on, you don't believe they are real?" She paused, looking up at Alana, who was so pale, and she had her hand over her heart, breathing fast. "Do you, Alana?"

"Aye," was all she said as she walked over to Tara's bed, grabbing Tara's newest book.

"Ye be a reading this book nay longer. Get ye in bed, Miss Tara," she said as she pulled back the covers.

"Get ye in," Alana said, and there would be no arguing at that point. Tara let out a deep, exasperated sigh as she flung herself on her bed and back onto her pillows.

Alana put the covers up for her. "Say ye prayers this night, Tara." She then mumbled something in Gaelic that Tara could not understand. "Pray fer ye family, 'tis no good thing ta see a Banshee." Tara gave a faint smile as Alana stood there fiddling with one of her curlers that had come loose. Another crack of thunder and some lightning made Tara look nervously at the window.

"Just stories," she said to herself as she turned onto her side. Alana pulled over a chair, setting the book in her lap. Tara pulled the covers past her mouth and up to her nose and tried not to think about what she had just seen, but images kept flashing in her head. Alana started singing a lullaby she would often sing to Tara when she was little. The Fairies lullaby it was called, and Tara listened as the rain quieted As Alana sang, Tara's mind also quieted, and her fear. Tara's eyes felt heavy, and she sighed as she felt Alana rest her hand on her shoulder. Then she was fast asleep.

At four o'clock in the morning, Tara's phone woke her. A man's voice was on the other end, and it seemed they had a poor connection.

"Is this a Miss Tara MacInnes?" he asked. She was still a bit groggy.

"I'm sorry, who? Oh yeah, this is Tara MacInnes."

"My name is Constable Flanagan. I'm sorry to have to tell ye this, but there has been a terrible accident." He paused.

"Accident?" Tara repeated.

"Your parents…they have been killed. I'm terribly sorry, miss."

Tara could not believe what she was hearing. She felt the whole world come to a halt, all except her heart which was beating way too fast and loud as it drummed in her ears. He rambled on in a thick accent. Scottish or Irish, she could not tell since the connection was bad. There was something about a bad storm, several cars, and a bridge. Tara dropped her phone as she struggled to breathe. She held onto her bed frame to keep from falling as a rush of panic went through her. She coughed, which helped catch her breath as she ran to open her door.

"Alana! Alana!" Tara screamed. She pounded on Alana's door. Alana came rushing out of her bedroom. She paused, looking at Tara. Tara ran back to her room and over to her bed, bent down, and found her phone. Alana followed her. With trembling fingers, Tara handed the phone to Alana.

"What is it, child?" Alana asked, furrowing her brow as she took the phone.

Tara just stared wide-eyed at her phone as Alana brought it up to her ear.

"Hello," Alana said. She listened for a few seconds, then she gasped and quickly ran from the room. Tara plopped down on her bed. She remembered the banshee, and shivered. Her door was still open, and the light from the hallway shone on the end of her bed. She could hear Alana wailing not so unlike the Banshee earlier. Tara just sat there in disbelief. She felt frozen.

How could they be dead? She had just talked to them earlier. No. It was a mistake. They were heading to the hospital to be with Gram and Gramps. She shook her head until it hurt. Alana came in. Some of her curlers were falling out, and her once-pale face was now red from crying.

"Yer parents, a'm sae sorry love." Alana sat down beside Tara and held her close and rocked her. Tara melted in the arms of her nanny and sobbed, her whole body shaking and Alana sang and cried over the loss of two people who she cared for deeply, and were now gone.

*
* *
# 3

Ettrick

The hopeless feeling of her parents being gone still lingered. Alana had told her that she was in shock. Of course, she was. Losing both parents so suddenly would put most people in that state. Tara sat at the island in the kitchen. It was already ten the next morning. Mark would be there in an hour. Breakfast sat untouched in front of her. She had cried the rest of the late night with Alana.

As Alana came into the kitchen, she took Tara's breakfast away and placed a cup of tea in its place. Tara noticed she looked pale, except for her blood-shot and puffy eyes, red nose and cheeks. She wondered what she looked like herself—probably worse.

The house phone kept ringing off the hook, and Alana kept answering it. "Why can't people just stop calling?" Tara said, annoyed, as she pushed her tea away, causing it to spill on the marble counter.

Charles, the groundskeeper, had come into the kitchen during her rant and had given Tara the mail. He quietly grabbed a towel, cleaned up the mess she had made, and then silently left the kitchen. He was always quietly going about his work, and always doing nice things for her. She would have to thank him somehow.

She put the mail in a box on the stool beside her. She then picked up the box and went to put it in the car. Not wanting to be bothered with it right now, she decided to go through it later.

As she approached the Beemer she glanced towards the woods where she had seen the Banshee, she shivered, remembering that horrible night. Then her eyes welled up with tears which threatened to brim over her lids, and run down her cheeks. She sighed as they did, and wiped at her cheeks with the back of her hand.

"Ya shouldn't weep so," she heard a young male voice say, and she stopped short. She looked around but saw no one.

"I'm down here," the voice said again. Tara looked down, and standing by the tire of the car was a small, young man. Tara yelled as she dropped the box, the contents spilling out all over the drive. The little man quickly ran over to help, and Tara took a few steps back as he approached. He quickly picked up the contents of the box. A few things had gotten a bit wet. He wiped the water off onto his shirt, then put the items back into the box and then held it up to Tara, smiling.

"Here ye are," he said with what she thought might be a strong Irish lilt, or maybe it was a Scottish accent she had never really heard before. No, it was definitely Irish. He stood about twenty inches tall; he had crazy blond hair that stuck out every which way from beneath a blue cap. He had on long brown shorts, a green t-shirt with a brown leather vest, and hiking boots. However, what struck Tara the most was his stunning good looks and sparkling green eyes.

She hesitantly took the box and set it down on the hood of the car. Tara rubbed at her eyes. "Am I going crazy now?" she thought to herself out loud.

"My name is Ettrick Aberfeldy." Tara quickly turned around; he was still there, standing in front of her with one hand on what looked to be a walking stick and the other's thumb hooked into his belt, and one leg was crossed over the other.

"I'm a brownie. We have been serving yer family fer centuries," he said, standing taller now.

She now noticed his slightly pointed ears and well-tanned skin. She had read lots of stories about brownies.

"A brownie, serving my family? Like in house chores?" she said, mostly said to herself. She was grieving losing her parents, and now her mind was playing tricks on her.

"Alana!" Tara yelled.

"Ah! Shush now, don't ya be callin' her," he said, coming closer to her and jumping up onto the hood of the car.

Alana opened the front door. "Tara! What is it ye be wantin'?" she yelled, leaning out of the doorway.

Tara turned around, backing into the Beemer and blocking the view of the box. The brownie had hunched down behind the box so that Alana could not see him.

Maybe she should not call Alana over, she thought. After all, it was her grief talking. That's why she was making the stories she had heard all her life come alive. "Just my grief," she said out loud to herself, but not so that Alana could hear.

"Um. Oh. Mark will be here soon," she said nervously, so Alana would not worry.

"Och, I'll call the club and—"

Tara interrupted her. "Oh, no, he can still come by."

Alana waved her hand. "All right, but ye need to come back inside or ye'll catch a cold," she said as she went back in, shaking her head.

Tara shivered, folding her arms in front of herself. The air was still chilled from the rain that had come down all night, and she wasn't wearing a jacket. Everything was still quite wet, and it was a cloudy, gloomy day.

"I am sorry ta hear about ye parents."

The sound caused Tara jump. She had forgetten all about the brownie, who still stood there. She turned around at the sound of his voice, which, for a brownie as small as he was, sounded like a grown man standing by her side.

"Who are you again?" she asked, getting a better look at him. She had definitely lost it, talking to brownies now. He looked fairly young, about her age, though she knew from stories that brownies can live for hundreds of years. His green eyes sparkled at her as she looked at him.

"My name's Ettrick Aberfeldy." Tara cut him off.

"Okay," She said hesitantly, waving her hand and rubbing at her temples. She suddenly had a headache.

A police car pulled up in the drive, and an officer got out. "Is this the MacInnes residence?" he asked, looking at a piece of paper.

"Yes," Tara answered back.

Alana came running out of the house just then, and over to the police officer. It was then that Tara saw Mark walking up the drive. "I gotta get out of here. Hearing things, seeing things, I am losing it," she said to herself as she grabbed the box. She opened the door and got in, setting the box down in the backseat. She luckily had the keys in her pocket, so she started the car and peeled out of the drive towards Mark.

"Tara! Officer Brown needs to be a speakin to ya!" Alana yelled.

Tara quickly pulled up next to Mark, who was walking up the long drive. "Get in the driver's seat," she said as she slid over into the passenger seat.

"There's a cop here," he said as he opened the door and climbed into the Beemer.

"Yeah, he wants to talk to me but I don't want to talk to him right now. " she said as she looked out the window into the mirror, watching Alana show the officer into the house. Mark smiled as he turned up the music and peeled down the driveway.

It did not take long before they were pulling into the park entrance. Mark pulled into a parking space and turned off the car. Tara looked in the back seat as she grabbed her sweater and saw no one. No brownie, just the box of mail. She sighed with relief, glad he was no longer there.

It was nice to be outside, and to take a walk along the water. The mansion felt too silent and still most of the time, more than usual. Her parents were hardly ever there when she was home. Her mother always went to the club and hung out with her friends. They liked to play tennis and gossip. Her Dad worked a lot. Now they were gone, and she felt a haunting realization that she would never get a chance to spend time with them again – ever. That was something that she had wished had happened more. Tara looked up at the sky in an attempt to keep the tears from spilling out. The clouds had begun to break up and you could see patches of blue sky.

Tara looked at Mark as the tears ran down her face. Mark grabbed her close, and hugged her.

"I am so sorry, Tara." He sighed into her hair as he held her. She knew that he knew how she felt in losing a parent—well, in her case, she had lost both.

Tara looked up at him. "What about the funerals?"

He frowned. "Do you want me to come with you to Ireland and Scotland? I could, my dad wouldn't mind, and I could get some more time off of work. They did just hire a few people."

Tara smiled faintly and nodded.

"That would be great if you could," she said as they pulled away from each other and started walking again. They walked around for a while—once around the pond and down a few paths that led into the trees nearby. They then sat on a bench just off the path that stood under a willow tree.

Tara's phone let her know she had a message. She took it out of her jacket pocket. "My lawyer," she told Mark, putting her phone away. Tara really did not want to talk to him, but knew she had to, eventually. Alana had told her she would need to sooner or later, and sooner was best. "I guess we should go. I have to set up a meeting with him and talk to the police."

"Yeah, okay," Mark said as he stood up.

Mark drove her back home, and it was a quiet drive. Tara did not have much to say; she was not really in a talkative mood. As Tara opened the car door, she looked at Mark. "You can drive the Beemer home, since you walked here, and I don't need it right now anyway." She got out, and before closing the door, she waved to him.

"Are you sure?" Mark asked.

"Yeah, go ahead, I will see you tomorrow."

"Okay, bye," Mark said as Tara closed the door.

Mark sat there in the car for a while before leaving. Tara watched him out of the window in the front living room. She really did not want him to go, but she did not want to have him dragged down with her in grief. Who was she kidding? She wanted him to stay. It was nice having him there. If anything, she did not see or hear anything unusual while he was there and that was comforting.

She slowly walked into the kitchen, not even realizing she was leaving muddy sneaker prints on the carpet and polished wooden floors. Tara found some Tablet and milk on the kitchen counter. She took a few tablets and drank the milk. Tara knew she needed to talk to the officer, but not now. He wasn't there anyway.

Tara walked up the stairs and down the hall, pausing just outside her parents' room. She stood there for a moment remembering her mom's voice asking for Tara's help to zip up her dress, or which outfit looked nicer as her mother stood holding two dresses. Tara went into the bedroom, which looked the same as it did every day. Except now there was stillness in the room, and it was very eerie. She shuddered.

She grabbed a sweater off the hook on the back of the door. Her mom's favorite sweater, hand knitted by her mom. It was light blue with a large collar and big coconut shell buttons. It was not Tara's style, but she put it on anyway. She wrapped her arms around herself as if her mom was giving her a huge hug. She could smell her mom's perfume on it: an expensive, spicy yet fruity scent.

Oh, what I wouldn't do for a hug from her right now, she thought. She absentmindedly put her hand in the pocket, where her fingers brushed against some paper. She pulled it out and unfolded it. It was a note to her mother from her dad. She quickly read the contents, and her heart felt heavy as she read of his love for her mom. She felt as if she were eavesdropping on a private conversation. She put the note back in the pocket.

She walked over to the closet where they kept their clothes. On one side were all of her father's suits hanging up. Organized by color, then brand. She took one of his shirts off of the hanger and held the fabric up to her face, inhaling the smell of his cologne. He must have worn this one recently and not had it dry cleaned yet. She caught herself thinking that she could take it to get cleaned for him. Her whole body ached at the thought that he would never wear it again. Tara walked past her mother's dresses, and she grabbed one off its hanger. She tried to hold back the tears as she felt the silky fabric slide between her fingers. She walked out of the closet and flung herself onto the bed, kicking off her sneakers. She had both garments now, burying her face in them and sobbing. She laid there in a fetal position and sobbed, her whole body shaking as she wept.

That's how Mark found her the next morning, her hair all tangled with the dress and shirt, asleep.

"Tara," he said softly in her ear. She stirred awake, slowly opening her eyes. They felt sticky and puffy. The phone was ringing.

"Mark?" she asked, a bit confused, and then reality slowly sunk in and her heart felt heavily weighed down.

There was a buzz of activity in the house. "What time is it?" she asked him, sitting up and leaving the shirt and dress on the bed.

"It's ten after eleven in the morning," he told her, looking out the window. "Your lawyer is here to meet with you." Tara slowly got off the bed.

"Oh, is he?" she said sleepily. "Okay, tell him I'll be down in a minute." He nodded and quietly left the room.

She went over to her mother's dressing counter, sat down in the plush chair, and looked in the mirror. Her hair was a mess, her eyes were puffy from crying, and she looked pale. She didn't even care that Mark had seen her this way. She grabbed her mother's hair brush and started combing through her knotted hair.

She then went into the closet and put on one of her mother's silky bathrobes over her sweats and tank top. She felt a bit chilled, so she also put on the slippers that matched the robe and then headed downstairs.

Tara neared the bottom of the stairs and saw Mr. Patton in the front room, which was off of the entryway.

"Mr. Patton," she greeted him, shaking his hand as he stood when she entered the room.

"Tara, I'm so sorry for your loss," he said, adjusting his glasses. He was wearing a brown suit, as always, and a bright, colorful tie. Mr. Patton was in his late thirties, single, and not too bad looking for his age, she thought. He was kind of skinny but she could tell he worked out. He had brown hair with flecks of gold, and blue eyes.

They both sat down as Alana brought in a tray carrying coffee, tea, and scones.

She set them on the table. "Here ye are Mr. Patton, Tara. Now if ye be a needin' anything more let me know." She then excused herself. Mr. Patton cleared his throat as he poured himself a cup of coffee.

Tara grabbed a scone and fiddled with it on her plate.

"The funerals have been arranged, as well as your plane tickets."

Tara absently nodded.

"Your parents left you everything, and Mrs. Alana will be your benefactor until you turn eighteen." She looked up at him then. He was sitting on the couch across from her, with the coffee table between them.

"Your parents requested that I continue my legal services for you, if you want them?" He set down his coffee cup and grabbed a scone. "Blueberry, my favorite." He smiled and took a bite then let out a sigh. Setting down his scone, he looked at Tara.

"It will get easier," he told her, and as he looked at her, she saw pain in his eyes. Her father had been his good friend.

"I lost my wife to cancer," he said, standing.

"Oh, I'm sorry. I didn't know," Tara said, looking at him as he walked over to the large windows. It seemed odd that she did not know about his wife; then again, he was her father's lawyer and friend.

"Yeah, it was before I had met your Dad. She died only a few short months after we were married." He turned and adjusted his glasses. "Believe me, it gets easier, but you will never forget them. How they looked, talked, laughed. Some memories will fade, and some will get stronger." He sat back down.

"I'm sorry to hear that you lost her, Mr. Patton. Have you ever thought about remarrying?" The question came out before she could stop it. "Oh, I'm sorry, it's none of my business."

"It's all right. Yes, I have thought about it. But I haven't really met anyone yet."

Tara nodded.

"You will miss him, won't you? My father?"

He looked at her and nodded back. "We have been friends for many years, Tara. I was the best man at your parents' wedding. He handed her an envelope. "Here are a bunch of documents, some properties that have already sold. Your father made sure if anything ever happened to him, they would be sold first."

Tara took the envelope.

"Properties where?" she asked, opening the large envelope.

"Mostly foreign properties—nothing with memories if that is what you are worried about. Your father was very specific as to what properties could be sold." She slightly smiled and set the envelope down. He handed her another envelope.

"This I need you to give to your Uncle Arland." She took the large envelope and added it to the other papers. He stood. "Well, you have my number if you need me for anything." Tara stood as well and walked with him to the door.

"Really, Tara, anything." He placed his hand on her arm, gave it a gentle squeeze, and then he walked down the steps, got into his car, and left. She did feel at that moment she could call him about anything.

Tara was still standing at the door when Mark walked up next to her. "Let's pack your things, Tara," he told her, closing the door.

"Yeah, I just need to put these papers in my Dad's study. These though," she said, handing the other papers to Mark, "Those are for my uncle; they need to go in my bag." Mark took them.

"I'll go put these away right now." She smiled faintly then opened the door to her father's study. Going into her father's study was an odd feeling. She never really went in very often before, however now it was so lonely. The whole house felt that way, as if it was morning the loss of her parents too. She sat at the large wooden desk, and opened a few drawers. She found some keys and looked around to see what they could be for. In the closet shoved up high on a shelf she found a box she tried a key. No luck. She tried the others, and the fourth key worked. As she heard it click, she opened the box. Nothing could have prepared her for what she found. Inside was her bracelet that she lost when she was twelve. She had had it ever since she was a baby, and was very attached to it. It was a small silver bracelet with white tiny pearls on either side of four small grayish stones that read TARA.

"I was wondering what happened to this," she thought. She took off her necklace and looped the small infant bracelet onto the chain. Then she saw some documents. She picked them up and looked at them, reading and re-reading their contents.

"Mark!" She called out, and he came in.

"Yeah, what's going on?" She held the papers out for him to take.

"Adoption papers. Mine," she said in disbelief. Mark was looking at the papers with a confused expression.

"These are yours?" he asked, reading the contents out loud. "It says you were adopted on May twentieth. That's your birthday."

"Yeah, and look at this." She held up the necklace to show him, with the bracelet on it.

"Hey, I thought you lost that one summer, while we were at day camp."
"Well, I guess it was found and my Dad put it in this box with these papers. Because it was in here." She pointed to the now empty box.

4

Family

The airplane ride to Ireland was long.

Mark shifted in his seat. Alana was asleep in her seat near the aisle. Tara opened her bag. "M&M's," she said as she pulled them out of her bag, opened them, and offered some to Mark, who gladly accepted. She hadn't eaten much, and Alana had expressed to Tara several times how she was quite worried about her. "Ah kin order something fur ye, I'll just git the stewardess." Alana had said it a few times before Tara politely declined.

Once they finally arrived in Ireland, Tara's grandfather was at the airport waiting for them. Tara ran to him, and his strong arms held her for a while as more tears ran down her cheeks.

"It's all right now, Tara. It will be alright," he said as he gently grabbed her arms and looked down at her. He looked tired.

Her grandfather took Alana's bag, and Mark grabbed Tara's. The drive to the funeral parlor was long as well, or at least it seemed to Tara.

Though her mother was an only child, and they did not have much extended family, there were a lot of people whom Tara didn't know at the funeral parlor: friends of her mother's and coworkers from her job before she left Ireland.

Her grandmother was unable to attend as she was still in the hospital. Tara thought her grandfather was holding things together fairly well. Tara's mother's casket was closed. Draped over it was the Irish flag, and some flowers lay across it as well. Tara had a white rose that she set atop the casket before sitting in a chair in the front row. She did not want to leave. She looked around as people greeted each other and they said their goodbyes. She felt drained. She needed to sleep. Her Grandfather came over to her and bent down to look at her face.

"Tara, it's time to go." Tara nodded as she got up. Out of the corner of her eye she thought she saw something just behind the casket. She quickly went over and looked but there was nothing. She rubbed at her eyes which were watering, as she yawned. She hadn't slept in twenty-four hours. After the service was over, they went back to her Grandparents house. It had been a lovely service. Many friends were there, but only a small number of family, as there were not many around anymore. Tara felt calm throughout the whole service as if her mother sat by her side. At the house, there were flowers, cards, and food all over—they seemed to kind of take over the entire small house.

"Well you won't have to cook for a while, Grandpa," Tara said, looking around.

He smiled and hugged her. "Come here, Tara. There are some things of your mother's we want you to have."

They walked upstairs to her mother's old room. It looked the same as it always had. Tara noticed her suit case. Her mother's favorite blue comforter with the stitched flowers on it was spread across the bed.

Various framed movie posters and pictures of places her mom had been still hung on the walls. Some things had been packed away, like her mom's small collection of snow globes and some jewelry. There were several boxes on the bed, and Tara looked through them. A lot of her mom's things were in there.

"I can ship these to you," her grandfather said as she found a photo album.

"That would be nice," Tara said, looking at a picture of her mother in high school. Tara did look a lot like her, except that her mother had blond hair. Tara realized how life could be going so well one minute, then snuffed out without any consideration to how everyone felt about it the next. Still, her mother had had a good life, and being in her old room Tara sensed that – saw reflections of that in the memoirs and pictures that were there. She would still miss her terribly, and there was now a big ache and hole were her mother had been and she doubted that it would ever go away.

They took the ferry to Scotland. The funerals were just days apart, so they had to leave Ireland before she had wanted to. As they drove through the country Tara felt a bit more relaxed. She leaned on Mark's arm as she stared out the window. Tara burst into tears when she saw Uncle Arland. He wore his jeans, as always, with his dark green hat, long-sleeved plaid shirt rolled up to his elbows, and his wool vest with gold buttons. She was in full sobbing mode, and she couldn't help it.

"There, there now lass," he said to her, his voice a soothing sound to her, always had been. He smelled of fresh heather, spices from his pipe, and fresh dirt.

Here in Scotland, her memories were of helping at the farm, long walks, days and nights filled with stories and pipe music, and mostly just playing with her cousins.

The funeral was at the farm, and it was quite a gathering. Tara loved the farm. Uncle Arland had a white stone cottage with a fence and trees surrounding it, with the Scotland hills behind. Tara knew a lot of people here, which made it harder for her, seeing them all mourning for her father, and also celebrating his life. She had always spent more time at Uncle Arland's in the summer than she did in Galway, Ireland with her grandparents. When she stayed with her grandparents, they would do a lot of shopping, or going to plays, or the theatre. There were many shops she loved to go to, especially book stores. Then she would spend hours reading. In Scotland, it was different. Yes, she went shopping, but it was a bit slower-paced here, which she liked.

Her father's college pipe band was playing at the service. Tara cried during every song.

How am I going to make it through this? she thought. Mark grabbed her hand, and she was glad Mark was there—he had been her rock, just being there, talking to her, but listening mostly. She did not know what she would do when it was time to go back to school.

After the funeral, friends and family who lingered celebrated her father's life by sharing memories and stories of him and the people and places he loved.

Uncle Arland told stories, played his fiddle along with others, and there was lots of food and drink. It was nice being here, seeing her new baby cousin, being around family. Except that two of the people she loved weren't there, and all she had was an empty void in her heart and soul like a great dark abyss.

Her father's urn sat on the fireplace mantel, and his pipes rested by the fireplace. It was an empty feeling, not having her father there. To think his body was reduced to ashes that sat on the mantle. It made her mad as well. That she would never hug him again, would never have a chance to connect with him and her mother on a deeper level like she always had wanted. For her to think that this was all that was left were ashes, memories, and tears, made being here in Scotland hard.

Tara left the cottage and walked down the pathway, as she liked to do on evenings like this. Calm and quiet. Well, except that she could still hear the music, talk, and laughter coming from the cottage. The distant sounds were comforting. She let her mind drift to happier times as she stood leaning on the fence.

"Ya all right, lass?" The brownie was back.

"Not now," she thought as she gave him a sullen look, and her head started pounding. He was sitting on the fence now beside her.

He shook his head. "I know this is hard for ye, Tara. You will pull through; you're a tough lass. There is more ta life than this, more to come." Tara closed her eyes as tight as she could, wishing the brownie to go away. She did not need a pep talk from an imaginary brownie. When she opened her eyes, he had vanished out of sight, along with her pounding headache.

Tara could hear a burst of laughter again coming from the cottage as the door opened and Uncle Arland came out walking towards her. He came and stood beside her and took out his pipe. Tara loved the smell of his pipe's sweet, woodsy aroma. It smelled of home. The smoke swirled up into the sky, the stars and moon were out, and she remembered how she used to stay outside for hours, just thinking.

Uncle Arland wrapped a tartan blanket around her shoulders, as the air was getting chilly.

"Uncle Arland, do you believe in brownies?"

He looked at her, cleared his throat, and took the pipe out of his mouth. "Uh, no, but they are there just the same," he said, puffing on his pipe again.

She smiled, as that was his answer to all of her questions about that kind of stuff.

"So, you think they are real?" she asked.

He raised his eyebrows. "Since when ye be a-believin' in them now, Tara?"

She leaned forward, her arms on the fence, and told him about the Banshee that she saw out of her bedroom window the night her parents were killed. "Alana saw it too, so I do not think I am going crazy." She told him about the brownie named Ettrick who kept appearing and disappearing.

"Sounds like to help ye cope, ye be a-seein' things," he said, smiling at her.

"Yes, but they are there just the same," she said, repeating his words. He laughed at her reply. "Aye," he said with a smile.

"You could have the Sight," he told her. She had heard about or Second Sight. Not only from him and Alana but others in town, where Uncle Arland lived. It was when you could see things that others couldn't, like fairies and Brownies. It was not very common. Tara did not really believe in it, but then again, she had not met anyone that claimed they had it. Although her Uncle Arland said he saw things as a kid on several occasions.

"You think I do?" Tara stood up and looked at him.

"Ye might Tara, can't say for sure." He casually puffed his pipe as they stood side by side.

"Dad didn't believe in the stories you told him, did he?"

Uncle Arland shook his head.

"Nay, he didn't." He set his right hand down on the fence holding his pipe.

"I do not think I do either," she told him. He smiled and nodded. After a few minutes, spoke.

"There is a festival tomorrow, also a tour of the castle there, and some of the kids in town you know are going. I said ye and Mark would go as well." He cleared his throat.

Tara turned so that her back was leaning against the fence.

"Dunvegan Castle?" Tara asked, her face lighting up with excitement. "Sounds like fun."

Uncle Arland motioned for them to head back towards the cottage. People started leaving to go back home. They said their well wishes, shaking hands, giving hugs, and a few pecks on Tara's cheek from a few of the older ladies. Once everyone was gone, Uncle Arland squeezed her tight. "Good night, Tara."

She slowly and sleepily walked up the stairs to her cousin Mary's room, where she always stayed when she was at Uncle Arland's. Mary was sleeping, so Tara was as quiet as she could be. Mary was getting so big now, at almost eight years old. She had straw-colored hair with a hint of red, green eyes, and freckles. She was going to be a heart breaker when she was older. Mary was the closest thing to a sister Tara would ever have.

During the night, Tara must have been crying because Mary had climbed into her bed, shushed her with her sweet little voice, and sang to her in Gaelic back into a more restful sleep.

5

Dunvegan Castle

In the morning, Tara woke up and found herself alone in the bed and the bedroom. Mary must have gone over to her friend's house, Tara thought. There was a friend of the family who watched Mary while Uncle Arland was at work. She went downstairs after she got dressed and found a letter from Alana.

"Oh, she went to go visit her family." Mark came up behind her and tapped her shoulder. Good morning," he said cheerfully.

"Good morning," Tara said back, swinging her long hair to the side so that she could look up at him.

There were oatmeal bannocks on the kitchen counter. "Your uncle left for work already. He reminds me of Alana. He likes to tell stories." Tara laughed and nodded her head as they both grabbed a few bannocks.

"Yes, they both like to tell stories, of fairies, and monsters and legends of Ireland and Scotland."

"My favorite so far has been about the hounds of Hell, and trolls," Mark said taking another bannock.

"Of course," Tara said, not surprised.

"What? I also like hearing about the Giants, and the Gods and Goddesses."

Tara sighed and grabbed her bag.

"Are you ready to go then?" Mark asked, scarfing down a bannock.

"Yeah, I just need to grab an umbrella," she said as Mark followed her to a closet.

"You know, these are better than you described, Tara!" Mark exclaimed. "I love it here. I see now why you do too. How are you doing? I mean, with everything?"

She sighed.

"It has been hard. I see my Dad everywhere. I hear him in the music, I hear him out in the Highlands, in the cottage, at the market – everywhere."

"I bet you do," Mark said as Tara grabbed her jacket and an umbrella. The weather this time of year could be very unpredictable. "It is very haunting." She shivered as they opened the door and stepped outside.

Two four-wheel drive vehicles pulled up to the cottage. Uncle Arland had planned everything for them.

"Are you ready to go?" asked one of the drivers, a young man named Matt. Tara had met him at the local bookstore one day a few years back. They had been on a few dates but They were better off as friends, they had decided.

"Yeah, we're ready. This is my friend, Mark. He is from Connecticut too," Tara said, getting in.

"How are ye, Mark?" Matt asked as he got in the car.

"Good, thanks."

"How do you like Scotland, ever been here before?" Matt asked as they pulled away from the cottage.

"Uh, no. This is my first time here. But I love it." Matt smiled, and nodded his head as he drove.

"Hey, so any bands playing today that I would know?" Mark looked around hopefully.

"No, not anyone you might know or anything. Mostly local bands," Matt said, grinning.

After the music festival they went to Dunvegan Castle for a tour.

The castle was huge, with many towers and windows, and was set atop a hill covered with bushes. The castle was situated next to a loch, and there was a paved road that led up to a path with white-washed walls that looked as if they were painted centuries ago. As they made their way through the gardens, Tara thought that they looked like a hidden oasis of different kinds of plants and was a stunning contrast to the surrounding barren moors and mountains. Tara especially liked the lily pond and the boat tour in which they got to see the colony of seals that lived near the castle on the loch. Tara enjoyed seeing the seals as well, as they lay on the rocky shores by the castle laying in the sun. The stories about the seals here were that they were Selkies – seals that could change into human form on land. They always looked so happy basking in the sun, as they laid there, or played in the water, their little round heads bobbing in the surf.

Tara had thought of going to the castle many times while visiting Scotland but never had until now. She was mesmerized, like she was drawn to it somehow. It was almost like she had been there before, or in her dreams maybe. They came to a part of the tour where they were looking at an old piece of cloth encased in glass. There were also a cup and a horn in a display case.

"This is called the Fairy Flag," the tour guide said. Tara listened intently to the different stories of how it came to be called the Fairy Flag. Tara had heard a few stories that Uncle Arland had told her, but these were more detailed. "It is known for its magical properties associated with it," the tour guide said as she wrapped up her presentation. "It is said that it was a gift from the fairies to an infant chieftain long ago. Some of the powers attributed to the flag are, to multiply a clan's forces, cure a plague on cattle, even to increase the chances of fertility."

As she stared at it, Tara did not notice the crowd moving on.

"Come on, Tara," Mark said, tugging on her jacket.

Tara reached and touched the glass, and as soon as she did so, she saw a soft glow inside the glass case. It started off low and then got brighter and brighter, causing the fabric to come to life and look as if it was brand new. It rippled and shined; it was a silky golden color with small crosses embroidered in gold thread and had small red dots on it.

"Tara, what the crap!" Mark yelled. Tara pulled her hand back. It felt like it weighed a ton as it dropped down by her side.

"I don't know, I –" Tara stammered. Maybe they had some trick lighting or something. She looked around and under the case. No wires, no lamps – nothing.

They were both so transfixed by the way the fabric looked that when they heard an elderly woman's voice behind them, they both jumped. "You have been protected by the fairies," she told them.

"Who, me?" Tara asked.

"Yes," the woman said as she smiled, causing her eyes to wrinkle and shine. She probably lived locally, or worked at the castle, Tara thought.

"Have ye enjoyed the tour? The old woman asked, still smiling. Her accent was unusual – a strong Scottish brogue, but with a slight hint of French as well.

"Yes, thank you," Tara told her, smiling back.

Tara briefly looked back at the flag. Turning back toward the old woman, she asked, "Do you—" but the woman was gone. They looked around a bit, however the old lady was nowhere to be seen. Tara reached up and rubbed at her temples as she felt a hint of a headache.

"Uh, okay, that was really weird," Tara said. "Stuff like this just doesn't happen – but then it did happen. Right?"

Mark shrugged his shoulders. "I don't know, seems to me someone rigged it to light up or something. They seem to like stories here."

"Yeah," Tara said in agreement.

Mark was looking at his watch. He tugged at Tara's arm. "We need to find the tour guide and finish our tour. It's getting late."

Tara looked back at the Fairy Flag as she left, which again now was old and grey. Something about the castle and the flag haunted her memories, but she could not place it. Flashes of memory crept in her mind, like old dreams. The fabric of the flag soft and silky next to her skin, the cold stone walls. A sense of warmth too, though, and a hearty meal, a warm fire. However, she had never been here before. She shivered and then turned to Mark, rubbing at her temples as her headache got worse.

"Let's go."

They soon caught up to the group, and Matt waved as he saw them.

"Hey, where did you two go?" Matt asked. Tara and Mark both shrugged their shoulders and listened to the guide. As they moved through the castle, Tara kept looking over her shoulder, and at one point she saw the old woman go into a room, but it was as if she was see-through, like not really there – like in a dream. Tara quietly left the tour group and followed her.

When Tara got into the spacious room, she saw the old lady sitting in a rocking chair. She smiled at Tara when Tara came in.

"I have waited a long time for you to arrive, Tara MacInnes," she said, smiling at Tara and motioning for her to come closer. Tara did move closer, but reluctantly.

"So," Said the old lady as she rocked. "Many strange things have taken place lately?" Tara did not know what to say, so she just stood there.

"I don't want to frighten you, lass, it's alright. Everything will be alright." She shakily got up from the rocking chair and walked closer to Tara, speaking softly as she did. "When you get back home, you need to find a young woman named Beira. She will help you." She stood in front of Tara now, and smiled as she gently placed her hands on Tara's shoulders. The woman appeared not as old or short as before.

Mark appeared in the doorway. As she turned to look at him, Tara felt the weight of the woman's hands leave her shoulders. Her head was feeling slightly off. She started to wonder if all the stress was getting to her. "I'll take some pain relief medicine when I get back to Uncle Arland's," She thought to herself.

"There you are, Tara. Come on, the tour is over," he said impatiently. Tara turned her head back around only to find the old woman had gone. She looked all around but did not see her. Tara reached up and touched her shoulders where the old woman had placed her hands and stood there for a moment.

"Mark, did you—" she started to say, but then stopped. She did not think he had seen the woman; she vanished too quickly. Tara went to grab her bag.

"Tara, what is it?" Mark asked with a puzzled expression on his face. He looked tired.

Tara rubbed her forehead. "Oh, nothing." She grabbed his arm as they left the room.

A part of her wanted to leave the castle as fast as she could, since she was a bit freaked out. How did that woman just vanish, and what was up with the fairy flag? However, somehow it felt like home. She couldn't think of the reasons why, so she did not tell Mark how she felt—not yet anyway.

After dinner at Uncle Arland's, Tara decided to tell him about the strange things that happened at the castle. She had taken some headache medicine, and it seemed to help, for now. She felt maybe her mind was losing grip with reality, except Mark had seen the flag, and what happened when she touched the glass. Hadn't he? He did think it was rigged or something, and he did not see the old lady the second time.

"That's all she said?" Mark asked when Tara had finished. "She probably was just a crazy old woman," he said, trying to brush it off. Tara thought he was over reacting.

"Shush boy," Uncle Arland said in a reprimanding tone. "'Tis said that us folk who live here can have what ye call Second Sight." He puffed on his pipe again.

"Second Sight?" asked Mark.

"Aye. 'Tis when ye can see the fair folk. That's what we call them." He sighed and then fiddled with his pipe.

"Fair Folk?" Mark asked.

"Fairies," Tara told him. "It's when humans can see fairies." Tara turned to Uncle Arland. "But those are just stories, Uncle Arland. They aren't real." Mark nodded and did not ask any more questions, for which Tara was grateful. To change the subject before Uncle Arland could start lecturing about the Fair Folk, she reached into her back pocket and pulled out some folded papers. She offered them to Uncle Arland.

"What's this?" He asked, taking the papers and opening them.

"Adoption papers," she answered him with a bit of sass. "Did you know, Uncle Arland?" Though she was sincere about her question, she couldn't be mad at him. Not after everything that had happened.

"Yes lassie, ah knew," He bowed his head as he sighed loudly.

Uncle Arland grabbed Tara's hands in his big strong ones. Tara sighed heavily as he squeezed her arms gently.

"It doesn't mean we loue ye ony less, Tara." He kissed her forehead.

"Why did they not tell me, and why did you keep it a secret?"

Uncle Arland took a deep breath. "Tara, they asked a' body tae keep it a secret. Th' circumstances o' howfur ye git in th' care o' th' adoption agency wis unknown 'n' aye under investigation."

"Well that's not comforting," Tara said. Uncle Arland seemed a bit unnerved, so she changed the subject. "This was also in the box in Dad's study with the adoption papers." She showed him the bracelet. Uncle Arland asked to get a better look at it, so she took it off her necklace.

"Ah haven't seen this sin ye wur a bairn." He was smiling as he gave it back to her. She took off her necklace and looped the bracelet through it.

"I had this when I was a baby, then lost it one summer when I was twelve." Tara touched one of the stones. He nodded his head.

"I remember when you lost it, you were heart broken," Uncle Arland said as Tara looked through more of the papers.

"I asked Mr. Patton, who is now my lawyer, to get more information about my adoption. He says to contact a Beira Monach. That's also who the old woman at the castle told me to find." She stood and rubbed her arms. Goose bumps had broken out all over them.

"How could the old woman have known about this?" Mark said, grabbing the letter. "Or this Beira person?" he asked, looking as shaken as Tara felt. They both looked at Uncle Arland.

"She could be a fairy. The old woman at the castle," Uncle Arland said as he stood and got a closer look at the bracelet that was now dangling from Tara's necklace.

"Uncle Arland, please," Tara pleaded. She did not want him teasing her now. He liked to tease her, it was all in good fun, but this was serious. She was adopted, some strange lady she had never met mentioned a Beira, and now this.

Uncle Arland started muttering in Scottish Gaelic. Tara and Mark just looked at each other and shrugged their shoulders. He was still muttering to himself as he walked into his cottage and closed the door.

"Now that my parents are gone, I can't even ask questions, or be mad at them really, or anything. I have my Grandparents, and Uncle Arland and all my cousins, but that's not the same thing." Tara was pacing, she felt restless, this new information and her parents not around to help her, it was frustrating. Mark put his hand on her arm, as he spoke.

"They were great parents, Tara. I'm sure they did have their reasons for not telling you." Tara was lost in her thoughts, thinking about what reasons they could possibly have had for not telling her. Were her birth parents dangerous somehow, she wondered. Drug dealers? What?

"I'm going to bed, Tara," Mark said, sighing. He gave her hand a gentle squeeze before he left.

Tara stood there for a while by herself.

"Well, that went well," Ettrick said, appearing down by Tara's shoe and making Tara jump.

"Oh! Ettrick. You scared me," Tara said, shoving the papers back into the envelope. "Are you following me?" she asked. "Shouldn't you be at my house doing all that stuff that brownies do?"

"Aye, Come on, lass. Ye be needin' your sleep, and yes I am keeping an eye out fer ye, doin me job," Ettrick said as he vanished out of sight.

Tara shook her head. "You are not real," she said as she walked towards the cottage, squeezing her eyes closed and willing her head to stop pounding. When she went in, she saw Uncle Arland sitting in his chair looking at the papers Mr.Patton had given her to give to him.

"Tara, come sit doon. A'm needin' tae tell ye something." Tara went over and sat down on the couch next to Uncle Arland's chair.

She sat there waiting patiently until her uncle addressed her. Her headache seemed to have eased.

"Your parents appointed me as yer guardian." Tara looked at him, waiting to hear more. Uncle Arland just handed her the papers.

"Really, they really did?" Tara asked, taking the papers from him. She read them over. It was all there in black and white, signed by her parents, that if anything ever happened to them then Arland MacInnes was to be her guardian, and she was to live with him. "I will be living here?" She didn't know what to say.

"Would ye like that, tae bide here with me n' Mary?" Tara jumped up and flung herself into his arms, which he wrapped tightly around her as they both began to cry.

She pulled away from him after a few minutes and they both wiped at their tear-stained faces. "Well, I am pretty tired. I think I will go to bed," Tara said as she smiled and headed for the stairs.

Tara laid in her bed, wide awake. She couldn't sleep. "Figures," she said to herself. She couldn't help but wonder about who she really was, and who her other family were. Did they want to know who she was, or where she was, or did they not care? All those questions were running through her head. Questions that did not seem to have any answers—in fact they didn't. Should she go looking for this Beira person? And if she found her, then what? Also, she was so happy that she would get to come live here with Uncle Arland and Mary, and she could see her grandparents more often. It was all she had ever wanted, besides spending more time with her parents. However, what about Mark? How would she tell him? Would she ever see him anymore?

She sighed, plopping her head back against the pillow. She finally fell into a restless sleep.

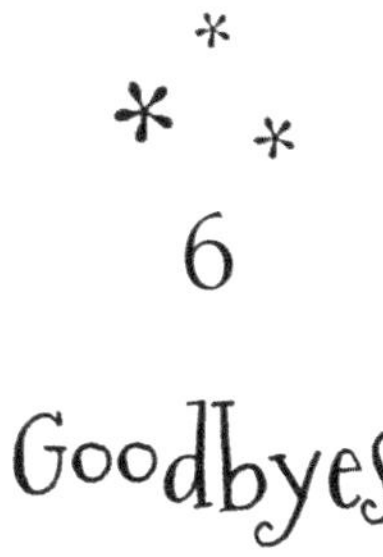

6

Goodbyes

Someone was nudging Tara's arm. She opened her eyes just as Ettrick was jumping off of the bed. Tara rubbed at her eyes. Surely, she was still dreaming. She sat up and saw that her bags had been packed. Tara got out of bed, grabbed her robe, and put it on as she went down the stairs. She saw Mark, Mary, and Uncle Arland all eating.

"Ooh, blossom honey," she said, grabbing the jar and a knife and smearing the sticky honey on a piece of bread. She took a huge bite.

"I'm glad ye at least have an appetite, lass," Uncle Arland said.

"Are we going to drop them off?" Mary asked Uncle Arland.

"You better be," Tara said through her mouthful of food.

"Tara, did you pack my bags?" Mark asked.

"No, why?" she asked, getting some juice.

"Well, Uncle Arland and Mary said that they didn't and—"

"Oh, it was probably Ettrick," Tara said with a hint of sarcasm, as if they all knew who she was talking about.

They all looked at her. "Who's Ettrick?" Mary asked.

Tara looked at Uncle Arland. He cleared his throat.

"We best be a-getting on. We have a long ride," Uncle Arland said as he got up, giving Tara a worried look. Tara got up and grabbed one of her bags. Mark had grabbed the other.

It was very hard to leave the comfort of Uncle Arland's home. Tara held him tight as she said goodbye. "You wull be back, afore ye ken it," he said as he gave her a quick squeeze. "Now, ye mind whit ah said," he told her as he kissed her cheek. "Also, we love ye very much, lass, and never forget it."

Mary ran over and hugged her as well. "We do love you, Tara!" Mary was squeezing her so tightly that Tara could hardly breathe. "I'll call you all the time, oh and I can't wait for ye to move here and live with us," Mary said.

"Text, Mary, text, and I can't wait either," Tara said, tears welling up in her eyes. Mary smiled and held up the phone that Tara had given her close to her heart. The whole flight back to Connecticut, Mark was asking questions about Scotland, Ireland, and her family – especially Uncle Arland, who she suspected Mark liked a lot. She did too. Uncle Arland was a likeable fellow.

"So, you would go back? To Ireland and Scotland?" Tara asked Mark as they sat side by side on the plane.

"Yes, I would." When they landed it was noisy and busy, and Tara longed for the comfort of Uncle Arland's cottage. Alana had stayed behind in Scotland, to spend more time with her kids and grandchildren.

On the plane, Tara and Mark had also found the adoption agency from the paperwork Tara had. It was in Alaska.

Tara was not excited to be home. She had to go to a big empty estate when she would rather have been in Scotland at Uncle Arland's. But she had to find out more about this adoption agency, and this Beira person. When Tara could turn on her phone, she saw that she had twenty messages. Most were from Mary. Tara smiled. There were a few from her lawyer and one recent one from Alana.

Tara called her. "Hi Alana," she said, happy to hear from her nanny.

"Ah wull be staying in bonnie Scotland fur at least anither week. Mah daughter needs me fur she isnae weel."

"Oh, I am sorry to hear that. Give her my best, and I will see you when you get back." Tara hung up as Mark grabbed Tara's new bags, and they headed for the car. Tara was sitting in the driver's seat and opening the CD her cousin had given her, and Mark was putting their luggage in the back. He got into the passenger seat.

"Tara, I have been thinking. What about if I come with you to Alaska?"

Tara looked at him briefly. "You would come with me? What about the club?"

"Oh, there are a lot of guys who want a job there. Besides, with Alana not around, someone has to be with you. Also, I…" He stopped short of what he was going to say.

"Yeah, I would love for you to come with me."

Mark smiled and rolled down his window once they were out of the parking garage.

"I really want to help you Tara, and with your parents gone and all…" His voice kind of trailed off again, leaving Tara wondering what he was going to say.

"I can take care of myself, really. But I am glad you have been around. Really, Mark." She smiled at him as he smiled back. It was going to be a great summer, with him around.

"Can you drive by the club before bringing me home?" Mark asked.

"Sure," Tara said, changing lanes and going down a different street. Tara pulled up to the club.

"I'll be right back," Mark told her, slamming the door closed.

"So," said a voice. Tara jumped. It was Ettrick, the brownie.

"You startled me," she told him.

"So, what if I show myself to Mark? Would you believe I was real then?" Tara was not sure she wanted to pull Mark more into her craziness.

"I don't think that is such a great idea," she told him.

They both looked up as Mark opened the door suddenly, and went to sit down. "No!" Tara yelled. Ettrick poked him in the butt with his walking stick so that Mark would not sit on him.

"Ow!" Mark yelled as he jumped back out of the Beemer, rubbing his bottom.

"Don't ye be sittin' on me," Ettrick said, standing up.

"What the—?" Mark exclaimed as he blinked a few times and then took a few steps back.

"Mark, this is Ettrick," Tara said smiling.

"'Tis a pleasure ta meet ye, Mark." Ettrick stuck out his hand.

Mark just stood there gaping. Then he leaned down a bit.

"What?" Tara laughed nervously. "Yeah, I thought he was all in my head, too. But you can see him. Right, Mark? You see him?"

"Yeah, but what the crap is it?"

Tara sighed. "He is a brownie. They are little goblin, or fairy creatures known to help out with household things."

"Okay, cool, I guess," Mark said as he turned and hesitantly held out his hand and Ettrick shook his finger.

"Is he just gonna stare at me all day?" Ettrick asked, jumping into the back seat as Mark's gaze followed him.

"Come on Mark, get in. We gotta go," Tara said, raising her head from the steering wheel where she had been resting it. Her headache was back. She turned on the engine.

By the time Tara looked in the rear-view mirror, Ettrick had already disappeared. As she started pulling away, Mark spoke.

"Everything is all set with the club manager. They already hired several new people, and so–"

"That's that," Tara finished. They both laughed. The rest of the drive to Mark's house was mostly quiet.

Tara pulled up in Mark's driveway. He got out and went around to the back of the car and got his bags. Then he leaned down by the open driver's window.

"Are you sure you will be okay?" he asked.

"Yes Mark, I will be fine. I will pick you up tomorrow before lunch, okay?" Mark looked in the back seat, but no Ettrick.

"Does he—?"

Tara looked back. "Oh, he leaves and shows up when he wants to. Don't worry, you will see him again."

He leaned in through the open window and kissed Tara's cheek. It wasn't a real kiss—well it was a real kiss, just not where she had wanted him to kiss her. Or did she want him to? She felt her face grow warm.

"Bye, I will see you tomorrow," he said, backing up so she could leave.

When Tara walked into the house, it seemed so empty to her. Alana was in Scotland, and Charles the groundskeeper was on vacation. His daughter was overseeing the estate duties while he was away. Her parents… Well, at least she had Ettrick.

He had started doing things around the house, and she let him do whatever it was. She was going to bed.

She started to climb the long staircase very slowly, and the house was fairly dark. She briefly paused by her parents' bedroom door. She stood there for a few moments before going to her own bedroom. The house was so quiet, it kind of gave her the shivers. It felt so empty and cold.

Tara was so exhausted. She lay down on her bed, not even bothering to change out of her clothes.

*

* *

7

Alaska

It took Tara and Mark a little over a week to drive to Anchorage. Their plan was to get more information if they could about Tara's adoption. Uncle Arland did not know much and neither did her Grandparents. She did not know what she would do with the info. Call her birth parents? Or try to visit them? However, she wasn't sure if she wanted to, or if they would be willing. After all, what if they had given her away and never wanted to see her again? They both were glad they were traveling during the summer—any other time might not have been so nice. The scenery was beautiful: a lot of trees, hills, winding roads, and lakes. The snowcapped mountains stood behind the city's skyline. The city seemed small in comparison to the mountains. Breathtaking, really.

Tara held the tiny bracelet that was on her necklace as they pulled up to the address, they had for the adoption agency. Tara and Mark got out of the car. Tara looked at the address on the building and then back at the address on the letter.

"Mark, is this the right place? Because there is no adoption agency here." They both stood there for a moment. Mark took the paper from Tara. "Well um, yeah. That's a bookstore, not an adoption agency. Let's go inside and ask someone."

Mark gave the paper back to her and headed for the door. He opened it, and as he did, an old-fashioned bell rang out. The store smelled of books and coffee: two scents Tara loved.

There were a few people in the store perusing about, and some sat in the coffee shop area.

"Can I help you?" asked a young woman wearing glasses, her black hair pulled back into a tight ponytail. She was wearing a cream-colored, frilly blouse, a tight, knee-length skirt, and high heels. Her outfit fit her curves just right, and you could tell she was athletic.

"Um, yeah. We're looking for the Alaskan Adoption Agency?" Tara asked, handing the young lady her paper.

She looked at the paper. "Oh, I'm sorry. The agency closed down several years ago. My boyfriend and I bought this old building after the agency were gone. I do not know what to tell you."

She handed the paper back to Tara. Someone was standing at the front desk.

"If you'll excuse me, I need to go help that gentleman. If you have any questions my name is Beira." She walked away towards the desk.

Tara and Mark stood there, her name not yet registering in Tara's mind.

"Did she say her name was Beira?" Mark asked, looking at Tara, who did not answer.

Mark gently grabbed her by the arms. "You're shaking," he said as Tara looked down.

"Am I?" She asked.

"Tara, we don't have to do this. We could go back home live our lives and…"

"No Mark, I need to find out. I need to know why that old lady knew stuff, and why she told me to talk to a Beira."

"This could just be a coincidence," Mark said, looking at the paper Tara held in her hand. "Well," he continued, "she said she bought the place. Maybe she knows more, and we can ask her after she is done helping her customers. Besides, if she is the one you need to talk to then I guess you should." He hesitated. "Well, if you want, anyway."

"I do, it's just…"

Mark took Tara's hand as he started walking around the shop. The girl named Beira was kept very busy though, until they saw someone else working instead, and Tara went to ask where the other girl had gone.

"Oh, she went on her break. She will be back later." The older woman was holding a big stack of books, she nodded and went back to sorting books in a cart.

Mark checked the time. "Come on, let's check into our hotel, get something to eat, and come back later," he said, putting a book back on the shelf.

When they returned to the bookstore later on, the streets were dark, and not many were about. A few people here and there strolled the wet sidewalks. It had rained earlier with some good lightning, and a thunderstorm to go with it.

When they got to the door, they saw that in the window it said closed. The times were posted on the door, and it was not closing time yet. However, now there was also a paper stating that they had closed early.

"You have got to be kidding me!" Tara practically screamed.

Mark hit the doorframe with his fist. "Wait, there is a light on inside," He said as he peered through the window.

He pounded on the door. Another light came on and the young lady appeared. She came up to the door and unlocked it.

"Oh hello," Beira said cheerfully. "Let me just get the door." It seemed to be stuck, but she opened it fairly quickly. "Sorry about earlier, I was swamped., and then went on my break. We are closed now but did you still want to come in?" she said, stepping aside.

As soon as Tara and Mark walked in, she closed and relocked the door.

"If you will follow me please," she said, smiling, as she walked ahead of them in her bare feet. They followed her to a back room. There was a huge, messy desk, a few chairs, and more bookshelves heaving with books and papers.

Beira grabbed a box of off one of the shelves, dusted it off, and handed it to Tara.

"Why do you still have papers here? Wouldn't they be at the station or in the state records department?" Mark asked.

"These were found recently, and since my boyfriend works at the station, we just have kept them here."

"You can sit down and look through the box if you would like. This is everything that is left from the adoption agency. Well, all the paperwork that was left here I should say."

Tara and Mark looked through the papers inside the box.

"So, you said you bought the place? From who?"

"Oh, from the city. No one in particular. My fiancé and I took over this place several months ago. It had been vacant for a while, so we fixed it up. I guess a woman ran it. She just left town one day, never bothered to close the building or anything," Beira said, shrugging her shoulders.

"So, you never met the woman who ran the agency?" Mark asked, wanting more answers.

"No, sorry, the city never found her. It's as if she just vanished."

"Look," Tara said, grabbing a folder labeled "Baby Girl Doe." Tara and Mark looked through the file.

"There is information about my parents in here," Tara said. There was a picture of her parents holding a baby, and around the baby's wrist was the bracelet Tara now wore around her neck.

"Are you sure there is no more information other than what is in this box?" Tara asked, getting up.

"There's no more here. However, my fiancé might have some more info down at the police station. He works there, like I said before," Beira told them.

Tara looked from Beira back to the file she held. "It only says here that I was left on the doorstep of the adoption agency."

Startled, Beira dropped her stack of papers, and they scattered all over the floor. She quickly walked over to Tara, slipping on the papers scattered on the floor, but she caught herself.

"You're the baby in the file?" she asked, looking very surprised.

"Um, yeah. My name is Tara MacInnes."

Beira backed away, seeming a bit startled.

"You think you are the baby in this photo?" Beira asked, glancing at it.

"Yes, those are my parents, and that is me as a baby."

"Is something wrong?" Tara asked.

"No! No. Um… Could you meet me and my fiancé for breakfast at Terra Bella tomorrow morning? Let's say around seven a.m.?" Tara and Mark looked at each other.

"Sure, if he can help us." Mark was cautious in answering her.

Beira smiled. "Yes, I think he can. I will see you there then." She started walking towards the front door. They followed her.

"I will see you both in the morning?" she asked, opening the door as Tara and Mark followed her.

"Yes," Tara told her confidently.

"Oh, and you can keep the file. I have no use for it," she said as she held the door open.

"Thanks," Tara said, walking out into the chilly night air.

"See ya," Beira said, closing the door and locking it. They watched as she walked hastily back to her office, and soon all the lights were out in the bookstore.

"Well, okay. I guess we shall see what more she knows in the morning then," Mark said as he took Tara's hand, and they walked to the car. Tara hesitantly walked with him, looking over her shoulder at the bookstore.

"I was left on the doorstep to the agency," Tara said out loud, trying to comprehend why someone would do that.

"Hey," Mark said, putting his hands on her shoulders and standing in front of her. "Your parents loved you, Tara."

She smiled. They did, but did her birth parents? she wondered.

They got into the car. Tara let Mark drive as she did not feel like driving.

Once back at the hotel, Tara took a long hot bath. She was feeling very drained. She lay in the bed as a million questions ran through her mind. She tossed and turned, trying to sleep.

"You know, your parents did love you. Still do," Ettrick said. He was sitting in a chair by the bed. Tara looked at him.

"Do you know my parents? I mean my birth parents?" she asked.

"I know of them Tara, but I have never met them. My great-great grandfather is their brownie."

She peered at him, not sure if she should believe what he was saying.

"I can tell you aren't sure whether to believe me or not, aye. Well I don't blame ya. Get some sleep now Tara, I believe tomorrow will be a busy day."

With that, he jumped down off the chair and vanished.

Tara shook her head and fell into a restless sleep. What was Ettrick hiding, and why would he not tell her more information?

* * *

8

Beira and Lou

The next morning, Mark and Tara met Beira and her fiancé at the organic coffee shop.

"This is my fiancé Louis, but he likes to go by Lou," Beira said as they stood to greet them.

Lou was pretty tall and fairly muscular with fair skin. He had very blond hair and green eyes. Tara thought he was gorgeous, and her initial impression was that they made a great couple. Tara and Mark sat down, although Tara noticed that Mark sat reluctantly.

As the waitress handed them menus, Tara decided that she was having at least two cups of coffee.

Beira waited until the waitress left. "We have more information. But it might not be safe to discuss it here."

"What do you mean isn't safe?" Tara asked behind her menu.

"We should order first," Lou said.

Beira nodded. Something was up, but Tara wasn't going to ask right then. "Let's order. I'm starving," Tara said as she looked at the menu.

After a few unsettling moments of silence, the waitress came back over. "What can I get you?" she asked.

"Ladies first," Lou said.

After they had all ordered, the waitress took the menus.

"All right, I'll take care of these."

"The information we have for you is classified. However, since I work at the station, I can get you all in to look," said Lou.

Tara sat up.

"What were my birth parents, murderers or something?"

Lou smiled. "No, nothing like that."

"Well, what then?" Tara asked.

"It's hard to explain," Beira said. "We just need to show you."

Their food came, and they all ate and talked a bit. Tara told them that her adoptive parents had been killed in a bad car accident in Scotland.

"Oh. We are sorry to hear that," Beira said as she put down her cup.

"Has anything odd happened since their passing?" Lou asked.

"Odd?" Tara asked. "Um, yeah I guess so," she said, wondering why they would ask a question like that.

"Why would you ask her that?" Mark asked, pushing his empty plate away.

"Look, we have info on the circumstances of where you were found, if all you are saying is true of who you are. Meet us at the police station at six tonight. That's when I can let you in. Park around the back." He handed Mark a card.

"Here is the address." Mark took the card and stared at Lou like he wanted to knock his head right off his shoulders.

"Six. That's a long time to wait," Tara said, drinking the last of her drink.

"Sorry. It's the best I can do for now."

The waitress came over and was talking to Beira and Lou. "We should get information from them now," Mark said to Tara in a hushed tone.

"Yeah well, if we have to wait until tonight to see what they have at the station, I will wait," Tara said. Even though she wanted to go now.

"Should we trust them though, Mark?" Tara asked. She felt she could; however, she still had an uneasy feeling.

He shrugged his shoulders.

Lou offered to pay for breakfast.

"We are going with you now, not waiting until later," Tara told Beira and Lou.

"Later at six is when I can get you into the classified old file room, not now."

"It's now or never," Mark said, standing in front of Tara protectively.

Lou sighed and got out his phone. He stepped far enough away from them that Tara could not hear what he was saying. He came back over, putting his phone away.

"The best I can do is lunch time, which will be at noon. The station will be quiet then, long enough for us to show you what we have."

Tara glanced up at the clock on the wall in the diner. It was nine.

"Now, or never," Tara said impatiently.

Beira pulled Lou aside and they talked very animatedly.

"Looks like they are arguing," Tara said as they concluded and came closer.

"Noon," Lou said, standing there adamantly.

Mark nodded.

"Fine," Tara said as they all went outside. Tara got into the passenger seat of the Beemer. She got out the business card and punched in the address for the police station.

They drove around town for a while, then decided to venture a bit out of town since they had time.

"Hey, what's up with the navigation system?" Mark asked as he started pushing buttons.

"I don't know, let me see," Tara said as she too pushed buttons and spoke commands to the computer.

"Unable to connect," the voice of the computer called out.

"Oh great, no signal," Tara said as Mark pulled over.

"We can't get lost, Mark. We have to meet them at noon," Tara said in a slightly panicked tone. She felt a tug on her shirt. It was Ettrick.

She bent down as he motioned for her to come in close. "You need help. Go for a walk to the river," Ettrick told her and then disappeared.

She started walking, all frustrated. "And why can't you help me, Ettrick? Lousy brownie."

Tara looked up. Sure enough, there was a river, which was flowing lazily over rocks and made little waterfalls.

"Hey, I'm going to see if anyone is around," Tara said as she opened the door. Mark had the manual out and was pushing more buttons.

"Yeah, okay," he said, not really paying attention.

She got out of the car and closed the door. She looked around. It did not seem as if anyone was around. She started walking down the road a bit.

The trees were pretty thick here, and before long she could no longer see the Beemer.

Then she thought she saw someone fishing in the river. She made her way toward the river's edge. The rush of the water was louder here. There was someone standing on a rock and fishing. Tara thought the person's posture was a bit weird.

He wore all the gear you would need to fish in a river, including a wide brimmed hat.

"Excuse me!" Tara yelled above the rush of the water. At first, he did not acknowledge she was there and just kept fishing.

"Hello!" Tara yelled.

Then he turned.

Tara stumbled backwards as she got a good look at him. Or it. She landed on her bottom with her arms behind her, supporting her upper body.

Staring back at her was not a man, but a wolf.

With one leap, he was on the river bank a few feet away from Tara. He looked like a man from the waist down, but his upper body looked like a wolf. He grunted at her and then grinned, showing all his sharp white teeth. Tara backed away a bit, and he held out his paw. Tara was a bit scared and unsure she wanted to get closer. He grunted again and set down his fishing pole. He then came closer to her, and offered his paw again. She reluctantly took it and, with strength like an ox, pulled her to her feet.

She brushed off her pants. She was breathing hard, and her heart was pounding in her chest.

"Um, we're lost, could you tell us were the highway is?" Tara asked, out of breath. She wasn't scared of him…well, not too much anyway, not anymore at least. At first yes. It was just—well, he was half wolf!

"So, who are you? I mean what are you? You look like a Wulver. Well from what I have read about them that is."

He nodded his head yes and took out a piece of paper and a stubby pencil from his pocket.

After a few moments, he handed the paper to her. She looked at the paper and then his paw with its long claws. Tara swallowed hard. He gestured for her to take the paper, so she took it quickly and looked at it.

There at the top was the word Wulver, and the word yes. Then there was a very detailed map of where she stood, where the car was, and where the highway was. When she looked up, he was standing there holding up a fish, still on some line. He extended his arm towards her.

"Oh, I just ate. Thank you though."

He still held it out. She slowly walked over to him and took it. It was a very large fish.

"Thank you. I have read about Wulver's. You don't usually contact people in person. I thought you were a myth." She chuckled nervously. He shook his head no, and patted his chest, she guessed to signify he was real. He grinned at her, again showing all of his sharp white teeth. He then turned and jumped into the water and started fishing again.

Tara stood there transfixed, her head felt a bit fuzzy.

"Wow," She said as it started drizzling a slightly cold rain. She looked at the fish and the map, then back at the wolf man. "Thank you!" she called out as she quickly climbed the bank up to the road.

"Yeah, strange things have been going on for sure." She just saw a Wulver. She was quite shocked and awed. It was her fourth encounter with a magical being of sorts. First the Banshee, then Ettrick, the flag at the castle, and the old woman, and now him, the Wulver.

Tara got back to the car, out of breath and shaking a bit from the encounter, and from the cold rain coming down, her head ached a bit too.

"Okay, so I got directions," she said, handing the small piece of paper to Mark through the window.

"Where did you get this?" he asked as he looked at the small piece of paper. She held up the fish still on some line, and it dangled between them.

"A guy fishing. He gave me this, too."

"A fish. He gave you a fish," Mark said, looking at it with his nose crinkled up a bit. "Yeah okay, how are we going to cook that?"

"You don't like fish?" she asked him.

"I do," he responded, looking at the little map.

"Are you okay?" Mark asked her as she looked back behind her towards the river.

"Um, the guy fishing…"

"Yeah…?" he prodded. He opened the car door, got out, and took the fish.

Tara shrugged her shoulders and went to open the trunk of the car. Ettrick was there.

"I'll take it and cook it up proper. That Wulver give you this?" he asked, grabbing the fish and putting it in the cooler they had.

"Uh yeah," Tara said, looking towards the river.

Maybe the fish was really for him anyway, Tara thought to herself. "Your sight abilities are growing." Ettrick said as the lid to the cooler closed, with Ettrick inside.

"What is a Wulver?" Mark must have heard her.

"Nothing, nobody," she said as she closed the trunk.

Tara sat in the passenger seat. Mark got back into the driver's seat and turned on the car and the windshield wipers. Then he turned around and drove in the direction of the highway.

"Who were you talking to?" Mark asked her.

"Ettrick," she said as she buckled her seatbelt. He sighed.

"Ettrick." He sounded fed up. "Tara, look, I know it's been hard losing your parents and finding out you were adopted but don't you think this is enough?"

"Mark, I was hoping you would believe me."

"Well I don't." Tara sensed his uneasiness.

"He wasn't going to hurt me or anything."

Mark shook his head. "Tara!" He seemed upset, so she just dropped it and looked out the window. She watched the landscape stream past her window.

"It's so beautiful here," Tara said as they drove through thick, very green forest. They even saw a few deer as they drove. "I am hungry, aren't you?" Tara asked. Mark just turned up the volume on the radio.

9

Proof

Once at the station, they parked around the back. They got out of the car and followed Lou over to a door. Tara had her adoption papers with her, along with her birth certificate and driver's license. Once inside, Beira closed the door behind them quietly. They followed Lou down a few hallways. Tara felt nervous.

"Are you sure this is okay?" Tara asked as Lou stopped in front of a door and punched in a code on the keypad. He put his finger up to his lips as Beira came around the corner. They all went inside a dark room and Beira stood by the door, which was now closed.

"Don't touch anything until you put these on," Lou said, handing them each a pair of plastic gloves.

He then turned on the flashlight that he held in his hands. They quickly put the gloves on.

Lou walked up to a huge filing cabinet, opened it, and started looking for a file. He pulled it out as soon as he found it.

"Here, take this," Lou said to Tara, giving her the file.

It was bigger than the file that Beira had given her. Tara looked through the file with Mark peering over her shoulder. Lou shined the flashlight so they could see. There were all kinds of paperwork, pictures, and articles about a baby girl found by some hikers in the woods. Some of the pictures were of massive prints in the mud. Speculations of Bigfoot ran throughout some of the articles. There was a newspaper about the police casting the prints.

"Do you have the castings?" Mark asked.

Lou's face lit up. "I was hoping you would ask," he said, motioning for them to follow him. He led them through another door into a storage room. It was huge, dark and musty smelling.

"What proof do you have that you are the baby girl in these documents?" Beira asked as Tara handed her the documents she had along with her driver's license. She showed them to Lou. He nodded as he looked at them.

"That's all I got, unless you want a DNA testing done or something." Tara felt insulted that they would doubt her. "Look. My parents are dead and I am here seeking answers, so if you can't help or don't believe me then we can go somewhere else."

"No," Lou said quickly. He shot Beira a warning look. "No, we will help you," he said, looking back at Tara.

"Not too many of us have access to this room," he said as he shone the flashlight around the room. He turned on a pull chain light, which was a low yellow light that swung back and forth casting weird shadows all over the room. He turned off his flashlight and secured it to his belt around his waist.

He brought them over to a huge crate when his pager went off. He held up his hand as he answered it. "Hey chief. Yeah. Okay, when I am done in the dungeon I will file that. Yeah, just checking on an old lead. Yeah, not much longer. Okay, thanks. Bye." He hung up.

Lou found a crowbar and got the lid off of the crate; it took a few minutes; his large muscles could be seen bulging under his short-sleeved uniform, but he got it. Crap, he must be strong, Tara thought as Mark set the lid down so that it leaned against a crate, which caused the dust from the top of the crate and the floor to rise and tickle Tara's nose. Mark must be fairly strong too—that lid was huge.

"Can you help me, Mark?" Lou asked as he started pulling straw out of the crate.

Then they both lifted a huge casting of a footprint. But not just a footprint—it was actually a huge boot print.

"That's a boot print," Tara said, looking at it from all angles.

"It sure is," Lou said as he put his hands on his hips.

"What could be that big?" Tara asked, touching the white plaster.

"Giants" was all Lou said as his pager went off again. This time it was Beira, as she came into the room.

"Giants. As in 'Fee-fi-fo-fum?'" Tara was not sure that the print was real.

They heard noises outside in the hall. Lou gestured for Mark to help him again.

"Wait!" yelled Tara as she took out her phone. "I want to take a picture." Tara handed Beira the phone and smiled as she and Mark held the casting up for the photo. Once she was done, they put it back into the crate, put the straw back in, and fastened the lid back on.

"Come on," he said, getting out his flashlight again and turning it on as he pulled the string for the light on the ceiling. They followed him out another door that Tara had not seen before.

"Beira will meet us outside," he said, opening the door. "I gotta go talk to the chief about something. Be right back."

The door led to outside—a few doors down to where they had entered earlier. Beira was waiting at the farthest corner of the building.

"Oh, I still have these," Tara said, trying to hand the files to Beira.

"Keep them. That case has been shelved for so long, no one will miss them. Besides, they are about you," she said, looking around nervously.

Tara grinned slightly back and held onto the files as they walked to the car.

"Nice car," Beira said as they approached.

"Thanks," Tara said as she got out the keys. She unlocked the car and put all the papers inside on the back seat in a box. Lou came jogging around the corner, his slightly wavy hair bouncing as he ran.

"All set," he said smiling.

Just then a group of people came into the alley where they were parked.

"Have you heard about the northern lights? Aurora borealis? Or ever seen them?" Beira asked them both.

"Heard of them yes, but I have never seen them. Have you, Mark?"

"I saw them as a kid," Mark replied watching the group get closer. Mark whispered to Tara. "Get in the car and lock it." She looked at him, just now noticing the crowd. Then all of a sudden, some people from the group grabbed Tara and Mark. They tied them up, tied scarves over their mouths so they could not yell and put them in the trunk of the cruiser. Tara was not sure how long they were in there, and they were not sure where they were going once the cruiser started. They were bumped around and even though Mark got off his scarf from around his mouth he could not untie the bonds on his wrists or ankles. Eventually, the cruiser stopped. They heard muffled talking and then the trunk was opened. Two men pulled Tara and Mark out of the car. Tara could not believe they had been tied up and taken. What did these people want?

They were in a field, and it was dark now. Tara and Mark sat side by side in the field as Beira and Lou stood nearby. The other people were standing about nearby.

"Why did you take us?" Mark asked. No answer. Lou came over and took the scarf off of Tara's mouth. She gave him a nasty look.

"How did you know Beira's name?" Lou asked, looking at Tara.

"You don't have to tell them anything, Tara," Mark said, trying to free himself of the bonds.

"Can you guys stop with the questions and answer some of ours?" Mark said through clenched teeth.

Lou spoke first. "We believe, Tara, that you are the abducted princess, granddaughter of the first King of Scotland."

Tara began to laugh. "Abducted, yeah by you two."

Beira turned and looked at Tara.

"Princess of the Dalriada," Lou said again

Tara was still laughing, a coping mechanism for all that had been going on she guessed.

"As in the Dagda, the high king of old, of Scotland?" She really laughed out loud now. "He is an ancient myth."

"Really. Are you guys on drugs or something? Really, the high kings of old," Mark added as he shifted his weight.

"Tara please, this is all new to you, we know. Just hear us out," Beira said, coming closer to her.

"You both are loony!" Mark said as he struggled to stand, pulling Tara up with him.

Tara looked at Mark. She hadn't said much. She was sifting it all out in her brain. Which hurt her brain. She closed her eyes. Then opened them. "Do you think they are lying?" She asked him. She really wanted to know what he thought.

"I don't know, Tara. All this crazy stuff and now they are saying you're some lost princess from—well, gosh only knows where."

"Fine, who are you two?" Tara had about all she could take.

Beira came closer as Lou followed. "My name is Beira Monach, daughter of King Frogal Monach, and he is Lou, son of King Cian of the sky Kingdom."

Tara nearly fell over with laughter. "Oh, this is just great." She stopped laughing and regained her composure. "Fine, I'm listening," she said, looking at them sternly.

"The king and queen held a celebration long ago," Beira started to say.

"Even the fairies came," Lou piped in as they walked closer.

"Fairies! Really?" Mark said.

Tara hit Mark's arm. "Shh," she said as Lou continued.

"The celebration was held in honor of their third born, a daughter. The princess was given a gift by the fairy queen and king. A blanket called the Fae Flag, or Fairy Flag as some call it."

Tara's eyes widened as she listened.

"You know about it?" Beira asked.

"Maybe," Tara said as she shifted her weight onto her right foot. "Well there is the story about the flag at a castle in Scotland."

Tara's head was starting to hurt.

"Sometime during the celebration, the princess was taken by giants," Lou said as he and Beira walked even closer. "The nursemaid had left the baby in her cradle and had rejoined the party."

"I – I mean the baby – was left alone," Tara said as she shifted her weight. If Mark was going to do anything, it would be soon. She could sense his anger building minute by minute.

"Yes. Well she got her punishment, but that's beside the point. The king called for his army to go search for the princess," said Beira, seemingly annoyed.

"The king and queen grieved for many months. They would often go check out leads that often ended up at dead ends. Recently, they went missing as well, causing the kingdoms to become divided," Lou told them.

"The clans and kingdoms are at war with the Stone Kingdom and the Sky Kingdom. Then there are the giants. The Fae Flag is missing, so the two fairy kings are using that as an excuse for a fight. Oh, and one of the kings has a ton of sons; three are triplets. They are missing as well. The fourth son went missing years ago, and he has not been found either," Beira finished telling them.

"Wow, sounds like you could use some good police there," Tara said as she looked at Lou. "So, if you think I am the princess, then how long have I been missing?"

Lou and Beira looked at each other.

"Time is different here than in the Higher Realms; it goes by slower there.

Mark interrupted. "Higher Realms, what is that again?" Mark's voice was a bit snarky.

"That is where the kings and queens of old still reside," Beira told him.

"Along with fairies and other mystical creatures?" Mark was now being really sarcastic.

"Yes," Beira told him very seriously.

"The infant princess has been missing for only a little while—a little over a year. A year is like a heartbeat here. So here you have aged many years," Beira said as she walked even closer to Tara.

"Maybe I'm not who you're looking for," she stated plainly.

"We believe you could be," Lou said as he walked closer as well.

"All the evidence pointed us to Alaska, and when you came and had evidence of your own, we agreed you had to come with us.

"Whether we wanted to or not," Mark said as Lou, who had been pacing, turned to look at him.

"All royalty has a piece of the coronation stone set in something like a brooch, or a necklace." Beira came closer. "Do you have anything like that?"

Tara remembered her small bracelet but was not going to tell them about it. There was no way she was going to show them, they might steal it. She shook her head no.

"Beira, can we untie them now? They won't get far if they try to run."

Beira nodded as Lou untied Mark first. As soon as he was free, he swung and hit Lou in the stomach. Lou just pushed him down. The punch did not seem to faze him. Mark was rubbing his knuckles. He then untied Tara. Lou went to get something from the cruiser as Beira stood nearby watching them.

Mark whispered in Tara's ear, "Run." Without looking, she pushed past and started running into the forest behind them. She heard a gunshot and yelling as she felt something strike the back of her head, and everything went black.

10

The Higher Realms

Tara awoke with her hands tied behind her back, again. She lifted her head, which was pounding. "Ahh," she said as she tried to focus.

"Don't struggle, Tara." It was Mark—he was sitting beside her, tied up as well.

"Oh good, you're awake. Wouldn't want you to miss anything, Princess. Also, don't try to run again. There is a lot at stake if you go missing again. I will not let that happen," Beira said as Tara tried to kick her, but her feet were tied as well. Beira backed away and stood upright, smiling.

"Where is this so-called place, anyway? The Higher Realms?" Mark asked, wondering if they were telling the truth or trying to trick them. Tara grabbed at the necklace under her shirt and then let go of it.

"It is here," Beira said, opening her arms wide, "and there." She pointed to the sky. "Then stretches far beyond our vision. It is all around us, it's just earthly mortals cannot see it."

Lou took over explaining. "The Higher Realms are connected to Earth like ribbons of time, space and magic. They are woven here and there and the aurora borealis is a connecting point. Well, one of them. There are several; some are fairy hills."

"Can you give us proof?" Mark asked.

"Yeah, proof," said a voice. Both Tara and Mark jumped. Tara's head pounded.

Ettrick appeared then.

"Ye be needing more proof than me? The old woman, the Fairy Flag, the Banshee, shall I go on?" he asked.

"Ettrick, go away," Tara whispered through clenched teeth. Mark looked down with an expression of disgust on his face.

"Again?" Mark tried swiping him away with his hand like a pesky fly.

Lou and Beira peered down at Ettrick as Tara saw Lou putting Mark's gun in his holster. "Ah, you have a brownie." Beira smiled. "Hello," she said as Ettrick bowed his head. Beira answered Tara's initial question. "It's a place where your ancestors live, through the mist and colors in the sky to a land full of fairies, trolls, and castles."

"Ah, hello," Ettrick said, planting his walking stick into the ground.

"My name is Ettrick Aberfeldy," he said. "And ye are Prince Lou, son of King Cian of the Light Kingdom, a.k.a. the Sun God." He bowed to Lou then turned and bowed to Beira. "Ye are Beira Monach, daughter of King Frogal Monach of the Stone Kingdom. Also known as 'The Queen of Winter.'"

"Very good," Lou said quickly as he smiled.

"And what about ye, Mark?" Ettrick asked.

"What about me?" Mark said, Tara could tell by the tone of his voice that he did not want to be in the conversation. Actually, Mark looked like he was going to explode right out of his bindings. He kept clenching up his fists.

"What is your name, and where are ye from?" Ettrick asked.

"I am from Arizona, and my name is Mark Weatherbee," he said, annoyed. "And it is looking better and better by the minute," Mark said, hitting Tara's shoulder with his own.

"They are all crazy," he said, not looking directly at Tara but slightly at the others.

"How long have you been serving Tara, Ettrick?" Beira asked.

"Ettrick, I don't think they can be trusted," Tara said, resting her head on Mark's shoulder.

Ettrick came over. "Don't be daft, of course they can be trusted."

"Then why are we tied up?!" Mark was mad and getting madder by the minute. "Don't tell them anything," he said through clenched teeth.

"Well I am not sure I trust them," Tara said. "Mark. You see Ettrick, you saw the flag at the castle. Come on, something is going on. Or we both are having nervous breakdowns. I mean, we both recently lost parents."

Mark sighed.

"She kind of has a point, ye know," Ettrick said and then disappeared.

Tara rolled her eyes into the back of her throbbing head. "I won't leave. At least, not without you." She snapped her head forward, and nudged Mark with her arm. Sighing, she said, "Well if we are losing it, we might as well enjoy the ride." She looked over to Beira and Lou.

"So, you said something about the northern lights?" She was very curious as to what they had to say. Beside her Mark was trying to get his hands free.

"That is how we travel from the Higher Realms to your world, or this world. Well, one of the ways I should say. Well, one of the ways. It is also where the Nimble Men dance with the Merry Maidens this time of year." She sighed then. "It is quite lovely." She was dreamily looking up into the sky and then looked at Tara. "All the proof you want and need will be here soon. Oh, and don't even try to get your bonds loose." She quickly looked at Mark, who gave her a dark, foreboding look.

Then Tara saw something as she looked up into the darkened sky. "Look."

She pointed to where a brilliant mixture of colors – green and pink and purple – danced and weaved across the dark sky, with a backdrop of stars. Tara sat there amazed at it all. Mark was looking up as well.

"It's beautiful, isn't it?" Mark asked her.

"Yeah it is. Wait, what's that?" She squinted her eyes to see.

It became more visible the longer they looked. It was moving, and moving fast. An army riding on large horses burst through the colors of the northern lights, and they were carrying spears and wearing shiny helmets. The colors of the northern lights reflected off of the horses and their riders causing them to look green, blue, purple, and some pink. The colors shifted and the group of them seemed to ebb and flow along with the colors. The horses were huge muscular war horses, wearing armor. The army was wearing a mix of leather and metal armor, and there were both men and women. The sight alarmed Tara, and she jumped up onto Mark's lap.

The army landed in the field, and one woman quickly dismounted from her horse, removed her helmet, and started walking their way. She had thick, long, straw-colored hair that was pulled back into a ponytail; she was tall and muscular, and she was wearing armor.

"Holy crap," Tara said as she sat there.

"Uh, yeah," Mark said as he looked at the army.

The female warrior stopped in front of Beira and bowed.

"You summoned us Beira," she said in a heavy accent that Tara could not quite place.

Tara whispered so only Mark could hear, "I think I believe them now, don't you?" He nodded, looking wide eyed at the army before them.

Beira pointed at them sitting there in the field. "Yes. I believe we have finally found the princess."

The woman looked at her as well. "Why are their limbs bound, then?" she asked.

"Merely a precautionary measure," Lou said, walking around to face them. "They tried running away already."

She bowed towards Tara. "His Highness would not be pleased to learn of his daughter being tied up." She stood and looked at Lou stiffly.

"Well now that we found her, we don't want her getting away," Lou said sharply.

"You think you have found her, it isn't until she sits upon the throne made of the coronation stone that we shall know for sure," the warrior stated. "I would untie them Beira, if I were you."

The blond-haired woman whistled and turned on her heel, smiling at the army now gathered all around them.

The whole army was staring at them now, as the blond warrior walked around talking to them. They all started to cheer. Beira whistled, and out of the army came three horses. One was absolutely stunning: a light caramel color with a rich, buttery mane and tail. Beira lovingly patted the horse's flank.

Beira looked at Mark. "Can you ride?" she asked him. "I mean, I know you ride for pleasure here, for competitions, races, but can you ride?"

Mark smiled. "Untie me and I can show you."

Tara laughed out loud. She couldn't help it. "He owns horses," she told them.

"What about you?" Beira asked.

Tara stopped laughing. "I um…"

Mark answered the question. "She is still getting used to horses."

Beira motioned with her head, and two armed warriors came over and helped them up, grabbing them firmly but gently by their upper arms as a wagon-type of chariot came rushing forward. One of the warriors brought Tara over to a carriage. It was filled with stuff. She had to step over several bundles which was hard because her legs were still kind of tied together. He sat her down into a corner where she felt squeezed, and the other warrior set Mark down opposite her and threw Tara's bag onto her lap.

"It will be okay," said the young girl, not much older than Tara who was holding the reins that were pulling the cart. Tara could see that the horse pulling it was very muscular and large, more than the others.

"We could ride, really, there is no need." She was interrupted as, all at once, the entire army of horses and people leaped into the air. Tara banged against the side of the cart as they soared into the sky. Now her whole head hurt. She looked at the sky as they flew past, and the colors seemed to move and shift with them, as if the bands of color were a road on which they traveled. She would occasionally see dancing couples dressed in gowns and fancy suits. They looked as if they were dancing on the colors of the northern lights and the sparkling stars that filled the sky. At one point the cart turned as a dancing couple were so close that Tara felt the fabric of the female dancer brush against her hand, which was resting on the edge of the cart. It felt soft and silky, and she even heard the rustling of the layers of her dress as they waltzed away from the cart. The gentlemen winked at her as she looked up at his handsome face. She turned in the cart, now facing backwards, watching the dancers as they floated up and up like they were also dancing on clouds.

"That is cool," Tara said as she watched them fade into the distance.

Before long, they seemed to be miles away until the field below was out of sight completely. Soon she saw the horses that were pulling the wagon break through the clouds and mist, and the wagon followed. On the other side was the sun, shining so brightly Tara had to cover her eyes to shield them.

Ahead of them in the sky, as if just floating there, she saw a huge mass of earth and stone, which she could not see the end of. As they flew towards it, Tara could make out trees and farms. Then she saw a huge city.

They landed in a thick forest.

"Welcome to the Sky Kingdom," Lou said with a huge grin on his face.

Quickly, the army dismounted their horses and surrounded the chariot. Beira came up and introduced Tara and Mark to the army. There were cheers again after they were introduced.

"We need a plan," said the woman warrior with the thick, straw-colored hair who had first greeted Beira.

"Yes Epona, we do."

"Epona!" Tara exclaimed in shocked wonder. "As in the Celtic Goddess Epona?"

"Yes Tara, it's Epona," Beira said smiling.

Beira smiled at Tara as she stood staring with her mouth gaping wide open.

"We do need a plan now that we are here. We can't stay long, Lou." Beira seemed a little jittery.

Beira sighed. "Yes, I am called that. But I am not queen yet." She held up her finger at Tara. "Also, I am not an ugly old woman or a giant with blue skin, as all the tales say."

"No, you aren't. So how can you still be alive? I mean, you are ancient, right?"

Lou laughed and Beira gave him a nasty look. "We are alive, yes, and as I said before, time is different in the Higher Realms. Here on mortal Earth we would age rapidly, and we are known as myths, or we are dead. But we are immortal actually, well at least in the Higher Realms."

"Oh, because you're gods and all," Tara said almost mockingly.

"Ah, ha. Yeah, well," Lou snickered.

Tara was kind of smiling; however, she wasn't sure whether or not they were telling her the truth about who they were.

Tara was recalling the stories Alana had told her growing up. Oh shoot! Alana! Tara thought to herself. What will she think if I am missing? And Uncle Arland! Maybe they will just think that we stayed in Alaska longer.

"Hey Beira, will my cell phone work here?" Tara wanted to know because, if it did, then she could send messages to people to let them know she was okay.

"Ah maybe. Depends on where you are," she told her.

The gal driving the cart came over holding a knife. "Here, let me cut those ropes." She gently reached in and cut them and then handed the knife to Tara. "You can cut the ropes by your feet and then untie Romeo here." Tara laughed. "How do you know about Romeo? Isn't that from the mortal realm?" she asked.

"We study and read about you as much as you do about us," the girl told her.

"Romeo." She repeated as she looked his way. Mark gave her a nasty look. Tara cut the ropes around her ankles. She then cut the ropes around Mark's wrist, then gave him the knife. Mark quickly cut the rope around his ankles as Lou came up to him, wanting the knife back.

Tara got out her phone. No signal. "Darn!" Tara said out loud.

The gal driving the chariot came closer. "It might not work here—possibly closer towards the city," she said smiling. Tara noticed all the gals were dressed similarly, had variations of blond and brown hair, and some were darker skinned with dark hair. They all had the same build. They were all different ages, though. The girl took out her phone.

"I love these things," she said all cheerfully. She was pretty young; Tara guessed around fourteen or so. "I text my BF all the time. She lives in the Stone Kingdom."

"But how do they work here?" Tara asked curiously.

"Oh, well in some places the cell phone signals break through and we can connect. Other places it doesn't."

"Sounds like home," Tara said, mostly to herself. Tara then smiled as the girl put her phone away. There were men of all different ages; and girls, however, none of them were older than about twenty years, or so it seemed to her. Someone called Tara over to where Beira, Lou and Mark were now standing.

"So now that we are here, you cut our bonds?" Mark asked still a bit upset.

Lou came closer. "We figured you don't know how to navigate around here, and with the king's army you surely wouldn't try to escape." He smiled as Mark came over to Tara.

Tara was looking around. She had been to the Redwoods in California, but these trees made them look small.

"Tara!"

Tara looked at Beira. "What?" she said, annoyed.

"Okay, so our goal now that we believe we have found princess Brigit, aka Tara, is to find out where our allies are." Beira pulled out a map. Epona sighed.

"What?" Beira said looking at Epona.

"We think we found adequate evidence for now, trust me." Epona looked angrily at Beira then at Tara but her expression softened.

"If you made a mistake, Beira, taking these kids, the king will be in an up roar."

Mark was looking at the map intently, and Lou talked about different places they could look. As Tara listened, she wanted to ask questions but thought better of it for now.

"We could try the Sea Kingdom," Lou suggested.

"That is possible, although it would be tricky to get there," Beira said as if she was thinking really hard. "Besides, King Lir is neutral."

"By Dunvegan Castle there are seals. If they are selkies they could help," Tara said as everyone stared silently at her.

"No, they would just think that we were trying to trick them," Beira stated.

"Mermaids?" asked Tara. Everyone shook their heads no, except Mark.

"Kelpies!" Tara shouted a little louder than she intended. They all looked at her with horrified faces. "Okay, maybe not," she said, mostly to herself, realizing her mistake. They did not want to ask any mermaids, selkies or Kelpies. Kelpies yeah, she understood, those demon water horses would drag you into the water to your death. However, mermaids, well maybe they weren't nice either. Most stories about mermaids were fairly nice stories. Selkies, they might think you were trying to trick them and to take their seal skins so they would be trapped as a human. Tara sighed.

Mark came closer to her. "Tara, we need to find a way back," he whispered.

"All right, we can think of something I'm sure. Tara did want to find out what was going on first, and why they think she was some lost princess. She wanted answers to who she really was.

"Did you get a good look at the map?" She asked hoping they could somehow find a way home at some point.

"Yes, but I have no idea." He stopped talking as a male warrior walked past. Mark smiled and nodded as the man passed by. He then looked back at Tara, moving in closer to her.

"I have no idea where exactly we are."

11

Lir and Cian

Over dinner by an open fire, everyone agreed that they would start looking for allies to the king by some big famous bodies of water, or places where there was water.

"Where are we going to sleep?" Tara asked, realizing they would be traveling around for a while. At least until they figured out where they were exactly. Tara though kind of wanted to stay. She leaned over to whisper in Mark's ear.

"When we figure out where we are, we can talk about getting out of here, but I kind of want to stay."

He looked at her like she was crazy and walked away fuming mad. That made Tara upset. Beira saw Mark's reaction and went over to Tara.

"Oh, we have tents and things," Beira told her as she ate. The fire was nice. The air had cooled off some so the fire helped her get warm. She only had her sweat shirt and that did not seem to be helping much with the damp cold.

"Will we be tied up while sleeping?" Mark asked as Tara gave him a horrified look.

"Not unless you give us a reason to," Lou said as he walked over to a group of men. Mark got even madder.

"Look!" He shouted. "You can't just take us, claiming Tara is some princess that needs to be rescued and brought here, and expect us to just believe you!" They were both yelling and shouting now and it was making Tara's head hurt. Lou turned full face and got into Mark's space.

"Look! This war started over the princess going missing, we have spent months searching! Putting our lives on hold.!"

"That's enough!" Yelled Beira, her face red as a beet. "Look. The king sent us on an important mission, and if we do not deliver you safely and in one piece, we will lose our positions."

Tara spoke now and felt a bit nervous. "What if your wrong? What will happen?"

Lou came closer to her, a bit more composed now. "We don't know. King Kenneth Dagda is an honorable king, but not to be trifled with."

Tara was thinking and another question popped in her head. "Why did you tie us up, me up if you think I am the princess?"

Lou sighed. "We aren't sure you are. Beira is but the rest of us aren't. Until we have more proof, we are just going on a hunch and the evidence we have." Tara did not think that was very comforting.

Someone called out that it was time to eat, but Tara was not very hungry.

After they ate, the tents were set up. They reminded Tara of old-fashioned circus tents, but not bright and colorful. They were mostly a type of thick linen draped around long poles gathered at the top like a tepee. The tent was large, with long pieces of linen stretched over big wooden poles which had lanterns hanging from them. Inside there were all kinds of blankets and big, fluffy pillows.

"Come on, Tara, you will sleep in my tent. Actually, it's the king's tent, so I guess in a way it belongs to you too," Beira told her as they walked into the tent. Beira fastened the tent's opening shut.

There were two hammocks hanging from the big middle beam of the tent. The hammocks had a mesh draping spread around them. There were thick blankets and pillows on them as well. Tara took off her shoes and her outer clothing and sat in the hammock. It gently swayed back and forth as she lay down and covered herself up. It was so cozy. Beira got in hers, which was across from Tara's.

"When the high king and queen travel, there is usually a big, log-framed bed in here," Beira told her as her hammock swayed a bit.

"This is amazing. How did they get these big wooden beams up so fast, and where did they come from?"

Beira looked around. "Oh, these are in another wagon pulled by two horses. It also holds lots of other stuff. That's why we had you in the smaller of the two." Tara thought they were pretty big, fancy wagons though. They are so fancy because they belong to the king, Tara realized.

Beira looked at her, her eyes half closed. "Look, I am sorry how things have turned out. I guess I did get carried away. It's just that I have more at stake than Lou does. If I don't find the princess, my life will be ruined. The king already replaced my position as head of the army while we were in Alaska, and it was a great risk staying there. Then you two showed up, our first hope at finding her. The math is about right as to how old she would be now, you had evidence that you were the baby in the photos and, well, we made a frantic desperate decision"

Tara sighed. "What if your wrong?" She asked Beira.

"If I am wrong, we are all in a lot of trouble." Beira closed her eyes. "Now try to get some sleep, Tara. It will be a long day tomorrow," Beira told her. But she did not fall asleep right away. She was in a strange place, and it wasn't Connecticut or Scotland.

She listened to the different sounds of the night creatures. Crickets, the hooting of an owl. A distant sound of a wolf made Tara jump a bit. Beira slept peacefully near her. Tara snuggled down further in her hammock, which felt enormous, full of fluffy down, and comfortable.

Beira had told her some of the army would take turns standing watch, and Lou would as well, with Mark right by his side. That at least was a bit comforting.

Tara fell asleep and had crazy dreams of fairies, kelpies and giants.

Beira was waking her up. "Tara come on, we have to get up."

Her hair was pulled back into a long braid down the middle of her back. She had changed her clothes; she now looked like all of the other women in the army. Yet she still looked feminine.

Tara stretched as she sat up, watching as Beira left the tent.

Tara got up and put on her Converse sneakers. They were cold. She quickly took them off and grabbed them and put them under the covers where they could warm up, along with her other clothes. She had slept in her underwear and bra only the night before and she had forgotten that if you were camping you put your clothes in the sleeping bag with you so they would be warm and dry in the morning. Once they were warm enough, she put on her denim capris and a t-shirt and threw on her hoodie, and put her sneakers on. As she was walking out of the tent, she noticed the camp was being broken down quite swiftly. She quickly braided her hair.

"What's going on?" she asked as Lou and Mark came over to her.

"We need to eat and move out fast. A small band of warriors was spotted about five miles from here, and they are not King Kenneth's," Lou told her as she looked around.

Once they had eaten and were all packed and ready, they mounted the horses. Tara rode with Mark this time on a very tall horse. The cart was full of equipment. Tara had wondered where they put it all, and she noticed that a lot of the warriors had packs on their backs and on the saddles.

Beira and Lou rode up to Mark and Tara. "We are going to the Great Lakes in the northern part of the United States," she told them.

"We're going back to my world?" Tara asked.

"Yes, and no," said Beira. "The ribbons and mists of time, which our army can travel in, connect the higher realms to Earth. Sometimes in the mist, you can see the Higher Realms overlaid with the Earth. The part of the Higher Realms that we are going to is connected to the Great Lakes area."

"We are looking for King Lir, the god of the sea kingdom," Lou said. "He is neutral as far as the war is concerned, but that's just because he's being stubborn. We plan to talk him into joining King Kenneth, and helping to determine your status, Tara McInnes."

The army started moving and began to lift into the air as they had when leaving Earth. They were soon surrounded by mists, and every now and again, through breaks in the mist, they could see glimpses of battles going on down below them on the ground as they flew through the air. The speed at which they could travel would vary: sometimes they went fast, and other times it seemed as if they were going in slow motion, and it made Tara's stomach feel queasy.

Once they arrived, they did not find King Lir there. Tara was thinking about where to go next. She figured the quicker she proved them wrong about who she was, the sooner she could go home. Her text to Alana still showed to be not delivered.

"What about Niagara Falls?" Tara asked.

"Okay, sounds like a good plan. What do you think, Beira?" asked Lou.

Beira nodded and they set out.

Once they got there, they spread out. There were a lot of people there, mostly tourists.

Tara ran towards the visitor center. "I need a map!" She yelled so that everyone heard her; she didn't want them to think she was trying to get away.

The men and woman in the army had changed their clothes into modern-day outfits so that they would not stand out or be conspicuous; however, people still stared at the blond-haired beauties and very muscular men. They probably thought they were part of a weight-lifting party or something.

Once Tara found the map she walked back outside as she looked at it.

"Nothing here, we should go set up camp," Beira told her, looking over Tara's shoulder at the map.

Ettrick poked his head out of Tara's bag. "Try Nova Scotia," he said and was gone as quickly as he had come.

"Here," Tara said, pointing. "The Bras d'Or Lake on Cape Breton. I used to go there all the time. My parents still have a cabin there." She looked hopeful but then the light in her eyes faded. Her parents' cabin was now her cabin.

"That could possibly be a good place to find King Lir," Beira said as Tara folded up the map.

"Let's go get to camp, Tara," Beira said soberly. "We will try there in the morning."

"We are close, we could leave after dinner and get there before it got too late?" Tara suggested.

Beira shrugged her shoulders. "Okay," she said smiling.

Tara didn't want to admit that she wanted to go somewhere safe and familiar.

After dinner, it did not take long to get to Nova Scotia. The air was cooler now as they traveled. Once at the cabin Tara found the spare key in the big pot on the porch. A fine mist was circling around her feet.

"Here it is," she said as she went to unlock the door. The door opened and she reached to turn on the light. It looked and smelled the same as she always remembered, and a tear ran down her cheek. She brushed it away and cleared her throat.

"My parents hire a local older couple to come clean and maintain the property," she told them as they all entered.

Soon the cabin was full of people. It was a very large cabin, bigger than most. It had three levels with stables and a huge field nearby. Not everyone stayed in the cabin—mostly some of the woman warriors, plus Tara, Mark, Lou and Beira.

"We'll start setting up and give everyone their sleeping arrangements," Lou said as Epona walked by.

"I will tend to the horses," Epona said, smiling at Lou as she walked past.

"Oh, there's a nice field behind the cabin," Tara told her. She nodded and left. Tara realized that she probably had already seen it, along with the stables but figured she would let her know anyway.

Once they were all settled in for the evening, Tara lay there looking out of her window at the stars, just like she would whenever she had been there before. The stars seemed numerous here. After a while she fell asleep, dreaming of her parents.

Tara woke up before anyone else. She felt strange waking up with her parents not there with her. Also, the air felt a bit heavy. She grabbed her bag and quietly left the cottage. She had slept in her clothes. She might have something in a box at the cabin. Most likely, they would be too small anyway, although some of her Mom's clothes could fit her.

It was so peaceful this time of day. Tara loved just sitting by the lake. She was sitting on the cool grass just staring out onto the lake. Its glass like surface had a smooth film of mist on it. She sat there looking at all the trees and listening to the chatter of the birds.

"Hello," Tara heard behind her. She turned to see a handsome older man standing there. He had dark brown hair, a hint of a beard, and was wearing a purple shirt and brown pants. He seemed a little overdressed for a morning on the lake, she thought. Probably a tourist.

"Hi," Tara said, a bit hesitant.

He squatted down by the water as some geese swam over to him, and she saw the mist fall away from them a bit. He was feeding them something from his pocket.

"What is your name?" he asked her.

"Tara," she stated. "What's yours?"

"My name is Lir."

"Okay," Tara said. She thought for a moment.

He smiled at her as he stood. "I am king of the waters and sea. I heard you were looking for me?"

Tara looked at him carefully.

"Uh, well the people I am with are, I guess. Looking for you, that is." Tara hesitated.

"I am actually a god, but right now I am just Lir."

"Yeah, okay," Tara said "Come on out, Mark!" she yelled, certain they were playing a joke on her. She was tired and grouchy and was hoping he was one of the army guys making fun.

The man looked around. No one came out from behind a tree or anywhere else.

"There is no one else here," he stated. Tara stood slowly; she would run if she had to.

"You used to be God of the underworld, what happened?" Tara was trying small talk. She was a bit nervous. , He stood there, looking at her and smiling.

Her question made his smile fade a bit. "Ahh. Bringing up my past, huh? Yes, yes. That post has been taken over by someone else now." He waved his hand dismissively. "So. Am I not mistaken in thinking you are in need of some assistance?"

"Maybe," Tara said, not sure if she should trust him.

"I know your story well, read it in many books."

"Books," he repeated then he sat down on the grass, motioning for Tara to come sit by him. "I can help." He smiled, getting more comfortable on the grass. "Look, I am here to help you."

Tara looked at him for a while not saying anything, and then she decided to go sit by him. He did not seem to be creepy or anything. "The people I am with need to speak with you." He looked at her as he rested his legs, letting them stretch out in front of him. Tara shifted her feet. She needed help. They needed help. "It's about the war."

"Well, I stand neutral for now unless I see a need to assist." He looked at her.

"They think I might be the princess of some king. Would you know anything about that?" Tara could not explain why, but she suddenly felt like she could trust him.

"So, the king's army thinks they have found the princess. If indeed you are the princess." He wiped at his chin. "Well I see a need to assist then." He smiled.

Tara smiled back. "How do I know I can trust you? I mean, Beira and Lou tied me and Mark up and hauled us here."

Lir sat up straighter. "They tied you up?" Tara nodded her head. "King Kenneth would not be pleased – I am not pleased! Poor girl, I bet this is all just shocking for you." Tara nodded her head again, not trusting her voice at the moment.

"You don't know if you can trust me. However, I am offering my help." He held up his hands. "I am not armed, and no, I am not going to kidnap you or tie you up. Of all things – those kids will get a stern talking to." It was as if he was talking to himself now, and Tara felt as if she should be going back. She heard Mark calling for her.

"That's Mark," she told Lir. "He came with me from…" She paused. She did not want to give this man too much information.

Lir held up his hand. "You do not have to explain."

"Wait. How did you find me, or why were you waiting here? Well, it seemed like you were waiting here." Tara wanted to know why it had not been hard to find him.

"Your friend Ettrick is quite persuasive."

"Ettrick! I should have known." She looked around, but of course he was nowhere to be found. Where was that brownie? She hadn't seen much of him lately.

"Are Beira and Lou with the king's army?" Lir asked. Tara nodded her head as she looked around.

"I saw them ride in. Quite an impressive army, don't you think?" he said as she heard Mark call her name again. He was closer now. "How old are you, Tara?" he asked.

"I'm sixteen. Why?"

He looked at her, puzzled. "You must be but…well, in earth years it could make sense." He was talking out loud as if to himself, rubbing his chin with his fingers and pacing around. He walked over to her. "Do you see this ring?" He held up his right hand.

She looked closely at it. It was a ring that had two swans on it with their necks entwined, and atop their beaks was a smooth stone. "This rock is part of a giant stone. The Coronation Stone—all royalty has something with a piece of the stone in it. Before, the stone was mounted in the high king's throne. Tara recognized the stone in his ring. It looked just like the stone pieces in her baby bracelet.

"Do you have something like this?" he asked her. Tara swallowed hard and just stared at him. He lowered his hand as Tara reached in the neck part of her blouse and pulled out her necklace, and on it was the tiny infant bracelet.

He looked at the bracelet and then back up to Tara's face. He smiled widely, causing his face to wrinkle a bit more than it already was. He was an attractive older man.

"Welcome home, Princess," he said, bowing to her. This made Tara quite uncomfortable. He stood up. "Sorry, has anyone else confirmed who you are?"

"Uh no, not exactly, but how can you just assume I am her. I mean, I have this bracelet, yes. But I know only if I sit on the throne made out of the coronation stone will my true identity be revealed. Or at least that's what I have read."

Tara said as she shifted uncomfortably.

He smiled.

"True. That's all true, however, only royalty have pieces of the stone. So then, I believe the High King's Army has finally found you, but the only way to know for sure is to find the Coronation Stone, and have you sit upon it. Then we shall know for sure. When it is found, that is." Just then, Mark came running up.

"Tara! I have been calling for you. Didn't you hear me?" She turned and looked at him. "Who's this?" he asked, pointing to Lir and then resting his hands on his thighs, slightly bent down to catch his breath.

"I am King Lir, and you must be Mark." Lir held out his hand, and Mark stood and shook hands with him.

"King Lir, huh?"

"He has told me he wants to help us," Tara told Mark as Mark stood there looking a bit defensive. "He's uh, the one we were looking for." Mark just stared back at her. "Ya know, the King of the Sea Kingdom."

"Oh yeah," Mark said as he bobbed his head up and down.

"I have a cabin nearby if you wish to talk further, and bring the others with you if you like," Lir said as Ettrick poked his head out of Tara's bag.

"I'd be goin' with him," he said and he vanished again.

"Ettrick!" Tara yelled as she opened her bag, but the brownie was nowhere in sight. "Uh!" she said, frustrated. "That darn little brownie."

Lir started to laugh a bit. "Brownies can be that way."

"Tara, the others are on the other side of the lake looking for you," Mark said, also sounding frustrated.

"Shouldn't we wait for Beira and Lou?" Mark asked.

"Biera and Lou will get by without us for a bit," Tara said. "Lead the way," she told Lir, and followed him. She felt she could trust him; the stone in his ring matched hers and maybe there was some truth in what he said. Mark followed as well, but a bit grudgingly.

"Tara," Mark said quietly into her ear. "What are you doing?" Tara was not sure, but he had not harmed her, yet at least.

"What if he can help us?"

Mark rolled his eyes as they kept walking. They walked down a few paths and came to a clearing. A huge cabin was there with an impressive water fountain on the lawn. The front of the cabin faced the water, which could be seen through the trees.

"I never knew this cabin was here." Tara was in awe. She had walked in these woods for as long as she could remember, and she had never seen it.

Two huge dogs got up from the porch and ran down the stairs towards them. "Those are Cian's dogs," Lir said as the dogs came up to them, wagging their tails. They ran right up to Mark.

"They act as if they know you, Mark," Lir said, smiling.

"I love dogs. I used to have one," Mark said as he petted the larger male's head.

"Who is Cian?" Tara asked.

"He is my friend, and the Sky Kingdom's king."

"Oh," Tara said, looking at the dogs as she joined Mark petting the dogs.

"The one that is at war with the…?"

"The Stone Kingdom actually, which is technically in your father's kingdom. The Earth Kingdom."

The dogs ran ahead and followed him up the stairs.

"We like to come here and hang out, as you would call it." He turned and smiled as he opened the door to the cabin. They went inside, and it was beautiful. A coat rack bench stood against the wall to the left with a huge entryway that led to the main room, and to the right was the kitchen. Straight ahead, past the entryway was a vast great room with vaulted ceilings and a massive, three-story stone fireplace. The room was furnished with leather couches, paintings and pictures, and heads of dead animals. There were lots of tall windows all around and bookshelves filled with books.

"Wow!" Tara exclaimed as she walked in further.

"So, Tara, have you seen a picture of the coronation stone?" Lir asked, walking over to one of the bookshelves.

"Ah, I think so. In a book I read at some point." Tara went over near where Lir was standing. He handed her a book.

"Go to page one hundred."

Tara flipped through the book to the page. "That is the Coronation stone?" she asked in amazement. "It is huge.How could someone steal that? Well I'm assuming it was stolen because you said it needs to be found," said Tara.

"There is a war because four treasured things that were stolen from the king. The first being the princess, then the coronation stone, then the fairy flag."

He told her to go to another page. "There is the Fairy Flag. King Fergus is holding it."

Tara looked at the king. King Fergus was tall, muscular and had dark hair and beard. He wore robes and he was standing by a throne.

"That throne was carved from the stone. All kings sit upon it," Lir said.

"With it missing, though, Beira and Lou cannot prove I am who they claim I am." Tara was looking at the picture. Mark was too.

"So, they need the stone to prove Tara is this princess?" Mark asked Lir.

"As a proper identification, yes," Lir told him.

Lir handed her another book, pointing to a picture of a giant. "You think the giants carried away a stone that size?" Tara asked.

"Oh yes, they could," Lir said, handing Mark a book also. Mark showed another picture to Tara. She raised her eyebrows a bit. It was a picture of a giant standing by a castle. The giant must have been twenty feet tall at least.

"Here, let's sit on the couches by the fireplace," Lir told them, motioning for them to sit. There was a fire going, and Tara sat down placing one book on the coffee table.

Tara whispered to Mark, "So that boot casting is real." He shrugged his shoulders.

"How can you be here? I mean, not in the Higher Realms, if you are a god and king?" Tara asked Lir.

Lir looked at her and smiled. "Well, that's the beauty of being immortal. We can come here as often as we wish. We generally don't stay long, though."

They were all talking and looking at the different pictures when the door to the cabin burst open. In came a large man carrying tons of fish hanging from a fishing line. He reminded Tara of a lumberjack; he was muscular with dark blond hair, a beard, and had a booming voice that announced, "Caught a bunch of fish. We will have a feast for sure." The dogs—whining and tails wagging—ran up to the man. "Oh! And look who I found wandering around the lake," the man said to Lir as he stepped further into the cabin, and Beira and Lou came in. The dogs were jumping all over Lou.

They bowed their heads at Lir. Oh, Tara thought. Have I been disrespectful? Well, I will need to improve on my manners.

"Beira and my wayward son, Lou," Cian said.

Lir took a few steps toward the new comers.

"Well Beira, it seems I have found some friends of yours." Beira looked at Tara like she was upset—her forehead was wrinkled. She then smiled at Lir.

"Yes sire, we have been looking for them all morning. Haven't we Lou?" Lou was petting the dogs and smiling nervously.

"Cian, this is Tara and Mark. They are from the Earth, the mortal world."

"They are in need of some assistance?" Cian asked, smiling. Tara swore she saw his eyes and teeth sparkle.

"Well, with what? We do not often help mortals," Cian said as he set down the fish on the kitchen counter. He then came over to where Lir, Mark, and Tara were sitting.

Lir picked up a book and showed it to Cian.

"Oh. I see. What do you want to know about those for?" Cian handed the book back to Lir.

"Father, I can explain," Lou said as he and Beira came closer to the couches, and the dogs had lain down by Tara's feet. Tara looked at Lou, then Cian. She recalled the story of Lou the sun god, and how his mother had been locked in a tower and Cian found her, rescued her and they fell in love. But to see them in the flesh standing in front of her – she had no words.

"Please, do!" Cian boomed at Lou as Tara jumped, breaking out of her thoughts. Lou looked as if he wanted to leave.

"Haven't heard a peep from you in months, and now you are here."

"Sorry, Father." He paused and then looked at Beira.

"They think they have found the missing princess," Lir said.

"This is Tara—well, that's her Earthly name," Lir said as Tara looked at Cian. Cian came closer towards her.

"Found her, you think, huh? She looks like she could fit the bill. Except she is no infant. Mortal Earth you said? Hmm." He ran his fingers through his beard. "Well, does she have a stone piece?" He was bending slightly down toward her.

"I do," Tara said, holding up her necklace. He looked intently at it and then raised his eyebrows. Beira and Lou looked as well. Tara quickly put it back under her shirt.

"Well, well then, that is an heirloom! It has four stones from the coronation stone," He told Tara as Lir nodded in agreement. He cleared his throat as he motioned for Mark to scoot over on the couch. He sat and Beira sat by him, as did Lou. Tara looked at it again, then grabbed the book that had a picture of the stone to examine it further. Sure enough, it looked like the exact same stone. Although it could have been stone from anywhere.

Lir sat by Tara on the smaller couch. Cian was staring at Tara with a sad yet surprised expression.

"Tara, tell them all the things that have happened to you, starting with the Banshee."

"Banshee!" Cian said loudly as the fire crackled.

Tara told them of the Banshee, losing her parents, the castle, the Fairy Flag, the old woman, and Ettrick.

"Oh, and I got directions from a Wulver."

"What!" Said Beira and Lou at the same time, surprised to hear the news.

Beira was frowning. "My cousin saw a Wulver once, when we were little. I have always wanted to see one."

"Yes, they are very reclusive," said Cian.

"Sorry to hear you lost your parents," Lir said with empathy.

"Yes, a terrible loss," Cian said as he coughed a bit.

"That would explain the Banshee. They appear to a loved one before someone dies. Terrible way to find out of someone's passing." Cian choked back his words. "I saw a Banshee right before my first wife passed. Terrible. Just terrible."

It was nice to hear of someone else claiming to have seen a banshee and knowing what that meant.

"Well, we believe your father possibly has the Stone," Cian told Beira.

"My father!" She looked surprised and mad.

"Well, if he has it, then it is very well hidden. I guess I should not be too surprised; he is fighting against the High King."

Cian patted her back. "Beira and her father had a quarrel. Haven't made up yet either."

Beira scowled, her face etched with lines that Tara had not seen before, and they made her look older.

"My father is greedy. I want the kingdoms to unite. I want peace back in the Higher Realms. He likes war," Beira told her and Mark.

"Yes, well your father has caused us some heartache already. He is in league with Don Pater, and he is gaining more favor in other smaller kingdoms," Lir told them as he started putting the books back on the shelf.

"Who is this Don Pater?" Mark asked. He had been so quiet, Tara almost forgot he was there.

"He is now the ruler of the underworld," Lir said, leaning forward.

"And he is helping Beira's father."

"What a mess," Tara said as she gave Beira a sympathetic glance.

"If we find the Fairy Flag, then what?" Tara wanted to know what she was getting herself into.

"It needs to be given to King Kenneth, to be brought to the castle. To where the high king is. To Tara," Cian told her.

"Tara?" Tara said out loud, looking up, confused.

"Tara is a place, where the castle is. The flag must be brought back there for there to be peace, well after it is unfurled and used during the battle," Beira said to her, standing now. Lir told them of other items that went missing not long after the king was gone.

Beira rolled her eyes. "So, the high royalty goes missing, and everyone steals their possessions!"

"I know where a few of those items are in my world," Tara said hopefully. But then her face fell. "They are in a glass enclosure at the old Dunvegan castle, though."

"Ah yes, we'll see, but they are in the Higher Realms, not really on earth. Those are replicas," Lir told her, sitting back down as Cian stood up. "We have also heard the triplet princes are possibly fighting on your father's side, and Don Pater's, Beira," said Lir, almost accusingly.

That was when Mark got up and went over to the fireplace and just stared into the flames.

Cian walked over to Beira. "The King of Erin has gathered an army also. Some of us," he looked at Lir, "have remained neutral."

Tara was wringing her hands and pacing. "Okay, so there is a war, and the flag can help end the war, and reunite the kingdoms, and—"

She was interrupted by Cian. "Yes. The flag can end the war."

"Okay," she said, pausing. "So we also need to find the high king and queen, and these three princes, along with the other prince. Have I missed anything?"

"That about sums it up. Well, and confirm you are the princess," Cian said as he walked towards the kitchen. Then Lir stood and followed Cian into the kitchen.

"Who's hungry?" Cian bellowed, bending down and getting something out of a cabinet. Lou and Beira joined him in the kitchen.

Lir was looking at Mark. He came out of the kitchen and walked over to Mark. "Is something troubling you, lad?" he asked, concerned.

"Oh, well this is just a lot of information. A few days ago, I was working at the golf course and now...well, I am Tara's friend and I don't want to see her get hurt."

Lir chuckled as he patted Mark on the back. "Sorry you got dragged into this mess, lad. You are a good friend to Tara, I can see that. Now let's go eat. First course!" he yelled, smiling, raising his hand, and pointing towards the kitchen.

Lir's smile helped Tara feel at ease and welcome, even though she still felt a bit confused. She kept going over things in her mind, sorting it all out. Losing her parents, finding out she was adopted. Learning she could be a princess, and had another family. A second chance at a family. She loved her parents no questioning that, and loved her extended family back in Ireland and Scotland, however other family that loved her, a war was started over this missing princess. That told Tara a lot.

She looked at Cian. He seemed familiar to her, like she had known him her whole life, and even though his voice was loud, she could tell he was fun to be around. Then there was Lir who, unlike Cian, was quiet and calm, and she felt comfortable around him. It was like they were her uncles or something.

12

Ness and Fenian

A few hours later they were again relaxing by the fire, their bellies full, all feeling a little more relaxed. Tara was petting the dogs that were lying by her feet.

Tara thought that the dogs looked like a cross between a Newfie, a Great Dane, and a Wolfhound. Or maybe a Leonberger.

"That is Ness," Lou said, pointing to the black and white one. "And that is Fenian." He was the larger, dark brown male. Fenian looked more wolfhound however not as skinny, Fenian was bulkier.

"Failinis is my dog from their first litter," Lou told her and then looked at Cian. "Dad, where is Failinis?"

Cian coughed and shifted in his chair; he was sitting closest to the fire. "Oh, he's around. You know

Failinis." He kind of chuckled then. Lou frowned. Tara felt as if Lou was not too happy, and his father was keeping something from him.

"Anyway," said Lou, "we gave one pup to Prince John-Keegan, and another to the High King's new infant daughter. They are being cared for but miss their owners. John-Keegan is the youngest of the princes that are missing. He went by Keegan, though. He has been missing since I was a kid, and he was my best friend. Unfortunately, Keegan's father is on Beira's father's side of the war, although he could possibly now be swayed to our side.

"Why?" Tara asked, not really understanding how one would choose sides.

"He actually blames King Kenneth, Tara, for his last-born son's disappearance. So, when the war started, he chose to fight against your father."

"Oh" was all she could say at that point. Lou looked so sad as he spoke that Tara had to choke back her emotions. Mark got up from the couch and left the cabin abruptly, and she stood up and watched him as he walked down by the lake.

She wondered what had gotten into him, and why he was being so quiet and moody.

"They have a new litter of pups if you are interested in one." Tara turned and looked at Lou.

"One!" Cian boomed. "How about the whole litter, if she wants them. She is, after all, the princess!" He cleared his throat. "Well, we think she is at least." His broad smile seemed to light up the whole room.

"I would love at least one," Tara admitted. She had always wanted a dog, but her parents never let her have one. Her mother was afraid of dogs, she was attached by one when she was little and never got over her fear of them. Tara loved dogs, and was excited to have one finally. Well, several.

"Done, then. You can meet them soon—they are only a few weeks old now, mind you," Cian told her as he stood up, stretching as he did. The dogs went over to him.

"Even if I am not who you think I am?" She wanted to not get her hopes up of getting a puppy and then have them change their minds.

"Oh, sure you can," Cian boomed, then called for the dogs.

"Come on, let's go for a walk before bed, shall we?" he said and then pet the dogs, grabbed his coat, opened the door, and off they went.

Tara wondered what Mark was doing for so long by the lake. "I am going to check on Mark," she told the others as she got up and headed for the door.

She did find him by the lake, just staring out at it. "Hey, are you okay?" she asked him as she walked up next to him. He continued to gaze out across the water. The stars and moon were out, and it was a beautiful night, though there was a bit of a chill in the air. The reflection of the moon was shining on the surface of the rippling water.

"Pretty messed up place, huh? These Higher Realms, I mean," Tara said to him, hoping she would get a chuckle out of him. But as he continued to stare out at the water she realized no, she wouldn't get that from him.

"Yeah, you could say that." He seemed distant, like was in deep thought when she approached him. The two dogs came running up. Mark took notice of them and picked up a stick and threw it out into the water. Fenian ran and jumped in after it. That put a small smile on his face. Tara saw Cian go inside the cabin, which was in clear sight from where they stood.

Ness was standing by Tara's side panting.

"I had a dog in Arizona," Mark said.

"You mentioned earlier having a dog, I never knew."

"His name was Jake, and he was a yellow Lab. Great dog."

"What happened?" Tara wanted to know more.

He looked at her then. "He was hit by a truck, killed instantly."

"I'm sorry to hear that."

Fenian came out of the water with the stick.

"Maybe you could have one of their puppies. They just had a litter."

"Yeah, can you imagine me having one of these dogs in our hometown?"

"Oh, I don't know. They aren't that big." She paused as Fenian shook off the water. He was a massive dog really, bigger than any other dog she had ever seen. "Okay they are huge, and people might be scared of them."

Tara patted Ness's head, her fur was so soft. "I was thinking about the four princes, I wonder what happened to them. Lir told me that the three older ones had a fight with their father."

Mark shrugged his shoulders. "Who knows? I had a blowout with my dad one time. It took two weeks to sort it out. My mom was mad at both of us."

At the mention of his mom, Tara felt bad. She had not been gone long.

"I'm sorry."

He turned to look at her then. "Hey, don't, okay?" He touched her arm then as Fenian was sitting at their feet looking hopefully up at Mark, probably thinking about when he would throw the stick again.

Mark smiled, took the stick, and threw it far out onto the water. The dog turned and jumped into the water, causing a big splash that got both Mark and Tara a bit wet, and he started swimming after it.

"Do you want to go back? To Connecticut I mean?" Tara asked, not sure if she really wanted to know the answer.

"Are you crazy? What, and leave you with all of them?" He looked out at Fenian as he was swimming back.

"I will not leave you here, though I have thought about leaving. At least there I am not always in danger like here, and I'm not risking my life. Well, unless Mr. Johns is playing golf. I swear that old man has it in for me." They both started laughing. "But seriously, no. I am staying with you."

She smiled at him then, and he smiled back.

Fenian brought the stick back, dropped it at Mark's feet, and stood there.

"Good boy," Mark said, petting his wet head. They heard a whistle, and the two dogs took off running towards the cabin.

"Ah! You're all wet, Fenian!" they heard Lou say. As they saw him, he Lou spotted them and waved. Tara waved back as he closed the door to the cabin. The lights from the windows and porch seemed to glow in the thick darkness of the night. Tara did love it here, on Cape Breton. The Bras d'Or Lake was like her third home.

"Do you think they are talking about me?" Tara asked.

"Probably." Mark was kind of joking; however, they knew the others were inside talking, if not about her, then at least about how to get the fairy flag and if she really was this stolen princess.

"What if we just left?"

"You want to leave?" Mark asked.

Tara shrugged her shoulders. "I don't know. I bet if we tried though they would probably send Don Pater and his Hounds of Hell after us." They both laughed.

"Hey what's that?" Tara asked, reaching up to touch the top of Mark's head where she thought she saw light blond.

"What?" He said reaching up as well, trying to knock her hand away.

Tara gasped. "You dye your hair!"

"Uh, no, it's just the light reflecting off the lake."

"No! You dye your hair." She tried looking closer on her tiptoes. He took a few steps away from her, his arm outstretched and pointing at her. "Don't touch my hair." Tara walked forward, and he kept stepping back.

"What are you doing?" she asked.

"What are you doing?" he asked back, grinning and walking back faster. All of a sudden, he turned and started sprinting away. Tara called after him.

"Wait up, Mark!"

When she caught up with him, he was laughing.

"And you were teasing me about dyeing my hair." She smacked his arm. He laughed as he rubbed where she had hit him on his bicep. "What color is yours?"

"Blond."

"Really, blond, huh? You would look good as a blond. Tell you what, if you let your hair grow out, I will too. Deal?" Tara extended her hand for him to shake it.

Mark grinned. "Deal." He took her hand and shook it, smiling.

Just then they heard Cian calling them in. They both sighed and started walking back to the cabin. When they opened the door and walked in, they saw that someone new was there.

"Oh good, there you two are," Cian said, waving them forward into the great room. "Someone is here to see you."

"Hello princess. My name is Titiana," the woman said as she turned around.

"Hi," Tara said at the beautiful woman standing in front of her. The whole room seemed to be brighter—her skin just glowed and sparkled.

"Wait. Do I know you?" Tara felt as though she should, but she wasn't sure. Mark was just standing there with his mouth gaped open. Tara shot him a disgusted look.

"You have met me before," Titiana said as her beautiful form changed into an old woman.

Tara gasped and grabbed onto Mark's arm. "The old lady at the castle," she said, grabbing Mark's arm tighter.

"This is Titiana, queen of the fairies," Lir said as he smiled their way.

"Tina, to those who know me well. It is good to see you again," she said, smiling.

"Queen, fairy?" Tara said under her breath, not meaning to say it out loud.

Titiana smiled and then turned towards Mark. "And who is your friend?"

"My name is Mark." He stepped forward and slightly bowed.

"He is my friend from Connecticut." Tara took a few steps forward. She had wanted to smack Mark for staring so.

Titiana was tall and slender. She had very dark hair that cascaded down her back in loose curls. She had high cheek bones, her eyes and ears were slightly pointed, and she had beautiful, almost purple eyes. She was wearing an elegant gown, as if to go to a dance or something. It was tight-fitting, except for at the wrists where it belled a bit, and at the hem where it fluttered out like a mermaid's tail. She wore high heels.

"Why are you here, Tina?" Lir asked.

The fairy queen turned on her heel quickly. "I wanted to see for myself if the rumors were true."

"Ah," said Cian. "Rumors running amuck already, are they?"

She turned to Tara, walked over to her, and gently fingered the necklace from beneath her blouse. "I guess they are," she said smiling.

"Rumors?" Tara asked.

Tina laughed. "Word travels fast here, when one has eyes and ears all over," she said.

"Now what about the flag?" she asked, looking at Lir and Cian.

"All we know is that it is missing," Cian told her.

"Yes, shortly after Tara visited the castle, she triggered something somehow and now it is no longer in our possession," Tina said, looking at Tara slightly.

Tara looked at her, wide eyed. "Well, I did not take it!"

"Of course not. It was yours anyway. A gift from me and my husband to you. Why would you steal it?" She gave a whimsical laugh and then fiddled with the hem of her sleeve.

"That's if I am who you all think I am. What if I am not her? You should be looking for her." Tara's temper was flaring.

"All evidence points to you, dearest," The fairy queen said in a soft tone that seemed to calm Tara's nerves.

"Who else could be involved, Tina?" Cian asked as he came closer to her. The fairy queen walked away a bit, turning her back on everyone and headed towards the door.

"Pater, the Famorians, Cullin. Just to name a few." She turned back around, a hint of mischievousness in her eyes. "I will let you know if I hear news." She opened the front door and, in a blink of an eye, was gone.

"She'll be back!" boomed Cian, smiling.

"Wow," Mark said.

Tara rolled her eyes, and yet found herself mesmerized by the tall, beautiful fairy queen whose light and shimmer still had an effect on those in the room. Tara was staring at the spot where the fairy queen had stood before she disappeared into thin air. She then came back to her senses, shook her head, and crinkled her brow as she turned around.

"Who are the Famorians? Are they the giants?" Tara asked.

"Yes, they are also called giants," Lou told her. Tara nodded her head; she did know a few stories about giants. "I bet either the other fairy king has the flag, or the giants do," Lou piped in.

"That's possible. They did steal the princess," Cian said, walking into the kitchen. He started preparing the fish to fry up. He was getting out pans, oil, bowls, eggs, and flour.

"Why would giants steal a new baby? Why did they take me?" Tara followed the small crowd into the kitchen area. Tara wanted to know, and if they knew, she had the right to know as well.

"It's my fault," Beira said as she stood and started walking towards the kitchen.

"Now do not go blaming yourself lass for what your father did. Nor for what Angus did," Cian told her.

Tara walked up to the counter, which was fairly high, and sat in a chair by the entryway to the cabin. "What are you talking about?" Tara asked.

"Well it is as long story, but we have time as I make us dinner," Cian told her, pushing up his sleeves to dip some fish into an egg batter. Mark sat next to Tara, and everyone else was standing around the kitchen. Lir smiled broadly as he entered the kitchen and started helping by peeling potatoes. He tossed a peeler and a potato to Lou, who began peeling it into a trash can.

"See, there was a girl named Granua Bride, and her father King Ben Bride, lived in a castle by the sea on the cliffs. Beira's father has a castle in the mountains behind the castle on the cliffs. There was a giant by the name of Fin McCool across the way over the sea. Two lovely castles by the sea, two kingdoms."

"Wait," Tara said. "McCool, as in Fingal's Cave?"

"Yes and no," Cian said.

"See, in our time, the great castles still stand. In your time, they are thousands and thousands of years old. Just rocks and ruins now. Have you been there?" he asked her.

"Yes once, when I was young. Both sides, there were castles! Really?"

Cian nodded. Tara sat there transfixed. Who would have imagined it—giants' castles, with a huge bridge! She sat there, more intent on listening to the story.

"Well just imagine two gigantic castles with their huge drawbridges facing the sea where there was a great stone road that connected the two. There you have it."

"The Giants Causeway!" Tara exclaimed.

"Very good," Cian said to her. "Anyway, Granua Bride, whom Beira just called Bride, is King Ben's daughter. She got into a bit of trouble and ended up being Beira's servant."

"What did she do? And why can't Beira tell the story?" Tara asked. Beira blushed but did not answer her question.

"Because," Lir said Cian likes telling the stories even if they are about someone who is perfectly capable of telling it themselves." Cian cleared his throat and continued as Tara smiled.

"She had stolen Beira's magic hammer," Cian said and set down the huge plate of fish.

Beira sighed and continued, "She lost it and broke my brother's heart, and she continued to stomp on it by marrying someone else. She was King Ben's only daughter, and hearing this news did not please him. And to make matters worse, there were rumors about her falling in love with one of the princes across the causeway. That caused some tension between the two kingdoms."

Cian turned the heat on under a big pot with oil in it. He then continued to stack battered fish on plates, waiting to be fried.

"Why though?" Tara asked.

Beira answered her. "Because my brother had already declared his love for her, and preparations were being made." Tara could tell Beira was annoyed at him telling them the story, she was mostly talking to Lou.

"What like for a wedding?" Tara asked.

Beira nodded her head. "Then it was found out that she had been seeing another across the way at Fin's castle."

"The stories I heard are a bit different," Tara said as Lir handed her carrots and a peeler. Beira was cutting up cabbage.

"Are we making coleslaw?" Tara asked.

Lir gave Mark a bowl, some seasonings, and other bottles. "Yes," Lir said as he placed another pot of oil on the stove.

"Fish, chips, and slaw. One of our favorite meals. Also, yes, stories you have heard or read are a bit off," Cian told them. It intrigued Tara to hear the stories she had read growing up told as facts.

Lir finished the story. "Now King Ben was very enraged that his daughter was a servant—after all, she was a princess. However, there was a debt to settle. Also, the young giant she fell for was to wed someone else, and Beira's brother was furious. It was a big mess."

As they talked, the food was cooking and Beira was setting the large wooden table in the dining hall of the large cabin. Once the food was done, they brought it to the table, and Lir filled two glass pitchers full of homemade lemonade. They all sat down and served themselves, and Beira started the story back up again.

"I might as well finish the story. So, Bride was my servant, and my brother had been away. I had an old woolen blanket that used to be white but in storage had turned brown. I had asked her to wash it. She took it outside and tried washing it in one of the pools by the waterfall on the castle grounds. Well, it would not get clean. I sent her out again with specific instructions, and she brought it back still dirty. I kind of lost my temper and yelled at her. She took it out a third time. From what she tells is that a king from the Green Isle, whose castle is near the Green Glenn in Erin, happened to be riding through and took pity on her, I guess. But he somehow got it clean and gave her snowdrop flowers to give me. In part to apologize for misplacing my hammer. However, he had told her to tell me, if I asked where she got them, that she found them by the banks of the stream where spring flowers and new grass were growing. Well I am not heartless, so one day I wanted her to show me where. We got lost and separated until Angus found her while he was riding his huge white horse." She stopped and took a sip of her drink.

"Angus only rides white horses, he feels they are the strongest," she continued.

"He was wearing his gold armor and a crimson robe. He said he had a dream with her in it and that she had needed his help. He said she had been crying and was sad. Probably because she was lost in the woods. I had, of course, found my way back to the castle." She stopped talking to eat some of her food.

"So, what happened?" Mark asked, eagerly listening to the story.

"Well accusations were thrown around, and things were said back and forth, and, well, then you were taken, Tara. It was a mess."

"You were supposed to be a bargaining tool. See, the giants wanted to rule over more land, and by abducting the new princess – well, they should have just talked to King Kenneth. I guess they tried and he was too busy. They got impatient as most giants do, and took action.

Tara felt like she was going to faint. "All of this trouble just because they wanted to rule over more land, and some lover's dispute?"

"Aye lass," Cian told her as his Scottish accent came out more.

"The tale goes on about Angus marrying Bride at the fairy queen's palace in a private wood, where there are fields and fields of flowers."

"That would be Queen Gloriana," Lir said, sighing. "And yes, Angus married Bride."

"Queen Gloriana likes to cause trouble sometimes," Lou said, finishing his fish.

Tara looked at him. "I still don't really understand why I would be taken. Also, what a confusing story. But now the Giants Causeway is ruined, they say because the two giants, Fingal and Benandonner, were yelling back and forth, and Fingal tricked Ben by pretending he was an infant. Benandonner thought, well if this is the king's infant son, then the king must be a huge giant," Tara told Mark.

"Yes they did fight. Also, Ben was really the bigger of the two. It is said that, later on in time, Ben and Fingal had another fight, and Ben had left as fast as he could, and Fingal broke up the causeway so Ben could not come back," Lir told him as he finished his dinner.

"Yes, but the castles still stand, and the Giants Causeway is still being used," Lou told them. "Well, at least here in the Higher Realms," he finished.

"I want to see it!" Tara exclaimed.

"Hey, what if one of the giants stole the flag?" Tara asked.

Beira sighed, stood, and grabbed her empty plate. "Well, Angus did steal you, so who knows. He confessed awhile later after they did not bring you back to their father. Their father was not happy either." She went and put her dishes in the dishwasher.

"I still want to see them," Tara burst out.

"Me too," Mark said as he too got up. "What happened to Bride?"

Beira brought in more lemonade. "She lives by the loch, Loch Ness as a matter of fact."

"You got so mad at her and threw her into the river, Beira," Lou said, taking another piece of fish.

"Yes we had an argument, and I threw her in the loch. I was just messing around really. I didn't know she couldn't swim. She would have drowned if it wasn't for the Nessies."

Tara stared at Beira. "Wait. Nessie, as in the Loch Ness Monster?"

Lou raised his eyebrows. "The one and only," she heard Lir say. "There is a whole community, or group of them. Water horses, we call them. They live in the loch."

Tara was so excited to hear about them. "What do they look like?" They all laughed—well, except for Mark. He looked just as intrigued as Tara.

Cian put down a plate of doughnuts on the table and answered her, "Oh, just like everyone thinks. Long necks and bodies with flippers or fins. They are beautiful water creatures, but shy. They keep to themselves."

Beira took one and finished her story. "Anyway, now Bride lives there by the loch with Angus."

"So the causeway is not in ruins here?"

"No," Lir told her. "It still stands, and even though the two kingdoms don't really get along well, they have their disputes. The Giants Causeway is still being used."

"Now is not a great time to go sightseeing though, Tara. Wars breaking out everywhere, the high king and queen missing. You just barely found," Lir said, bending down with his eyebrows raised as he stared at Tara. He picked up his and Tara's empty plates and headed for the kitchen. "Besides, you are no longer an infant, and if they caught you, they could still use you as a bargaining tool."

"Yes, and how would we explain that you were missing again to the king and queen? "Cian asked, standing and grabbing a bunch of dishes, including Mark's.

Lou looked at Tara. "Great idea though. I bet they do have the flag. Or maybe the stone at least."

"How do we get there?" Tara asked.

"Persistent, aren't we Princess," Cian said as he took the dishes to the kitchen.

"Well the other fairy king could have them too," Beira piped in.

"Or Don Pater," Lou said. Just then there was a tapping on the window. It was a small male fairy, and he had something in his hands.

Cian looked and leaned up to the window. "Oh, hello there," he said with a grin as he opened the window, and the fairy flew in. He was wearing brown clothes and had light brown hair with flecks of blond and gold. He held out the little rolled-up paper to Tara. She looked at Cian, who told her, "Take it, Tara."

"Are you Princess Tara-Brigit?" the fairy asked with a hopeful voice.

"I guess," Tara answered reluctantly. He bowed and held out the paper.

"Then this is for you, and a Master Mark Weatherbee?"

She took the little scroll, which had a small seal of a butterfly and was all glittery. "Thank you," Tara said as the fairy bowed again and quickly flew out the window.

"Should I open this?" Tara held up the scroll.

"Just a minute, Princess," Cian said as he stood and went and looked out of one of the front windows. "Come in here and sit by the fire."

"Sounds like we need a plan," Mark told them.

"Yes, and some sleep," Cian said, yawning as he turned and came back from looking out the window over to where they all were sitting.

"We will take the King's Army with Tara and Mark and start with the Fairy Kingdom," Lou told them.

"Mortals like Mark going in there is not that great of an idea," Lir told them. "Unless invited."

Cian smiled as he walked into the kitchen and started loading the dishwasher.

"You should open that scroll," Beira told her. Tara nodded and opened the scroll. "Well here is an invitation from the fairy queen. It's only for Mark and me, though."

"Ha! Well there ya go," Cian boomed. Tara had to get used to that.

Mark looked over her shoulder at the small piece of parchment.

"Well I guess we will be attending other business." Beira seemed annoyed, Tara thought.

"All right. We also have other business to attend to as well, so we will all head out in the morning." Lir was standing and stretching.

"Let's get some shut-eye. There are many rooms here, just pick one. Some of us can share if you like."

"I will share with Mark," Lou stated. Cian nodded, and they all found a room.

"Why, so you can keep an eye on me?" Mark asked Lou as he walked past Tara and stood next to Lou.

Lou smiled. "Something like that. No messing around, you two do not have a clue how much trouble you can get into, or us for that matter."
Cian laughed. "Ah yes. King Kenneth would not be very pleased, would he son?"

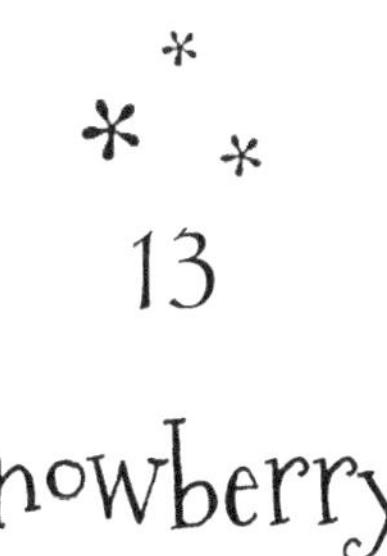

13

Snowberry

Tara woke up to Ettrick tapping her shoulder. She yawned and sat up. She could smell bacon, and she thought maybe pancakes as well. Her stomach rumbled. She got out of bed and went into the bathroom. She showered, got dressed and found her hair dye.

"Red," she said out loud. "I thought I grabbed black." Sighing, she looked at the label again. The label said light red. Couldn't hurt, she thought as she opened the box. She smiled in the mirror and decided to go for it.

Once she was dressed, her hair dyed back to its original color (which she knew for certain because of the two-inch roots that were showing, she had started dying her hair in fifth grade, only because her friend convinced her that it would be cool. She liked it and so kept doing it. Tara pulled it back and braided it, once it was dry. She turned around and noticed her bags were packed.

"Ettrick, I am going down for breakfast!" she shouted as she left the room.

When she went into the kitchen everyone was awake and ready to go, and some were still eating.

"Whoa!" Mark said as she came in.

"Well would you look at that," Cian said, handing her a plate full of yummy food.

She smiled and sat down to eat. Beira and Lou walked in.

"Well I briefed the army, and told them that the Fairy Queen wanted to see Tara. Whoa..." Beira stopped and looked at Tara. "Now you look like Princess Brigit – at least how I would have pictured and older version of her looking," she said, raising her eyebrows towards Lou. Lou stared wide-eyed as well.

"Come on, eat up. We have to go. Cian, let's close up the cabin," Lir told them as he started turning off lights and grabbing bags, and Cian frantically loaded and ran the dishwasher.

They were standing in the front yard of the cabin, the army in a field further down the path.

"Oh, wait is my—" Tara started to ask, but Beira interrupted and told her that her cabin was all sparkly clean and locked up. "The key is in its proper hiding place."

Tara nodded and smiled. "Thanks."

Lou and Mark were playing around with the dogs.

"Well, Princess, this is where we part," Lir told Tara.

Cian set down his bags and spread his arms open wide. Tara walked over to him, and he hugged her. "Your father is one of our dearest friends. We will help find him as much as we can."

They parted, and Lir hugged Tara as well. "Now go with our blessing. Watch out for the many armies of the Foal. They have acquired many nasty recruits."

"The Foal?" Tara asked, not too sure she remembered who or what they were.

"The army fighting against the King, which is made up of beasts and other nasty creatures."

"Oh." Tara knew now what he meant. The darkest of beasts were in the army. Tara shuddered, then watched as Lou approached his father as they shook forearms and hugged, then slapped each other on the back.

"Come Ness, Fenian." Cian whistled. Cian was wearing jeans, a t-shirt, and large hiking boots. Lir winked at Tara and smiled as he picked up his bags. He was wearing shorts, flip flops, and a red Hawaiian shirt. Tara giggled as she watched them walk away down the dirt path. The dogs walked behind them, wagging their tails.

"Will we see them again?" Tara asked.

"I believe so," Beira told her as she started walking on the path in the opposite direction. Tara, Lou, and Mark followed. When they got to the army, one of the men came over leading two horses by the reins. He stopped in front of Beira, who took the reins of one of the horses. It was cream-colored, with a black mane and tail. With a gesture, she indicated that the soldier should lead the other horse to Tara.

"This is Snowberry," Beira said. "She will let you ride her into the fairy realm." Snowberry was a beautiful horse. She was a small black horse with patches of white. Her mane and tail were black with a bit of white. Her hooves were white with long hair covering them. "We will be finding out more information. You will be fine. Once there you will be guarded," Beira told them. Tara frowned.

Beira continued, "Go straight down the path until you come to the Fairy Mound. Snowberry will guide you in, she knows the way. Oh, and she will alert us if you get off her before entering the fairy kingdom. Or if something happens."

"Of course," Tara said smiling.

"Here is a map if you get lost. Oh, and don't uh, get lost, captured, or killed," Lou smiled.

"Great. Yeah, we'll try not to," Mark said, taking the map. It was rolled up and tied with string.

"By the time you are done in the fairy kingdom, we will do our best to meet up with you when you exit the Fairy Mound," Beira told her as she walked away, catching up with Lou.

Mark got up into the saddle. "Come on Tara," he called to her as she watched Beira and Lou walk away. She got up in the saddle behind him. She noticed that rolled-up sacks and hanging sacks were dangling from the saddle. Mark urged the horse forward. Tara was nervous; as they went down the path, the trees were closing them in a thick forest.

"Don't be nervous," Tara heard Ettrick say. His head was poking out of one of the bags.

"The fairies are great, well most of them anyway."

"Shh," Mark said as he held the reins. He must be nervous, thought Tara as the path in front of them wound up and down and through a small meadow. It started getting dark and misty. Tara shivered slightly.

They were approaching a big mound of dirt and grass. The horse stopped as the fog swirled around them.

"Hey Mark, did you ever see the movie Brigadoon?"

"No," Mark answered. "Why?" He definitely was not calm.

"Oh, well this fog and everything that has happened reminds me of that movie a bit."

Mark sighed. The horse breathed loudly, blowing air out through her nostrils. The fog lifted, and an opening could be seen now in front of them.

"Whoa." Tara was transfixed on the opening to the hill. The horse walked forward.

"Snowberry used to belong to the fairy king, but now she is yours, Tara," Ettrick told her.

"Great. I can't even ride well yet. Is she yours to give?

Ettrick looked up at her. "No. She belonged to the Fairy Queen and now she is gifted to you. The fairy queen is my queen, I do as she bids me."

They entered the mound. The opening was tall and wide enough that Tara could not touch the sides. The floor at first was packed-down dirt but then changed to paved stones. The horse's shoes made noise that echoed off the walls. It was kind of dark; small lanterns hung on the walls here and there, giving off just enough light to see a bit. There were roots of all sizes hanging down or poking through the sides of the Fairy Mound tunnel.

"What if this is a waste of time?" Mark asked. "What information would the fairy king have that the fairy queen did not have, or did not tell us?"

Tara looked back behind them, where she saw fog coming into the tunnel. "I don't know. Lir told me that they have information worth listening to."

Every now and again they could hear music that sounded like the tinkling of little bells. The light at the end of the tunnel made them squint their eyes, it was so bright. As they emerged out of the tunnel, they found themselves in a field. On the other side was a thick wood, and in the distance, Tara could barely see the top spires of a castle.

Ettrick popped out of the bag. "Dismount here, and leave Snowberry to graze. She will be okay," he reassured them. They did as Ettrick suggested and dismounted.

"Why will she be okay here?" Tara asked as she looked at Ettrick.

"She was born in these fields, grazed here a many a day. Trust me, she'll be fine."

Mark went to grab some of the gear.

"Ya won't be a needin' that. The fairy king and queen will be quite hospitable." He was grinning up at them. He had his walking stick in one hand and turned and waved them to follow him.

As they walked through the meadow, Tara slowly started to see fairies of all shapes and sizes. One fluttered up to her, and she was small. Tara held up her hand, and the fairy fluttered just above her palm.

With a tinkling voice the fairy said, "It is her. Princess Brigit."

Tara heard a bunch of tinkling noises like the chatter of birds. The way she pronounced her birth name sounded like a French lady saying the words "bridge" and "eat" together. Tara smiled, and the fairy fluttered away. They followed Ettrick through the meadow to a path that led into the woods.

"Now stay close behind me," Ettrick told them as they walked.

"Ettrick, how many fairies live here?"

"Oh, a great variety. We have wood nymphs, pixies, trolls, toadstools, gnomes, water nymphs." Tara thought she even saw a leprechaun. They kept walking.

"Aye, so just about everything you could think of. Except dragons and unicorns. They live in a different part of the kingdom."

Tara looked all around as they walked. At one point, she thought she saw a huge creature with a big nose peek out from behind a tree trunk. He had a grin on his face, but once she looked at his eyes, he ducked behind the tree bashfully.

"Some fairies are more like elves, some are tall and slender like the fairy king and queen, then some are very tiny—the size of buttercups. Or smaller," Ettrick told them as they followed him down winding pathways.

Once through the wood, they came to another, larger meadow. Tons of flowers lined the meadow as bees and butterflies flew about. Fairies also fluttered here and there. They did not seem to notice Tara and Mark very much at this point.

"There is the fairy castle," Ettrick said, pointing into the sky. More of it could be seen now above the tree line. It was beautiful, and Tara had to catch her breath. Several tall, white sparkling towers rose up to the sky. She also could see tall stained-glass windows and parapets that jutted outwards from the sides of the pillars. It was huge. The castle was surrounded by huge gardens and thick, wooden forests as well.

"Wow." Tara was absolutely mesmerized.

"We will take the path around the edge of this meadow and pond area," he told them, walking ahead. Tara noticed a bridge, which looked so lovely over the water.

"But there is a path, and a bridge," Tara said as she quickly caught up to Ettrick and Mark.

"We need to go this way, it is safer," Ettrick said again.

Tara pointed to the bridge. "Why can't we go that way? It looks like a lovely way to go."

Ettrick paused and pointed to the bridge. "Trolls. Big, nasty ones, too. Also, there are other treacherous races of fairies, and the further in we travel the more trouble you two can find yourselves in," he warned them. So, they followed Ettrick and walked all the way around the huge meadow, even though Tara still wanted to walk across the bridge. Once they approached the edge of the castle gardens,

Tara and Mark stood there, gaping. The gardens were really big and beautiful—bigger than Tara could have pictured. The castle was larger than Tara had originally thought, now that they were right by it. There was a huge gate at the other end of the gardens. Gnomes attended to the different bushes, shrubs and trees.

"Look Tara, gnomes." Mark laughed almost giddily, as if he could not believe what he saw. One gnome tipped his hat while another gave Mark a grumpy face and stuck out his tongue. Mark frowned as Tara giggled.

Standing as guards were two very tall, lean but muscular elves. "State your business," one said, peering down at them. They were in full battle gear, wearing capes and holding long spears. Their light, long blond hair cascaded down their shoulders and backs. They had long, thin noses and pointy ears.

"This is Princess Tara-Brigit and guest, accompanied by Ettrick Abberfeldy. Queen Titiana requested our company."

The elf smiled, showing a perfect white smile. "Sure Ettrick. Sorry, just doing our duty."

The other one opened the gate wide so they could walk through. They each smiled and bowed as Tara passed. Then the gate closed with a clang. It made Tara jump.

Before them stretched a long field lined with trees and shrubs and bushes. There was a huge fountain with a walking path.

"I bet this place is amazing at night," Tara said as they walked towards the stony path that led to the drawbridge.

Ettrick smiled. "Aye. Everything is lit up, and the castle seems to twinkle in the night light."

They came across a drawbridge, and it was pulled down so they walked onto it.

"Any trolls here, at the castle?" Tara asked.

"No. The Queen would nay allow it." Tara was disappointed. Like with most magical creatures, Tara was curious about trolls, having read many stories. She imagined them to be huge ugly creatures that were also playful in nature.

Once they were to the two huge, high wooden doors, Ettrick tapped on the door with his walking stick three times. The left door swung open. Out came a young boy, or elf, Tara guessed.

"Ettrick! Come on in. Mother is expecting you," greeted a boy fairy. He was a bit shorter than Tara, kind of skinny, and knobby kneed. His reddish-brown hair stuck every which way, just as bad as Ettrick's. He had blue eyes and freckles.

"Princess," the fairy said smiling as he opened the door wider and stood taller as Tara walked past. "And who are you?" he asked Mark.

"My name is Mark."

"You may call him Master Mark, Cyphris," a woman said. Descending the long, narrow, windy staircase was the fairy queen. Tara could not help but gasp as she saw her. She was wearing a lovely lavender long, flowing dress. She had flowers in her long, black, loosely curled hair, and she was barefoot.

"Welcome to my palace and my kingdom," she said, smiling as she greeted them. It did not take her long to come down all those stairs; she was fast yet graceful. "Come. We do not have much time. Cyphris, you may return to your studies." The young prince frowned and turned to go down a hallway.

The queen opened a door, and she ushered them inside. She then closed the door and exhaled. "Now that you are safely here, let's discuss why I asked you here."

"Yes, that would be good," Ettrick told her.

"Please sit." She stretched out her arm; there were several sitting chairs and sofas. It was a huge library and study. It had a desk, lots of books, and armor and weapons hanging on the walls or leaning on things, like vases, or trunks, or on shields. There were several bookshelves full of books, some were very aged leather-bound books, some looked new with shiny covers.

The queen clasped her hands together. "Now Ettrick, I know you have some private business to attend to. After refreshments, I shall not keep you here." Ettrick gave a small grunt of frustration, then nodded his head.

"You work for her?" Tara asked. Ettrick nodded his head when the queen was looking away. The queen snapped her fingers and in came a girl fairy who was flying and carrying a tray of cakes, cookies and tea, and some other fruity smelling drink.

"Help yourself," the queen said as the smaller fairy poured some tea and handed the queen a small cake. The queen smiled, and the smaller fairy curtsied and left. Queen Titiana pointed to the sweet-smelling juice and said, "That is fairy nectar juice. It is quite delicious." Tara grinned and poured herself a cup. It was very refreshing and not too sweet.

"Only one cup, mind you," warned Ettrick. "It is quite addicting."

The queen gave a lighthearted laugh as she sat by Tara. "Tell me Tara-Brigit," she said, again sounding very French. "How are you coping with the news of yourself being a princess? Good, I hope." She smiled as she popped a very small cake in her mouth.

"Fine I guess," Tara told her.

"I trust Cian and Lir made you feel welcome?"

"Yes, they did." Tara told her.

"And you, Mark. How are you holding up?"

Mark put down his drink. "Fine," he said as she smiled at him.

Ettrick stood. "I must leave, your highness," he said, grabbing his walking stick.

"Tell your mother I have a bunch of grapes awaiting her pickup to make into jam."

Ettrick beamed. "I will tell her. Thank you." He turned. "I should not be too long, Tara. When it is time to go, do not fret. I will be close behind you." Then he was gone.

"So. You are here to find out what I know." She stood. She looked quite tall to Tara, but now with Tara sitting down she seemed to loom over her.

"Do you know who has the Fairy Flag? Or—" Tara stopped short.

"Or your birth parents?" the queen said as she continued the conversation. She looked out the huge glass windows, where you could see the drawbridge from the room, plus the lawn and the stone path.

"My husband was supposed to be here by now to confirm our information." She turned to look at them. "But no worries, he should be here any moment." She smiled slightly, but Tara could tell she was worried.

"Isn't he fighting the other fairy king or something?" Mark asked, going over to look through the window.

She raised her eyebrows. "Ah, he can speak. Well yes, and no. They were fighting. However, now that we think we have found the princess, they are joining together to help find King Kenneth and the queen. Also, they should have some information on the whereabouts of the flag."

"How do you—?" Tara started to ask, but decided to let them think what they wanted at this point. It was no use trying to tell them all that she was not who they thought. Just then, they heard the faint sounds of a galloping horse off in the distance outside. Queen Titiana looked up nervously.

"Excuse me," she said as she left the room quickly.

Tara looked at Mark and asked, "So do you think they know something?"

"I don't know, Tara," Mark said, sighing as he stood.

"All this." He held out his hands. "Everything that has happened, I am not sure of anything anymore."

Tara felt bad for dragging him along. Well, he would say he came willingly. Tara stood and walked over to the huge fireplace. Hanging above it was a huge horn.

"Hey Mark, does this not look like the horn from the castle?" He came over as well.

"Yeah it does, just not as old."

Tara reached up to touch it.

"Back away slowly" they heard someone say as Tara felt something sharp in her side. Tara folded her arms and backed away. Two elves—or fairies—were holding Mark, one on each arm.

"Whoa! Where did you guys come from?" Mark asked.

"Wouldn't you like to know, human?" said one. Tara noticed his grip on Mark got tighter, and Mark let out a grumble.

"I wasn't going to take it," Tara said as the doors burst open and a handsome, tall fairy rushed in, his facial expression serious. The fairy queen was on his heels.

"Let me explain," the queen said. "Oh, for goodness sake, Oberon! That is the princess!"

He raised his eyebrows. "Is it, now?" he said, looking at Tara from top to bottom.

"Call off your watch dogs! Husband! She isn't going to steal anything.

He looked at them with suspicious eyes, then cleared his facial expression.

The fairy king dismissed the guards with a gesture of his chin. Mark started straightening out his shirt where the guards had wrinkled it.

"You?" Oberon walked over until he was close to Tara. "You are the princess?" He was very tall, muscular, and very handsome. He had jet black hair that was short and spiked a bit on top. He had piercing green eyes that seemed to Tara to change from an emerald green to a darker green.

"Hmm," he said as he continued to observe her. He smiled widely at Tara as he bent down a bit. Smiling made his eyes sparkle. The queen hit his arm as she passed and stood by Tara.

"It is her. Show him your necklace, dearest," Tina said. Tara pulled out her necklace with the small bracelet on it. The king reached out to touch one of the small stones. He had fairly large hands and long fingers. The stones sparkled and a faint sound of a voice calling out could be heard. Tara looked down at the tiny bracelet. He stood abruptly, letting the bracelet fall back onto her chest. Tara reached for it and examined it carefully.

"What was that?" she asked, not sure what she had heard. Not answering her question, the fairy king stood tall.

"Well!" he said as he put his arms behind him, one hand on top of the other and started walking around the room. "Seems I was mistaken, clearly the stones know who she is, and now we know as well. My touch proved that. A fairy king and queen have magic no one else knows about. Touching these stones, my magic can engage the stones to call out. Quite remarkable, actually," he said as he turned to face the queen. "Don't you think, dearest?"

Queen Tina looked as if she was a sly fox beat at her own game.

"Sorry about my guards. No harm done though." He was walking past Mark, grinning mischievously.

"Who is this?"

"My name is Mark, King Oberon." Mark quickly bowed his head as the king walked over to Tina.

"Got dragged into this mess, did you?" Oberon asked as he laughed.

"Kind of," Mark said as Tara came closer towards Mark.

A tall fairy – or was it an elf – came in, handing Oberon a piece of parchment. It was kind of hard for Tara to distinguish between the elves and the fairies. The order of things here was quite complex.

"Ah, very good." He tried opening it but was having trouble. "Blasted seal has a magical lock." He snapped his fingers and the parchment opened.

"What news, husband?" Tina asked as he was reading it.

"It's not good, Tina my love. Pater has about half the Fomorians on his side, the Foal, and now the Red Caps." He hit his leg with the parchment. "Blast!" He stood there staring at the floor.

"The Fairy Flag was last seen in the Green Glenn though, my love." He looked up towards her, and the queen sighed.

"All those long days and nights searching the Green Glenn and you never found a thing."

"Yes. You were right. All the long hours we have spent. Hours roaming that blasted forest! And that is all we have, when we should have more information." Oberon was pacing now, flinging the parchment about as he paced.

"Sorry, my love," Tina said, trying to console him as she ran her finger along his shoulders.

"We cannot send these two out now, unguarded, for sure."

"I agree. What do you two say?" Tina asked, looking at Mark and Tara.

"Red Caps?" Tara asked, she had read about some in a book once, but she now wanted clarification. She saw the queen shiver. Maybe she didn't need to know more information after all.

"Oh, they are nasty goblins."

"Goblins?" Tara asked as King Oberon loomed above Tara; his mood had shifted to dark, causing the room to be cast in a bit of shadow as if the weather had changed. "They crave blood, and once it is shed, they will not stop. They even pigmented their hats in the blood of their victims. They are very fast, even though they wear those blasted iron boots."

"Pigment, as in dye?" Tara asked. Oberon nodded.

"That's disgusting!" Tara scrunched up her face like she had just bit into a lemon. She was now sorry she had asked.

"That's enough Oberon, no need to scare the children," Tina said. Tara could feel her disgust and fear; her whole countenance seemed a bit darker.

"Well they need to know who the enemy is."

"I agree," said Mark. "Knowing who our enemy is and what they can do is a good thing to know. Especially for us. Here were we have no magic, or any way to defend ourselves." He looked at Tara, all the color from her face draining away. She felt a bit sick.

The fairy king chuckled. "Ah. But what of your gun, Master Mark?"

Mark got it out. "I have no bullets, so it is completely useless. Besides, it is not mine, I just snagged it."

"Snagged it?" The king asked as he gestured to Mark to see it.

"Yeah, I borrowed it."

Tara noticed the room seemed not as gloomy as before. Like a kid with a new toy, the king took the gun and inspected it. He then handed it back to Mark, smiling widely. He then got out a piece of parchment.

"The Fomorians must have the stone," Oberon said, holding up the parchment so that Tina could see. He traced his finger along some writing.

"The Fomorians have been busy building another castle," said the queen, holding up her arms.

"Those blasted Fomorians! Can't they tell the difference between regular stone and the coronation stone?"

"Apparently not love, for Oren saw, with his own eyes mind you, the giants dragging the stone away."

Tara started to look a bit better. "Fomorians?"

The king glanced in her direction. "Giants."

Tara looked at him. "Yes, I know, I have read about them. Who is Oren?"

King Oberon nodded. He then embraced the queen, who seemed tired. He did not answer her question right away. The king seemed pre-occupied.

"Oren is our army's captain."

"How would we get a huge stone away from the giants? Also, I don't suppose that is the High King's horn?" Tara pointed at the horn on the wall.

Oberon raised his eyebrows, let go of his queen, and walked over to the fireplace.

"Oh this?" he asked, taking it down from the shelf. "This is Sir Rory's horn. It is indeed the kings. I took it when the king went missing. A few of us took items to protect them—we are all friends after all. Although some items were not protected enough and were stolen."

He handed it to Tara, and she took it and almost dropped it. It was a bit heavier than she thought. The king caught it in his hand under hers. He helped her lift it until he was sure she had it.

"It is a drinking horn. If you were not the princess you could not touch it, since I enchanted it." He smiled wildly at her.

Tara looked up into his green eyes. "What would it do if I was not the princess?"

He took a few steps away from her. "Any number of things. It might spurt out wine until this whole room was flooded, and you drowned, or it might—"

Tina came forward waving her hand, then took the horn from Tara and set it back on the shelf. "That's enough, Oberon. There are things we need to discuss." She seemed bored by his childlike antics.

"What you really need is the Fairy Flag. When held up high in battle, the army who raises it shall be victorious." Tina turned and looked very serious.

"Ah, but you, Princess, can find it, no?" King Oberon said as he came closer to Tara, quickly touching the tip of her nose with his finger and smiling at her. Tara smiled back. "And that, my dear princess, is how we shall win." He turned around and pointed to the horn the queen had just put back. "Let her have the horn. She could use it, I bet. Besides, it does belong to the king, her father."

"Fine. You can get it down for her," the queen said and then sat down on a chair, wiping at her forehead like she was sweating, even though Tara saw no evidence of such.

The doors to the room they were in creaked slowly open a bit. A little head full of light blond, long curls popped into view. "Daddy!" yelled a little girl fairy as she ran into the room, her curly hair bouncing as she ran. She was wearing a white nightdress and had bare feet. Tara thought she looked to be about two or three years old. Oberon bent down and scooped her up into his arms. "Now Una, why are you not napping?" She wrapped her little arms around his neck and pouted.

"All the children were worried about you. They missed their father. Especially since he was on a dangerous mission," Tina said as she raised her eyebrows. She stood and walked slowly over to Oberon and picked up the little fairy princess.

"Well I am fine, Una, as you can see." He turned to Tara. "Now the business of finding you two a guard."

"Is that the princess?" Una asked as her mother put her down. She walked over to Tara, looked up at her, and smiled.

"Yes Una. This is Princess Tara- Brigit," Tina told her as the little fairy curtsied.

"Mother. I am older than she, why is she bigger?"

The Queen laughed. "She was raised by mortal humans, Una, and that is why."

"Oh," Una said, not smiling. Tara squatted down in front of the fairy child. "It is nice to meet you Una." The little girl fairy smiled and touched Tara's hand with her own small, plump, and velvety soft one.

"Well I will take Mark to the stables, Tina. Una, you should go run along, find your brothers, and get ready for your afternoon class." Tara stood as Oberon gestured for Mark to follow him, and they left. Tara followed Tina out as the queen gently took Una's hand. They walked down a hallway, and then a young fairy about Tara's age came up to the queen. She let go of her daughter's hand and looked down.

"Now Una, be good for Beth and listen to her instructions." The little fairy princess looked back and smiled. "Yes Mommy," she said as she took the hand of the other fairy named Beth. They kept walking down the hall.

The fairy queen looked at Tara and smiled with a sigh. "Now Tara, you are in need of some riding clothes. Follow me." Tara followed her into a large room that had three vanity tables with mirrors. The queen turned away from Tara and walked toward the door. "Now just wait here and I will send in someone with the things you shall need. It seems I am in need of a rest." She smiled as she closed the door. Tara looked around. There was a huge four-poster bed, dressers, a sitting sofa, and long, elegant curtains on the windows. The door opened, and in came a girl fairy wearing a yellow dress, her brown, loosely curled hair pulled back by yellow flowers. She looked as if she could be about Tara's age.

"Here you are, Princess," she said as she walked over to the bed and laid the clothing down. She turned to Tara and smiled, and Tara noticed that her long, pointy ears had silver rings and dangling chains on them. "I can help you if you like?"

Tara walked over to the fairy. They were almost the same height, but the fairy was a little bit shorter. "No, I will be fine. Thank you, though."

The fairy's smile faded a bit and she curtsied. "Very well, I will be just outside the door. My name is Brin."

Tara knew that she let the fairy maid down, so she smiled in an attempt to make amends as the fairy walked to the door. "Thank you, Brin." The fairy smiled back and closed the door behind her.

14

Fairies, Trolls, and Trouble

Tara walked over to the bed. There was an elegant blouse, tan riding pants, and riding boots. She changed quickly and folded her other clothes and set them on the bed, leaving her sneakers on the floor. After a few minutes there was a knock on the door. "Princess, it's me Brin, can I come in?"

"Yes," Tara called out. The door opened and Brin came in holding a basket full of stuff. She pulled out a bag with a pull string. "This is for your other clothes." She set it down on the bed.

"What's in the basket?" Tara asked.

"I was hoping you would at least let me do your hair?"

She hadn't let anyone touch her hair, except for Mark, since her mother had died. She hesitantly said okay, and when the fairy's face lit up, she smiled. Tara was reluctant but did not want to offend the fairy. Brin gestured for her to sit down at one of the vanities. Brin set the basket down on the smooth surface of the vanity, and she opened the drawer. There were combs, brushes, and handheld mirrors. She grabbed a big brush and started brushing Tara's hair. It felt nice to have it brushed, and Tara closed her eyes. The clink of the brush set down on the wood made Tara open her eyes. Brin proceeded to braid her long hair, adding combs, clips, ribbons, and tiny little bells that made soft, light tinkling sounds. When she was done, she opened the drawer, put the brush back, and handed Tara a mirror so she could see the back of her head. Tara was surprised at how nice it looked. Beautiful actually. It made Tara smile to see her hair look so nice. It looked even better now than when she had let her mom pay for someone to do her hair for prom. "It looks so nice. Thank you, Brin."

Brin smiled. "I am glad you like it. Now you really look like a princess. Well not that you didn't before." A light knock on the door interrupted them.

"It's just me, Queen Tina." The door opened as the fairy queen came in.

She walked over to where Tara was sitting. The queen wore a different dress now, more of a deep blue color. Brin grabbed the basket and stood aside. "You did a lovely job Brin, as always."

Brin curtsied. "Thank you, your majesty." She then looked at Tara. "Good luck, princess." Then she was out the door. Tara looked up at the fairy queen's reflection in the mirror. Tina smiled.

"When I first met you and held you in my arms, you were the most beautiful human baby I had ever seen." Tina pulled over a chair and sat next to Tara. "Now you are grown and even lovelier." Tara smiled.

"You, Princess Tara-Brigit, are fairy blessed, and as such have and will be protected." She turned to look into the mirror. "There are those, Tara, who wish to harm you. Others, well…" She fiddled with a piece of hair on Tara's head and re-tucked the tiny bell clip into it. "Well, not everyone will be excited that you have been found. I, on the other hand am simply past relieved, and happy." She took a few steps away from Tara. "Now if only the king and queen could be found." Her voice sounded so sad, and her face took on a forlorn look. However, she then smiled again.

"You were so small when I first met you at the High King's castle, during your naming celebration. King Oberon and I had traveled far and presented your parents with a gift for you. The Fairy Flag. I sang along with my kin, and everything was right in the world. Until it was discovered you were missing, and nothing has been the same since. I blame myself. I should have done more." She sucked in breath and let it out in a huge sigh.

"Only you, Tara, can find the flag. I don't even know where it is, and neither does Oberon." She leaned in a bit and whispered into Tara's ear, "And I am the one who enchanted it."

"Why only me? I mean, why am I the only one who can find it?" Tara asked, a bit confused.

"It is magical, connected to you. It was a gift from me and Oberon to you, and as such you are bonded with it." Tara stood also and followed Tina to the bed.

"This cloak," she said, picking it up and handing it to Tara, "will protect you if you wear it with the hood up."

"It's really nice," Tara said, holding it up to herself. It was a light blue color, with a spring green edging that was silky; the inside had a similar fabric as the edging but was a bit darker. It had a butterfly fairy clasp.

"How will it protect me?" She asked.

"Well, it will shield you from danger, and keep you warm."

Tara smiled as she touched the fabric. It felt sturdy yet soft.

Tina then, out of thin air or so it seemed to Tara, held out a small silver whistle. "This whistle when blown will alert my army, if you need assistance." She reached and took the necklace off of Tara and added the whistle to it. "Do not blow it unless you are in dire need. No crying wolf."

Tara nodded. "No crying wolf," she repeated as Tina turned and walked towards the door. She turned slightly.

"There are those who will protect you with their lives, Tara. Those who want to help you. There are also those who would harm you. I am sorry, but you are not in your peaceful world anymore." The lines to The Wizard of Oz started playing in Tara's head.

Queen Tina opened the door more. "Follow me, and we will go down to the stables."

Once at the stables they saw Mark and King Oberon talking to another elf or fairy. It was hard for Tara to tell. Some fairies were as tall or taller than herself, some as tiny as bees. There were so many different magical races. She just would never assume what one was until she was told. It could take her a life time to sort it all out. Tara was amazed when they got to the stables because the they were some of the biggest, grandest ones she had ever seen. They were also very clean. One male fairy opened a stall and led a horse out and handed the reins to Mark.

Mark walked the horse out, smiling at Tara as he passed by her. Mark was wearing fairy armor. Tara thought he looked pretty hot, even though she let out a giggle when she saw him.

"That's a beautiful horse," Tara said, looking at the dark chocolate coat and its black tail and mane.

Mark came up to Tara. "Your hair looks amazing." He reached up and flicked a tiny bell with his finger. She felt her face grow warm. "Thanks," she said smiling.

King Oberon walked up, kissed Tina, and smiled at Tara. "We will be sending one of our best warriors with you. He will get you to the Green Glen. Oh, and here is the horn." Tara took it by the strap.

"Thanks," she said as she swung it onto her shoulder. A fairy came walking up, holding the reins to a huge horse. The horse reminded Tara of a Clydesdale, but a bit bigger. The fairy warrior on the horse's back was very tall, with long blond hair that was partially braided back. He had dark brown eyes and wore dark blue and brown leather armor. Tara could not help but stare. He was drop-dead gorgeous.

"This is Oren," Oberon told Tara. Oren bowed to Tara and then Mark. "He also happens to be my brother," Oberon told them.

"Nice to meet you, Oren," Tara said as Mark held out his hand. Oren looked around, not knowing what to do. Mark pulled back his hand and put it behind his back.

"That's a human gesture of greeting, Oren," Queen Tina told him. Oren nodded his head. A female fairy came out of the stables with Snowberry. Snowberry had been freshly cleaned and brushed, and she had decorations in her mane and tail that were similar to the ones in Tara's hair. The fairy handed the reins to Tina, who then handed them to Tara. Another younger female fairy flew up quickly and handed a bag to Mark and then one to Tara.

"Sorry I'm late, there was a bit of a mess in the kitchens." She seemed flustered as she bowed to Tina.

Tina looked at the fairy. "Oh goodness."

The fairy nodded her head.

Mark mounted his horse. Oren jumped off of his horse when he saw Tara struggling to get up and onto the saddle, and then he helped her mount Snowberry. She smiled at him and said, "Thank you, Oren."

He smiled back. "You are quite welcome." He had a velvety smooth voice, yet it sounded young. She thought he must be a younger brother to the king. Tara wondered how many siblings the king had. Maybe she could ask Oren later. Now did not seem to be a good time.

The fairy who had given her the bag came over to Tara. "There is food in there, and a pouch with fairy dust for cleaning your drinking water, or for wounds."

Tara's eyes widened. "Like real fairy dust, really?" The fairy giggled, curtsied, and then flew away. She was about the size of a five-year-old human child; her wings were big, although they did not make much noise as she flew away, just a light swooshing sound.

"All right then, be off with you," Oberon said, patted Snowberry's rump and then stood with Tina. They both were waving to the small party.

"Oren, be mindful of the Red Caps. Oh, and there is a full moon tonight!" Oberon yelled. Oren gave a quick nod. Tara was riding in between Oren and Mark.

"Why did he mention a full moon?" Tara asked, but Oren did not answer her right away. Further down the path they switched to traveling single file down the path. Many fairies came to see them off, including a very tall, elegant fairy. She was wearing a golden dress, her long blond hair glistening in the sun that was starting to set. She waved and blew Oren a kiss. He smiled at her and bowed his head as he passed.

"Who is she?" Tara asked as she rode by. The fairy smiled and waved at Tara. Tara smiled and waved back.

"That is Centry. She is my –" He paused. "My admirer."

"Oh," Tara said as she passed the beautiful fairy. Oren clicked his tongue and his horse picked it up as they went up a hill. Tara tried to get closer to Oren to ask about the full moon again. There was never a good moment to ask as they traveled up and down hills, through the woods and streams.

As it grew dark, they crossed over streams that had bridges and stayed away from the main roads. They hadn't talked much—it was not very easy to do anyway, riding the way they were. Finally, they came to a path wide enough for Tara to ride next to Oren. "Why did King Oberon warn you about the full moon?" Tara glanced up at it. Its huge sphere was so bright it lit up the wilderness.

"There are dangerous creatures that come out during a full moon," he said, riding by her side. Now she wished she never asked. As a child, her imagination would sweep her away, and still did sometimes. She needed more questions answered, so she asked another.

"How far is it to the Green Glenn?"

"A few more hours. We cannot rest until we are safe within the Glenn." The stretch of land between the Fairy Kingdom and there was treacherous. Tara looked around the forest, which seemed perfectly calm to her, but then again, she was not a fairy, and fairies had sensitive hearing, keen eyesight, and reflexes to match. "We are now in the lands of the Stone Kingdom. Be on guard."

Tara froze. They were in enemy territory. "Ugh! Is this a good idea? I mean, what if something happens?"

"That is why they sent me with you." Tara was slightly comforted, even though she never had met him before. What were they doing?

She did not have any special gifts to sense danger or anything. Beira and Lou were supposed to meet us, she now remembered. Oren must have sensed her uneasiness.

"Don't worry Princess, I shall warn you if there is any trouble." She must have had a worried look on her face, because Mark leaned towards her.

"He'd better be as great of a warrior as Oberon says he is." Tara nodded her head in agreement. Then, as if reading her mind, Oren spoke to her in a kind, calm voice. "As for Beira and Lou, well they are busy. They have been informed of the change in plans. Also, I am a very skilled warrior. I have trained almost my whole life and have been in many battles." Tara smiled faintly as she looked at Mark.

"How are you?" he asked.

"Fin," Tara sighed. "Tina told me some stuff."

"Yeah, Oberon told me some stuff too. We aren't in Kansas anymore," Mark said as Tara swallowed, her throat feeling dry. Tara was really becoming aware of how dangerous a place the Higher Realms were, and she realized that she wanted to go home. She reached for her water bag and took a sip. It was getting really dark, and the moon was already shining brightly. Oren slowed his pace a bit and then stopped. Mark and Tara stopped as well.

"If we need to run the horses, secure your life line around your waist so you will not fall off." He held up a long leather strap, kind of like a belt. "Should the need arise." He smiled faintly and clicked his tongue as his horse began to trot slowly. As they went under a cluster of trees, Oren turned and put his finger up to his mouth. He then looked around and listened. Mark and Tara stopped their horses and Snowberry pawed at the ground nervously. Then they heard a howl in the distance. The hairs on Tara's arms stood on end, and Snowberry whinnied. Oren gestured for them to fasten their life lines. She wrapped her life line around her waist but fumbled with the clasp. Mark reached over to help her. Oren got out his longbow and then sat up stiffly in his saddle.

"Ride! Now!" He then gave a short loud whistle as the horses took off.

Tara quickly finished fastening her belt around her waist, just in time because Snowberry had taken off right behind Oren's horse. Something was chasing them, and it was fast. It ran alongside them, several feet away in the dense forest, she could only make out big black shapes. Tara could barely hold on as the horses ran and jumped over fallen trees and low bushes. Snowberry and Mark's horse listened to Oren's commands as he made short clicks with his tongue and low, sharp whistles. The horses moved as if they were one as they ran through a small clearing. Oren yelled as the horses went even faster as they each jumped over a huge fallen tree and back into the forest.

At one-point Tara looked back to see what was chasing them and realized they were wolves. Huge, massive scary wolves. One jumped down from a rock ledge near Oren. It almost knocked Oren off his horse, and that's when he shot his longbow, which had huge, silver-tipped arrows. He loaded it and shot arrow after arrow. They made whizzing sounds like fireworks do on the fourth of July. One hit the wolf straight in the chest. It let out a strangled sounding howl and then tumbled to the ground. Tara screamed as her horse flew by the beast lying on the ground. The wolf was trying to dislodge the arrow, his long-clawed paw trying to swipe at her legs as they ran past it. Luckily it missed. There were two chasing alongside them now, one on the left and one on the right. Oren quickly and gracefully, without breaking stride, stood up in the saddle, reloaded his bow, and fired shots one after the other in the directions of the wolves. Mark was riding alongside Tara, and they both were behind Oren by only a few feet. If Oren lost control of his horse, they would become a giant heap of horses' hooves and mangled arms and legs. However, the horses were well trained and knew to stay a generous distance from one another. Oren shot another arrow that lodged in the chest of one of the wolves, and he went down. Howls and ferocious growling could be heard all around.

"We're almost there, just a few more yards!" Oren yelled as he kept shooting, but his quiver of arrows looked as if it was getting sparse.

The forest thickened, and they crashed through a shallow but wide stream. The wolves seemed to have stopped pursuing them. Oren slowed his horse down slowly to a canter, and the other two horses did the same. Oren was breathing heavily, his chest heaving as much as the horses. Tara's heart was beating fast, and her hands were numb from gripping the reins too hard for too long.

"Everyone all right?" he asked as he circled around them. "Tara, your right arm is bleeding." Tara briefly looked down, then looked up when they heard howling; however, it was not too close. Tara looked down and saw that her jacket was torn through her shirt and blood was seeping through. Oren hastily got out a satchel, poured something in his hand, poured a bit of water into it, used his finger to mix it, and came up to Tara. "Let's see," he said as Mark helped her take her arm out of the sleeves. "A branch must have caught you, not the beast's claws, right?" Tara looked at him, horrified to think of one of those massive claws cutting her.

"No, you would be more wounded than this," he said reassuring himself and her. He put the paste on the cut, ripped a piece of cloth, and tied it around her arm.

It instantly felt better. "Thank you," Tara said quietly, as she was still breathing kind of fast. She looked around, wondering if, at any moment, the beasts would lunge from out of somewhere. But nothing happened. They dismounted the horses and let them walk slowly to cool down as they walked out of the stream and into even thicker wooded areas.

"They need water. There should be another stream nearby," Oren told them as they walked. The moon was still bright, giving the forest a weird murky greenish-silver tone. They would occasionally hear a howl far away, and Tara shivered each time. They came to a big pond, and Mark offered to take the horses over to get a drink. It was a nice night, and it was peaceful where they were. Tara thought, even after what had just happened. The woods were quiet except for the chirping of crickets and the croaking of frogs, and the occasional hoot of an owl.

"Oren, what were those?" asked Tara. "I mean, they looked like huge wolves."

He took a sip of his water, capping his pouch as he answered her. "That was Sawney Bean and his family. Cannibals they are, and werewolves to boot."

Tara swallowed hard, and her arms started shaking. "Here." Oren got out a blanket and set it down. "Sit. You are worn out."

Tara looked around.

"You are safe, we are in the Green Glenn now. They won't follow us in here."

"Why not?" Mark asked, looking around.

Tara sat as Oren got out a little pot and explained, "It is not their territory. If they came in here, they would be hunted. There are even more frightful things here." He noticed Tara's facial expression. "Nothing that will harm you if you listen and stick with me." He looked down at Tara, who looked wide-eyed up at him. "We are safe," he reassured her.

Tara looked around; the greenery of the grass and trees were almost unnatural, yet beautiful like a picture that was enhanced by some kind of photo-editing program.

"Where are we exactly?" Tara asked as Oren got up. "I mean, where is the Green Glenn on earth?"

He raised his eyebrows as he looked back—he was bending over the small fire getting them some tea. "The Green Glen is in Ireland."

"We are in Ireland?" Mark asked, looking around. "This does not look like Ireland."

Oren passed by Mark. "No, I expect it does not to you." Oren smiled and handed Mark a cup and then one to Tara. He then came up and sat by Tara.

"Well that almost made me wet my pants, running away from those things," she said as Mark reached over and touched Tara's hand.

"Are you all right, Tara?" Mark noticed that her hands were still shaking.

"She'll be fine once I give her some more tea, and she rests," Oren said as he stood and started gathering sticks to make a fire.

Tara leaned into Mark and repeated, "Werewolves." Her face was ghost white.

Mark nodded. "Yeah, thinking about going back now, aren't you?"

Tara nodded her head as she straightened out her legs.

"Tara, your leg," Mark said, looking terrified.

Tara looked down. Her right leg was bleeding, a piece of a branch still stuck in her pants. She could not feel it because her leg was a bit numb. Oren walked over to her as the fire blazed.

"Her leg is hurt too," Mark told him.

Oren knelt down and looked at Tara's leg. She winced when he moved the fabric of her pants aside a bit. The fabric had been like a compression, and now that it was moved, she felt her leg stinging. "Tara, this was not a claw, right?"

She shook her head. "I don't think so." Fear was draped around every word. She hoped not at least. He grabbed the piece of tree branch and pulled it out of her pants where it clung. "No, those things did not touch me." She was horrified at the thought. She would have remembered if it was a claw.

Oren nodded and got out a small first aid kit. "This needs stitches. I can do it, but I need to clean it and numb it first." Tara nodded her head, glad that he had what was needed. "You both have a kit in your satchels. Tina did not let us come unprepared."

"What can I do?" Mark asked.

"You can get the tea ready. She will need at least two cups after this, and you will need some as well."

The cut was on the side of her calf; luckily, the blood would not stain her socks, since they were a dark brownish-grey color. Oren cleaned her cut, which stung. "Ouch!" Tara yelled. Mark finished pouring the cup of the tea. He brought it over to her and set it down. Oren got out a packet, opened it and applied some kind of salve to the cut. Within a few minutes it was numb.

Oren got supplies ready to sew up the wound. "Tara," Mark said, sitting on her left side but slightly behind her. "Hold my hand and look at me, okay?" Tara nodded and gripped his hand.

When Oren started stitching, she felt tugging at first, but then a sharp pain. The cut was deeper than they had believed, and they didn't have adequate numbing medicine. She sucked in her breath and held it.

"Tara, breathe, I don't want you passing out on me," Oren said as he continued to stitch up the large cut. She was breathing but in shallow breaths. The pain had gone, but she still felt the tugging. After

Oren was done stitching her up, her hands were trembling. She was going into shock. He bandaged her, and Tara let go of Mark's hand as he kissed her sweaty forehead, and Oren then handed her the tin mug. "Drink all of it, and then you will need a second cup."

He then poured a cup for Mark and then for himself last.

"They can't come in here, right?" Tara asked Oren again.

"No, don't worry. As I said before, we are safe. We are in the area of a group of warriors who know we are coming. They probably already know we are here. We are under their protection."

Oren stood and got out his rolled-up blanket. "We should turn in soon. Mark, you take first watch, then I will. Tara, drink another cup of tea." Mark got it for her. She was feeling really drowsy.
Mark got Tara's bed roll and helped her lie down. She yawned. "What was in that tea?" That was the last thing she said until morning.

$$* \atop {* \ *}$$

15

The Bear Village

"Good morning," Mark said as Tara sat up slowly. Tara looked around. The sun was barely up, and she saw the horses grazing in the small meadow nearby. They were all groomed. Oren was asleep near her by the fire that was barely glowing. "How did you sleep?" Mark asked.

Tara scrunched up her face. "Fine, I guess. She had had a strange dream of a big room, full of stuff, and a huge bear statue."

"Good," smiled Mark as he was packing up his gear.

"You seem chipper," she said as she stood, wincing and feeling the pain in her leg, her arm, and her muscles.

Mark handed her a cup of water and two Tylenol. "Here." She took them and sighed. "There's food in your bag. Let me get some for you." Tara sat back down.

Oren stirred in his sleep and then rolled over, waking up and looking at Tara. "Good morning," he said, resting his head in his hand and propped up on his elbow.

Tara kind of smiled. "I thought I might have nightmares all night and not sleep."

Oren sat up. "Not with the special tea I gave you. Both of you slept really well." He got up and started rolling up his blanket.

"Well," Tara sighed, looking around. Everything was very green, and the sparkling sun shone through the leaves and made the grass and small plants seem to sparkle. "I know why they call this the Green Glenn." Because all she saw, besides the blue sky, was green. Everything was lush and beautiful: the many different kinds of trees, the smaller bushes, ferns, moss on the rocks and the fallen trees. Everything actually.

Mark handed her some food. "Thanks," she said as she started eating it. Birds were chirping, and the sun was becoming bright in the sky above, filtering through the trees.

"How much longer before we get to where we are going?" Mark asked Oren.

"Oh, a few hours on horseback. Lord Marty McMahon's village is pretty big though.

Mark nodded.

"A few more hours," he repeated.

"Is that who is protecting us?" Tara asked.

"Yes," Oren replied as he got a drink and some food and then excused himself.

Tara stood. "I need to, uh…"

"Oh, you go that way." Mark pointed in the opposite direction Oren went. "Just beyond that cluster of darker trees." Tara nodded put on her cloak and walked over to where he told her to go.

After she was done, she was buttoning her pants when she heard something behind her. She froze. Oren had said the wolves could not come here, but she was still scared. Then she saw something small move in the bushes.

"Hello," Tara called out.

"Hello" came a small, childlike voice. Tara walked a bit in the direction of where the greeting came from.

"Hello," she called out again. Then she saw two ears peek up from behind a bush, and then a nose. It was a very small deer.

"Oh, a deer." Tara looked around. "Hello," she said again, looking around. Surely there was someone there. The dear walked cautiously closer towards Tara as Tara took a step forward. The deer stepped back a bit.

"Where are you?" she asked but heard nothing. She was looking into the bushes. Tara did not think that the deer would actually speak to her, but it was the only other being around, and its eyes looked intelligent.

"I am just a deer, but you are a princess," it said, kind of giggling as it started to walk around Tara.

"You can talk," Tara said, amazed.

The deer stopped walking and crinkled up its nose.

"It's just I have never met a talking deer."

The deer giggled again. "And I have never met a princess." The deer started slowly walking away.

"So how do you know I am one if you have never met one?" Tara asked.

"Well you look like one," said the small deer. Tara followed the deer, fascinated. "Are all princesses as pretty as you?" the deer asked as they walked along in the woods.

"I wouldn't know really," Tara told her. The deer suddenly looked up, moving her ears back and forth.

"Is something wrong?" Tara asked, looking around.

"A bear—run!" the deer squeaked out before darting off into the forest brush. Tara heard a snorting sound which could have been a bear but she wasn't going to hang around to find out. Tara ran in the direction the deer went. After a while, she stopped to catch her breath, and she didn't see the deer anywhere. There was also no sign of a bear. She bent down to rub her leg near the stitches, it throbbed.

"Hello!" she yelled and then realized that maybe she should not yell. Frustrated, she tried going back the way she came. "Mark!" she yelled and stopped to listen. Nothing. She kept walking. "Oren!" she yelled. Still nothing but the silence of a dense forest. She was very hot, so she took off her cloak. She passed a waterfall, thinking that she had not seen that before. I am lost, she thought as she walked, hoping that she would run into Mark and Oren or maybe even the village. But no such luck. The sun was now casting long shadows on the ground. It must be late noon, she thought as she also realized she was tired of walking. She came to a wide path through the trees, but it wasn't a very worn one. At one point as she walked, she saw a bunch of birds take flight and saw the trees in front of her sway. She stopped walking, holding her breath. But she saw nothing and continued through the path.

"Oh, why did I have to follow that deer?" she asked out loud to no one after she had been walking for most of the day. She shivered at the thought of what else could be out there and put her cloak back on. The path led to a clearing. She walked in a bit and noticed that, in the trees, there were large balls of sticks. One in every other tree. They all were quite a way up and had wooden ladders attached that led to openings. The sun was setting fast now as the air had a bit of chill to it. Her stomach grumbled as she walked towards one. She looked closer and realized that they looked like nests. She decided to climb up one of the ladders. When she reached the top, two large beaks popped out and pecked at her hands.

"Ouch!" she yelled, almost losing her grip on the ladder. The two baby birds looked at her, their big eyes looking startled. "I won't hurt you," she said softly. They were huge birds with long, skinny legs. Their fluffy fur was white except for their necks and heads, which were black. They tipped their heads sideways and just stared at her. Then they nestled back down in the fluffy feathers they were lying on. She made her way back down the ladder, and the baby birds poked their heads out and looked down at her, softly chirping.

"I am sure your parents will be here soon, and I wouldn't want to be between you and them, now would I?" she asked as the two baby birds shook their heads as if to answer her. She kind of laughed. "Silly birds, I think you can understand me but can't talk to me."

Once she got down, she sat on a rock near the tree. Then she heard the fluttering of wings, and the next things she saw were several big, tall birds landing in the clearing. They were towering, and twice as tall as Tara. One by one, they each climbed a ladder with stuff in their beaks. They all looked at her but did not seem scared or concerned of her presence. One nest did not have a bird climbing its ladder. She waited a bit to see if a bird would land and go in. She watched as the birds climbed up and in, and then they pulled up the ladders and everything was quiet. It was getting almost too dark to see, and so she took a chance and climbed the remaining ladder. She hesitantly peeked in, hoping no baby birds would be startled and poke her eyes out. The nest was empty. Tara climbed all the way up and into the nest. It was full of white fluffy feathers. She looked out, reached down and grabbed the ladder, which came up easily enough, and she found it fit nicely up and out of the way.

"Well at least I have shelter," she said to herself quietly. The wind picked up a bit, rocking the tree a little, and then it started to rain. A few minutes later the rain came down harder, so she wrapped her cloak around her. She looked up and noticed that the rain had hit some of the long, entwined sticks and rolled down away from the nest. Clever, she thought as she got comfortable, and she quickly fell asleep. She woke up with a start, screaming when she heard the clap of thunder and saw a big flash of lightning. She was breathing hard, and she wrapped the cloak around her more and felt warmer but not very safe. She was alone in a strange place and did not have any provisions. She grabbed her necklace with the whistle. Then remembered the fairy queen's warning, No crying wolf. "Ha, funny. Wolf. Not funny! Tara! Oh gosh." She swallowed hard, and her throat felt dry. She drifted off to sleep and then woke up with a start again. waking up suddenly, then going back to sleep went on for the rest of the evening.

Tara sat up quickly. She had had an awful dream; those wolves were chasing her, and she was on foot but couldn't run fast. "It was just a dream," she told herself. She was still in the nest. She thought she heard her name being called from a far distance. She poked her head out, and she noticed that all of the ladders were down except for hers. The sun was up and everything sparkled from the previous night's rainstorm. She was high up enough that she could see for a far distance. All she saw were trees and hills, and it was a beautiful view. The sky was a forget-me-not blue, clear and bright. She felt safer now that it was daylight. She reached down and rubbed her stomach as it rumbled and ached. She tried to ignore it. Also, her leg hurt. She was thinking of how at home she could raid the fridge whenever she wanted, or that Alana could make her whatever she wanted. Out here she was on her own. Not such a happy thought. She shuddered when she thought again of being chased by hungry werewolves, so she tried thinking of more pleasant things. Like the fairies—they seemed nice enough. Cian and Lir were nice and even fed her, and gave her advice. Still this place was very different: talking animals, things that wanted to eat her, or harm her. She wondered how big the

Higher Realms really were. She wondered if it would take her a lifetime to explore them, or a lifetime to get back home.

Then she heard her name again, and she saw baby birds pop their heads out of their nests, looking around. "Here!" she called out as all of the birds looked her way and then quickly pulled their heads back in. She then listened but heard nothing. Tara sighed and sat down. She absentmindedly reached up and felt for her necklace and on it the whistle. The fairy queen had told her to use it only if she was in dire need, but that was hardly the case right now. She let it drop back down onto her chest. She started throwing feathers out of the nest. She was bored and hungry, but she really did not want to leave the nest, fearful of what she would come across and of getting even more lost. She laughed. I wonder if baby birds get that same feeling. She wondered were Ettrick was—probably still in the fairy kingdom. Blasted brownie. She watched as a few birds came and went, feeding their babies, now really wishing she could eat. She was leaning her head on the opening of the nest just staring out. It was beautiful here, with the green rolling hills far off in the distance, and the thick, lush forest. Home was beautiful too, but this was different. It was magical here. Something caught her eye at the far side of the clearing. It was a bear, slowly entering the clearing. Tara sat up slowly and pulled her head inside the nest. She looked sideways out of a crack to look at the bear. It was in the clearing, and it walked slowly and would stick its nose up in the air and sniff. It paused, and Tara closed her eyes. Oh gosh, please go away, bear, she thought. Then she heard someone calling her name, but it was not a voice she recognized, and it was close. She did not dare call back—what if she got the attention of the bear? She hoped that the bear gone.

"I know you're up there in that nest! Won't you come down, Please?"

Tara opened her eyes. Whoever he was, he was in the clearing and knew who she was and where she was. Maybe the bear was gone. She looked. Nope, the bear was still there. The bear walked forward, and it was close to the tree now. "Are you going to make me come up there?" the bear asked. Tara looked down, and her eyes bugged out. She shook her head no, and went back into the nest. "Please do not make me come up."

She peeked her head out of the nest. "I certainly do not want to come down and I do not want you coming up here," she called down to the bear.

"Then you must come down," it said.

"I will not come down! What if you hurt me, or want to eat me? Nope, staying right here," she said, folding her arms. She knew that bears could climb trees, and if he decided to come up, she would get out of the nest and get on top of it and climb higher. She thought she probably weighed less, and the bear would not get far.

The bear laughed. "I will not eat, or harm you." Tara looked down. He had a paw on the tree but stood on his hind legs, kind of leaning on the tree trunk. That's odd behavior, but then again, he is a talking bear, she thought.

"We have been looking for you for hours, now please come down."

"Who's we?" Tara asked, because if it was someone, she knew then she would reluctantly get down. If not, there was no way she was going down there.

"Would it help if I told you your friends Mark and Oren are safe at the village? That we have been looking for you all night?"

Tara sat up straighter. She looked down at the bear. It had soft brown eyes and reddish-brown fur. "How are they?"

The bear laughed and then sat down. "You are the one lost and you ask me if they are okay." Tara sighed and looked up at the sky. Looking down, she looked at the bear. He had a pleasant face, he seemed nice enough.

"Who are you?" Tara asked. She wanted to know, since after all he had found her, and knew who Mark and Oren were.

"My name is Ryan Bres McMahon. At your service, Tara. Now could you please come down," he told her, bowing.

She looked at the ladder. "As in The McMahon village?"

"Yes." He had backed away a bit from the tree.

"If I come down, promise not to eat me or chase me." Tara was nervous as she grabbed the ladder.

"I promise, unless you try to run from me, then I will chase you."

Tara slightly smiled and then let it fade as she looked at him straight faced. She slowly lowered the ladder and hesitantly stepped out onto it backwards. She peered over her shoulder and saw that the bear stayed where it was. She slowly made her way down and, once she was on the grass, she slowly turned. The bear was sitting in the clearing, and he waved. She raised her hand and slowly waved back.

"How do you know Mark and Oren?" she asked as she still held onto the ladder.

"Oh, they are in the village, resting. They are worried about you; however, my father's army has told them not to fear and that we would find you."

"How far?" Tara asked as she slowly walked forward.

"It's about an hour's walk," he said as he stood up. "Come on." He started walking away from her and into the forest.

Tara slowly followed. "The last time I followed a talking animal I got lost."

The bear laughed. "Was it a deer?"

"Maybe," Tara replied as she still followed him.

"Yeah, they can be little pranksters, but they wouldn't hurt you. However, it was, I suspect, just curious and probably did not mean for you to get lost."

"No. I guess not. So, you live in the village?" Tara was pushing away tree branches as they walked.

"Yes, my whole family lives there, and others." He was walking ahead of her on all fours. He looked like a regular, reddish-brown bear. Maybe a bit bigger, though.

"Are you all talking bears?" He laughed again as he stopped and turned to look at her. She came up closer to him, and she noticed that his fur looked very thick.

"Yes, and no. We, ah, can change from human form to bear form very easily."

"So, you are human too? So, like a 'werebear'? Is there such a thing?"

He shrugged his shoulders. "Well we do not call ourselves 'werebears,' but yes we are human too."

"Are you hungry?" he asked, pausing. "There are berries up ahead." He ran a bit forward and then stepped slightly off the trail they were on. There were huge bushes filled with berries. All kinds too: blackberries, raspberries, and blueberries. The bear picked some with his clawed paws, and Tara also picked some. They were warm and juicy, and she got some juice on her hands. "Hmm. These are delicious. I am starving," she said as she ate more, the warm juice filling her mouth and running down her throat.

"Race you," he said as he paused.

Tara looked at him and smiled. "You're on," she said as they both frantically started picking and eating berries. They were so succulent that the warm juice was running down her arms and her chin. They both laughed as they ate. He was so much faster than she was. Then they both stopped and sat down, still laughing.

"There is a stream near here, we can wash up there." He stood again.

"Oh wait." Tara held up the corner of her cape. "I want to pick some to give to Mark and Oren." She picked a bunch and carefully folded them into the hem of her cape. Once they got to the stream, she carefully took off her cape and set it down on the ground. She went over and started cleaning her hands, arms, and face. The water felt cool and refreshing. The bear was drinking the water. Tara frowned when she realized she did not have her fairy dust.

Ryan came over to her and explained, "If you are thirsty, you can drink from this stream. It runs from the mountain just there. Don't worry, there is nothing in the water that will harm you or make you sick. Well, I hope not anyway." He pointed to a peak that they could see now over the tree line. Tara went over, cupped her hands, and took a small sip. It was cold and invigorating. She then went over, picked up her cape, and they started walking some more. "So, you are really the princess?" he asked as they walked.

"I guess so. I mean, several people say that I am." They kept walking.

"But you don't think you are?"

Tara shrugged her shoulders. "I don't know. So much has happened. It's a long story."

"Were have you been, and why are you about my age?"

She looked at the bear. "Your age? How old are you?" she asked, curious.

"I am eighteen."

She smiled. "Well I have a birthday coming up, and I will be sixteen."

"Oh, well happy birthday then." They walked a bit more as the trees and underbrush thinned. They now were walking along a dirt road.

"I was raised in Connecticut. Not here."

"Oh. The earth kingdom, so that would explain it then," Ryan the bear said as they walked along the road. It was wider now, and smoother. Tara grabbed her necklace.

"Here, look," she said as she held out her small bracelet that was dangling from the necklace like a big charm. "Pieces of the coronation stone."

He came closer to her, his big black nose almost touching the necklace. "You know, if you stand or sit upon the stone it will ring out if you are royalty."

Yeah, I have heard that, but what about pieces of it?"

"I believe so," he said as they continued to walk. "Also, don't show that to just anybody, okay?"

Tara shrugged her shoulders. "Yeah, okay."

They soon came to a bend in the road, and on one side was a huge tree, the trunk carved into a bear. It held a sign that read McMahon Village.

"Well here we are, just a few more minutes up that way to the upper gate, you were actually just outside our borders. You were very close," he said, pointing with his paw towards the road that led to the village. Tara saw the village gates and walls in between trees, long before they reached them. They were huge, tall wooden gates that had huge parapets on either side that were connected to very thick, tall walls. The tall parapets were in the shape of bears that held huge lanterns that now emitted a little light as the sun was going down. There were platforms up high on the walls with guards.

Tara heard shouts as Ryan roared, and Tara jumped. "Oh sorry, I was announcing our coming."

She stood there for a moment, frozen stiff. She had never had a bear roar like that by her side.

"Again, sorry," he said, smiling. Tara chuckled a bit. A talking, laughing, smiling bear.

"The gates will be open by the time we get up there." A horn was blown and, sure enough, the huge gates slowly opened as they came forward. Tara did not realize how huge they really were, and she felt dwarfed by their size, even the trees were bigger here.

"We call it a village, but really it's a castle town. We have our own mill, orchards, and gardens. We also have lakes and streams to fish, and land where we have cattle and other animals that we raise to eat or make leather and such. The whole village where most of us live and work is enclosed inside the walls. Some land is outside the gated walls, though."

As they entered, Tara could see a huge water fountain in the middle of what she assumed was the village square, and the cobblestone walkway was not too bumpy under her feet. Many people walked about, carrying parcels and baskets. The streets were lined with shops and houses, and the walkways had street lamps with tall, slender bears holding lanterns that were shaped like honey hives and were all lit up.

There were benches along the sidewalks, potted flowers and plants, and some of the buildings had signs hanging out on the brick or wooden fronts. It reminded Tara of a fairytale village. She laughed to herself.

"Is something funny?" Ryan the bear asked.

"Oh sorry. No, nothing." She had already felt, even before coming to this village, that she was in a fairytale.

A gentleman approached them. He wore a coat that looked like it was made of corduroy and had tails, and he was wearing a vest, a nice shirt, and a top hat. He announced, "Ryan, your father awaits your arrival in the Great Hall tavern."

"Thank you, Fred," Ryan replied.

Fred then turned to Tara and proceeded to bow, taking off his hat. "Welcome to McMahon Village." He then stood, smiled, and quickly walked away. Then Tara saw Mark and Oren. "Mark!" She waved, and her smile was so big there was not much that could make it go away.

"I will see you later, Tara-Brigit," Ryan said as he ran off. She yelled Mark's name again as she ran over to him, wrapping her left arm around his neck. They were laughing, and when she pulled away Oren did not look pleased.

"We looked all over for you," he said as his frown made his face look longer.

"I'm sorry. I followed this talking deer and—"

He held up his hand. "No worries, you were found. I shall keep my head."

"Look," she said, happily opening her cloak. "I found some berries. Well, Ryan the bear found them." Oren laughed and then came closer. Oren smiled, took a few berries, and popped them in his mouth. He bowed and then walked into the building they were close to; she guessed it was the Great Hall Tavern, but she could only see the front of the building. The rest went back into the thick trees.

Mark looked at Tara. "Tell me you were safe the whole time."

"Yes, I was actually. Here, take some berries." He took a few and put them in his mouth, chewed, swallowed, and then took some more. "You?"

He shifted his leg to stand differently. "No, we ran into some giants. Luckily for us we weren't too far from the village. Do you have any idea what danger you were in? That's why Oren was guiding us, and yes, Oren could have lost his head by losing you."

"No Mark, I didn't! Really. What's gotten into you?" She backed away from him. "Besides, Ryan found me." Mark rolled his eyes. They both took a few minutes to calm down.

"Giants, really? How big were they?" she asked quietly. They heard cheering coming from inside the building they stood by.

"They were pretty big, and they're fast too."

Oren came back out grinning. "Tara, your presence is requested by Lord McMahon." He escorted them inside. It was crowded as they walked in, and there were long tables and a section that looked like a bar or a counter. A tall, handsome man was standing at the head of one of the larger tables. He was dressed nicely, had dark brown hair with flecks of grey. He smiled more as they got closer.

"Lord McMahon, may I present Princess Tara MacInnes, or also known as Tara-Brigit, daughter of King Kenneth the Third, son of King Fergus," Oren announced.

The man stepped out from behind the table, his arms outstretched. "Welcome, princess. My name is Lord Marty McMahon." He put his hands on her shoulders and squeezed slightly. Tara smiled.

"You have grown a bit since we saw you last, has she not, Cara?"

A lovely woman came and stood by his side. She smiled. She had light copper colored hair with a hint of light brown that was in a thick braid, and she wore a nice cotton dress. She was not thin, but full-figured with large hips. "Welcome, Princess," she said as she bowed her head. "I am Lady McMahon."

"Hello," Tara said as Lord McMahon waved over a young girl.

"Sarah, can you get the princess some food?"

"Yes, my Lord," she said, bowed and then quickly walked through double swinging doors.

"Please. Sit." The king motioned for them all to sit. Oren sat across from her, with Mark by his side. Tara sat by two girls who were about thirteen and fourteen years old. Freshly baked bread was set down on the table, along with cheese and butter, and big goblets of cider also.

"We are glad you were found, Tara." The king said as he handed her a plate of bread. Tara took a piece and then put some butter on her plate. Someone reached over her shoulder and poured her some cider.

Lord McMahon continued to talk. "Some of the enemy's army was spotted near here, and we have been looking for you cautiously, and quietly." A plate full of roasted chicken, mashed potatoes, gravy, corn, and green beans were set in front of her. It smelled heavenly. "Eat up now, you must be quite famished after your ordeal," he said as the doors to the hall opened. Standing there was a tall young man who looked like a younger version of Lord McMahon.

"Ah! There he is. The man of the hour!" Lord McMahon boomed as everyone cheered.

Who is this guy? Tara wondered as he walked over. He was wearing dark pants, a dark blue shirt that had silky ties down part of the front like a Ghillie shirt, and brown boots. The lord and everyone stood. Mark and Tara also stood as the young man approached. Lord McMahon raised his glass, and Tara quickly grabbed her glass.

"To young Lord Ryan!" He boomed as cheers rang out all over the hall. Tara almost spit out her cider while taking a sip. When he walked past her, he bowed, winked, and smiled, and then continued to walk up to his father. They embraced with a quick, rough hug, and then the young lord sat down. Tara was having a hard time breathing. He was very nice looking. They all sat down, and Mark kicked her foot. She abruptly looked at him and scowled. There was a lot of talking and laughing as they ate. Tara noticed another young lady sitting by Ryan, and saw that they looked alike. She had long, dark brown hair, and she was beautiful. As they ate and people started to leave, Mark came and sat by her.

"That's Anne, Ryan's sister," he told her as he must have seen how she stared at the royal family. Tara continued to eat. She looked just like Ryan; she had long dark straight hair, and they looked like twins sitting there.

"Oren needs to leave, and I am going with him." Tara almost choked on her food. "What? What do you mean leave? Where to?"

Oren came over and he sat by her as well. "Sorry Tara, I must go. You will be safe here until I return."

"Why does Mark need to go with you?"

Oren looked at Mark. "He doesn't have to really." Oren paused. "Mark can stay here with you, if that is what you want, what he wants?" he said standing. Mark stood too.

"What? Oren, you—"

Oren held up his hand. "You will stay here with her, understood?"

Mark nodded reluctantly. Tara was confused. Why would Mark want to leave her? He had promised her he wouldn't. Tara and Mark followed Oren outside.

"Lord McMahon and his army will look out for you while I am gone. One of our units was attacked last night, so King Oberon wants me to check it out."

"Oh, I am sorry to hear that."

Oren leaned into Tara and whispered in her ear, "It is your job to find the flag. You have two days." He raised his eyebrows as he stood still looking into her eyes. "Oren, I had a dream about some kind of storage place."

"Start with that then, dreams can be powerful. So, ask to see their storage buildings. You have two days."

She looked at him as he slowly backed away. She forced a smile. "Two days, okay. Well, I hope you will be safe, too. Wait." Her smile faded. "Will we see you back here in two days?"

"Can't say," Oren said as he looked out of a window into the darkening sky. There were deep reds and oranges in a beautiful sun set. He left the hall, and Tara, Mark and Ryan followed. Oren's horse was brought to him, and he jumped up in the saddle. "Remember, if you are in trouble, blow that whistle. Then you will see me." He smiled and Tara smiled back nervously. Oren looked at Mark, not smiling now, and nodded. Mark nodded back. Tara wondered what was going on with those two.

"Good luck!" she yelled as she watched him go. The doors to the hall opened as a woman and three bear cubs left.

"Okay, what's going on with you and Oren?" Tara asked. Mark looked at Ryan, who was walking their way.

"Oh, he, ah, just helped me out with my fighting skills, and told me I could go with him.

Tara looked at him and smirked. "Fighting skills?"

"Yeah, I took fencing."

Tara laughed. "That's fencing, not using real swords."

"Well, I will have you know that Oren passed me with flying colors, and he is a skilled warrior."

Tara rolled her eyes. "So that's why you wanted to go with him, and leave me. To help fight?"

"Why? Are you afraid I will get hurt?"

"You could die, Mark! This is not a game!" She sighed and lowered her voice as Ryan slowed his pace coming towards them. "Look. We are not from here. Well, you aren't. Anyway, we have lived a pampered life compared to here." Tara had a point, and Mark knew it.

"So do you want to leave?" he asked her.

Tara shook her head. "No, not yet. I have to help."

"You could die too, you know. You're right, this isn't home for us." Mark was getting mad, his face turning red. "What you are doing is risky too."

"Fine!" Tara said as Mark huffed, turned around, and stormed away towards the fountain. Tara went inside the tavern, passing Ryan who stood by watching. She sat down and got some more cider. She was kind of mad, and she needed some good sleep. She put her hand on her forehead.

"So," said a familiar voice as Ryan sat down beside her. Tara was expecting to see the bear.

"What's up with him?"

Tara shrugged her shoulders, grabbed some more bread, and smothered it with honey butter. She then took a huge bite.

He smiled. "Nothing fixes a bad mood like fresh bread with our special honey butter." He grabbed a napkin and wiped off her chin, which had honey butter running down.

"Thanks," she said and then took a sip of cider.

"I was surprised to see you earlier in, uh, your human form, and now."

He looked down at his hands. "Oh yeah, I guess you didn't recognize me." They both smiled.

Then Tara leaned closer to him and said, "Ryan, I need your help finding something."

"Sure, I will help if I can." He smiled at her as she sat up more, cleared her throat, and took another sip of cider. "What are we looking for?"

Tara scooted closer to him, leaned in closely, and whispered in his ear. "The Fairy Flag."

He cleared his throat this time and looked at her. Their faces were very close. He smiled and said, "I am sure I can help you with that."

16

McMahon Mansion

"So you think it's here?" Ryan asked her, standing up and stretching.

Tara shrugged her shoulders. "I have two days to find it, so yeah I hope it's here."

Ryan sat back down, moving his chair so that it faced Tara.

"King Oberon and Queen Tina believe it's in the Green Glenn, and well, this village is here, so…"

"Yeah, smack in the middle of the Green Glenn is our village. My father is lord of only a small portion of it. There are a few more kings and lords too."

Tara sighed, looking up at the ceiling. "It could be anywhere?"

"Yeah, sorry. We can look though, in here I mean. What about Mark?"

"What about him?" Tara looked at him.

"Oh, it's just something Oren said."

Tara leaned forward. "What did Oren say?"

"He doesn't trust him. Well, not completely."

Tara looked confused. "He doesn't trust him? They just met." She thought maybe Ryan was a bit jealous of Mark. "Well, I trust him."

"Do you though?"

Tara stood, getting a bit wary. "Yes, I trust him. Why?"

Ryan stood as well. "Your brownie. Ettrick, he ah, has some info on him."

"What like a rap sheet?"

"Like what?"

Tara began to laugh. "Whatever! Never mind. It wouldn't be anything here. He is from Arizona."

"Are you sure?" Tara was pretty sure; when she first met him years ago he said that he had moved to Connecticut from Arizona. Why was that in question now? "Oh great. Well, whatever he did, I am sure there is an explanation."

"Also, there was word that Don Pater has your parents in the underworld. I mean the king and queen."

"The underworld? Oh, things just keep getting better and better. Have you heard anything about the coronation stone?" she asked, since he seemed to know so much other stuff.

"I know that it was stolen, along with many other of the king's prized possessions. Tara, we have a lot of ground to cover."

"We, as in you and me?"

He smiled. "Yeah, at least until Beira and Lou or Oren can assist you. Until then, I'm your guy." Tara felt her insides go queasy.

Tara started tapping her left foot. She always did this during tests at school—a nervous habit. "Great."

"The stone should not be hard to find, but first I need to find the flag."

"How come?" She stopped tapping her foot. "I need it. What about the stone?"

She stopped tapping her foot. "Well I guess it is needed too, to prove to everyone I am or not this princess everyone keeps talking about."

"Do you know a lot about the higher realms?"

"Yes, all royalty are required to have studies. About here and mortal earth. All royalty have a stone piece, as well. Besides, if I am to be a lord one day I need to be in the loop." He raised his eyebrows.

Ryan held up his hand, and on his right ring finger was a ring. It had a bear symbol on it, and the bear's belly was a stone piece. "Oh wow, that's a cool ring." She looked at it closer.

"Get your necklace out." Tara did, and he gently placed his ringed hand on top of hers, holding the small bracelet.

"I don't—" she began to say.

"Wait," Ryan said. Then she felt a small vibration, and she heard a faint humming noise. Then she heard a faint cry—no, a call. A voice. Ryan let go of her hand and cleared his throat. "Well there you have it."

"Am I interrupting something?" Mark asked. He was standing there, and Tara did not even hear him come up to them. Tara turned around. She did not want to see Mark or talk to him.

"Tara, we need to talk."

"Oh, yeah okay. Sure." She smiled at Ryan and told him, "I will be right back."

He nodded and then went to talk to someone. Tara's smile faded as she faced Mark.

"Outside," Mark said, grabbing her arm.

"Hey, wait. Let go, Mark." He did, and Tara followed him out. "Gosh, what is wrong with you?"

"Have you checked your phone recently?"

"No, why?"

"I have. My dad sent me a text over two weeks ago." He turned on his phone and showed Tara the message.

"What?" She looked at him confused. "Wait, over two weeks ago?" The date said July twenty-second.

He nodded his head and said, "Yeah."

"But we have only been here for a few days. Wait! They said time is slower here." Tara looked at Mark. "Oh gosh, how long have we been gone? Oh! Alana! She will be worried sick. Where is phone" She said to herself.

" it's at the mansion. Well it looks like a mansion, not a castle. Where the McMahons live."

Tara looked at him, confused. "I already had a quick tour."

"Oh. Um, does your cell give the date? Now that's the weird thing on my phone. By the fountain here it usually works, but other places the date and time keeps changing. Okay see? Like right now." He showed her his phone. He was right—the date and time kept changing.

"Weird," Tara said, confused.

"Well that gal in the King's Army did say it worked in some places but not others."

Tara looked at Mark as she sat on the edge of the fountain.

"You want to go back, don't you?" he asked her.

She had a feeling he did. "Yeah, kind of. I mean, fairies, castles, giants and all, and magic. Yeah, cool. But..." She folded her arms, pouting.

"But. You want to go home." He looked at her and took her hand. "Don't you?"

"Yeah kind of, but...they need me. I need to help them." He let go of her hand. "How would you get back, Mark?"

"I don't know, I could think of something."

Tara looked at the fountain, into the water. "You would leave me here?"

"Oh gosh, Tara! No! I mean, definitely not, if you didn't want me to."

Ettrick appeared just then. "You aren't leaving, Tara. You can't."

Tara looked at the brownie, who was standing on the edge of the fountain. I could push him in, she thought, feeling annoyed.

"I know that look. You could Tara, but what then, aye?" She shook her head—he knew what she was thinking.

"So, Ettrick, Ryan says you have some info on—"

She was interrupted by Ettrick, who was pointing his walking stick at her. "Don't ye be a-sayin' another word, Tara-Brigit," he said sternly. She shut her mouth. He turned to Mark. "Mark, how are ye with a sword?" Ettrick jumped down and was standing by Mark's feet.

"Uh, not bad actually."

"Aye. Stay. We need you both." He picked up a coin and threw it into the fountain. It made a cool kerplunk noise. "Oh Mark, can ye do me a favor? Go warn young Lord McMahon that the Red Caps have been spotted two miles from the border of the Green Glenn." He disappeared.

"I really would like to know how he does that." Mark said, looking around.

"I would too, but as always you can't get much out of him." Tara said, feeling let down by the conversation. It left her feeling a bit torn to stay or go.

Ryan was walking towards them. "Tell him. Go." Tara was anxious—she could feel the panic creeping up inside her, making her insides feel like a jumbled mess. Mark ran up to Ryan, stopped, and told him as Tara watched his reaction. She saw Ryan clench his fists, which were starting to grow fur, and then Mark ran into the hall.

Ryan came over to Tara, walking quickly, and said, "So Mark will need a sword and some gear."

What she knew about the Red Caps was very disturbing. There was nothing like them where she was from, and that was a relief. "I guess so, but…" It was all happening too fast. Tara felt a panicky sensation rising in her even more. She felt a wave of nausea.

Ryan put his hand on her arm, and by then it had returned to a human hand and not a bear's paw. "It's okay, he will be suited tomorrow. Right now, it is my father's army and a few others nearby who will protect you and the people who live in the village. We need to get those blasted Red Caps away from here. Or kill them."

Then the doors to the hall burst open as a huge black bear burst through. Like really big—Tara had never seen a bear that big, not up that close at least. Seeing him made Tara jump behind Ryan.

"Ryan, have the archers at the gate get ready! I will ready the others," the bear said as he passed. It was Lord McMahon, and he practically roared as he ran off down the street.

"Yes father!" Ryan called back, turning towards the guards. Tara was so alarmed at seeing him she froze where she was.

"Tara, wait here," Ryan said as Mark came over to her.

"Yeah, sure. No problem." She could barely speak as he walked away. Ryan was yelling up at men on the walls, in the battlements, and in the framed guarded forts, or hourds, that were on the wall. Huge torches shaped like bears were lit, lighting the night sky on the towers that were set along the wall.

Tara fingered her necklace nervously. When Ryan was done, he walked over to where Tara and Mark were standing and told them, "My father has everything under control. He has sent some men to the border." He looked up at the sky. "We will not hear anything until tomorrow."

"All right. Now what?" Tara wasn't sure how to take this all in; she felt drained.

"We will go back to the mansion and get some food, and sleep. Come on," said Ryan.

Sleep—how was Tara going to sleep? She hadn't slept well the night before. The stress was getting to her, but she tried to hold it together. If not for Mark's sake, then at least for her own.

Tara and Mark followed Ryan down many streets as people were rushing about, locking doors, and armed men and a few bears were now walking the streets. It did not seem to be like a fairy tale anymore to Tara. More like the start of a nightmare.

"The mansion is in another part of the village," Ryan said as they walked. At one-point Ryan was handed a cross bow and a huge quiver filled with arrows.

"I know how to use one of those too," Tara told him nervously as they walked.

"Really? Then we will have to get you one tomorrow. Have you ever shot anything living?"

"Uh, yeah, I went turkey hunting once," Tara replied, and Ryan smiled.

"Turkey. Yum!" This made Tara laugh, which lessened the tension.

They saw the mansion before getting there. It was huge, and it looked like a grand log cabin but with stained glass windows like Tara saw at the fairy castle. Two very tall wooden bear carvings stood at the top of the enormous stairs where you entered, which held beehive lanterns like Tara had seen throughout the village. However, these were bigger. There was a covered wraparound porch, and there were two tall, thick wooden doors that Ryan opened without any trouble that led to a huge entryway. Mark could barely hold one open for Tara to walk through.

"Mum!" Ryan yelled as they walked in, but there was no answer. He turned to look at Tara and Mark. "Cover your ears." Tara and Mark did as he said. He then yelled extremely loudly, although it sounded more like a roar of a bear. Lady McMahon appeared at the top of the grand wooden staircase. It actually looked like a huge tree with its branches going up and outward, creating the staircase. All of the furnishings were amazing. There were chairs, and tables carved from wood. Rich tapestries hung on the walls along with paintings.

"Ryan! What is it?" Lady McMahon called down.

"Red Caps near our border."

She nodded and ran towards the window behind her. Ryan turned and went over to the double front doors. "We need to secure the mansion, and it's best if you just stay where you are." Where am I going to go anyway? Tara thought as Ryan lifted a long metal lever, and it swung down in front of the doors, locking them into place. He then ran over to a panel that was hidden behind a painting and punched in a code. They heard clicks and sliding sounds coming from all over. Then the light on the panel flashed red.

"All set, Mum," he said as Lady McMahon came down a huge staircase, which looked like a huge tree stretching up as the branches seemed to reach out across the walls. Two small bear cubs followed her down the wooden staircase, going down clumsily one step at a time.

"Are they camped?" she asked, a bit out of breath.

"Yes, Mum. They are."

Lady McMahon shook her head. The two bear cubs stood in front of Tara. "I will go call the stables to make sure they are on lock down," she said as she quickly walked away.

The bear cubs made a noise, and Tara reached down and picked them up. They were so small and did not seem to weigh too much.

"Those are my newest siblings, and they are twins," Ryan said and pointed to the one in Tara's left arm. "This is Jaeneen," he said and then pointed to the other. "This is Jeanelle." Three larger bear cubs appeared at the top of the stairs. Ryan laughed. "All of the excitement has gotten you all out of bed, hasn't it?"

The three came down the stairs, and then Tara noticed they were all three different sizes, and they were also different colors—varying shades of black, brown, and reddish brown. The cubs were followed by a girl. Tara realized she was the same one who was sitting by Ryan in the hall tavern.

"Tara, Mark. This is Anne," Ryan said.

Anne smiled and held out her hand. "Hi," she said as Tara shook her hand, and then Mark did as well.

"Hi," Tara said as Mark took a minute to say anything.

"Uh, yeah. Hi," Mark said as one of the bear cubs started playing with his shoe laces.

Anne bent down. "No Alec," she said, swatting him away.

"These are my younger brothers. Alec is the youngest of the three, he's ten. Then there is Tom who is twelve, and Sam is fourteen." They started tumbling over each other in the entryway as their mother came back.

"All is well at the stables." She looked around.

"All the commotion got you three worked up, huh?" She bent down and patted one of them on his backside. "Off with you now to the kitchen to get some warm honey milk. Then it's off to bed." One stomped away, staying clear of his mother. "Uh, those three," she said as the two cubs in Tara's arms leaned out to get held by their mother.

"Sorry about that. Well now, Tara," she said, smiling, "you will sleep in Anne's room, and Mark, you will take the guest room down the hall from Ryan. Your things are already there." Tara smiled.

"Let's go into the family room. I don't know about you guys, but I am not tired yet," Ryan said as he led them into the family room. The room was off of the entryway, and it had a three-story stone fireplace, vaulted ceilings with wooden beams, and a huge wall of windows overlooking the forest. There was an enormous chandelier hanging from the vaulted ceiling. The place was amazing.

"Would you all like some berry custard? I made it earlier today," Anne asked getting up.

"Sure," they all replied as Ryan got up to help.

"I'll help you sis," he said as they disappeared into the kitchen.

"Tara?" Mark asked. "Notice anything about this place?" She looked around. It was very nice.

"Look at the lights," he told her.

She looked, and at first, she didn't notice, but then she saw it. Electricity.

"Cool. They have, like, real lights."

Tara excitedly got out her phone and charger.

"Ryan can Mark and I charge our phones?"

"Yeah sure, right here," he said, pointing to an outlet.

Anne and Ryan came in carrying bowls of custard. Ryan handed one to Tara and Anne gave one to Mark.

"Look!" Tara said holding up her charging phone.

"We can charge our phones here."

"Sweet," Mark said, getting out his as well.

"How do you have electricity here?" Mark asked as he sat down.

"Um, well we can tap into it here. We also get great cell phone coverage."

"Really," Mark said, taking a big bite of custard. His eyes got wide, he smiled, and took another huge bite.

"Well in most parts of the village at least."

"This is really good," Tara told Anne.

"Thanks. It is my grandmother's recipe."

Ryan opened a drawer and got out a remote. A huge cabinet opened, showing a huge flat-screen TV.

"Is that a seventy inch?" Mark asked.

"Yeah. We sometimes get channels, just not all the time."

"Not everywhere is like here. I mean, some of the Higher Realms is," Anne explained.

"In the dark ages," Ryan finished for her. Tara smiled as she took another bite of her custard.

"So. Tomorrow I will be getting a sword?" Mark asked as he set his empty bowl down on the coffee table.

"Yeah. They will be able to get one that is just right for you, or close anyway."

"Good. Because if we come across any more werewolves, I will need one." Tara shivered at

Mark's mention of the werewolves, and at the thought of seeing them again.

"Werewolves?" Anne asked, setting her bowl down slowly.

"It was a full moon. Remember, sis?" Ryan reminded her.

"Yeah, but here?"

"Oh. No, before we came to the Green Glenn," Mark told them.

"Don't worry, they won't come here," Ryan reassured them all, including his sister, who had never left the Glenn.

The doors to the living room opened.

"Oh, I see you are all still awake," said a voice.

"Father!" Anne got up and ran over to him. He was in his human form and looked tired.

"What's going on, Father?" Ryan asked as his mother came into the room and stood beside Lord McMahon.

"Well. The Red Caps are camped two miles west of us. They had attacked a small army that was going to join King Kenneth's army the night before. A few of King Kenneth's army got away, but most, well…"

Lady McMahon linked her arm through her husband's as she came in shaking her head.

"We will be traveling north along the border. If they leave before us, great. If not, then that could be a problem, however nothing we can't handle."

"Father, if you run into them, make sure your small band can take them out," Anne said as she collected the dishes and went to put them in the kitchen.

"Well I am hoping they leave before there is any fighting," Lady McMahon said. Tara couldn't agree more—they sounded nasty. Anne came back into the room.

"Well, we are going to try to get a few hours of sleep before we have to head out. You four should do the same. Don't worry. We will either kill them all or drive them out," Lord MacMahon said, placing his hand delicately on Anne's cheek. Lord and Lady McMahon left and went to their room.

"In the morning Tara, I will help you find what it is you came here looking for. Anne will go with Mark to the armory, and we will go if we are needed," Ryan said. The thought of them fighting the

Red Caps nearly made Tara's custard come back up. Ryan stood up, and so Tara and Mark did as well.

Ryan saw Tara's worried expression. "Don't worry, we are well guarded here," Ryan told Tara as they started walking towards the stairs. Once they were at the top of the stairs, Anne went down a different hallway than Ryan, and Tara followed Anne. Just as Anne was opening her bedroom door, Tara heard, "Psst."

She turned, and Ryan was standing near another door. "You need a bow, don't you?" he asked.

"Yeah," Tara answered, wondering what he was up to.

"I will get you a bow and a few daggers." He paused and came closer. "This flag. I have heard about it, but could you describe it to me, so I know what to look for tomorrow?"

Tara explained what it looked like, remembering her experience in the castle.

"Ryan, do you have storage buildings?"

"Yeah, a few."

"Good. Could we start with those, looking in them, I mean?"

He nodded and said goodnight as she went into Anne's room. When she closed the door, she leaned against it. Anne's room looked like a teen Pottery Barn catalog.

"Oh my gosh!" Tara squealed as she walked into the room. The floor was wooden, and in front of her was a vaulted section with stained glass windows. The scene was a castle by some woods and fields, and the ocean. To the left were two beds nestled in a little alcove. The bed on the right was decorated with pillows and quilts and had a purple theme. The one on the left was similar but had a teal theme. The wooden beams had hanging white lights in the shape of small stars strung on them, outlining the area were the beds were. Each bed had a trunk at the foot with various things like books and such on them. By the beds were small wooden tables with lamps in the shape of rabbits. Various pictures, memorabilia, and dried flowers covered the walls.

"Come on, I will show you the other side," said Anne. In the middle of the large room, to the right of the door, was a tall wall and in the center was a vanity bigger than hers back home. On either side were hallways, and Anne led Tara through the left side, which had dressers and shelves lined with baskets and drawers, and clothes hung on hangers. At the end was a huge sitting room complete with chairs, a cozy couch, a table, and a huge flat-screen TV. There was also a large desk at the far right, near a small window.

"Did you want to take a shower?"

Tara stood frozen. Did she really just say shower? Tara thought. "A shower? Really?"

Anne laughed and went into the hallway and got out a t-shirt and a pair of sweatpants. She grabbed a new package of underwear, a matching bra and some socks. "Here. The bathroom is in the other hallway just past the vanity. There are towels in there, soaps and stuff."

Tara grabbed the clothes and smiled.

"I will be in the study room, which is what I call it. Mum made us some honey hot chocolate, and we could talk for a bit."

"Okay." Tara was so excited to have a real shower, her first in what seemed like weeks. She found a set of soap, shampoo, and conditioner in the bathroom.

It was labeled "milk, honey, and snowberries." She liked the smell. Tara carefully took all the stuff out of her hair, including the small tinkling bells, and set them in a small basket on the bathroom counter. Once she was all showered and had gotten dressed, she came out and found a note, slippers and a robe sitting on a stool by the bathroom. The note was from Anne. It read,

Dear Tara,

I hope you enjoy your stay. I don't have many princesses stay here. Enjoy the slipper and bathrobe set.

Your new friend,

Anne

Tara put the set on and went into the study room. Anne was there reading a book.

"What are you reading?"

"Oh. Ah, Wuthering Heights."

"Oh, I read that a few years ago. I love books."

"You need to see our library. My parents love books too. We all like to read." Anne pointed to a huge mug. "That's your hot cocoa, with my mum's special honey blend."

Tara picked up the mug. It had a tall pile of whipped cream with honey drizzled on top. She took a sip. It was creamy, sweet, and very chocolaty with a hint of honey. "Oh, wow that is good," Tara exclaimed.

Anne laughed. They sat up talking about movies, music, books, and boys. "I can redo your hair if you would like?" Anne got up.

"Oh, I put all my hair stuff in a basket on the bathroom counter."

"I can do your hair in the morning then, is that okay?"

"Yeah, I wouldn't want it to get messed up while I slept."

Anne yawned. "Speaking about sleeping, I am tired." She looked at Tara. "You?"

Tara nodded and stood. "I am dead."

They went over to where the beds were, and Anne told her, "Mine is the purple bed, and you can sleep in the blue bed."

"Okay," Tara said, taking off the bathrobe and her slippers. Her hair was mostly dry, and she ran her fingers through it as she got into bed and then lay down.

"Oh, this is so much better than sleeping on the ground or in a nest."

"A nest?" Anne kind of sat up, propped up by her many pillows, and she turned out the lights. She was going to turn off the stringed light when Tara asked, "Oh, leave them on, would you Anne? I like them on."

Anne smiled. "Me too."

Tara got cozy. "Yeah, when I was lost in the woods, I found a huge nest to sleep in."

"The raven headed swans."

Tara shifted onto her side. "Is that what kind of birds they are? I was wondering. They seem very intelligent."

"Oh, they are," Anne told her as she shifted and lay on her back. "Too smart sometimes. They don't talk, though they can understand everything you say. They are used as messengers."

A few minutes went by, and it became quiet. Anne broke the silence by saying, "This all must seem strange and scary for you. I can't imagine."

"Scary. Yeah, a bit." Tara sat up slightly. "What is weird, though, is it all seems a bit familiar. Even though I was taken when I was a baby."

Anne nodded her head. "I have never left the Green Glenn. I tried once. But Father's army caught me. Good thing too, because my best friend and a group of kids went off wandering and the werewolves got them."

"That's awful." Tara was horrified at the thought. "Maybe they would let me take you to my world?" Tara did not think it was too absurd.

Anne laughed. "Not likely, but I would love to. One day." She sighed and sank into her pillows. "Tara, how old are you?"

"Oh, I am sixteen, almost sixteen I mean. You?"

"I am nineteen. How old is Mark?"

"He is eighteen." Tara still lay on her side, facing Anne. "Ryan, your brother is...?" She could not remember how old he said he was.

"Oh, he's eighteen. He is old enough to be married but hasn't found anyone yet. He is learning how to be the next Lord. For when my father retires."

"Sounds busy." Anne nodded.

They both were getting drowsy as they looked at the small star lights.

"Tara?"

"Yeah."

"I am glad you were found."

"Me too, Anne. Me too."

*
* *

17

Storage Units

When Tara woke up, she heard the shower running. She sat up and stretched.

"Good morning, Princess Tara-Brigit." It was Ettrick, and he looked tired and filthy.

"Where have you been?"

"Ah, I won't be a-worryin' ya. I have been running errands for King Oberon. You look well rested."

"Yeah, I slept like a rock, once I was asleep. I crashed hard."

Ettrick smiled. "Good. I had hoped to find you well. The McMahons are great people, so you stick close to Ryan. He is there to protect you when Oren is not around."

"I have Mark too," Tara said, putting on her slippers. The floor was cold.

"Och! Mark, ye have him all right. Let's see if he can use a sword, shall we?" Ettrick winked and jumped off the bed.

"I am going to find that flag, Ettrick."

"I know ye are. As soon as ye do, you will be a-meetin' Beira and Lou. Just be careful, Tara. Look, I have to be goin'."

"You be careful too, Ettrick."

He nodded and then disappeared. Anne came into the small alcove. "Who were you talking to?"

"Oh, uh Ettrick, my brownie."

"Oh. Well, that's cool. What's he like?"

Tara smiled. "He's nice, young, and disappears way too soon sometimes."

Anne started laughing. "That's a brownie for you. My friend's family had a Brownie for a long time. He would not talk much; just do his work. But he would warn them of trouble. She was towel drying her hair. She was wearing short denim shorts, a t-shirt, and cute Converse sneakers that matched her shirt.

"So, they do not talk much?" Tara asked since Anne seemed to know some about Brownies.

"They aren't allowed to. It's in their contract that they do not interfere or meddle, at least not too much." She put the wet towel in a laundry basket.

"Let's go over to the vanity and do our hair," Anne suggested.

Tara nodded.

"Oh, and you can look through all my clothes and pick something. We are about the same size." They looked at their reflections in the mirror. "Well I am a bit taller, but yeah we're about the same size."

Anne sat next to Tara on the wide bench seat at the vanity, and they got ready. Anne had grabbed all of Tara's hair stuff and it was now sitting on the vanity, she got out a brush, hair dryer, and curling iron.

"You can curl your hair while I dry mine. Mum wants us downstairs in ten minutes."

"Oh, okay."

Anne smiled. "Breakfast."

They talked as they worked on each other's hair. To Tara's surprise Anne had used every last hair piece that was given to her by the fairies.

"I figured you would want all of this in your hair. How do you like it?"

Tara looked in the mirror. Her hair looked amazing: all clean, dry, curled and partly pinned up. Tara smiled, and so did Anne.

"You are beautiful, Tara."

Tara turned around and looked at Anne. She was pulling up her long, thick and wavy dark hair.

"You are, too."

Anne smiled. "Thanks. Go pick some clothes, get dressed, and meet us in the kitchen," she said and grabbed a sweatshirt off of a hanger and left. Tara stood and started looking through clothes. She found a pair of capris, a t-shirt, and socks. She also grabbed a new set of matching undergarments, and a pair of Converse sneakers. She got dressed, grabbed her bag, and got out her phone. There were tons of messages. She started listening to them as she headed down the stairs. She realized she had to call her lawyer, her cousin, and Alana. She paused on a landing on the stairs, made her first call, and looked out of the huge window as she talked.

"Yes, Mary, I am fine. No. My car is at the estate. Tell Uncle Arland I am fine. Okay. Bye." She noticed a huge field with what she thought were beehives, and she quickly called Alana. She had to leave a message. Then her lawyer, and again got voicemail.

"Oh, well." Tara heard someone clearing their throat at the bottom of the stairs. She looked down to see Ryan standing there. He was wearing jeans, a t-shirt, sneakers, and a dark grey hoodie.

"Hey," Ryan said as he took a few steps closer. Tara smiled. He looked gorgeous, and she thought she would say something ridiculous, so she just said, "Hi."

"Do you want breakfast? My mum cooked up some pancakes and stuff."

"Sure." Tara was pretty hungry, so she followed him towards the kitchen. She could smell something sweet and some bacon cooking. Her stomach rumbled. A small boy came running around the corner, crashing into Ryan. "Hey Sam, what's the hurry?"

"Oh, Mum wants to know—" He saw Tara and froze.

"Mum wants to know what, Sam?"

"Ah, nothing." He turned around, and Ryan ruffled Sam's hair as they walked into the kitchen. It was a huge gourmet kitchen, bigger than hers at home.

"Hey, Mum. Everyone." Ryan sat down, and Tara sat by him. Mark and Anne were already eating, and it looked like they were almost done. The twins were in highchairs eating, and they had jam smeared all over themselves. It was good to see the kids in their human forms. The three other boys were eating as well.

Lady McMahon set a fresh stack of pancakes on the table.

"How many, Tara?" Ryan asked as he grabbed her a plate.

"Oh, uh. Two." He gave her two and handed her the plate.

There were all kinds of syrup on the table, and milk, juice, and fruit. Then Lady McMahon set a plate full of sausage and bacon down. "Now Ryan, serve Princess Tara-Brigit first," she said, wiping her hands on her apron. She looked pretty even though she had been cooking; her cheeks were rosy, and she had a huge, friendly smile.

Tara almost choked on her food as her eyes suddenly filled with tears. Ryan's family was very close, like she had wished her family was. Sure, she was close to her parents, but not very bonded. Not as much as she had wanted. She felt the aching in her heart grow, and she grabbed her glass of juice.

"We will need to walk awhile before we get to the first storage place," Ryan told her as she drank some of her juice.

Anne stood. "Well, we are done. We'll see you all later." She went over and kissed her mother's cheek.

"Here." Lady McMahon grabbed a towel and put biscuits and other breakfast stuff into it. "Give this to Fred."

Anne smiled. "Sure will, Mum." She turned towards Mark. "Come on Mark, we will go have you fitted for some armor and get you a sword."

Mark looked at Tara before he stood, smiling as he grabbed a few more pieces of bacon. "I guess I will see you later."

Tara smiled and finished chewing her food, swallowed, and barely got out a reply before Anne grabbed his arm and pulled him away. "Yeah, see you later." Tara grabbed a scone and smothered it with a glaze that was in a bowl.

"This tastes amazing! Lady McMahon." Tara took another bite, the scone almost melting in her mouth. The twins laughed as one kicked Tara's leg. They were sitting near her. Tara looked up.

"Can I give her one?"

"Oh yeah sure, if she wants another," Lady McMahon told her as she herself sat down to eat.

A maid came in and checked on the children. "Who's done?" she asked. The twins smiled at her—they were a mess.

"Come back in a few minutes Marcy, I think the twins will be done then."

The maid named Marcy curtsied and said, "Yes, my Lady." Then she left the kitchen in a hurry.

"Are you really the stolen princess?" one of the boys asked.

"Shh, Samual," Lady McMahon said as she stood up and started clearing the table. Ryan stood to help her.

Tara looked at Sam. "I think I am. Well, that's what everyone thinks anyway."

"Prove it," Tom said suddenly.

"She doesn't have to prove anything to you, Thomas," Ryan said, whacking him on the head with a dish towel. Tara thought it wouldn't hurt anything or anybody if she showed them her bracelet. All three boys' eyes grew wide when she showed them her small bracelet with pieces of the stone in it.

Lady McMahon came over to her. "Ah, so there you go, boys. Now off to the stables with you." Each got up and kissed her cheek as she bent down, and then they ran off.

"We should get going too Mum," Ryan said as he too kissed her cheek. Tara waved and thanked her for a yummy breakfast. Ryan kissed the twins, and they headed out of the kitchen. When they got outside, the air was a bit chilly. "Do you want my sweatshirt?" he asked as he started taking it off. She saw his muscles through his shirt and had to clear her throat as he handed the sweatshirt to her and then got out a map from his back pocket. Tara put the sweatshirt on, and it was big on her but very cozy. It smelled of cedar and pine.

"Are we walking?" Tara asked, looking around.

"We can walk, or I can get the horses?"

"Uh, walking is good," Tara quickly replied.

"What, you don't like horses?" Tara was about to answer him, but Ryan said, "Never mind, we can walk."

As they walked Tara asked questions about the village. "So how big is the village?"

"Oh, pretty big, it would take about four days to go through it. However, the grounds are larger. They go for miles."

"And you always have it patrolled?"

"Yes, mostly our guards are in bear form. They can cover more ground that way."

"You seem to be more modern than other places. Like you have lights. I mean real lights."

Ryan laughed. "You mean electricity. Yeah. We are more modern than most."

"But you also seem timeless." Tara was caught up in the fairytale aspect of it all.

They passed by several shops, homes, and the watermill. As they left the main section of town, the road became more like a dirt road, and it wound around and through the trees and hills.

"You are going to find the Fairy Flag, and then what?" Ryan asked.

"Oh, uh, find the king and queen, and stop the war."

"Oh. That's all, huh?"

He smiled. Tara smiled back. It was getting warm, so Tara gave Ryan back his sweatshirt. He tied it around his waist and told her, "We will be passing by the beehives you were asking about." They crested the hill when Tara saw them. The hives. There were thousands of them. She could hear the buzzing from where she was. After they walked a bit out of the trees and down the hill, Tara turned around. She saw the big mansion with its glass-stained windows.

"I saw these hives from the stairs in the mansion," Tara told Ryan. They walked between the fields, which were on the right, and the woods, which were on the left side of the road.

"Hi Peter!" Ryan yelled as a huge bear stood up from stooping over a hive. He waved his big brown paw in their direction.

"I feel like I'm on a set of a movie about the three bears," Tara said as they walked. Ryan chuckled, wiping at his mouth.

"We have freshly made honey sticks in the store. Go grab a few," the bear named Peter said as Tara and Ryan kept walking. Ryan waved as they walked away further down the dirt road. They must have walked down the road for about twenty minutes when, on their left, they reached a clearing of the trees and they could see what looked like a little white house. As they got closer, Tara realized it was a fairly large house with a huge sign by the road that was in the shape of a beehive with the words The Bear Country Store and Café on it. Tara liked the name of the place. It reminded her of a Country store you would find in an old New England town, or in the West. Or maybe in Pennsylvania.

As they went inside, there was a bell on the door that rang out when they opened it. A tall, slender, darker brown bear was behind the counter wearing a white apron, and she turned to see who had come in.

"Oh, young Lord Ryan! It's good to see you." She looked at Tara. "And who is this?"

"Hi Adelia. This is Princess Tara-Brigit."

"Oh!" she said in surprise. "Welcome then princess."

"Thank you," Tara said, still not comfortable with the idea of talking bears.

"Let me get you guys a cold drink. Help yourselves to some honey sticks as well."

"Peter said you made a fresh batch today."

She smiled. "Yes, pies too."

"They have the best food here, and everyone comes here after work or school. They also make takeout orders and mail orders to other kingdoms," Ryan explained.

"Awesome, so if I was in another kingdom I could order, say, this jar of honey?" Tara held up a jar of honey that had a label on it.

"Yeah," Ryan said as Tara set it back down.

"Other things too?"

"Yes, just about anything as long as it could keep."

"How do they order, and who delivers?" Tara was now wanting to know more.

"They take orders by phone, or birds fly in with orders. We have several that deliver, some in bear form, others on horses, or birds like the ones whose nest you were sleeping when I found you."

"That is just the coolest," Tara said as they were now standing in front of a huge shelf with glass jars filled with honey sticks. The store reminded Tara of a Cracker Barrel restaurant. There were tables all over with red and white checkered table cloths, and there were honey hive glass lanterns as centerpieces. Adelia came over to Tara and Ryan with two glass mugs filled with frothy root bear.

"Root beer?" she offered. Tara took hers and took a huge sip. Ryan and Adelia laughed as Tara realized she had root beer foam on her face. She wiped the foam off her upper lip.

"This place just keeps getting better and better. I could get used to this," Tara said with a grin.

Ryan cleared his throat.

"What are you up to today?" Adelia asked as she went on busily readjusting shelves and moving things around. Tara saw soaps, lotions, jarred jams, and all kinds of honey. Creamed, honey soap, all kinds of stuff.

"Oh, we need to check on a few things in the storage units."

Tara picked a regular honey stick, and a strawberry one, and a cinnamon one. They finished off their root beer, put the glasses on top of a tray that was sitting on a huge barrel, and said goodbye to Adelia.

"Stop by later for something to eat," she called out as the bell on the door rang out.

"Thanks, Adelia!" they shouted back, and the door closed.

"Okay, let me get this straight. You can you change into a bear whenever you want?" Tara was curious to know, for it seemed to her they could.

"Yeah, pretty much."

"Cool."

They started walking down the road again, and it was quiet.

"Do you miss home?" Ryan asked as they came up to a group of buildings.

"Yeah, but I am fine really. I think Mark misses home. He wants to go back."

"Yeah, I don't blame him. This place isn't always a nice place."

"Neither is earth. We have problems too."

"True, however here." He paused.

"Here, it is complicated. On one hand like here we have modern technology, but in other places it is like the stone age."

Tara chuckled. "Yeah I noticed that."

"Plus," Ryan went on. "We have monsters, and magical beings. It's complicated."

"Yeah, but you have magic!" Tara thought that was one of the coolest things.

"Some would say your technology is magic."

"I guess you're right, Ryan," Tara said as they approached a huge storage unit.

"Yeah, I guess where you came from, they have problems too. This is called West Side," Ryan told her as he got out some keys from his pocket. "Storage building number one," he said, unlocking the door. It was cold inside, and musty-smelling. "You look over there Tara, and I will start here." He turned on the lights, and they flickered before turning on, and not very brightly.

Tara started opening boxes and crates. They had been looking for a few hours when Tara found a small jewelry box. "Hey, look at this." She held up a bracelet. It had a small wooden bear charm on it.

Ryan came over. "Oh wow. I haven't seen that in a while." He took it from her, dangling the bear charm in front of his face. "It belonged to my great aunt Daisy. My uncle made it for her. They are both gone now."

"Oh, sorry," Tara said as he looked at her.

"You can have it," he said as he started putting it on her wrist.

"Oh, no! What if your mother or Anne wants it? I—"

"No, they have their own. Besides, my aunt would have liked you, so I want you to have it."

"Do you miss them?" she asked, feeling an ache in her own heart.

He looked away a bit. "Yeah, you never really get over losing someone you love. It gets easier to bear not having them around, but still you miss them."

"Yeah, my parents died a few..." She paused. "Recently."

"I'm sorry, Tara. I am assuming you mean your earth parents," he said, securing the box shut. He stood upright. She nodded her head.

"How?"

Tara stood and took a deep breath. "They died in a terrible car accident. Do you know what cars are?"

"Oh yeah, I know a lot about your world actually." Ryan said as he walked over to a case and closed the door. He then came back over to her.

"I'm sorry to hear about your parents, how are you coping?"

Tara shrugged her shoulders. "Okay, I guess. It is a bit better now. We should move on to the next storage unit, I think." She really did not want to talk about it with him now.

"How many do we have to go through?"

Ryan reached over as they got closer to the door and flipped off the light switch. "Four more to go."

* 329 *

18

The Bear Country Store and Cafe

Ryan Closed the door to the storage unit making sure it was locked before they headed down the dirt road. Ryan looked up at the sky. The sun made everything look hazy. "I was hoping it would rain," he said as they walked down another road. "Shall we go eat lunch?" he asked her.

He was taller than Mark, and more built, she noticed as she walked beside him. She found herself squinting to look at him in the sun's light. "Yeah, I am hungry, although we just had breakfast. Didn't we?"

He laughed. "All this walking and fresh air makes me hungry." When they got to the Bear Country

Store and Café, Tara noticed it was very busy, unlike earlier when she and Ryan were the only ones there. Ryan opened the door, and the door's bell rang out. Everyone in the place looked their way.

They got in line. "Hey Ryan," said a tall, skinny guy about Ryan's age.

"Hey Paul, how's it going?" Paul ruffled up his hair with his hand.

"Uh. Well those Red Caps started moving out, but they are not far enough away to let our guard down."

Ryan put his hands on his hips, and he stood with one knee cocked forward. "Yeah well, my father will not lower defenses until they are miles away." The line was getting shorter. Ryan turned to Tara. "Oh, hey Paul, this is Tara-Brigit."

"The princess. Oh, yeah. Word has gotten around about you," said Paul.

Paul and Tara shook hands. "Nice to meet you," she said. "Are you on the guard?" she asked.

"Yeah a bit down the road. I am off right now. For a few hours." Tara smiled, and Paul and Ryan started talking, so she just started looking at the menu as Ryan and Paul strategized about their defenses. She would cringe when they spoke about something she wasn't used to, like guards that would get their paws cut off by swords. Or traveling for days when you could not rest and the living conditions weren't the best, also running into trolls or other not so friendly magical creatures. Stuff a teenage girl from Connecticut would never really talk about.

"So. What looks good to you?" Ryan asked.

She looked at Ryan, making sure he was talking to her. "Uh. The biscuits and gravy."

He smiled. "Good choice. That's my favorite. I will order two." She nodded as they approached the counter. A young teenage girl with light brown hair pulled back into a ponytail turned around, smiling widely at Ryan.

"Hello Ryan. What do you want to order today?"

He was smiling back. "We will have two biscuits and gravy specials."

"Oh. Is she with you then?"

Ryan moved aside slightly and pulled Tara forward. "Yeah this is—" The girl behind the counter interrupted him by calling back their order.

"Sorry. Go find a seat and I will bring it out shortly." She kind of smiled at Ryan, but when he turned around, she gave Tara a not-so-friendly look. Tara raised her eyebrows and turned to follow Ryan. Wow she's a bit rude, Tara thought.

They approached a table, and he pulled out her chair. "Thank you," said Tara. She sat down, and he sat across from her. Tara noticed salt and pepper shakers in the shapes of bears. She picked one up, looking at it. "Is everything made out of the shape of bears here?"

Ryan laughed. "No," he replied, taking it from her and setting it down.

The girl from the counter came over to their table and asked, "What will you have to drink then?" She was wearing short, cut-off denim shorts. Very short. She wore sneakers and no socks. She had on a tight-fitting red cotton blouse that was short-sleeved and unbuttoned a bit low. She was also wearing a short, white, frilly apron. She seemed to be flirting with Ryan as Tara noticed how she looked at him, and how she talked.

"Um, well I'll have a root beer." Ryan looked at Tara.

"I'll have the same," she said as the girl nodded and turned abruptly on her heel.

"Sorry, Jen is usually friendlier."

Tara scrunched up her nose. "Oh, I'm sure she is," she said, almost sarcastically. "Maybe she doesn't like strangers."

He smiled and leaned forward. "You aren't a stranger." She smiled back, feeling her ears grow warm. Tara had a feeling this Jen girl and Ryan had dated at some point, or at least she really liked him. A lot. Jen brought them their sodas and then went to a different table. Adelia brought them their food. Well, Ryan had to tell her it was Adelia, the bear they saw in the store earlier. This time she was in human form, and she was tall and had long brown hair. She looked fairly young possibly late twenties.

"Thank you, Adelia," said Ryan.

"Sure thing. Enjoy," she said, smiling as she walked away.

Tara gave Ryan a puzzled look. "Why would you choose one form over the other? I mean, is there a reason to be in one form or another? Why would someone come to the café as a bear rather than as a human?"

He smiled. "In bear form, we can protect others, our homes and stuff better. It is not easy to switch forms. It takes a lot out of you, so we only do it when we have to, or when it suits the situation best. Once we're in one form, we usually don't switch unless there is a good reason."

"Adelia is Jen's older sister, and she is Peter's wife," Ryan explained.

Tara scrunched her forehead trying to think who Peter was. Ryan explained, "The bear we saw in the beehive field."

"Oh. Yeah," Tara said, recollecting seeing him. She took a bite of her meal and raised her eyebrows as she smiled. She chewed her food and then smiled again. "Wow, this is amazing."

Ryan smiled while he shoved a huge bite into his mouth. They talked while they ate, and he told her that they were skipping one of the storage units because it was full of food. Tara leaned back in her chair. "Oh gosh. I am stuffed." She had eaten the whole thing.

Ryan grinned as he wiped his mouth with a napkin. "I'll be right back," he said, getting up. She watched him go up to the counter, where he talked to that Jen gal. She watched as Jen kept smiling and tossing her head around, making her ponytail swing back and forth. "Wow, is she flirting bad," Tara said to herself as she watched. They talked for a few minutes as people came and went. Tara looked down at the bracelet, gently using her finger to make the bear charm rock from side to side.

"All set then?" he asked her, and Tara turned around and stood up.

"Yeah, let's go." They walked out of the café, noticing some clouds had rolled in.

Ryan looked up. "Well maybe it will rain." Tara looked up as well. They didn't look like storm clouds, but then again she was not from there. They soon came to a huge storage unit. Ryan unlocked the door. There were plenty of windows, so they did not need to turn on lights yet. "Okay, let's start looking," he said as he started opening boxes.

Tara began looking around. She found some furniture and end tables that had drawers full of things. Ryan found a pirate hat and put it on. Its large plume hung in his face. "How can I help you me lady?" he asked, blowing the plume out of his face.

Tara laughed. "Help me find that fairy flag."

He bowed. "As you wish," he said in a pirate accent that made Tara laugh. She laughed even harder as Ryan chased her around with a big stuffed lion, making roaring and snarling noises. At one-point Tara tripped and landed on some floor pillows. "Whoa, watch out," he said as he pulled her up and into his arms. He brought his face close to hers and quickly brushed his lips with hers in a quick, soft kiss. He then let her go. She could feel her face turn bright red. Ryan cleared his throat as one of the huge doors opened and light from outside filtered in.

"Ryan! Son! Are you in here?" called Lord McMahon.

"Yes Father. Over here," Ryan called out.

Soon Lord McMahon was standing near them. "So it seems that the young Prince of Erin has been found. Also, his brothers are fighting in the war, on

Don Pater's side. It seems they had tried to kill their younger brother years ago, and he went missing."

"Oh yeah, I remember hearing he had gone missing. When was he found?" Ryan asked his father.

"Recently. However, now they apparently have tried to kill him again."

"Well they are not nice brothers, are they?' Tara said as she stood by Ryan. Lord McMahon raised his eye brows.

"Well that's not good news, is it?" Ryan asked.

"No. But news it still is. How are you two holding up?"

"Well we haven't found it yet. We will keep looking," Ryan told his father.

Lord McMahon grabbed Ryan's shoulder, squeezed it, and smiled. "All right then. Dinner is at seven sharp." He let go of Ryan's shoulder. "Also, there are rumors that the high king and queen are in the underworld."

Tara wasn't too thrilled to hear that, and the thought of going there gave her the chills. But she would if she had to. "Yeah, got that already."

"Oh, okay. Well, see you two later." Lord McMahon started leaving.

"Yes father, we won't be late," Ryan said.

Lord McMahon waved before exiting the storage unit. They took another hour looking, and after they had looked through everything they decided to leave. Tara felt frustrated.

"We'll find it. One way or another." Ryan nudged her shoulder, making her smile just a bit. "Let's stop by the artolater's shop and get you a bow and quiver. Okay?"

Tara shrugged her shoulders. "Sure. But that won't help find the flag."

"No, but if you need to defend yourself, it will help." They talked as they went along the path, and Ryan explained what an artolater was. "Cyrus is our master archer. He makes all of our bows and arrows, and he is very good at his craft. He even helps design the fairies' bows and arrows." Tara was excited to meet the man named Cyrus, and Ryan went on to say that he had even designed massive bows that sat atop the walls that protected the village.

They walked down the path into some trees, and when they rounded the corner, they came to a few buildings near a field with targets set up.

"Hey, young Lord Ryan. What can I do for you?" The man was leaning through the top part of a hinged door of one of the buildings. He was a short older man, skinny, with a scruffy little beard. Friendly looking though.

"Hi, Cyrus. Tara here needs a bow."

The man smiled, showing a silver tooth. He opened the bottom half of the door and said, "Come on in." They walked in, and Tara looked around the little shop. The man hobbled towards a wall and took down a simple wooden bow. "This here bow is made of hickory wood. I also have a bow made of ash." He walked over to a shelf and held up another bow. The ash bow was a bit darker.

"I like the hickory one," Tara said.

Cyrus smiled. "Good choice," he said and handed it to her. "Here. Take it out and shoot with it for a bit. See if you still like it."

Ryan was filling a quiver full of arrows. "Thanks Cyrus, we will be back." The man waved and started working on a piece of wood.

Tara and Ryan walked out onto the field, and Tara set her arrow. Her first shot was inside the marked lines.

"Very good," Ryan said, smiling.

"I took archery in school." The next three shots were even better as she got used to the feel of the bow.

"So. Do you like it?" Ryan asked her.

She smiled as she went to go get the arrows. "Yes."

"Fine, they're yours. Except I think we should get you an arm guard. You might need it later on."

Tara shrugged her shoulders. "Okay." She followed him back inside the workshop.

"So. What did you think?'

"I like it," Tara said, smiling as she held up the bow.

"We'll take them, the quiver and arrows. Also, an arm guard."

Cyrus nodded and motioned for Tara to follow him over to a counter. He took out a few leather arm guards and fitted her with one.

"Thanks Cyrus, see ya." The man waved and went back to work.

"Don't we have to pay him?" Tara asked.

"No. We have an account. Besides, he knows who you are."

"Oh." Tara didn't feel right not paying the man. "My father will order him some more hickory wood. He gave you his last one. He makes some of the finest bows around. Well, besides the fairies." Tara felt better about not paying him and that he would be paid in new hickory wood.

*
* *
# 19

Blood and Stone

Soon they came to the main square of the village. It was getting dark by now, and it seemed a little quiet.

"Everyone closed up their shops early, looks like. It's part of our defenses. Ya know, so the guards don't have to worry about people running about."

"I thought you said it was safe here?" Tara asked.

"Well sure, it is. However, we still could get attacked."

They stopped talking, and their footsteps echoed off of the cobblestone walkway. Ryan waved to a guard in human form as they passed, and when they turned the corner there were several bear guards in the bigger part of the courtyard. They kept walking towards the mansion. As soon as they walked in, they knew something was wrong.

There were several guards, and Anne was lying on the sofa in the entryway. "What happened?" he asked, running over to her.

One of the guards stepped aside. Anne's head was bandaged, and Mark was not there.

"Where's Mark?" Tara asked. Everyone stood still as Lord McMahon came into the foyer with Cian.

"Cian!" Tara ran over to him. "Where's Mark?" The panicked feeling returned, making her voice sound higher pitched.

"He's gone," Anne said sleepily.

"Shh Anne," Lady McMahon said as she rushed to her side, and Anne started to cry.

"Gone. What?" Tara looked around.

"What do you mean gone?" Ryan asked, looking at his father.

Cian stepped forward. "I found your Anne unconscious in the northwestern field. I was coming here for a meeting. A very small group of Red Caps was seen hastily leaving the area." He pulled out a letter. "This was found by the wall. Two of the guards there are dead, and the third is in critical condition."

Lady MacMahon turned her head. "I thought you told me you had driven those Red Caps away, Marty!"

"We had, blast it! This small group must have slipped past us."

Tara ran over as Cian handed the letter to Ryan. When she saw that it was covered in blood, she backed away, shaking her head and feeling bile rise from her stomach.

"We're sorry Tara, the Red Caps captured Mark. I wanted to tell you this myself as Oren has not been able to get here yet," said Cian.

Tara looked at Lord McMahon as everything around her became fuzzy. "Tara!" she faintly heard Ryan say as she felt her head hit the wooden floor.

When Tara woke up, she was on the floor. Ryan was cradling her head in his arms. She stood. "Whoa Tara, easy now. You passed out." Ryan was trying to calm her.

Mark, she thought in alarm. She broke free from Ryan's arms and tried opening the door, but it was closed up nice and tight.

"Let me out! Mark!" she yelled as Cian came over, setting a huge hand on her shoulder.

"It's no use, Tara. They have him."

She abruptly turned around. "They'll kill him!"

Ryan held up the letter. Tara looked at it, the sickened feeling coming back. "Whose blood is that?" she asked as she closed her eyes to try to calm her stomach. "Never mind, I don't think I want to know," she said, walked towards a chair and sat down, shaking.

Lady McMahon came over to her and wrapped a loving arm around her shoulders. Tara looked at Anne. "Oh gosh Anne! Are you oaky?"

Anne faintly smiled as fresh tears ran down her face.

"How badly did they hurt you?"

"She has a concussion," Lady McMahon told her as Anne's eyes closed.

"What did they do to her?"

"I found this by her head." Cian pulled out a huge rock from a bag that was covered with blood.

Tara felt like she was going to be sick. She put her head between her legs as Lady McMahon rubbed her back. It was no use. She emptied the contents of her stomach onto the floor between her feet.

"Sarah!" Called Lady MacMahon. "We need some towels and wet rags, please!"

"Yes, My Lady," Tara heard the maid as she quickly ran up the stairs.

After a few minutes she sat up, wiping at her face where the tears had been running down.

"This is my fault." She stood as the maid came to clean up the mess.

"Nonsense, my dear," Lady McMahon said, trying to comfort her.

"The closest army has been alerted, and Oren is on his way here to pick up Cian. Our meeting will be short," Lord McMahon said as Ryan added the letter to the bag with the rock. Tara shivered.

"Father, we haven't found the flag and..." Ryan started to say, and Lord McMahon pulled him aside.

They were talking, but Tara couldn't hear what they were saying.

"How about I go make some tea?" Lady McMahon said as she hastily left the grand foyer. Cian came over to Tara.

"Cian. What should I do?" Tara asked him.

He looked at her solemnly. "Find the flag, Tara. You are the only one who can. Tina said you are connected to it. You will know where to look. Leave us to find Mark. There is not much you can do about that. We will find him, Tara."

Fresh tears started running down her cheeks. "What if they…" She couldn't finish what she had to say. Cian held her in his strong arms as she sobbed. How could she go on without him? He had always been there for her. He was her best friend.

There was a pounding on the heavy wooden doors. Ryan walked over and climbed up onto the door to look out of the barred glass. "It's Oren." He jumped down as Lord McMahon disengaged the security on the doors. Oren and a few other fairy warriors rushed in.

"Oh good, Cian! You did make it here," Oren said hastily.

"What news do you have for us?" Cian asked as Oren looked around.

"The Red Caps have Mark, and they are making their way to the Stone Kingdom as we speak," Oren told them. "Mark is still alive as far as we could tell. We need to leave now to catch up with them. They will not have gone too far." Relief poured over Tara. "However, he is of course in danger. We need to ride out now to meet with the Sky kingdom's two armies to intercede them. How is Anne?" Oren looked at her on the sofa.

"She is resting but has a concussion," Lord McMahon explained.

Oren went over and felt her cheek. "She is running a fever. Check her for internal bleeding."

Lady McMahon came in just then, dropped the tea tray, and ran over to Anne. She knelt down and started crying. Hearing that she might have internal bleeding upset her greatly.

"Martha!" Lord McMahon roared. Tara almost jumped out of her skin. Soon a maid came in. "Clean this up!" He demanded, pointing to the spilt tea and broken china. "Make a fresh pot."

"Yes, my Lord," she said as she hastily went into the kitchen. Lord McMahon turned around, and his demeaner changed to a more pleasant one. "Sorry about that."

"I will get Doctor Moss, Father," Ryan said, taking off at a run out the front doors. Lord McMahon nodded as Oren came over to Tara, who was feeling a bit numb by now. "Tara." He looked down at her.

"I need to find that flag Oren. This needs to stop." Tara felt almost helpless. He guided her into the large great room. The fireplace was lit, and the room felt stuffy. Cian followed.

"We have two more storage units to look through. I have a feeling it's here somewhere," Tara said.

Oren nodded his head. "Good, that's good Tara. But listen to me." She looked up at him. "None of this is your fault."

Cian came closer to her. "That's right. This all started long before you were born."

"Okay fine, but I am going to end it!" Tara exclaimed.

Cian nodded.

"That's the spirit," Cian said as Oren put a hand on Tara's shoulder. "Remember the whistle Tara, and keep close to young Lord McMahon," Oren told her.

She looked at him then, remembering what she was told about Mark. "What is going on with Mark? I mean, besides being captured."

Oren looked at Cian. He lifted his hand off of her shoulder. "The letter was a ransom note, Tara. Someone saw you two exiting the Fairy Realm and word spread. You were followed here. Mark is the fourth prince of the King of Erin."

Tara stood there, not sure her ears heard him right. She shook her head. "What are you talking about?" she yelled. "What prince?"

"That is why he was taken, someone recognized him. They are taking him to his brother's."

"No! Cian, he is my friend from Connecticut!"

"Whoa, what's all the yelling? Keep it down! Anne is being moved to her room," Ryan said as he came into the great room.

Tara sighed loudly. "Sorry Ryan."

Cian walked over to Ryan. "We told her about Mark." Ryan just nodded.

Tara started pacing the room like an animal at the zoo, her arms folded over her chest, her head hanging down.

"The fourth prince, the older brothers wanted him dead. I have heard the story. It's real." She stopped pacing and looked up.

"He never told me any of this. Mistaken identity. Again. What is it with you people?"

Oren came over then and cupped his hands around her upper arms.

"Tara. Cian and I have to go. Stay here, find the flag. Send word to us when you have found it. Then we will arrange for Beira and Lou to go to the underground kingdom with you."

"But I need to get Mark back." Fresh tears threatened to spill. Oren sighed and bent down to look Tara in the eyes.

"I will send Beira and Lou to meet you." With the mention of Beira and Lou again, Tara's head jerked up. She stopped short. "Why couldn't they have just left us alone!" Tara pulled away from Oren.

"Because, Tara," Cian said, walking towards her, "they had an order, and you have a duty as the princess to help if you can."

"My name is Tara MacInnes! I am the daughter of Brian MacInnes, and I am from Connecticut!" She stood with her arms at her sides, her hands clenched in fists. Oren swiftly came over and grabbed at her necklace.

"Enough of this nonsense!" he said as he boldly grabbed at her necklace. Holding it up, he said something in a language she did not recognize. The stones began to glow. They heard a faint cry at first, then a loud declaration.

"Princess Tara-Brigit MacInnes MacLeod. Treasured and beloved daughter of Sean MacInnes and King Dagda Kenneth the third of the Higher Realms." The glowing stopped as the voice went still.

She relaxed her posture, letting out a huge sigh. She had no idea that she had been holding her breath.

She felt the muscles in her trunk area hurting from tension. She rubbed at her ribs.

"We will be hearing from you. Hopefully soon," Oren said as he shook hands with Ryan. Then he briefly hugged Tara who now stood in disbelief and shock. Cian also quickly embraced her. Tara watched them as they left the room, Ryan followed, and then Oren and Cian left the mansion. Tara slowly lowered herself into the closest chair. She was staring at the front doors as a cup of tea was placed on the side table by her. Then she heard a familiar voice.

"Let them go, Tara. They will get Mark back." Tara looked over. Standing on the table by the tea cup was Ettrick.

"You have an important duty as well. Find that flag, Tara. Find that flag and the war will be at its end, it will."

Tara turned to look at Ettrick with a new fire burning inside her. They would not take her friend and bring him to harm! they would not hurt the people she cared about! Ettrick must have seen the look in her eyes as he stood there, grinning from ear to ear. Ryan came into the room as Tara stood. Tara looked him straight in the eyes. "Let's go find that flag." He nodded and smiled as Ettrick gave out a yip and a holler and vanished into thin air. Tara and Ryan headed towards the massive foyer.

Lord McMahon was giving orders to his guards when they came into the foyer. The guards left in a hurry. Lord MacMahon turned as they came in. "Anne is resting. Doctor Moss is with her."

"Thank you, father," Ryan said as he sounded relieved.

"We are going to the last two storage sheds, tell Mother we will be on guard," Ryan said. Lord McMahon nodded.

"I will grab my sword, and," he said as he handed Tara her bow, "Tara has her bow."

"Very good, son." He came over and hugged Ryan and then did the same to Tara. He stepped back and looked at them both. "Now be safe, cautious, and alert."

"Yes, Father," Ryan said as two guards opened the front doors, and they walked out onto the massive porch. It had begun to rain lightly, and little wet spots dotted the walkway. Tara put up the hood on her sweatshirt. Tara heard a rustle of skirts behind her, but Ryan pulled her along. "Keep walking, Tara. Do not look back. It will make it harder to leave."

"Okay," she nodded. She could not believe what was happening. She knew Mark—he was her crush, the boy from Arizona who hated the cold. He was not some missing prince. They had made a mistake. They walked in silence for a while, Ryan pausing every now and again listening, but all they could hear was the rain coming down.

They soon came to a storage unit. However, mostly what they found was stored grains and other foods. There was a smaller one near it. "This one is a food storage unit as well." He looked at Tara, and her expression was solemn. "I'm sorry about Mark," he said, closing and relocking the doors.

"It's not your fault."

"It's not yours, either. Look, his brothers left the kingdom, tried to kill him. In the letter, he said he had run away. Far away."

"Why did he not tell me? It might not even be true."

Ryan sighed as he got out a rain poncho and placed it over her. The rain was coming down more now. "I don't know, Tara. Maybe he was afraid you would think he was crazy."

She laughed at his comment, and then thought for a minute. "He was acting strangely when we went to Alaska. He definitely did not seem thrilled to be here. It's just I…" She paused as they got to the last unit. Ryan was unlocking the doors.

"This one we use as an overflow library." She could almost feel a buzz about the storage unit. "But it also holds all kinds of stuff."

He turned on some lights. There was so much stuff to look through, and Tara felt drained.

"Here, sit down. I can bring boxes to you to look through," Ryan offered. Tara sat, feeling her weight pull her down. Soon there were several boxes in front of her. She sucked in her breath, let it out, and set to work.

"Hey Tara," Ryan called out, walking towards her and holding something. "Check out this dagger." The blade was about six inches long, and the handle was in the shape of a bear. Its eyes were two ruby red stones.

"Wow, that's cool," she said as he bent down to show her. He flipped it over. Engraved on the back was the McMahon name and some other words she did not recognize. "Hey look, the bear has a tail," she pointed out.

"I want you to have it, besides the bow."

"Oh Ryan. I don't..." He put it back into its little leather sheath and placed it in her hand.

"Look, you need to be able to protect yourself."

She nodded her head. "Thanks."

Ryan smiled and packed up another box. "I am going to go over there to look," she told him as she walked over to a big pile of rugs and clothes. She started moving the rugs off of one box and onto the floor. When she moved another box aside, she found a large wooden bear statue, its friendly face staring down at her. She smiled. Then she remembered her dream. Something caught her eye. Underneath the statue she saw a little piece of gold fabric. She tried pushing the bear statue out of the way; however, it would not budge. "Ryan! Come here!" she yelled out to him.

He came over to where she was standing. "What?"

She stood aside and pointed, smiling. "Look. I think I found it."

He looked closer to where she was pointing. "Do you think you could move this statue?" she asked him.

He looked at it and nodded. "Yeah, I think so." It was about three feet taller than he was. "Yeah, not a problem," he said, sucking in a deep breath, and then he grabbed the bear statue and lifted it. It came off of the floor a few inches, and Tara reached down and grabbed at the fabric.

"It's still stuck."

Ryan let down the statue, grunting. "Okay, I will try to move it a bit more, but man, that thing weighs a ton."

He went to grab it again and moved it enough so that this time she got the fabric out from under it. He set the bear statue down with a thud.

Tara stared wide-eyed at the fabric now in her hands.

"The Fairy Flag." She was actually holding it. She held it up high so he could see. "I don't see how a piece of cloth can end the war. I mean, I have heard it's enchanted, but…" Ryan looked more closely at it. Tara ran her fingers along its silky edge as it shimmered and shined, causing him to squint his eyes.

"Don't unfold it." Ryan quickly set his hand atop hers.

"I wasn't going to."

He relaxed and started looking around. "I have heard that once it is unfurled it will draw you to the battle."

"Great. Let's go," Tara said half-jokingly.

"Here let's put it in this bag." He grabbed a small fabric backpack that had a Nike logo on it.

"You got this from my world," she said as he put the flag into the backpack. She just smiled.

"What? I like Nike. Here." He started putting the bag on her back under her sweatshirt that by now was mostly dry. "When we are traveling, keep this under your cloak."

She nodded. "How are we going to let the others know we found it?" she asked him.

"I am sending my falcon named Arrow. I usually have him with me, but he has been busy delivering messages already," he said casually as he started turning off lights.

"You mean like a big bird of prey?"

"Yeah, and I use him for hunting sometimes."

They walked out of the building, and as Ryan was locking the door he looked around. "Okay, all seems to be good." They could see some lanterns turned on and guards walking about. Tara saw at one point a bear handing over a lantern to a human guard. "Let's go to the Falconry building. My father said to come back to the mansion before we leave the Green Glenn, to say goodbye."

"We have to leave?" Tara said apprehensively. The thought of leaving made her realize how safe she felt there.

"Well yeah, since you found the flag." They kept walking down a street she hadn't been down before. "Okay, here we are." They walked into the building, and there were several birds inside. Ryan put on a big glove and made a whistling noise. A beautiful bird of prey came and landed on his arm. He had a piece of meat for him. "This is Arrow. Now I need you to write a note and we will put it in this little pouch attached to his leg and let him go."

Ryan spoke to the bird softly, but with a commanding tone. "Arrow, you will deliver this message to Oren."

Tara found a small desk and some paper and a quill pen. She wrote the note and gave it to Ryan. He put it in the little leather pouch and secured it to Arrow's leg. "Okay, let's let him go." They went outside and Ryan whispered to the falcon, and then let him go.

"Is he as intelligent as those birds I was staying with?" Tara asked.

Ryan shrugged his shoulders. "I think so. Smaller but still brilliant."

They walked down the road and up to the mansion. Lights were on inside, and outside as it had started to get dark. Two guards stood at the front entrance. "Young Lord Ryan," one said, bowing before knocking three times. Then they heard the latch and the doors opened. They walked in.

"Oh good, you're back," Lady McMahon said.

"We started packing your gear," Lord McMahon said as Ryan's brothers came into the grand foyer, along with two maids carrying the twins. Confused, Tara looked at the bags on the floor.

"We were briefed, dear," Lady MacMahon said, smiling.

"How is Anne doing, Mum?" Ryan asked.

"She is resting. She feels terrible that Mark was taken," she said, looking at Tara.

"It wasn't her fault, just like it wasn't Tara's," Lord McMahon said, hugging his wife. He brought two packs to Tara and Ryan. "Now the bigger pack is for you to carry, Son, and the smaller is for Tara. Although you will be able to attach them to the saddles." Ryan lifted the huge pack and swung it onto his back. Tara picked up the smaller one.

"Can we go see Anne before we go?" Tara asked.

"Oh yes, of course. She would like that," Lady McMahon said, smiling.

Tara and Ryan left their packs on the floor and went up the huge staircase. When they reached Anne's room, Ryan slowly opened the door. A nurse was sitting on a chair in the hall. "Hey Anne, it's me and Tara," he said quietly. The room was dimly lit, and very quiet. They walked over to the bed.

Anne slowly opened her eyes. "Ryan, Tara, have you heard anything?" she asked.

Ryan knelt down by her bed. "As far as we know, Mark is still alive."

She smiled slightly.

"We found the flag," Tara told her.

"You did? I'm glad. But that means you're leaving."

Ryan took her hand. "Yes, we are, but we will be back soon."

She looked at Tara. "You should change before you go. Both of you."

Ryan hugged her gently. "Yes, we should. I'll meet you downstairs, Tara." He left, and Tara went to change. Anne fell back asleep.

Tara put on clean socks, undergarments, a long-sleeved shirt, and jeans. She grabbed some riding boots and a thick sweater. She also grabbed her cloak that was hanging on a hook by the door. "Bye, my sweet friend. I hope you get better soon," she said quietly to a sleeping Anne as she left the room and closed the door quietly. She ran down the hall and down the stairs, where Ryan was already saying goodbye to his family. She grabbed her pack. Lady McMahon helped her with her cloak, and the dagger fell onto the floor.

Lord McMahon came over and picked it up. "What's this?" he asked.

Ryan came over to him. "Oh, I found that in one of the storage units. I figured Tara should have it for protection since she can't wield a sword."

Lord McMahon unsheathed the small dagger. "Artair Arktos," he said, holding it up.

Lady McMahon sucked in her breath. "We haven't seen that for ages," she said as Lord McMahon turned it around in his huge hands. He made the dagger look small. "The name means Bear Guardian." He handed it back to Tara after he put it back in its leather sheathe.

"Bear Guardian. Wow, cool name," she said, fastening it to her thigh by a leather strap.

Lady McMahon adjusted the straps on Ryan's pack. "Now I packed first aid kits and food in your packs. Be careful, alert, and as safe as possible."

Ryan smiled. "Yes, Mum."

Lord and Lady McMahon hugged their son, and then all of his siblings came over to him. Tara too got her fair share of hugs, plus kisses from the twin babies. The doors were opened and their horses were waiting for them at the top of the walkway. A guard helped Tara up into the saddle. Snowberry was happy to see her. Tara leaned over and hugged the horse's neck. As they started walking the horses away, Ryan looked at her. "Don't turn around Tara, just keep on moving forward." She could hear Lady McMahon's sobs from where she was and decided not to turn around and look. Although she had wondered if she had, would she see a family of bears or humans standing there?

20

Giant Country

Tara's pack felt as big as Ryan's by the time they stopped. The whole day's events had caught up with her. They had traveled up into the more mountainous region. The air felt cooler up here, so Tara had her cloak on over her other jacket. She slid out of Snowberry's saddle and let her pack slide off her back and onto the ground.

"Ah, I am so tired." Ryan walked over to her, got ahold of Snowberry's reins, and tethered up both horses. "We can rest here for a while. I can set up camp." He was already getting stuff out of his pack. Two sleeping bags and a small pot.

"I can go find some wood for a fire," she said, walking over to where the sleeping bags were.

"No. I'll go," he said, grabbing a flashlight. The moon was bright in the sky, giving off some light, but the forest looked pretty dark.

Tara swallowed hard. "Are there wolves here?" she asked, looking around nervously.

"In these parts, yeah there are regular wolves, not werewolves. But there aren't any around, believe me." He started walking further away. "I won't go far. Can you keep an eye on the camp and horses?" he asked, flicking on the flashlight as he disappeared into the forest. Tara stood in silence, listening for any sound. It was quiet. She jumped when, a few minutes later, Ryan came out of the forest holding a bunch of firewood. Tara started laying out the sleeping bags. "You will love the view in the morning," he said as he started to make a fire. There were rock formations around them, which helped Tara to feel a bit safer, but she couldn't see much, which did not calm her nerves.

Once the fire was going it didn't take long before Tara was asleep. She dreamt of Mark, and he was lost and she couldn't find him. When she woke up, she sat up slowly. Letting her mind and body wake up.

Sleeping outdoors was hard on your body, Tara felt that she was a little more used to it though now. Ryan was already at the fire cooking.

"Hey. How did you sleep?" he asked her.

Tara stretched and yawned and looked around. "Okay I guess." He brought her over a steaming mug. The air was cool—cool enough for her fingers to feel cold and stiff.

"Hot chocolate, my mum's recipe," he said, handing her the mug.

Tara wrapped her hands around the mug, letting the warmth seep into her cold fingers. She took a sip and sighed. "This has got to be the best hot chocolate I have ever tasted."

Ryan smiled and sat down near her. "I made some eggs and ham." Tara nodded as she took another sip of her hot chocolate. "We need to get going soon, though," he said, standing.

"Yeah, okay." She got out of her sleeping bag and stood as well. Ryan went over to the fire and then gave Tara a small bowl with her food in it. She ate quickly, and afterwards they put out the fire and packed up their stuff. They mounted the horses, and Ryan led the way further up into the mountains.

"At this next ridge, we should be able to see the great view," he called out, as they were single file at this point.

Tara was surprised at how well the horses traveled on the rocky terrain. As they came out through the trees, they could see the view down below. Tara had to catch her breath. "It's beautiful!" She came up alongside Ryan as they both looked down.

He pointed and told her, "That's the Giants Causeway, and Fingal's Cave." Far off in the distance Tara could see it; however, it did look different. She saw the two huge castles, and the causeway was like an enormous bridge across the sea. She could also see massive cottages and trees.

"Everything is so big."

Ryan laughed. "What did you expect? They're giants." He tugged on the reins of his horse as they started to descend the rocky slope. For a good chunk of the morning they kept at a slow, steady pace. "There is a lake coming up ahead, and we can let the horses graze for a while in the meadow there," he said as they trotted along.

Soon it was hard to keep the horses from going a full gallop. Tara had to really pull on Snowberry's reins. "She knows what's up ahead," Tara said as Ryan laughed.

"Yeah. There is some of the best grass around here." He was right; as soon as they got to the field Tara saw thick, very green, lush grass. She jumped down and let Snowberry run off with Bone, Ryan's horse.

Tara looked up in the sky and saw Arrow flying. "Oh, looks like Arrow found us. He must have a message." Ryan got out his big glove and held up his arm. Soon Arrow landed on him, and Ryan gave the bird a piece of meat. The bird ripped at it quickly, swallowing pieces. Ryan got out the small message. Tara moved in closer. "What does it say?"

"Our numbers are gaining. Oren has some new recruits." He looked at her.

"Who?" she asked, trying to see.

"Fomorians."

Tara looked at the falcon, which was now eyeing her. "Giants?"

Ryan shook his head. "Not all Fomorians are bad, Tara."

"Okay, I didn't say they were. It's just…" She fiddled with Arrow's feathers on his tail. The bird quickly looked down and tried pecking at her hand. "That's who took me, and I can't help but think how my life would be different if…" She shook her head and then suddenly looked up at him.

He gave Arrow another piece of meat. "You will find a few who are neutral, or will only fight for their own causes." He got his pack and set Arrow down on it. The bird looked around, still eyeing Tara. "I am going to get some water. Look in the pack for what we can have for lunch."

Tara wasn't particularly hungry, but she didn't know when they would stop again. Ryan had told her that, since they were closer to the giants' towns, they could not risk making a fire. She found some chicken sandwiches and juice. By the time he came back, she was definitely hungry.

Ryan smiled as he took a big bite of his sandwich, and then he took a big gulp of juice. "Well, you have been eating well since I met you." Tara rolled her eyes. Ryan finished his lunch before Tara. "Come on, we have to make it to the cave entrance before it gets dark. We need to go the rest of the way on foot, though."

Tara looked at him like he was crazy. "We're walking the rest of the way?" He nodded as he put his pack on. She grabbed her small pack and walked over to him, slinging her bow over her shoulder. "Fine," she said with exasperation.

They started down the trail, the tall grass in the field shielding the horses. They came to another point on the trail where they could see the Giants Causeway a lot better. Tara could see giants walking and driving cattle carts. She could faintly hear cattle and sheep as they made their way down from the mountains. The sun warmed the cooler air, and Tara saw it sparkling on the water. "It looks so different from where I grew up." She could see more details of the castles now as they walked. "So, the giants want more land than this?"

Ryan nodded. "Yeah, everyone always wants more land. Even my father." She stumbled over some loose rocks. "Careful," Ryan said, catching her. Tara felt her cheeks grow warm as she straightened herself and started walking again. They came to another field that was covered in flowers, and the air felt like summer now that they were out of the mountains.

Tara looked back behind her. "We didn't go all the way up into the mountains, did we?"

Ryan laughed. "No, we didn't." When they turned back around, they saw the boots of a giant in their path. "Run!" yelled Ryan as Tara grabbed her pack and started running. The giant was not far behind them.

"Pick a tree and climb!" yelled Ryan, hoisting himself up onto a branch and hastily started climbing. Tara looked around. There were no other places to hide. She ran to the nearest tree and started climbing, It wasn't easy, but she was soon making her way up. When she thought she was high enough, and that the thickness of the branches would conceal her, she stopped. She stood on the thick branch, breathing fast from the workout. However, she underestimated just how tall giants were. For when she turned around, staring back at her was the giant. His eyes widened when she looked at him.

"Hello," the giant said smiling. His huge white teeth glared back at her. Tara slowly moved backwards on the huge tree limb. "What is your name?" he asked, his light brown hair sticking out from under a knitted hat.

"My name?" she asked him back, as if not hearing him right. He smiled as Tara cleared her throat. Should she tell him her real name? She hesitantly took a step forward. "My name is Tara."

"Tara, that's it? Just Tara?" He cocked his head just a bit.

"Princess Tara-Brigit." She didn't get to finish before the giant's whole face lit up, and he smiled. "The Princess. I knew it. I knew you would come visit me one day."

Tara smiled slightly. "Who are you?"

"My name is Leonard. Some just call me Leo." Tara took another step towards him. "My brother Angus and I took you. But Father was going to do something mean to you, so I hid you."

"Wait. You took me. You mean when I was small?" Tara stood very still.

"I left you by the lake. Oh, you were so tiny and cute." He cupped his hand and pretended to hold a tiny baby. "I would sing to you, and…" He stopped, looked around, and then whispered, "I have kept this for you. It fell off of your wee itty-bitty foot." He reached in his pocket and took out a tiny, pink crocheted baby bootie.

"Tara?" She heard someone say, and she turned and looked to her left. Standing on a branch, at about her same height in the tree next to her, was Ryan. "Who are you talking to?"

Tara realized that, with the thick branches and leaves, Ryan couldn't see the giant. Leonard pushed aside some of the branches. "Whoa! Oh, it's you, Leo," Ryan said as he saw the giant.

"Ryan," Leonard said, recognizing him.

Ryan climbed over to where Tara was. "Hi. How have you been?"

"Wait. You two know each other?" Tara asked, feeling a bit confused.

"Yeah we have been friends for a while. Right, Leo?"

The young giant nodded his head.

"Leonard was just telling me that it was his brother and him who kidnapped me when I was a baby."

"You and your brother?" Ryan asked. He was now standing right in front of Tara.

"Oh yeah, and that he didn't want anything bad to happen to me so he left me by the lake? Isn't that right Leonard?" Tara asked

"Really, Leo, why do you always let your brothers talk you into stuff?"

Leonard took off his hat, wringing it in his hands. "Yeah."

Ryan relaxed and stood aside so that he was no longer shielding Tara. "Okay well, Tara and I are meeting some friends, so uh…we need to go." Ryan turned to Tara as the giant put his hat back on and let go of the big branch he had been blocking with his shoulder.

"I could help you. Where are you meeting them?"

Ryan turned around as Tara walked closer to the giant. "A cave entrance near here," Ryan said, walking up beside Tara. "Why do you want to help us, Leonard? You aren't allowed." However, the young giant cut him off.

The giant wiggled his nose. "Some of my family are fighting in the war, on both sides. I was not allowed to. I want to help you if I can."

Ryan nodded his head. "I get it. You want to feel like you are contributing somehow."

The giant nodded back. He then held out his hand. "Get on," he said as Ryan helped Tara up, and he jumped up next to her. Leonard carefully lifted them up and started walking into the forest.

"What was your brother going to do to me? The baby?" Tara asked.

Leonard thought for a moment then told them his story while they walked.

"Well, Angus said that father wanted to use you as a, ummm," He was thinking again, and Tara wished she could give his memory a shove.

"A bargnin tool. Yeah. So, we got to the castle and there was a big party. I could smell the food. Oh, it smelt so good. I could hear people talking. Angus broke the window and was reaching in with his big hands and I thought he would hurt you. He yelled at me and told me to get the baby. So, I did. You were so tiny and cute," he repeated. He held up his hand and with his thumb and pointer finger showed how little the baby was.

"Then we had to run, and fast. I thought your wee little body would get all jumbled so I told Angus we had to slow down."

"Then what happened, Leo?" Ryan asked, encouraging him to continue.

"He yelled at me while I was checking on her. I thought he would scare her. But she kept sleeping in my pocket. Yeah, that's where I had her, in my pocket," he said as he patted his pocket with his hand gently. Then, as if remembering something, his face lit up and he reached into his pocket. Tara noticed at the bottom edge it had been roughly sewn. Leonard pulled out a tiny baby bootie.

"I have saved this. It fell off your wee little foot." He gave it to her. Astounded, Tara took it and held it in front of her. She had the matching one. Then Leonard continued his story.

"When I found out what father wanted with the baby, I did not want her to get hurt or dead, so I cut a hole in my pocket. I took the baby out, wrapped her up and left her there by the lake. Oh, she was so little and helpless. I did not want to, but I had to do it. Father would hurt her."

Tara's eyes filled to the brim with tears as he told the story. She had been taken. "My poor parents," she thought.

"Don't be mad at Angus, okay. He was doing what father wanted. Angus is on your side. Father can be mean." Leonard was pouting now as they came near the caves.

"Leo," Ryan said as Leonard stopped walking. "You did the right thing, in the end." Ryan's encouraging words put a smile back on the young giant's face.

"There is a cave opening near here, but it goes to the underworld."

"That's where we're going."

"Why do you want to go there?" Leonard scratched at his head with his left hand. Tara wasn't sure how much they should tell him. After all, they were not in friendly territory. Not exactly enemy territory either.

"We need to find someone, and we think they are there," Tara told him. "Okay," Leonard said, walking again. "You need to be careful though. Don Pater is a nasty man."

"We will," Tara told him as he stopped again.

"I will let you down here. The cave is a few yards that way." He pointed in the direction they should go.

"Thank you, Leonard." Tara was smiling up at the giant.

"Yeah, thanks Leo, I'll see you around," Ryan said as he adjusted his pack. They started walking away. Tara was waving back as the giant waved to them. His face looked kind of sad.

"Do you think he wants to help us more?" Tara asked as Ryan turned to look at the sad giant. Tara felt bad for leaving him when he wanted to help. She felt as if she was leaving a very younger brother behind.

"Come on Tara," Ryan said, tugging at her sleeve. "Beira and Lou are waiting for us."

Tara sighed but followed him down a hill to the cave. Beira and Lou were waiting for them there, and Tara spotted Arrow flying up in the sky above them.

"Hi." Beira was waving to them. Beira and Lou were both decked out in armor, and they were filthy.

"So," Lou asked, "ready to go in?"

Tara wasn't really ready; she actually felt scared. Ryan must have felt her hesitation. "What if it's a trap?" He got out his bow and repositioned his quiver.

Tara took a deep breath. "If the King and queen are in there, they need us."
With that, the four of them entered the cave entrance.

21

The Cave

As soon as they walked in it felt cold, damp, and very dark. Beira grabbed a torch off of the wall, lit it, and they started walking.

"Is it weird to anyone else that the cave isn't guarded?" Tara asked. That comment made Ryan get out his sword. Beira and Lou were ready to fight as well. They soon came to a small crossroads. Three different paths spread out into three different directions.

"You pick which way to go, Tara," Lou told her as they stood there.

"I think we should split up," Tara answered, and all three of the others nodded.

"Sounds good," Beira said, grabbing another torch and, using the flame from hers, lit it and handed it to

Tara. She then joined Lou as they walked towards the right, and Tara and Ryan took the left passageway. The deeper they got, the colder and creepier it got. Weird rock formations caused the light to cast creepy shadows on the walls, making Tara jump a few times.

They passed by a few water pools. The first one had a weird iridescent blue hue, and the second one was black and motionless. It looked like a big, black piece of glass and made Tara shiver. They carefully walked around the large pool so they were now at the opposite end from where they came in. They walked around and passed some stalagmites—huge ones.

"Those are pretty big," Tara said as they walked away from them, only to come across more. Then it opened into an enormous, underground city. However, there was still no one around. Tara thought she saw some movement. Then she saw a light, and they could barely make out the two figures that were chained to the rock wall.

"Look," Tara said as she pointed to a far wall in the cave. "Do you think it's them?" Tara asked very quietly as she squinted her eyes.

"The king and Queen?"

"Well if it is," Ryan whispered back, "they don't seem guarded." Ryan looked around cautiously, as did Tara. They slowly walked a bit closer. "Stay here," Ryan said as he walked forward.

Tara stepped back, and a loose rock made her twist her foot. "Ouch!" she called out before thinking. Just then a giant, black dog jumped out in front of Ryan. Tara screamed, which stirred the man who was chained to the wall. He was standing with his head drooped in front of him. He slowly raised his head, his long strawberry blond hair hanging in his face. The woman was chained to the wall as well but was halfway kneeling on the ground towards the man. She slowly looked their way as well, but just like the man, Tara could not make out her face.

"They are guarded by a hellhound," Ryan said as he held his sword in front of himself.

The dog's barking caused Tara to cover her ears. He was enormous, towering over both of their heads. He had dark black fur and glowing red eyes. The barks echoed off of the cave's walls, making it seem louder. "How will we get by him?" Tara yelled as Ryan was looking around. He walked towards the right, and the dog lunged forward but then stopped. He was chained. Ryan smiled as he picked up a rock. The Hellhound stopped barking and eyed the rock in his hand. Ryan waved it back and forth, the dog following.

"Ah. So, you like to play catch, do you?" he asked, throwing the rock. The dog caught it with his slobbery mouth. Ryan picked up another. This time, when he threw it, he threw it a bit farther, giving them a better view of how much space there was. "Tara. When I throw this rock, wait for him to catch it, then run over to were those people are." She nodded, getting her bow ready as well. Ryan threw the rock high up into the air, and the dog had to practically jump to catch it.

"Use the dagger!" he yelled as Tara began to run under the dog's body. She got out the dagger, and just when she thought she was clear, the dog's tail swiped at her legs, causing Tara to fall flat on her chest. The hard ground knocked the air out of her lungs. The dagger went sliding across the hard ground and stopped a few feet in front of her but closer to the dog. She struggled to breathe as she started seeing small flecks of white circles. She closed her eyes as all the noise went quiet.

"Tara!" yelled Ryan as she sat up. "Are you all right?" Ryan was looking at her with a worried expression on his face. The dog's attention was now on her. Ryan whistled as the dog turned his way. Tara used that chance to get her dagger—she got up, ran over, and grabbed it. That's when she saw the shackles on the dog's paws. They glowed a weird color. She looked at the two people chained up. Even if they weren't the king and queen, no one deserved to be chained to a cold cave wall.

"I am here to free you," Tara said as she held up the dagger and swung it down onto the metal of the shackles that glowed the same eerie pulsing color. The contact of the blade to metal made a loud pinging noise that made the dog yelp, and the two people cried out in pain. Sparks flew everywhere, and the red eyes of the bear on the grip glowed a bright red. The lady looked up at her. Her pale ivory skin was a contrast to her black, long, wavy hair. She was dirty and looked so tired. The woman gritted her teeth and nodded to Tara to try again. Tara hit the shackles again, and this time they fell to the ground. She then turned to the man, who was quite a bit taller than she was.

Ryan was trying to keep the dog distracted, which Tara noticed was getting more difficult as it would continue to try to get at Tara. Tara raised the dagger and hit the shackles on the man's wrists. They broke free at once. The dog was right behind Tara now, snarling. She could here its hot breath on her back.

She raised the dagger. The dog's reflection could be seen on the blade. It looked distorted, and she only saw a smaller, light-brown-colored shaggy dog. It was still big, but not monstrous. It seemed to look at her as if it was sad. She suddenly felt bad for him. She ran towards the cave's wall where the chains held the dog.

"Tara! What are you doing?" Ryan was frantically trying to get to her, but the dog was doing its job. No one was going anywhere.

"He's a prisoner too!" Tara yelled before slamming the dagger into the bulk of the metal chains. There was a huge spark, a loud noise, and an explosion. Tara and everyone else were blown away from the dog. When Tara stood, with some help from the man standing near her, she saw before them a normal dog. It looked like an Irish Wolfhound mixed with a Great Dane, but a bit bigger. The dog barked a few times and wagged its tail.

Beira and Lou came running into the cavern. "What did you guys do?" They both stopped short and bowed. Standing behind Tara, tall and proud, stood the man and the woman. Ryan bowed as well.

"King Kenneth," Ryan said as he straightened and stood tall.

The dog turned and ran excitedly over to Lou. "Failinis!" he yelled as the dog jumped up on him, whining and licking Lou's face, his tail going back and forth vigorously.

Beira came over. "Tara! You found them." Awe was all over her face. Beira bowed again. "Your majesties."

Tara turned and also bowed. Ryan had come over with Lou, with Failinis running circles around them. The king and queen smiled. Lou handed the king a sword. "Come on, we need to get out of here."

Just then the cavern floor and walls began to shake, and they heard distant shouting and screeching. Tara looked at Lou and asked, "What is that?"

"That is what we were running from," Lou said, grabbing her arm. "Run!" he yelled as they all fled down a tunnel. The screeching was loud and made the hairs on Tara's arms stand on end. She tried covering her ears. The sound almost reminded her of the Banshee's screams, except more of a shrill cry.

They were coming out of the darkness, through cracks in the walls. Ghosts and ghouls.

Ryan grabbed Tara's arm. "Come on, Tara," he said as he pulled her along. They were all running. He pushed her forward as they came to another cavern. The ghosts were coming from everywhere. They were all in the cavern now: Lou, Beira, Ryan and the king, surrounding Tara and the queen, with Failinis circling them and growling at the bluish-green ghosts and ghouls coming towards them. Then a dark figure came into the cavern, followed by a group of warriors.

"Don Pater," said the king as he held his sword high. They were surrounded with nowhere to go. The man approaching them was dark and menacing. He reminded Tara of her history teacher, but a thousand times worse. His face was ashen white, and his dark, penetrating eyes looked about, scanning the cave. Tara reached for her necklace, fingering for the tiny whistle. She found it, held it up to her lips. She blew into it, causing all the ghosts and ghouls to screech and yell and cover their ears, as if they had them. Don Pater did the same; he seemed to bend and contort as she blew. Tara, though, didn't hear anything. So, she blew on it again. Still she heard nothing but the ghosts and ghouls screaming. Don Pater looked Tara's way, then lunged for her. Ryan, in bear form now, was quicker and knocked him off his feet, sending him flying a good ten feet from where Tara stood. Then she heard fighting, and Tara saw a bright light enter the cavern. She had to shield her eyes a bit, it was so bright.

Lou yelled to Failinis, "Guard!" and the dog stood in front of Tara and the queen. Tara and the queen had retreated to a small alcove away from the fighting. Everything was in chaos—screaming, yelling, sparks flying, and loud clanging noises. She covered her eyes and ears. When she let her arm drop from shielding her eyes, she saw Oren atop his horse, fighting.

"Oren!" she yelled out. He briefly looked her way, and then Tara saw the fairies. They were all over, fighting the ghosts and ghouls. Tara's heart was pounding rapidly as she watched. It felt as if she were watching a movie in a huge theater with the sound turned up way too loud. She had to look away a few times as ghosts and ghouls were slain. Then several ghosts tried to get past Failinis. He barked, growled, and bit at them. As soon as he bit them, they disintegrated. Then something grabbed at Tara's arm. She turned and screamed when she saw the arm coming from a crack in the cavern wall, and it grabbed her arm with an iron grip. She grabbed her dagger and sliced straight through its arm. The ghost screamed as the part of its arm that had Tara's in a deathly grip turned to smoke, the ghost pulled the rest of its arm away and retreated back through the wall. Tara shuddered as she turned back around towards the queen, who was standing by Failinis. She had a dagger as well, held out ready to strike.

Well, she can defend herself, Tara thought as she took a few deep breaths. Just then Tara saw several ghouls ram Ryan into a pillar of rock, causing it to break. Some kind of gas was now leaking from it into the air.

"Ryan!" Tara could barely call out. The gas was causing everyone to start coughing. Then the ceiling started shaking, and pieces of it were falling down. They could see light breaking through the darkness of the cave. The ghosts and ghouls screamed and retreated into the cracks and tunnels of the cavern. The huge face of Leonard peered down to them.

"Leonard!" Ryan yelled, standing and shaking his head. Oren yelled as he still fought Don Pater, who was not giving up quickly. "Quick, grab the queen and Tara!" Then Leonard's huge hand came down, grabbing Tara and the queen. They were lifted up and out of the cavern. Leonard set them down on the grass. They were both coughing. Tara had to support herself on a tree trunk. She felt sick, as she coughed and coughed. Then, out of the cave fleeing were Don Pater's warriors, followed by Oren and his warriors, Lou, Beira, Failinis, and a bear.

"Leonard!" yelled Oren. "Take them to safety!"

Leonard nodded, and again scooped Tara and the queen up and started running. The jarring motion did not help Tara's stomach, and she felt like her whole insides were mush. He then set them back down when they were near a castle. "There, Queen Moorigan. Tara."

The queen turned to Tara.

Tara breathed in the fresh air.

*
* *

22

Prince Keegan

The queen just stood there. Then she rushed over to Tara and embraced her. Even though Tara was surprised by this action, she did hug the queen back. "Oh, my sweet girl." She let Tara go and smiled. Small wrinkles could be seen around her eyes, but otherwise she looked fairly young.

"You will be safe here. I am sure that was not easy for you, fighting and freeing us as you did." The queen's expression was one of gratitude. She turned to look up at Leonard.

"Thank you, Leonard," the queen said.

Tara was a bit surprised. "You know each other?"

"Oh yes. Leonard has been a huge help to us during the war." The queen adjusted the belt around her waist. It could have been the light, but Tara thought it looked as though the queen was expecting.

"What about the others?" Tara looked around, but there was no one was in sight.

"This is my brother's castle. But he is fighting, so we will be safe here." Leonard looked around. 9

The queen smiled at Tara. "You must be hungry, thirsty, and tired. Come, we will find what we need inside." The queen then started walking closer to the castle, her hair glistening in the sunlight.

"This is my mother?" Tara was not sure she believed it, she did not mention that others claimed she was the missing princess. Also, the stones on her necklace confirmed it. .

The queen looked back at Tara as they climbed a huge hill and smiled. She was very beautiful. As they crested the hill, Tara could see the bigger view of the castle. The castle was enormous, and Tara stared at it in awe .

Leonard greeted a giant who was guarding the castle. "Hi, Hubert. Queen Moorigan and guest need some refreshments." The guard bowed as they walked past, but he stood where he was. Leonard led them to a kitchen. "I will find you something to eat and drink." He bent down and whispered, "Oh don't worry. Since we entertain all the time we have small dishes and seating." He stood back up and disappeared through a door.

Tara looked around at everything: massive tables, chairs, and other things. She laughed out loud.

"What is so funny?" the queen asked.

Tara turned to her. "Have you heard of the story of Jack and the Beanstalk?"

The queen looked at her, puzzled. "No, I have not."

Tara shrugged her shoulders. "Never mind," she said as Leonard came in with a small table, chairs, and food in a basket. He set everything down. "Let me go get the drinks," he told them. He left again, but shortly came back with a tiny pitcher of milk and a basket full of glasses. They sat down and ate, but it felt a bit awkward. The queen did not eat much, but Tara was starved. She filled her plate and her glass full of milk. Leonard sat at the huge table, and he only had a drink and an apple.

"Leonard!" someone called. The loud voice made Tara and the queen jump. The kitchen door opened. "Oh, there you are. Oberon is wanting to see the three of you." It was a giant Tara had never seen. He left as quickly as he came.

"Come on, your majesty," Leonard said, bending down.

"We can't keep the king waiting."

"All right, Leonard. We're coming," she said, getting up. Tara followed closely behind them.

When they got outside, Tara was not prepared for what she saw. Sitting on a warrior's horse, dressed for battle, was Mark.

"Mark!" Tara cried, and ran toward him. He jumped down off of his horse and they embraced.

Oberon was beside him on his own horse. Tara had never imagined seeing Mark atop a warrior's horse, dressed in battle gear. His blond, wavy hair seemed to glisten in the sunlight.

"Your majesty, so glad you are found and are safe," Oberon said as he bowed and then got off his own horse. Tara and Mark broke their embrace.

"May I present Prince Keegan of Erin," said Oberon. Mark bowed, and the queen, who had caught up with them, lowered her head and smiled.

"So, the missing prince has been found. So good to have your safe return as well Prince Keegan."

"Ah, yes," Oberon said, forcing a smile holding up his pointer finger and then pulling the queen aside.

Mark looked at Tara. "Tara, I can explain," he said.

Tara backed away. "Explain! Yeah, you should! But I'm not sure I want to hear it! You knew this whole time! All about the Higher realms and –" She started walking away from him towards the gardens.

"I'm sorry, Tara." He came up alongside her. "Really." Tara walked faster, trying to keep a distance from him. However, he had no problem catching up to her. "Tara, just hear me out."

She stopped walking but kept her back to him. "I don't even know if I can trust you."

Tara heard Mark sigh. "I don't blame you." He walked until he was in front of her. "Look. I am sorry. It's complicated."

Tara laughed. "Complicated. Yeah, okay." She went over and sat on a rock near a huge hedge.

"Look, I left my kingdom because my brothers tried to kill me. I ran from them. I was only eight. I ran and got lost and I found myself in Arizona. I was scared, alone, and in a strange place." He was walking around in front of Tara, kind of pacing in a circle. She listened to him as he continued. "The police found me, and I ended up in the system. I was placed with the Weatherbees. They took me in, no questions asked, and then adopted me. I was very young. Most of what I remember are bits and pieces."

Tara looked at him then. "Still. All this time you knew."

He walked closer to her. "What, about you? No. Well, not until the castle. Then I knew – well, I suspected. I was going to tell you, several times. What do you want? I was eight. I did not remember a lot about where I came from. A few things, yeah, but not enough to convince you of anything." He sighed. "Besides. I was trying to forget."

Tara stood. "And yet you said nothing! Even when we met Beira and Lou, or when you met

Ettrick." Her hands were trembling. She folded her arms to hopefully make them stop.

Mark ruffled his hair with his fingers. "Look. I had a lot at stake, Tara. Your safety was at stake as well. I did tell Oberon, who then told Oren, and, well it got around." His cheeks turned red.

"Really?" Tara started walking away.

"What was I going to say to you? Oh, by the way I am from a place called Erin, in the Higher Realms. I am a prince actually." He came up alongside her almost laughing. "You wouldn't have believed me." His face turned somber. "Besides, I was scared to come back, and I did not even know how to, anyway."

Tara was not laughing. Tears ran down her face. He stopped her by touching her arm. "Tara. I truly am sorry." She whirled around and faced him.

"Come on, Mark. We have known each other for a long time. Could you not trust me?"

"You're right. We have, and I should have told you."

She just stood there, stiff as a statue. She was taking in everything he had told her. She started to realize how awful and scary it probably was for him to come back.

"Did they hurt you?" she asked him in a softer tone.

"Who? The Red Caps?" He let his arm fall to his side. "Uh, not too bad, I guess. They brought me to my brothers." Tara sucked in her breath. "Yeah, I bet you can guess how well that went. I escaped. Barely alive though. My father's army found me, thank goodness." Tara felt a bit guilty for being mad at him.

"How did that go?"

"What? Seeing my Dad?"

"Yeah." Tara pushed a rock away from her foot with the front part of her shoe.

"It was great, but weird. He was happy, He thought I was dead."

"How awful!" Tara exclaimed.

"I am fine though. Really." He nudged her arm. "How are you?"

Tara shrugged her shoulders. "I'm okay, I guess." They started walking up to the castle.

"Tara, I would have told you, really I would have," Mark said, and Tara let out a huge sigh. She realized that she could not really be angry with him. She also realized that if he had told her, she might not have believed him. She probably would have thought he was crazy. At least until they came to the Higher Realms.

"How is Anne?" he asked as they kept walking.

"Anne is okay. She had a pretty bad concussion. Ryan told me she is still recovering."

Mark's face contorted, and he looked like he was in pain. "I had told her to run. I told her to change into a bear. She kept saying she couldn't. I knew they had done something to her but I didn't know what. I was knocked out cold and I guess they took me. Oren told me that she had been hurt."

"Cian found her covered in blood, left for dead. She was in pretty bad shape," Tara told him. He sighed and his shoulders heaved forward.

They walked in silence for a while, turning a corner when they saw the castle. Leonard, the queen, and several warriors were waiting for them. Oberon had left, or so it seemed but waiting there was Oren and Ryan.

"Where is King Kenneth?" Tara asked.

"Probably joined his army, to engage in the war," Mark said to her.

"Of course," Tara thought. The High King had gone missing, he now was found and freed, and needed to fight in the war."

"So, your real name is Keegan," Tara said as they walked closer.

"Yeah. Prince Keegan of Erin."

They walked up the hill where they were greeted by Oren. "Tara," he said as she smiled and hugged him.

"Hello, Oren."

He bowed slightly at Mark. "Prince Mark-Keegan."

"Hello, Oren."

"So." Oren leaned in towards Tara. "You had a talk?"

Tara nodded her head. "Yeah, we did."

"Good," he said, smiling. Mark called over his horse, and several warriors came as well.

"Did he also tell you that he is leaving?" Oren asked her.

Tara looked at Mark. "Leaving? Why?"

Mark walked over to her, holding the reins to his horse. "I need to join my father. He has joined King Kenneth's army. The battle is still going on."

Tara's eyes widened. "You don't know." She got out the bag from underneath her cape. "I found it. The Fairy Flag." She pulled it out, and the queen gasped and rushed over. Oren grinned, and Mark looked stunned.

The queen came closer and reached out to touch the silky fabric.

"You found the flag?" The queen looked stunned. "Oberon tells me you are the princess, and only my daughter could have found the flag. Yet you are older."

Tara shrugged. "I did find it." She held up her necklace. "I have this too."

The queen looked closely at the necklace and shook her head and sucked in her breath quickly. "That is the bracelet King Kenneth had made for baby Brigette." She started sobbing and a guard came over and had her sit down.

"Will she be alright?" Tara asked Oren as he came closer.

"She will be, in time." He looked over at Queen Moorigan then back at Tara.

"We must get that to King Kenneth," Oren told her.

"How though?" Tara asked. She knew King Kenneth was a great distance away by this point.

"Where is Snowberry?" Oren asked.

"Here," Ryan said, coming up from behind him and holding Snowberry and his horse's reins. A wave of relief washed over her when she saw him, and she smiled. Mark smiled back at her. He looked pretty good – a bit dirty, but otherwise fine. Mark got up on his horse. She saw that Ryan had her pack, and his as well. She went over and patted Snowberry, and as she grabbed her pack she smiled again at Ryan.

Oren came over to where they stood. "It is my duty to see you all to safety."

"What about Mark?" Tara asked, getting up into the saddle.

"Sorry Tara, I have to go."

"You promised me –" she broke off what she was going to say.

Mark frowned. "Sorry Tara, I..."

A warrior rode over to Mark. "Come, Prince Keegan. Your father awaits." Tara watched as he left, riding his horse and surrounded by many warriors. She wanted to yell, or call out to him. Anything to stop him from going, but she hesitated. He briefly looked back at her, then urged his horse to greater speed. She felt the tears coming, heat rising in her chest. Ryan's horse whinnied as he came up alongside hers. She looked at him briefly before wiping at her face and followed as Oren led the way.

23

Enemies and Allies

Tara followed Oren quietly. She did not want to make a scene. The queen rode a beautiful dark horse slightly behind her, and Leonard walked beside the queen's horse.

Ettrick poked his head from out of her bag. "Well, that went rather well." Tara was surprised to see him. "Ettrick! Where have you been?"

He got a bit comfortable before answering her, "Fighting of course. You know, there is a war going on."

Tara rolled her eyes. "Yes. I know there is a war going on."

"I had to check on ye. Also, you found the flag."

Tara nodded. "Yes. Also, Mark was here."

"You mean Prince Keegan." Ettrick sat up straighter.

"Yeah, Prince Keegan." She didn't really want to talk about him, even though she brought him up.

"Ye know Tara. He really couldn't tell you."

She shot him a nasty look. "No? Okay, and how long did you know who he was?"

His face fell. "I suspected it. Not long after he came to the Higher Realms." He shifted in the bag. "Look Tara, I don't want to be arguing with ya."

Ryan had slowed down and was now by Tara. "What's wrong?" he asked as Ettrick peeked out of her bag further. "Ah Ettrick. How's it goin'?"

"Fine, young Lord McMahon. Just checking in with Tara."

"Has Oberon given you a break?"

The brownie laughed a bit. "He has told me to keep an eye out fer Tara and get back to helping her, but he keeps me running around so I barely can catch me breath." Ryan laughed.

"Sounds like him." Ettrick stayed where he was for a while, and even fell asleep. Tara let him sleep. For once it was nice that he did not just disappear.

It was getting dark as they came to a small clearing in the trees. "We will rest here for a bit," Oren told them, jumping off his horse. A mist was drifting in. Ryan looked around, sniffing the air.

Ettrick jumped out of Tara's bag. "Trouble?"

Ryan looked at him and jumped off his horse. "Nah, we're good. Oren will take first shift as lookout." He helped Tara down and got out their sleeping bags from his pack. The mist was really rolling in now. Oren was patrolling around on foot, as Queen Moorigan was making a fire. She was pretty self-reliant, or at least she seemed to be. There was no way Tara could ever build a fire, not on her own at least. She supposed she could learn. The queen kept her distance, but occasionally Tara would catch the queen staring at her. Tara thought about how difficult it must be to have had your infant daughter stolen, then some stranger come along with others claiming she is the lost baby. Tara wanted to be accepted and loved, however so far it wasn't going well. She hoped in time everything would smooth out, and once the king and queen got confirmation that she was who others said she was that everything would be better.

Tara was trying to sleep, lying in her sleeping bag and looking at the fire. The ground was hard, and her body ached for her comfy bed at home. The fire would occasionally crackle and send up sparks into the mist. Then she thought she heard her name. Tara looked around. No one else seemed to have heard it. She saw Oren standing on a huge rock several feet from the campsite. Tara was curious as to who or what was calling to her. She grabbed the horn and slung it over her neck. She grabbed her cloak, her dagger, and her bow and quiver. She quickly put her hood up as she quietly stepped away from the fire and into the mist. The mist seemed to swirl all around her. She soon found herself going in circles.

"Where are you headed to?"

Tara turned around with a start. "Ugh. Ryan, you scared me."

He stood there, not amused. "So. Where do you think you are going?" She looked around. "These are the Clohinne Hills, Tara. You just can't go wandering around." He held up a torch. "Really, what on earth were you thinking?"

She rolled her eyes. "Oh, I don't know."

Ryan got out his sword. "I thought I heard—" She paused. "I am not sure of anything, or of anywhere, or anyone."

Ryan sighed. "Look I am here to protect you, and because I want to be. It's Prince Keegan, isn't it?"

Tara felt bad for sneaking off. "I don't know. Anyway, I thought I heard my name being called."

Ryan looked at her. "Really. And you just thought, 'Oh, let me find out who, or what is calling me'?"

Tara shrugged her shoulders.

It was Ryan's turn to roll his eyes. "So, what?! You thought you would just go check it out on your own? Really, Tara." He stood there, holding the torch high above him.

"Come on, we are not safe here." He went to grab her arm. "Wait. Listen. Did you hear that?" Ryan looked around, holding out his torch. Then they heard it. Tara's name in the mist. "Okay, and that doesn't creep you out?" He started walking. "Come on let's keep moving," he said firmly, looking wearily about. They heard it again. Ryan growled, which made Tara jump.

"Don't do that Ryan."

He looked at her and sniffed the air. Then he sneezed. "Fairies." He sniffed the air again. "Smell that?" He stopped walking, putting his finger up to his mouth. She could smell it now. It was wood burning.

Tara leaned into him. "What is it?"

He pointed to the left. Tara could barely make out a campfire. It wasn't theirs, though. "A fairy camp." They slowly moved in the direction of the fire. Ryan stopped short. "Trolls," he told her. As the mist cleared away a bit, she could see them. They were sitting around the fire. The trolls were huge—almost as big as giants. They had huge noses and long, straggly hair and wore big, baggy clothes. However, they did not look scary. Sitting among them were fairies, and they were all talking. Then one fairy paused and looked their way.

"Who's there?" the queen asked, standing as the mist cleared away from her. Everyone was silent, although Tara was sure they all could hear her heart beating. It was a female fairy, and she had long, wavy blond hair. On top of her head was a tall crown. She had on a long, flowing cream-colored dress with a blue outer dress, which looked kind of like a jacket.

Then Tara felt a sharp blade to her back. "Don't move," she heard a female's voice say. Tara noticed Ryan grimace, and he had something in his back too. Possibly the end of a sword, thought Tara.

"Come forward," the female fairy said as they were nudged ahead.

Tara tripped on her own feet. "Easy," said the female voice behind her.

"We mean no harm, Queen Gloriana," Ryan said.

The queen looked at Tara. "I recognize her from some meetings she attended with my father at the manor." Tara nodded.

The female fairy glided forward, the mist swirling around her. "At ease, Britomart." Tara felt the sharp blade leave her back. Ryan shook himself and stood closer to Tara.

"Britomart," Ryan said with clenched teeth. The woman warrior gave him a stern look, but said nothing. Tara got the feeling they were not friends.

Britomart stood by the fairy queen. Britomart was dressed like a warrior in full battle gear. She had two swords, and Tara saw she too was a fairy. The trolls stood behind them.

The fairy queen smiled. "So. We finally meet, young Lord McMahon." She then looked at Tara. "This is the princess?"

She smiled at Tara.

"Yes. This is Princess Tara-Brigit," Ryan said, pushing Tara forward slightly. Tara lowered her hood

"It hasn't been confirmed yet," Tara said smiling nervously.

The fairy queen nodded. "Come. Join me by the fire. We haven't much time."

Tara and Ryan walked over as the mist became thick behind them. "Were you the one calling me?" Tara asked the fairy queen.

Queen Gloriana smiled and nodded. "I have something to read to you. It is an old scroll" She paused and looked around. The trolls stayed standing. Tara found herself looking at them often as the conversation went on. "You are traveling as I am," the fairy queen said. "As we speak, my husband joins King Oberon. These are not safe passageways we take. Hence the mist." She held up her hand as a sheet of mist rolled off her palm and onto the ground as it spread.

"You made the mist?" Tara found herself asking.

The queen smiled. "It protects me and my company." She put her arm down as the mist swirled away from her. "I don't really make it; it just responds to my call." She stiffened for an instant and then relaxed. "You must listen and then rejoin your party."

A troll came over and handed the queen a scroll. The queen thanked the troll, who smiled, bowed, and then turned to Tara and Ryan and bowed again. "Princess. Lord McMahon." He then rejoined the other trolls. He had a kind voice, which made Tara kind of smile.

"So, Princess. Missing your home, are you not?"

Tara looked at the fairy queen, and Ryan put an arm around Tara's shoulders. "She is not from here. She—"

The fairy queen cut him off. "I am well aware, young Lord McMahon, where she came from, and her circumstances." She opened the scroll. "I will read this now, if I may?" Tara sat on the edge of the stump she sat on by the fire. "You are restless, and we have tarried here far too long. However, I think you need to hear what this scroll says."

Tara nodded, her throat feeling dry as she tried to swallow. The fairy queen held up the scroll and cleared her throat. She then began to read, "The Earth, the Sky, and the Sea Realms are ever present. The Center is Tara, where the ancient kings dwell. The three realms are sacred to the ancient Celts. They are the powers by which our ancestors—" she stopped, looked at Tara and said, "your ancestors," and then continued reading the scroll, "swore oaths. Powers that make up this world and the otherworld. The mists of Ireland shall shield the four treasures for all time until such hour as the need shall arise to defend once more Enchanted Emerald Shores."

She then rolled up the scroll and stood, and then she handed the scroll to Tara. The trolls circled the fairy queen, as did her warrior Britomart. "Go now! mountain trolls are near," the fairy queen said as the mist grew thick. It became so thick that Tara no longer could see the fairy queen or her company, or the light the fire had given.

"Tara, put my clothes in your bag," Ryan said. Tara shook her head, looking his way and then looking away again. "Hurry! Come on!" Ryan shoved his clothes in her hand. She quickly bent down and put them in her bag as he gave her more. She did not dare look at him, knowing he stood before her naked. She then heard a snorting sound as the wet nose of a bear touched her cheek. Tara quickly stood as she heard grunting noises and yelling through the mist. She quickly put the scroll in her bag as well.

"Get on," Ryan said quietly as the grunting noise got louder. Once she was on his back, she had to lean down and grab the fur on his neck to keep from falling off as he started running. Tara closed her eyes as the mist parted for a second. Standing there were three huge, dark green trolls. Ryan skidded to a halt and started running in a different direction. The trolls had shiny green skin; some had spikes on their backs and long arms with huge clawed hands. They also had long, sharp teeth.

"Those are nothing like the rock trolls," Tara called out as Ryan ran. They wore crude armor and had crude weapons. But Tara guessed they could still kill them. Tara was looking around just as Ryan was changing direction, and out of the mist came a huge, clawed green hand and grabbed Ryan's front leg. Tara screamed as she fell off of his back.

"Tara! Run!" Ryan yelled. Tara quickly got up and started running, but she couldn't tell where she was going because the fog was so thick. She tripped over a rock that jutted out from somewhere and fell on her knees. The palms of her hands hit the ground hard. "Ouch!"

Just as she was getting up, there stood a troll. "Got you now, my sweet," he said as Tara looked at him, horrified, and then started running to his right. With the troll right behind her, she did not see the cliff's edge until she went to step and nothing was there. She screamed as she fell, her cries echoing off the cliff's side. Her hand hit a tree root, and she grabbed it. She saw her bow slide off her back, and she tried grabbing it but missed.

"Son of a biscuit!" she yelled as she heard the distant roar of a bear. She grabbed the root with her other hand, and her left foot found a foothold. She then tried several times to get her right foot secure. Once it was, she leaned in close to the cliff's side, and it smelled of wet earth. She tried to slow her breathing and her heart. She heard loud yells and hollering from the trolls, but the fog made it hard to hear clearly. She started shaking, even though her cloak hid her from the cool, misty fog. She did not know how long she had been there; she only knew her body was getting weak. She didn't have enough energy to climb up, nor did she want to. Those trolls were scary, and Ryan was nowhere to be seen or heard. She couldn't even grab her whistle to blow it, since she did not dare let go of the tree's root. Her head bobbed up as she slipped a bit. She was dozing off to sleep.

"Come on Tara, stay awake," she told herself out loud. Then she heard a whooshing sound and then her name being called. "Here! I'm here!" she called out to Oren, who was now next to her. The fog was receding now she noticed, and the morning's sun was trying to break through the mist.

Oren had wings. Huge, black, beautiful wings, which were tipped with a cream color that matched his hair. How come she had never noticed them before? He came closer to her. "Oren?"

"Oh, Tara, thank goodness you are alive." He grabbed ahold of her shaking body as he carried and flew her up to the top of the cliff. The sun was just barely burning away the mist as he set her down, and she just collapsed onto the ground.

"I thought they would kill me," she said, looking up at him.

"They would have, if they had gotten ahold of you," Oren said as he started pacing. "And what business do you have going off wandering again! The king would have had my head, had I not found you!"

Tara stood on shaky legs. "What king?"

He stopped pacing. "Take your pick, princess. There's only about seven who would gladly take my head if you were harmed or killed!" He came closer, pointing and shaking his finger at her. "You have caused me more grief wandering off." He looked up into the sky, which was getting clearer now. "Guard the princess,' they said, 'it will be a piece of cake they said. Yeah right."

Tara stood in front of Oren, about to burst into tears. He came closer and looked down at her. "I'm sorry," Tara said apologetically. She looked down at the ground then at her hands. They were bleeding.

Oren sighed relaxing his stance. "Oh look at you, you're bleeding. Here." He came over and lifted her hands in his. "Come on, let's go back to the camp. I will bandage you up, and then we need to leave."

"Where's Ryan?"

"Don't you worry about him. He can take care of himself." However, she was worried—what if those big, ugly trolls took him away?

"Come on," Oren said gently as he comfortingly pulled her along and led the way, cautiously at first, and then he walked faster. Tara was having a hard time keeping up, her pants were rubbing on her knees, and she was sure they were injured as well.

"Oren!" Tara called out, not able to keep up. Oren slowed down.

"I didn't know you had wings," she said as he walked beside her now.

"I do. I do not use them often, as they use up more of my energy."

They walked side by side for a while.

"Well they're amazing." She shyly smiled at him, and he smiled back. Tara had her arms folded, shielding her bloody palms. They were hurting now. Throbbing, actually. Oren stopped her. "Let me see." She held out her hands. Oren got out some cloth and some kind of ointment, which he put on the cloth and then wrapped up her hands. "This will take some of the sting away, at least until we get back." He then abruptly stopped talking, as if he had something else to say. However, he must have thought better of it. He looked at her, all of a sudden angry like an older brother who was mad at a younger sibling. "Why on earth would you go running off in the Clohinne Hills?"

Tara now felt guilty as she realized what could have happened, and where was Ryan?

"These hills, Tara, there is powerful magic here."

"I thought I heard my name being called." Oren did not lecture her anymore, he just listened. "Someone was. A fairy named Gloriana."

Oren stopped walking. "Gloriana. Of course. Blast."

Tara was not sure what he was upset about, so she continued. "She gave me a scroll, and—"

"Keep walking," he told her. He seemed annoyed. She had to catch up with him again. He was tall, so he took long strides. "Let me guess, she didn't help you when the trolls came?"

"She warned us," Tara told him.

He laughed a throaty laugh. "Right. Why should she risk her own neck?" He stomped more when he walked, talking to himself. "When I see her next, I am going to *wring* her neck."

He was obviously mad, so Tara decided it was best to just be quiet and follow him. They got to the camp, but no one was there. Oren quickly gathered his things. "Grab your pack." He whistled and his horse came out of the thicket, along with Snowberry. He grabbed their reins.

She looked over at Ryan's pack. "Leave it. He will come back for it." She got out Ryan's clothes from her bag, wincing from the pain in her hands. She set the clothes on top of his pack. Oren kicked at the fire, and once he was done and it was completely out, they couldn't even tell people had camped there.

He got out a small satchel and said, "Come here, let me have a look at you."

She held up her hands. He sighed. The blood was seeping through. "I will rebandage your hands. Are you hurt anywhere else?"

"I think my knees." He looked down at her dirty knees. Blood was seeping through her pants, and one bloody knee was exposed were the pant leg was ripped a bit. He tore some cloth and applied the same salve ointment he had for her hands onto the cloth.

"Drop your drawers."

Tara looked at him, horrified. He smirked and held out a blanket. "I won't look." He turned around. "Wrap the blanket around yourself after you sit down. I need to look at your knees."

She did as he instructed and was waiting for him to turn around. However, when she looked up, he was already waiting to clean her knee wounds. It stung when he put the salve on her cut and bloody knees.

"Sorry. There." He got out clean pieces of cloth and placed them on her knees, and then he ripped some more and wrapped them up. He then put stuff back in his satchel and walked over to his horse.

"So much for bedside manners," she thought. "Great warrior, not so great a doctor." Still, he got the job done.

"Your leg is healing nicely though," he told her.

Tara looked around as she pulled up her pants. Her cut on her leg where she had stitches actually was healing nicely. She did not even see the stitches anymore. "Must be magic," she thought to herself.

"Where is everyone else?"

He got up onto his horse. "They left. When you and Ryan didn't return, I sent them on. Then I went looking for you." He trotted over, handing her Snowberry's reins. She handed him the blanket. She had trouble climbing up, so Oren got off his horse and picked her up, then set her in the saddle.

"We have a three-day journey. Let's hope for no more excitement, shall we?" He smiled and then got up on his horse, then turned his horse as he trotted down the path. Tara looked behind her. She saw Ryan's pack sitting there in the clearing. It looked so lonely sitting there by itself with the mist lingering a bit but now starting to clear away. "Come on, princess. Don't worry about young Lord McMahon." Tara gently kicked Snowberry's sides so she could catch up to Oren.

*
* *
# 24

Oren

They traveled all day, only taking short breaks. Now they were stopping to eat and rest.

"Will Ryan catch up to us?" Tara asked.

Oren looked up at her. He was bent over the fire, adding more wood. "Most likely, but not until we reach the castle."

This didn't make Tara happy at all. "So, you think he is alive and okay?"

He nodded. "Yes, I am sure he is fine. He was only guarding you while I was away. He was supposed to keep an eye on you while I was on patrol. Now I'm here, and you will not escape me a third time." He made it sound as if she was his prisoner. No—more like he was an older, protective brother. He stood and stretched.

"Ryan came with me."

He shot her a look. "Only a fool would go out in the mist in the hills." He paused. "He was doing what was asked of him."

"Oh," Tara said. "I thought…" She didn't finish, but she had wanted to say that Ryan had come to look for her to protect her and help her because he cared for her.

Oren went over to his horse and got out a rolled-up blanket. He set it on the ground. They were near some trees in a field.

"I am going to get some rest. Do not, under any circumstances, leave. Got it?"

She smiled. "I won't." He lay down and let out a huge sigh. Soon he was sleeping, occasionally grunting in his sleep. Tara quietly heated some food and ate it, watching the sun go down. She watched as Snowberry and Oren's horse grazed in the field. The last golden rays of the sun, with magnificent oranges and reds, glistened on the tall grass and the horses. and she was daydreaming when Oren cleared his throat.

She looked over at him. "It really is beautiful here," she told him as he sat up and looked out across the field.

"Beautiful and dangerous," Oren said and then stood. Tara nodded. "I'm going to get more firewood," Oren said. Tara watched him go into the woods. If she was older, she would probably want to date him, even though he was not human. She shook her head and thought, Crap. Crushing on a fairy. An older fairy too, although if he were human, he would be about twenty or so. Then again, he was drop-dead gorgeous. Long blond hair, very nice detailed facial features, like his strong chin. Muscles. She shook her head. Tara sighed and looked at her hands. The blood was seeping through the bandages a lot more.

Oren came back, holding a pile of wood. He added some to the fire and then looked over at her. He grabbed his satchel. "Bled through, did it?"

"Yeah." Tara nodded as he knelt down. She watched as he got fresh bandages and winced when he removed the old ones. "When you hold the reins, only do so with the tips of your fingers, Princess." He paused.

"Snowberry does not need you to guide her when she will follow me." He started to bandage her left hand. She hadn't realized while they rode that she had clutched on tightly to Snowberry's reins.

"I'm sorry," she said softly.

He looked at her earnestly. "It's okay. I am just glad you are alive." He sat by her on the ground.

"Can I see what Gloriana gave you?"

Tara looked at her bag, which was close to her side. "It's in my bag."

He grabbed it. "May I?" Tara nodded as he looked in it. Getting out the scroll, he opened it. When he was done, he looked at her.

"An ancient scroll." He leaned in closer. She saw now that it was written in gold ink, and not in English. It was a very flowery writing.

"Did she read it to you?'

"Yeah. She told me it would help me."

He got more comfortable by her side and let out a deep breath. "And yet she would not help you and Ryan when the trolls came. She just fled," he muttered. He held up the scroll. He read it out loud, first in fairy language. Or was it some form of elfish language? She didn't know. Then he read it in English. It sounded so dreamy and ancient.

He looked at her. "Do you ever wonder, why all the fuss? About you, or the flag?"

She looked at him with a puzzled look. "I don't know, I guess so."

"There are those who are born to do great things Tara, and those who do small things—many small things that lead to big results. You may not know it, but for you it is all in the same."

She laughed a bit as he sat next to her. "I am not a hero, if that's what you mean."

"Say what you like, but I know you, and I know a bit of your destiny." He stretched out his legs and got out a stone from a bag he had tied around his waist.

He held it up to her and said, "This is a seeing stone. Or seer stone. Ever seen one?" Tara shook her head. "My father gave this to me after Oberon was crowned king. Right before my father died, he told me that, even though I would not be king, I still would do great things." He smiled then as he held up the stone in the dwindling twilight. The light seemed to soak through the stone when Tara saw an image—

just a fleeting image of a woman standing proud and tall, wearing a beautiful, green dress with gold trim, a crown on her head, her long red hair gently flowing in the breeze. Tara was mesmerized. "Who is she?" Tara asked as the image faded with the last of the brighter twilight.

"It is you. Or will be you." Tara just stared at him in awe. How could that be? She was only just barely turning sixteen. That woman was easily in her late twenties: a queen, strong, proud, and regal.

"This stone aids me in seeing the past, present and future. It was with this stone that I was able to track the Famorians, and track were the babe had gone. However, traveling to the mortal world is tricky for a fairy of my size. So, my brother Oberon, Tina and I devised a plan. Many years had passed in the mortal world before we actually found you, and we had to be sure. You going to see the Fairy flag at that castle triggered my stone, and Queen Titiana decided to contact you first." He handed her the stone, which felt soft and smooth and warm.

"I have dreams. Most never made sense until I came here."

Oren nodded his head. "You have many gifts, Tara. Others will come as you figure out how to use them." Tara handed him back the stone. Oren sat back against a rock. They both looked up as the last of the sun's rays clung to the horizon.

"Tell you one thing, princess. When King Kenneth raises that flag, the other kingdom's army will crumble, and that will be a glorious sight to see and the start of something good. You'll see." He smiled as Tara watched the last of the sun's rays fade away until the stars came out, one by one.

"You should rest now, Tara-Brigit," he grunted as he stood. "I will stand watch. I got enough rest earlier." She nodded and laid down on her sleeping bag. It was a warm night as she lay there listening to the crackle of the fire and the sounds of the night bugs. She wondered what Mark was doing now and thought about all of the stuff she had been through. She was worried about Ryan; was he okay? Was he hurt? She also wondered how her family back home was. Did they miss her? Did they even know she was gone?

Oren got out a small musical flute type of instrument and started playing. The peaceful music lulled Tara to sleep. The next morning, she felt very stiff and sore. Her hands hurt too much to do anything.

Oren was packing up camp when Tara stood up slowly. Oren handed her a mug of warm tea and some pain medicine. "Drink the whole cup." He smiled at her then. The tea had an awful bitter taste, but she drank the whole thing.

"Thank you for the music last night. It was beautiful."

"You're welcome."

He started packing his saddle and then hers. "We ride again all day." Tara rolled her eyes. The combination of the heat of the day and the pain meds were causing Tara to feel sleepy in the saddle. Every now and again Oren would click his tongue, and Snowberry would trot faster, jolting Tara awake. She wasn't even really holding onto the reins. At one point, she gave in and rested on Snowberry's neck. They didn't talk much as they rode on the dusty paths and then through fields, streams, and woods. As they rode, they saw a herd of deer grazing far in a field, but otherwise they came across no one. By the time they stopped that evening, Tara could hardly keep her eyes open, and her bottom was sore. Again, that night she slept fine, and there was a slight breeze that cooled her as she slept. On the third day, they again were on rocky terrain. At one point, Tara got off of Snowberry's back and walked beside her instead.

"Oren. Have you ever been to Earth? I mean, where I was raised?"

He looked back at her, puzzled. "Your Earth?"

"Yeah. I was just curious if fairies went there."

He smiled. "We do all the time, it's just people in your world are so busy. You scarcely even notice."

That made her sad as she thought about it. "Oren? Why did you agree to be my guard? I mean, you could have said no, then you could be fighting in the war."

Oren stopped his horse. "I have been fighting in the war. Besides, there are greater things in this life than fighting in a war. I look at it like this: you needed a guard, I was asked, I am honored, and your well-being is important in the grand scheme of things. I have and will still use my skills in battle."

"But you agreed without even knowing me."

He smiled. "True. If I had known you would have a tendency to run off and be such a nuisance, I would have asked for more backup." He laughed and prodded his horse to keep going. Tara made a face, but he did not see it.

When they came around a bend, sitting high up on a rock by the path was Ryan. "Ah. Young Lord McMahon," Oren greeted him.

Tara was so relieved and thrilled to see him there that she couldn't contain her happiness. She ran up to him as he jumped down, pack still on his back.

"Oh, come on, Oren. You didn't think I would let you escort the princess all the way alone, did you?" Ryan teased. Oren laughed as Tara and Ryan embraced. Ryan placed the warm palm of his hand on her cheek. He had a large bandage on his arm. "It's nothing," he told her as they started walking. Ryan hung back and walked alongside Snowberry right by Tara's side. Arrow flew overhead.

"Where is my horse?" Ryan asked.

Tara shrugged her shoulders.

Oren looked back. "I sent him back, young Lord. You don't mind walking now, do you?"

Tara stopped Snowberry as Ryan jumped on and tied his pack to the saddle. He then pulled Tara up, and she sat behind him.

"Ah, so he does mind," Oren said, chuckling to himself.

"I have been running for two days, so no way am I walking." Ryan's tone made it clear he was not amused. That made Oren laugh even harder.

Tara leaned forward. "I lost my bow and quiver when I fell off the cliff."

"I found it," Ryan said as he leaned sideways. "It's tied to my pack." Tara was relieved to hear that. She glanced down and saw a part of it sticking out behind his pack. "You fell off the cliff? By the look of your hands, you caught hold of the thorn vines."

She looked down at her hands. The bleeding had stopped somewhat. "Oh, is that what they were? I didn't know. I was just glad they were there so I didn't fall."

"They give nasty cuts with their poisonous thorns. The fall is a thousand-foot drop to the sea below, with nasty rocks."

"Oh." Tara hadn't known. There was so much she didn't know. She could have died.

"Those details are not helpful now, young Lord McMahon," Oren said.

"Of course, you didn't realize," Ryan said. "You were running for your life, and you do not know that much about The Higher Realms." He kissed her cheek as they rode along. Tara's face turned bright red. "Oren didn't tell you?" He asked. Tara shook her head.

"I was saving her the worry, young Lord," Oren called out. By the time they reached the castle it was getting dark. It was a huge castle, with many sections of dark stone. The guards let them pass, and the path that led to the bridge was fairly long. They all dismounted as a stable boy came and got the horses.

The queen came out to greet them. "Welcome to my home," she said, smiling. She looked well rested, and her hair looked like it had been braided and then taken out of braids; it was very wavy, and she had the front and sides pulled back. She was wearing a beautiful, velvet, dark green dress. Tara realized that she herself didn't look so presentable. She was filthy and smelled of horses. She'd had a long day on the trail, and was covered with sweat, dirt, and blood.

A few servants came and took their bags. "Come, you must freshen up and join me for dinner," the queen said and turned and walked up the stairs. Tara was floored when they walked into the brightly lit castle. They didn't have electricity, but had lots of lanterns and candles. Three servants were waiting in the hall, lined up and awaiting the queen's orders. "Delphi, take the princess to her room please, and help her wash and dress."

The servant curtsied and spoke softly. "Yes, your majesty." She came up to Tara. "This way, princess." They walked down several hallways and then Delphi opened French doors, and they walked down a few more halls before she paused in front of white doors. "This way please," she said as she opened the doors. Tara gaped at the enormous room. It had a huge chandelier hanging from the ceiling and a plush bed with beautiful bedding. She motioned for Tara to follow her into a massive bathroom. "It will take me a bit to draw you a bath. Would you like refreshments before I get started?"

Tara looked at the girl, who was not much older than herself. "Um, yes, that would be nice." The maid went over near the fireplace and pulled a cord that hanging there. She smiled, curtsied, and then disappeared into the bathroom. A few minutes went by when there was a knock on the door.

"Refreshments." Tara turned to see Alana entering the room, tray in her hands.

"ALANA!" Tara ran towards her, forgetting the pain from her wounds, and Alana quickly set down the tray.

"Tara!"

They embraced. "What! Why are you here? How are you here?" Tara stood there, totally confused.

"Foremaist cuppa 'n' cakes, then ah wull explain." She smiled, and Tara was bursting with excitement. "Och! Whit did ye dae tae yer hauns, Tara?" Alana gently lifted Tara's hands.

"I fell off a cliff." Alana sucked in her breath. "I'm fine, really, just glad the mountain trolls didn't get me."

Alana sucked in her breath again. "Goodness! Mountain Trolls! Cliffs! Guid gracious, bairn." She stood and walked over to the wall near the fireplace and pulled a hanging cord.

"Oh Alana! There is so much to tell you."

"Ah. Hauld yer horses a minute, Tara. Foremaist ah mist tell ye how come a'm 'ere, 'n' a'm needin' tae tak' a keek at yer wounds," she said, walking back over to Tara.

"Oren already cleaned and dressed them," Tara protested. Alana sat down clicking her tongue, and no sooner did she sit than another maid came in. "Lucy, gang 'n' git a wee wash basin, fill it wi' warm water, 'n' add some o' mah cuts 'n' scrapes salts," Alana directed and then smiled at Tara.

"Shall I bring some cotton, Ms. Alana?"

"Aye, 'n' hurry up, lass."

Alana looked at Tara. "Ah wull rewash they wance ah tell ye aboot how come a'm here." Tara just sat there, unable to form a coherent question in her mind. Everything was all jumbled. She just couldn't really register that Alana was there.

"Noo. Ye see, Tara, ah wis a servant in this castle. A nursemaid tae be exact. We wur celebratin' yer birth. Oh, wit a wee babe ye wur, tae." Tara smiled when Alana did, remembering. "Och! Ah wis young, foolish."

"I was stolen, Alana."

"Aye. Ye wur. Richt oot o' yer wee cradle, ye wur."

The maid came in and set down the small wash basin and cloths. Alana set to work undoing the bandages Oren had put on her. "Oren used some yarrow salve, ah see." She cleaned her hands with the warm, soothing mixture while talking, telling Tara how she was very young and foolish for leaving her sleeping in her cradle, and how the king and queen had punished her.

"They banned you from the castle? From the kingdom?" Tara asked, surprised at such a punishment.

"Dinnae blame thaim, thay wur grieving." Tara fidgeted on the sofa. "Aye. That thay did. Ah think mah sister hud a say in that decision. Noo stoap yer fidgetin'." Alana sighed heavily before she put on fresh, clean bandages. "Lea thae oan while ye bathe, mynd ye."

"Yes, I'll leave them on," Tara said. She didn't tell her about her knees. She wasn't about to drop her pants here. "But how did you find me?" she asked.

"Yer fairy blessed, child."

"And by being so, Alana was able to find you," the fairy queen said, entering the room. Tara stood, as did Alana.

"Queen Titiania." Alana bowed her head.

"Even though my sister was forbidden from telling you anything."

"Or telling a'body fur that maiter," Alana piped in. She then mumbled something in Gaelic. Tara turned to face them both as Queen Tina put her arm around Alana's shoulders.

"Alana is my older half-sister, Tara-Brigit."

Tara scrunched up her face. "You two are sisters?"

"Aye," Alana said, smiling. Tara couldn't see a resemblance except maybe that Alana used to have dark hair. "Ah aged rapidly in yer world, Tara." For that Tara felt sorry.

Tara sat down, grabbed a cinnamon flavored cake, and eagerly took a bite. Queen Moorigan came in then, looking refreshed and beautiful. Tara felt like she could use a bath and some clean clothes right away.

The maid came out of the bathroom and was surprised to see others there. "Oh, your majesty." She curtsied to the queen. "And your majesty." She curtsied to the fairy queen. Then she turned to Alana. "The princess's bath is ready."

"Braw, Delphi," Alana said as the maid stood awaiting further instruction.

The queen smiled and stepped towards the door. "I guess we shall leave you to it then." The fairy queen and Alana started to follow her out.

"Come princess, your bath awaits." The maid gestured for Tara to go into the bathroom. Once she was in the tub, she let out a huge sigh. All the stress and tension she had been under started to go away. She lazily looked at her Nike bag that still held the Fairy Flag in it. She never let it leave her side, even while being chased by those gruesome trolls. She repositioned her head, leaning it back against the cool, smooth edge of the porcelain tub. She let the warm water soothe her aching muscles and bones from days of riding on horseback and sleeping on the ground. She started dozing off when the maid gently tapped her on the shoulder.

"Time to get out, Princess." She stood there, holding up a large, plush towel. "You will turn into an old prune if I let you sleep in the tub any longer." She held it so high Tara couldn't see her face. Tara carefully got out, and the maid wrapped the towel around her shoulders. Then she got another towel and started drying Tara's hair. She was very good at what she did, and before Tara knew it she was dressed in a simple yet elegant white cotton dress with light blue trim, and she was sitting at the huge vanity while the maid did her hair. She had said nothing about Tara's skinned up knees but proceeded to bandage them just as how Alana had bandaged her hands.

"You are all grown up, Princess. I used to help Alana give you baths when you were such a tiny baby."

Tara looked at her in the mirror. "Does it bother you I am no longer a baby?"

The maid shrugged her shoulders. "Me? No. Queen Moorigan, Queen Tina, Alana – Yes, I think it bothers them a bit."

"How old are you, Delphi?" Tara paused. "I can call you Delphi?"

The maid laughed. "Yes, you may call me Delphi, Princess. To answer your question, I will be seventeen in a few weeks."

"Oh, well then happy birthday."

"Thank you, Princess," she said, handing Tara a hand mirror. Tara looked at her red hair. It was all up in a French braid that cascaded down the center of her back.

"It looks lovely."

The maid held out a pair of leather flat-soled shoes. "These are yours as well."

Tara slipped her feet into them. They were very comfortable; more than she thought they would be.

"Come Princess, I will show you to the study where the Queen Moorigan awaits your arrival." Tara nodded, grabbed her Nike bag, and followed the maid through the castle. It was grand and, well, amazing. Large tapestries hung on the walls, alongside exquisite paintings and furnishings. It was very grand, even more so than her estate at home.

They approached two guards who were talking just outside of a room. Tara caught a little of their conversation.

"Yes. In the king's tower," said one.

"I would not want that post right now, even if you can kind of see the battle far off," said the other.

The maid touched Tara's sleeve. "Come, Princess." As soon as they were seen and heard, the guards stopped talking and stood up straight at attention like they were their generals approaching. Tara had wanted to hear more, such as where this tower was. However, the maid walked fast, and Tara didn't want to get separated from her. Soon she was in a room that had a huge desk, many bookshelves, a huge fireplace, and windows.

The queen stood; she had been sitting on a coach. "Thank you, Delphi. That will be all for now." The maid curtsied and then left.

"You look nice," the queen said, taking a few steps forward. This was the first time they had been alone, and Tara felt a bit awkward.

"Thank you," she said—if anything she had to be polite. "I really enjoyed the bath. I haven't taken one in weeks." That statement was true; she hadn't had a bath in a while. She did have a shower at the McMahon mansion, though. Gosh, was that the last time I had washed? She thought. Yes, it was. Wow. She didn't like that since coming to the Higher Realms, she hadn't had much downtime.

Her thoughts were interrupted by the queen, "It struck me as odd at first why your mortal parents called you Tara. Then I remembered your bracelet." Tara fingered it under her dress at her neckline. "You know that Tara is a place?" Tara nodded a bit, but she was a little confused.

"You see," the queen walked closer to her, "Tara is where the High King rules. This castle is one of many in his kingdom."

"You mean we are in Tara now?"

The queen smiled. "Yes, your name has more meaning than you thought."

The doors to the study opened, and in came the fairy queen and Alana.

"Any news, Queen Moorigan?" Queen Tina asked.

The queen sighed. "I'm afraid not."

"Oh, just dreadful," the fairy queen said as she walked over to the windows.

"Oh, look! It's Oren!" Queen Tina said, sounding grateful to see him.

That's all Tara needed to here. She ran out of the room, down the hall, and out into the courtyard. Oren saw her and slowed his horse so she could follow him to the stables. Tara stood there in front of him. He got off his horse, handing the reins to a stable worker. He then strode over towards Tara. He looked a bit tired, and his skin was a bit paler than she remembered.

"You look refreshed, Princess. How are you feeling?"

She smiled. "Better."

He nodded his head. Tara quickly pulled off her backpack and got out the flag when a man came up to Oren. Oren leaned down, whispered something, and then handed the man a scroll. The man quickly took off up the hill towards the castle.

"Good news I hope," Tara said nervously. Oren didn't smile or respond; he just stood in front of her. Tara swallowed hard, like food was stuck in her throat. She held out the Fairy Flag. "You must take this to the king. It would be foolish for me to."

Oren raised an eyebrow. Did he believe what she had just said? Probably not. He stepped forward and held out his arms with the palms of his hands facing upwards. "You must place the flag in my hands of your own free will, Princess." She stepped forward and noticed Ryan coming down the hill on the path. She slowly placed it in his hands. He quickly put it in a satchel and tied to his waist. "It is in good hands, Princess." He got up on his horse. "Ryan, you will join us when you can."

"Yes, when I can."

Oren nodded. "Very well then. Farewell, princess." He started riding away, sitting tall in the saddle. He didn't look back but called back to them, "See you at the victory feast."

Tara started running for the stables, and Ryan followed her. "Where are you going?"

Tara hastily opened Snowberry's stall and grabbed her reins. "I am going with him." Ryan grabbed the reins from Tara's hand. "He's long gone by now."

She glared at him. "Really? You're going to go there."

"No, really Tara. You can't go. Besides, Oren gave me strict orders to keep you here."

Tara laughed. "Women can go into battle just as much as—"

Ryan cut her off. "Yes, but not usually princesses."

"Well, what if I don't want to stay?" She walked over to the stable doors and leaned against the frame of the door. She could see part of the castle through the trees. "How can I stay here and do nothing?"

Ryan walked over to her and placed his hand on her upper arm. Then he put his other hand on her other arm and stood close, facing her. He leaned his head down, touching his forehead to hers. Tara wasn't used to this helpless feeling. The tears burned as they ran down her face.

"Tara, you have done the king and everyone living here a huge service. Don't discredit yourself. No one else could have found the flag." He let go of her and backed away. "Who knows? It could have sat in that storage unit until it rotted."

"How did it get there?" Tara asked. Ryan shrugged his shoulders. Just then a black raven flew and landed on the fencepost nearby. Tara looked at the raven as it walked about on the fence. Ryan stepped away from Tara as she relaxed. Thinking for a moment, she sprang to life.

"Come on," Tara said, practically running up the hill. She only paused as she got to the gate as the guards let her through, the raven following them, though Tara scarcely noticed.

"Tara! Where are you going?" Ryan called after her.

"I overheard some of the guards talking about a place where you can see the edge of the battlefield," she told Ryan as they ran.

She ran up the steps and into the castle, almost knocking into a maid she didn't recognize. "Where is the Queen?" she asked the maid.

The maid pointed and said, "In there, my lady." Tara ran in the direction she sent her, and Ryan followed her. She burst through the door, and the fairy queen and Alana stood abruptly as the Queen Moorigan came into the room through French doors from outside.

"Tara?" Alana came forward towards her.

Tara looked around. "Where can I see the battle from?".

The queen's face looked shocked and worried. "That would be the King's Tower, but—"

"Take me there, please?"

"Tara, maybe it's best if—" Ryan started.

Tara whirled around and cut him off. "Please Ryan, I must see something, do something. You understand. Right?"

Ryan shrugged his shoulders as the queen whisked by. "Wait here," she said and quickly left the room.

The fairy queen came forward. "What must you see, Princess? Only those that the King approves can go in the tower."

Tara couldn't explain it; she just knew she had to see for herself.

The queen came back with a guard, who walked over to Tara. "I am to take you to the King's Tower." He was about Ryan's age, maybe a few years older. Tara nodded and followed him as they left the room. Ryan followed as well. They walked through the castle with the guard leading the way, his cape trailing behind him. They came to a stairway. The walls of the castle were white stone, as were the stairs, which wound their way upward. Once they were on a platform, Tara noticed a door, which the guard knocked on. A maid answered, and she looked surprised to see them.

"The queen has asked me to escort Princess Tara-Brigit and young Lord McMahon to the King's Tower." The maid nodded and stood aside, letting them in. Tara noticed the room was very plain; there were lots of linens, blankets, and tapestries.

"This way," the guard told them as they followed. They entered and went through another room, which had a fireplace, a few tables, chairs, and some nice rugs and tapestry on the walls. Tara saw a very old chess set on one of the tables. She noticed no modern conveniences. They went through a doorway and up more stairs, and these were wooden stairs. There were lanterns and sconces on the walls with candles lighting the way up. They passed a doorway covered with a heavy curtain.

"That is the High King and Queen's quarters, and bed chamber," the guard told her, noticing that she had paused in front of it. "We will pass the maids' chambers as well before we reach the top."

Tara's legs were aching from climbing all of the stairs; however, she pressed on. They reached the top, and the guard opened the door that led out onto a balcony type of building off of the tower. There were two other guards there.

"Hello, boys. This is the princess, and you know young Lord McMahon." The guards nodded as they all stepped out onto the balcony. The guard that had brought them up pointed out past the fields and trees to a faraway clearing. "That is where you will see it."

Tara looked at him, confused. "Where?" she asked, squinting her eyes.

"The battle, my lady. Looks like nothing is going on right now."

One of the other guards came forward. "They are probably taking a reprieve for now. Don't worry. The war will start again soon."

"Well, I need to go back to my post, Princess." He bowed to her and then to Ryan. "Young Lord McMahon." He turned and smiled at the other guards. "See ya boys at dinner." Then he left. Ryan stood by Tara, who was looking out onto the distant field.

"Tara, I need to—" She held up her hand as she tried to focus. She saw something. "Tara?" She ignored Ryan as she squinted her eyes. There seemed to be a mist that rolled in. Then she saw an army descending out of the forest on the left, from the west going down the huge hill onto the field. Dark clouds came in from the right, or east, as the other army came forward. Tara had a strange feeling; she didn't see the king in the front of the line holding the Fairy Flag high.

"Tara!" Ryan was shaking her shoulders. She closed her eyes and then turned to look at him, and then back at the field, where it stood empty. The sun was shining once more, and there was no mist. The guards were looking out as well.

"I saw something. The armies, they…" She looked out onto the field again but saw nothing. She quickly looked at Ryan again. "Something is wrong." Ryan came closer to her.

"You have Second Sight, Tara." She looked up at him, and then his words reminded her of Uncle Arland's.

"You just saw the future, and you're right. Something is wrong. I need to go." Ryan kissed her cheek and started going over to the door. Then he was gone before Tara could respond. The next thing they saw was a huge, reddish-brown bear running into the forest.

"Good luck, young lord!" one of the guards called down, and Tara could only watch from high above. Tara felt her heart lurch forward, and her mind reeled.

"What if the flag was a bust? What if it wasn't enchanted?" She felt an arm go across her shoulders. Standing by her was the fairy queen.

"You doubt who you are, and so by doubting that, you doubt the flag can deliver the king's army."

Tara looked at her. Thoughts ran through her mind, causing her stomach to heave. She felt nauseated. She was worried about Ryan, Cian, Lir. And about her friends Oren, Leonard, and others. Mark. She did doubt who she was, but she didn't want to admit it to the fairy queen. Yet she did feel a tinge of hope that she was the princess. She wanted to believe it. Could she believe it?

"It's not your fault, really. Who could blame you?"

"So, you're saying that the flag will not work if I don't believe in it?"

Queen Tina raised her eyebrows and slid her arm off of Tara's shoulders. "It is connected to you, Tara. You gave it to Oren for safekeeping and to deliver it. What happens now is still in your hands, although my enchantment still could work without you believing. Most importantly you need to believe in yourself." Tara acknowledged what she said, and after Tina left, Tara stood for a long time looking out onto the field. It was quite dark when she finally went into the castle, down the many flights of stairs and out into the stables, where she found Snowberry. She grabbed a brush and started grooming her.

"Ye know Tara, the king believes in the flag." Tara dropped the brush—she was not expecting to hear from Ettrick. She looked down to see Ettrick there, holding the brush up to her.

"Sorry," he said. She grabbed it and put it on the shelf. His face and clothes were smudged with dirt.

"I need to go. I need to see the king."

Ettrick jumped up onto Snowberry's stall door frame. "There'll be none of that. Ye need to stay here, Tara. Stay safe."

"Where have you been, and what have you been doing?" Tara tried to stifle a yawn. She was so tired, but she had to stay awake.

"You're tired. Let me show you the way to your room. Come on. I will not be answering any questions. You need rest." Tara sleepily followed Ettrick into the castle.

"I don't want to sleep, Ettrick."

He chuckled. "Sure, ya don't." He led her into her dimly lit room. She paused by the window, but she couldn't see the far-off field. She really needed to get some sleep, but seeing the king was more urgent. She slid down onto the cushioned bench that was nestled in the base of the window.

"Where is Mark?"

"You mean Prince Keegan, aye? He is busy doing princely duties. His father was overjoyed at his return, and he is unable to see you right now." Tara frowned. Was it always going to be like this now? she wondered. Would it not ever be back how it was? Going to school, worrying about things like homework or what music to listen to.

"Ettrick, I…"

He put a plate of tablet, shortbread, and warm honey milk on the table by the bench. "Now come, Tara. Eat some of this and drink the milk." She smiled and lazily sat up. "Sweet dreams, Princess." Then he was gone.

The next morning, she awoke still at the window. The sun had just started to rise. "Ah, I fell asleep sitting here. Great," she said to herself as she stretched. Before everyone else awoke, she quickly ran down to the stables. She had grabbed a sack of food on the way, and she was now tightening the saddle strap. She also grabbed her bow and quiver full of arrows. Making sure she had the bear knife as well, she opened Snowberry's stall. "Come on, Snowberry. We need to leave before others wake." Tara gently guided Snowberry out of her stall, mounted, and rode off. She had a general idea of where she was going and hoped she would see the king's camp soon. She rode all day and was starting to think she had made a mistake, and she realized she hadn't even eaten.

The camp and fighting fields were farther away than she had anticipated. However, that seemed to not matter at the moment because, once she saw smoke, she slowly approached the camp. She jumped down from the saddle and poked her head through some bushes to see more clearly. It was a camp alright, but whose? She hoped she hadn't stumbled upon the enemy's camp. Now she realized her reckless decision could cost her, and possibly her life.

She saw men and other folk from the Higher Realms, and some women too. They were eating and packing. Then she saw Oren, his arm in a sling, and he was approaching a tent. The king came out of the tent and talked to Oren. She was about to go into the camp when someone grabbed her arm, and a hand covered her mouth.

"Going somewhere, Princess?" It was Ryan. He then quickly let go.

"Oh gosh Ryan, you scared me."

"Tara, I'm patrolling. Did you think you could really just sneak up to camp? What are you doing here?"

She shrugged her shoulders and grabbed Snowberry's reins. "I needed to see."

"If Oren finds out you're here, he will not be happy. Shoot, if the king finds out."

Tara rolled her eyes. "I don't care. I have to talk to him. The king, I mean." She stood firm. "I need to speak with the king." Ryan just stood there, holding Snowberry's reins out to her. "Look. I need to tell the king something." Ryan didn't look very pleased, though she thought he would be happy to see her.

"Look. He needs to know something that only I can tell him."

"This is not the way, Tara. You are in danger here."

"What, in the camp? Come on, Ryan."

He sighed. "Not, just here. Near the battlefield."

"As soon as I tell him what I came here to tell him, I will leave."

Ryan stood, tapping his foot on the ground with his hands on his hips and looking up to the sky, mumbling to himself.

"Are you going to take me, or do I have to go unescorted?" He shot past her then. She quickly followed. They were on a path now, and Ryan was leading the way. "Where are we going?"

"I am taking you to the king's tent. Now be quiet and follow me," he said sternly. He didn't even look at her—he just kept walking. When they entered the camp, all eyes were on her. Some men were sitting down eating, but when they saw her, their mouths gaped open. Some even stood quickly to their feet. She felt awkward. She smelled the food, and her stomach rumbled. When they reached the tent, Tara saw the flag on a long pole, rippling gently in the slight breeze. It was huge and amazing.

"Wait here," he said before going over to the tent where he talked to the guard and was then let into the tent. She heard the king greet Ryan, and then it was silent. Ryan came out and, right before she went in, she saw that Oren had spotted her. He stopped in his tracks when he saw her. His handsome face had a long cut along his left cheek and down past his collar. Tara winced. Then Ryan pulled her into the tent. It was huge, and there was a large wooden pole in the center. Tapestries hung on the walls of the tent, and there were maps all over—on tables, on the floor. There was a bed and some other bedroom furniture. It almost looked like a cabin.

King Kenneth was sitting at a table eating. He smiled when he saw her. "Come in, Tara-Brigit. To what do I owe this honor?" The first and last time she had seen him was chained to a wall in a cave. He looked so different now. Ryan bowed. "I shall leave you two alone, sire." Then he left Tara standing there, feeling a bit awkward. The king stood with some difficulty. He walked with a walking stick from behind the table. She then noticed his leg was bound up with dressings. He had been injured.

Tara looked up, not meaning to stare.

"First, I want to thank you for helping rescue me and my wife."

"Oh, that. Yeah, um, you're welcome," she said, still a bit nervous. There were a few awkward quiet moments before the King sat back down.

"So. Why are you here?" he asked as he moved maps aside on his desk.

"Ah. I had a vision. Second Sight, I was told."

The king's smile faded. He motioned for her to come closer. "Tara, it is very dangerous for you to be here. When did you leave the castle?"

She pushed some dirt around with her shoe. "Ah, early this morning," she sighed loudly. "Look. I felt useless there. I needed to do something. I should have delivered the flag myself."

He nodded. "So that's what this is about. Have you eaten?" He got up and went over to a tray full of food.

She looked up as he started making her a plate of food. "Ah, no, but…"

He came over to her. "Sit, eat this." He handed the plate to her as she sat down, and then handed her a goblet of cider. Tara looked around the tent. Behind her the doors were open letting the sunshine in.

"It's the flag, it won't work. You are going to your death," she told him bluntly as she quickly ate.

"What's all this nonsense about the flag?" someone behind them asked. It was Oren. Tara turned around to see him come in.

"Who told you this?" the king asked as Oren came and stood by the king.

"Queen Tina told me about the flag. It's my fault." Oren came closer and smiled as he placed his hand on her shoulder. "It is not your fault, Tara."

Tara pulled away, and Oren frowned.

"Yes, it is!" she blurted that out, more forcefully than she had intended. "I had a vision Oren, and Queen Tina told me it was from the future."

"You have Second Site," Oren said, scratching his chin.

"Yes," Tara said taking a bite of food.

"I see." He looked at King Kenneth.

The king was smiling. "You are my daughter, and as such it is no surprise that you have gifts." The king stood up and limped forward, using his walking stick. Tara frowned. She did not consider herself his daughter. She barely knew him.

"Come outside, Tara." She followed him, as did Oren. The king stood by the flag. The sun shone in his hair, making it look redder. Ryan was standing nearby as well, Tara noticed. "Now. What's all this about the flag, the war and my impending doom?"

Tara squinted to look up at him in the sun. "The flag won't win the battle for you."

The king frowned. "And why not?"

Tara walked closer. "Because I don't really believe I am who everyone thinks I am. There are a lot of people who claim I am, but –" she paused. "I am just a girl from Connecticut, a girl in high school. I was supposed to get a job over the summer. My parents, they –" Remembering them at that moment and everything that had happened opened the flood gate for her emotions, and tears ran down her face. "I should have gone with them, why did they make me stay? Why did they leave me behind? Why was I adopted? Did you not love me?"

She heard the queen gasp as she put her hands up to her face. She ran over and placed a hand on Tara's shoulder. Tara turned and was surprised to see her there. She had thought she was at the castle.

"I came as soon as we saw you were missing," the queen explained.

All of her questions came pouring out into deep sobs. She then saw the raw emotion of a strong proud king turn into a loving father, and an elegant queen to a loving mother. Parents she never knew she had. "Of course, we love you! You are our daughter!" Queen Moorigan said as she hugged Tara.

The king sighed, then motioned her closer, He grabbed onto the pole with his right hand and placed his left on her shoulder. "Grab the post, Tara." Just then a raven flew and landed nearby on a tree branch. She noticed it this time but said nothing. The queen no longer stood among them. She reached up with her left hand and grabbed onto the pole just under the king's hand. "Now. Tell me what you saw."

Tara looked up into the king's face and then closed her eyes, and the scene she saw came to her mind. She opened her eyes and looked into the king's eyes as the vision unfolded. She told him what she saw when she was out on the king's tower.

He lowered his head. "I see. You have Second Sight. A great and powerful gift, Tara. One of many, I believe." He looked at her. "You still do not believe you are the princess. Why? Is it because you are afraid?" He was right. She was afraid, afraid of losing more family. Afraid that if she accepted this reality the other one would go away. Tara nodded her head. He squeezed her shoulder firmly but gently as he smiled. Tara looked into his eyes. They were such a handsome shade of blue; they reminded her of Uncle Arland's eyes. She gasped. "Uncle Arland." She thought, then her father's face came into view. As soon as that thought came to her mind, the king's eyes sparkled. She saw her reflection in his eyes and a burning in her chest. "You are my daughter, Tara-Brigit. I knew the moment I saw you in the cave. I also believe in the flag; it holds a powerful weapon."

Tara crinkled her brow. "A weapon?"

The king smiled. "Love, and you Tara."

"Love?" she repeated, not understanding.

"Me?"

He bent down towards her ear. "Love is the strongest magic. Love brought you into this world. You were born at daybreak just as the sun's rays came and as they touched your wee face, you smiled. It was foretold that you would bring unity to a kingdom divided. It was love that went into making the flag to begin with. Queen Titiana made and blessed this gift for you. It was love that held us together when you went missing. Love that drove us to find you. Love that will now carry us into battle – a battle where the odds tip in our enemy's favor. However, it is love for our kingdoms, our lands, our people, not greed and bitterness, that make us strong."

"Just love?" Tara asked. The king smiled.

"Well, and maybe a bit of magic." He stood back up, standing proudly. She looked in his face again, and the king was glowing with love and pride. He looked even more like Uncle Arland and her father when they were young, just taller and more muscular.

"Uncle Arland? Father?" she muttered under her breath.

"What's that Princess?" the king asked.

She placed her right hand on the king's cheek as tears ran down her face.

"You remind me of my uncle. And my father." She blinked hard as more tears were squeezed out of her eyes.

He smiled slightly. "Yes. Arland MacInnes/MacLeod., and your father. Aye lass, they are my kin, my descendants. My family, as are you."

Tara felt happiness burst within her as a glow started from their hands into the pole and traveled upward towards the flag. It reached the flag and burst out into a sparkling brilliant light. Everyone had to shield their eyes.

"Now because you believe in yourself and us, no darkness or enemies can look upon this flag or on our army and not fear it. For love and light drives away the darkness, the fear, greed and doubt."

"Like magic," Tara said as he hugged her then, and she hugged back.

"Now." He looked around—they had gathered quite the crowd. He took out a small dagger. "Here, I give this to you so you can protect yourself."

Tara smiled and got out her own dagger. "I have one." The king looked surprised, but then he smiled. "Ah. Artair Arktos. Yes, a fine weapon." He was smiling and looked like a proud king.

"But how will the flag work?" Tara needed to know.

"Well," the king started to say. "Now that it has been unfurled, and you touched it with your light within, it can be carried into battle by the king – who happens to be me."

Ryan had walked closer, bowing to the king when he addressed him, "Young Lord McMahon."

"Yes, your majesty."

"Escort the princess back to the castle, and make haste now. We have a war to win."

"Yes, my lord." Ryan smiled, bowed, and grabbed Tara's arm.

"Wait!" Tara yelled as the king had started walking away. "What if it will not work if I leave?" The king turned then and sighed.

Then someone blew a horn, and everyone was running about. "Come on Tara, let's get Snowberry and get out of here. It's going to get ugly. Fast." Ryan started dragging her away.

"Wait! No!" she yelled, however it was no use. Ryan was too strong, but she dug her heels into the ground. He sighed loudly and let go of her arm.

"I need to stay," she demanded. Ryan was looking up to the sky with his hands on his hips. "Fine, we will go to the western forest and sit atop the hill by the tree line."

As soon as they mounted Snowberry, Oren flew towards them. He handed Tara a quiver of silver-tipped arrows and a bow. "Extra protection," he said as he smiled, winked, and flew off as she and Ryan galloped away from the camp.

25

Battle

Tara and Ryan left the camp quietly, careful not to call too much attention to themselves. It wasn't hard with everyone was preparing for battle. Arrow, Ryan's hawk, was flying above them as they walked. He circled around and occasionally flew ahead. It was a warm evening, not particularly hot or stuffy.

"So how long has the war been going on?" Tara couldn't remember. She knew from her history classes in school that wars can last for years.

"Almost a year," Ryan answered as he called to Arrow, who flew down and landed on his arm. Ryan let him rest for a bit before lifting his arm up high so Arrow could scout ahead for them some more. Ryan also stopped walking sometimes, looking around and sniffing the air. At one point, he told Tara to wait as he changed from human form into a bear. He had Tara stand with her back to him as he went a bit more into the forest. When he came out he was carrying his clothes. She put them in his pack, which was now tied around him.

They got to a top of a large foothill, where they could see the battle below. They were still far enough away that Tara was pretty sure they couldn't be seen, however. She had on her two bows and quivers and her knife Artair Arktos that Ryan had given her.

"Wouldn't you rather be down there, than sitting here with me?" Tara asked.

"Nope," Ryan said as he sat by her in bear form. He really was a massive bear, and still growing. He plucked a wildflower smelled its sweet aroma then threw it aside.

"Is Mark down there?" Tara asked, sounding somewhat anxious.

"Yes, he is fighting alongside his father."

A wave of fear and dread spread through Tara's whole body. What if he got injured, or died? She shook her head. Looking over to Ryan, she asked,

"Wouldn't you like to be fighting alongside your father?"

"I would," he answered. "I am old enough." He paused and looked down at her. "But being here with you, protecting you, is worth it. Making sure you are safe and all." He smiled at her, and she returned the smile.

The sun started to set behind the mountains. It was beautiful; hues of gold, red, yellow, orange, pinks and purples against the dark mountains. When she looked back down at the battle below them, she saw her vision unfolding right in front of her. The king's army was descending from the West, and Don Pater and most of the Famorians from the East, except this time the battle had already begun as the dead and injured were strewn all over the field. Tara sat up straighter, and Ryan did the same.

"What is it, Tara?" he asked as she narrowed her eyes to see more clearly. Tara could barely see the king, holding the flag. He was at the front of the line. The flag was unfurled. It should be doing something, shouldn't it? She asked herself as she anxiously looked on.

"Ryan, the flag isn't doing anything. Why isn't it doing anything?" She asked him frantically.

"I don't know." Tara turned to look at him.

"You don't know what it is supposed to do?" Ryan shrugged his shoulders.

Tara was thinking. The flag glowed when she touched it at the castle, it glowed brighter when she held it with King Kenneth when she realized he was family, and she truly was he princess. Then it occurred to her. Even though the king unfurled it, and was carrying it into battle, she had to engage it somehow. But what if she already did enough? She found the flag like everyone kept telling her she should. Could she risk doing nothing and lose another father?

"Ryan, take me closer," she said as she stood, adjusting her bows and quivers.

"No way!"

"Ryan, please!" She begged, but Ryan did not budge. He just shook his big furry bear head back and forth. Tara walked behind him and got out the bow that she had received as a gift from him. She knocked an arrow, drew, and aimed at him. He turned his head, then hastily stood.

"Tara, what –"

She cut him off. "Take me down there, Ryan Bres McMahon, or I swear, I will put an arrow in your backside."

Ryan snorted. "Fine, get on!"

Tara jumped on his back then put the arrow back into her quiver and swung the bow over her shoulder onto her back. Ryan ran partway down the hillside. There were plenty of low-lying trees and shrubs where they could hide if they had to.

"Here," Tara said, and jumped off of Ryan's back as he came to a stop. She got her bow and pulled an arrow from its quiver. She was not losing another family member if she had anything to say about it. Action was needed, and so once she spotted the king, she kissed the tip of the arrow head. Her kiss caused a spark to ignite onto the tip of the arrow, and she drew her bow. She focused on the flag and let the arrow fly. It went whizzing through the almost pitch-black night like a small rocket. The arrow lodged deep within the pole that the flag was attached to. The king did not seem to notice the impact of the arrow on the pole, or if he did it did not cause him to slow down. In fact, he seemed to ride harder, and he rode on. As Tara watched, flag started to glow. It got brighter and brighter as the king rode forward. The light that came from it became so bright that it looked as if it was making a huge shield or barrier up and to each side of the king along the front lines of his army. As it came crashing into the enemy's army, Tara saw their front lines crumble and fall as the High King was fighting, driving forward.

Tara heard a noise below them just at the base of the hillside. "Enemy Scouts!" Ryan said urgently. "Run!" They both started running up the mountainside. Tara got out a silver-tipped arrow as she ran, almost stumbling over roots and low bushes. Ryan noticed and ran alongside her.

"Get on, Tara!" He yelled. Tara grabbed skin and fur and hoisted herself onto his back.

"They're getting closer!" Tara yelled. She could see them clearly now. There were wolves and other strange creatures. Tara let an arrow fly but it ricocheted off a tree and missed her target. "Oren made this look so easy," she thought as she knocked another arrow. This time when she aimed and let the arrow go it hit its target square in the chest. The beast stumbled, causing a few others to stumble as well.

When Tara turned back around a wolf collided into Ryan, knocking Tara off his back. She barely got out of the way before she was crushed underneath them as they fought each other. Tara got out her knife and cut the wolf's leg just as Ryan's claw sliced through its neck. Tara stood and started running as more creatures came their way. As she ran, she could hear howls and other noises. It reminded her of the dream she had. They were gaining on her fast. She heard Ryan roar, but he was not close. Then she smacked into a Giant's boot.

Stunned, Tara stood back and shook her head as a huge hand reached down for her.

"Hello, Princess," Leonard said in his kind tone. Relief flooded through Tara. Leonard quickly picked her up, and as soon as he did, several creatures were at his feet. He kicked them away like little pebbles.

"Thank you, Leonard," Tara said as he started walking briskly away. He put her in his pocket, and she climbed up the fabric to peak out, resting her arms over the edge for support. Soon Leonard walked into a clearing, and standing there was a massively tall figure.

"Balor," Leonard said stopping abruptly, pushing Tara into his pocket. Tara got out her knife and cut a very small slit in the fabric to look out. So, this was Balor, also known as Balor of the evil eye for the third eye on his forehead. He was also the king of the Fomorians, or giants. The moon cast a white eerie glow on his black armor, his helmet low over his forehead covering his third eye so that his two eyes could barely be seen. Another piece of his helmet went over the bridge of his nose. He was massive, and she saw his bulk of muscles through his armor.

"Leonard," Balor said in a tone of surprise. Balor's voice was deep like rolling thunder. "Why are you not back at the castle? How many times must I tell you to stay put?" He did not sound angry; just annoyed.

"I- I just wanted to see," Leonard said shyly. Tara pictured him wringing his hat in his hands nervously, as he did when confronted. Balor moved a bit closer as a huge black bear came into the clearing. Tara could not believe her eyes. It was Lord McMahon, Ryan's father.

"Lost track of them," Lord McMahon told Balor, breathing heavily. Looking around, he said, "What's Leo doing here, Balor?"

Balor cleared his throat and answered. "He says he wanted a peak at the battle."

Lord McMahon snorted. "Well, it is not going well for us. The High King had the Fairy Flag."

Balor came closer to Leonard. Tara held her breath. "Did you see any of King Kenneth's scouts, Leonard?" Leonard shook his head. Balor sighed. "I will leave you to do what I asked of you, Marty. As for you, Leonard, you must go back to the castle and finish your chores. Do I make myself clear?"

"Yes, my lord Balor." Leonard answered back. Balor let out a big sigh and turned, as Tara quietly exhaled slowly.

"I am going back to camp, Marty. See that those scouts are never found."

"Yes Balor," Lord McMahon said as he left the clearing.

Tara climbed up almost out of Leonard's pocket. "Leonard, Lord McMahon is a traitor!" she said, still full of disbelief. "And, Balor – I was scared."

"He scares me too," Leonard said as he kept walking at a fast pace through the forest.

"Leonard, wait. Ryan is out here somewhere, we have to find him."

Leonard came to a big clearing and sat on a bog boulder to rest. He lifted Tara carefully out of his pocket and set her on the ground. Tara uneasily looked around.

"I think we are safe, for now," Leonard said, also looking around. Tara was tired but did not let it show.

"Leonard, does Ryan know about his father?" Leonard shook his head.

"I don't think so, but he does not like the fighting."

"What fighting Leonard?"

"Lord McMahon and King Kenneth."

"Oh," Tara said, looking at her two quivers. She still had plenty of arrows. "There must be another way to get more land, besides a war."

"There is," said a new voice. Tara turned to see Ryan approaching. He was dirty and a bit bloody but otherwise looked fine.

"My father is looking for us. We should go," Ryan said, coming closer.

"Your father –" Tara's words were stopped short by Lord McMahon, who had entered the clearing.

"Ryan Bres McMahon!" he yelled, as he came charging towards Ryan. Tara barely jumped out of the way in time.

"Father, please!" Ryan pleaded as his father pinned him to the ground.

"You should have obeyed me, son," Lord McMahon said, letting Ryan get up.

"You could have negotiated with King Kenneth," Ryan said. "Why join the Fomorian army?"

"Negotiations did not go as planned," was the reply.

"Father!"

Lord McMahon, easily twice Ryan's size, stared down his son, silencing him. Tara hid behind Leonard's boot, peering out.

"And you!" Lord McMahon said, looking at Leonard. "You should have listened to Balor. Are you helping them, Leo?" Leonard did not answer. "Go back to the castle, Leonard! Now!"

"No," Leonard said.

"What did you say?" Lord McMahon said, spitting froth from his mouth.

"He said no, father."

Lord McMahon turned to Ryan, jumping on him. They tumbled about, growling and fighting, and then Ryan was pinned to the ground again. Tara saw Lord McMahon raise a clawed paw. She quickly stepped out from behind Leonard's boot and grabbed an arrow, knocked her bow and stood there aimed and ready at Lord McMahon.

"Let him go."

Lord McMahon looked her way. "Ah, princess. I was wondering when you would show your face."

"I said let him go." However, Lord McMahon pushed with all his strength on Ryan's chest, causing a gurgling sound to come from Ryan's lips. Fearing for Ryan's life, Tara shot an arrow into the leg that held Ryan down. This made Lord McMahon pull back, but he was more enraged.

"How dare you strike a Lord!" He started running for her but Ryan plowed into him. They were both on hind legs now, roaring at each other.

"Leonard! Get Tara away from here!" Ryan yelled.

"No, I am staying!" Tara called up. Leonard tried grabbing her but she was like a pesky fly swirling around his feet.

When Tara looked back, she saw Lord McMahon strike Ryan down with one blow. Tara knocked her bow again and this time aimed for his chest. When the arrow struck, Lord McMahon fell back. It had hit his shoulder. He ripped the arrow out and now sneered at her, but before he could charge, someone on a horse came riding onto the field crashing into Lord McMahon. It was Mark. He got out his sword and swung, slicing Lord McMahon's side. He swayed and fell, blood pooling around him.

Ryan lifted his head slightly. "Leo," He said with a forced voice. "Take Father home." Leonard nodded, grabbed Lord McMahon's body and ran from the clearing, calling out as he ran, "I'll be back, Ryan, okay? I'll be back."

Tara ran over to Ryan, as did Mark. She hugged Mark, and they helped Ryan sit up. He had blood running down the side of his jaw. "Mark," he asked. "Can you ride and get help?"

"Yeah, uh, Oren is not too far away," Mark said. Arrow was flying overhead. Tara called to the hawk. "Fly ahead, Arrow! Help Mark!" The hawk called out and started flying towards the edge of the clearing. Tara nodded as Mark got on his horse and galloped speedily out of the clearing, using arrow as a guide. When Mark came back, he had about a dozen men, elves and faerie warriors. Oren was among them. He came riding up to them, jumping from his horse gracefully.

"Are you hurt, Tara?" he asked.

"No, it's Ryan," she answered. Ryan seemed to be going in and out of consciousness. A stretcher was brought over and Ryan loaded onto it as Oren attended to him. Arrow landed on the stretcher occasionally, carefully pecking at Ryan's paw. Mark came over, taking off his helmet. Tara fell to her knees, and when Oren saw, he came running over.

"Let me check you," Oren said. Tara had not noticed that her leg was bleeding. "You ripped open a section of your leg where the stitches are." Oren observed. He grabbed some fabric from his bag, ripped a length of it and tied it around her leg. He then rested his hand on her shoulder. He was dirty, bloody, and looked tired. Everyone did.

Tara looked up at him. "Will Ryan be okay?"

Oren nodded, looking at the stretcher. "Yeah, he'll be fine."

"How is the king?" She asked as he helped her stand. "How is my father?"
Oren smiled. "He is alive." Tara sighed and smiled back. "Welcome home, Princess Tara-Brigit," he said as he bowed, and everyone cheered. Then Oren stood and got onto his horse. Mark helped Tara mount his horse and they left the clearing.

26

The King

It had been a few days since she left the clearing were Tara first saw Balor, and the traitor Lord McMahon. The king's army were coming to the castle in big groups. They brought the dead, the living, and the wounded. Even Tara's minor wounds had been attended to. Tara was busy helping the overflowed infirmary. There were cases she could not help with like cut off limbs, or deep wounds, broken bones. She did help carry away dirty used linens, replenish them, fill water bowls for medical reasons as well as drinking. Carrying away waste pots, that was the worst. The king still had not come back to the castle, and she wondered if he just was making sure none of his men were left behind. . Ryan was being treated as well. Oren and many other healers were there to help. Ryan had a concussion, and some wounds that needed extra care. When Tara needed a break, she wound go change, wash up and go to the library. She had read many books and journals in the massive library that the castle had. She had read about her father, the king, and his extended family. Tara was standing on the castle grounds now, watching her sisters play with Ness and Fenian's puppies. The puppies had gotten bigger. She had three sisters, and it was strange that she was supposed to be an infant still, yet here she was all grown up, with her sisters quite a bit younger than she was. The queen came and stood by her.

"Brenta is the youngest, then Brant. The oldest is Braint. You, of course Brigit, were the youngest. However, now you are the oldest." They all had different shades of brown hair. Brenta's had a light, reddish-brown color, the closest to Tara's hair color.

The sisters were laughing and running, and Tara felt happy watching them. The queen placed her arm around Tara's shoulders as they stood and watched together. She hated waiting. It was like on Christmas morning when she would wake up hours before her parents, just waiting to open presents. Except this was worse. It had been weeks since the battle was over. They had not heard any news, other than the king was safe and helping his troops. Tara wished they had cell phones here, though she had tried hers. No service.

"How do they feel about their baby sister being all grown up?" she asked the queen.

The queen folded her arms. "Well, Braint is not so sure about you. When you were taken, she had to help a lot with the other two, since I was grieving so. She seems a bit put off that you are so much older than she. The younger two are just excited you are here and safe. I think they like that you are older." The queen smiled, watching her girls play.

Then there was some commotion down the hill as the girls and puppies ran towards the edge of the gardens. "Father!" yelled Braint as the girls all ran into their father's outstretched arms. The queen gasped, ran down the stairs and across the gardens, and embraced him as well. Then Tara saw Leonard, with Ettrick sitting on his shoulder. Mark, and many others. She too ran down the stairs and onto the grass of the gardens. The king saw her, and came forward, holding the flag. He bowed before her.

"This belongs to you, Princess Tara-Brigit." He smiled as Tara smiled back, nodded and took the flag.

"Here," Mark said and handed her the Nike bag, and she smiled. Tara put the flag safely in the bag, then slung it over her shoulder. The king hugged each of his girls again, then they darted off once again playing with the puppies. He hugged the queen as she pulled back from their embrace, she upped his face in her hands, nodded, smiled and went to watch the girls play.

Cian, Lou, and Beira came up the hill, and Tara waved and smiled as they came closer. Cian pointed through the woods and said, "There is someone who wants to see you if you go down the path to the lake, Tara." Tara nodded.

"I will take you down, Tara," Mark told her as he walked by her side.

"How are your father and brothers? I mean, are they—?"

Mark smiled. "Oh, they are fine. Wounded, but they will live."

"And your father?"

"He is fine too, and King Oberon, just so you know."

That was a relief to hear, Tara thought as they walked. "I was thinking I might not ever see you again."

Mark put his arm around her and pulled her towards him. "Look. I'm sorry I wasn't straightforward with you. Can you forgive me?"

Tara smiled as he let her go. "Yes, of course. How can I stay mad at you, when we have been through so much and…"? She stopped talking as they came to the lake and Tara saw a magnificent sight. Lir was clinging to a water horse's long neck. There were tons of them actually, their long necks protruding out of the water. The water horse set him on the land. Lir bowed and the whole herd of them slowly went into the water and disappeared under its sparkling depths.

"Beautiful, aren't they?" King Lir said as he came over and hugged Tara. "They sure are," she said, as they now were gone.

"So, Princess." He turned to look at her, one arm still around her shoulder, his bellowing sleeves rippling in the breeze. "You found the flag, and in doing so found yourself."

"Yes, I sure did."

Lir laughed hard, showing off his dazzling white teeth. His eyes were wrinkled yet sparkled brightly. Cian came down the hill. "Come! We feast at last!" he bellowed as Mark and King Lir laughed again, and Tara smiled.

They all walked up towards the castle, which was bustling with excitement and activity. Wagons full of people, food, and drink in barrels were conjoining. "A feast like ye have never seen," Lir said, his eyes shining, grinning ear to ear. He then ran ahead to catch up with Cian. Tara stopped near the castle, sat on a big boulder, and watched the castle come to life. The wounded were moved, and on the mend. The dead had been burned or buried. Queen Moorigan told her that since the king had returned, they would have a big burial ceremony once families arrived and were settled.

"I will see you in there," Mark said as he left her sitting there.

"Hey," Ryan said, sitting by her.

"Ryan, should you be up and around?" She smiled when he nudged her arm with his. He smiled back. "I am fine."

"So, when are you going back?"

She looked at him, her facial expression questioning his comment. "Back?"

"Yeah. To your home. On Earth." She smiled, which made him smile. "Well, not here I mean."

"I don't know."

He stood and offered her his hand. She took it as he pulled her off the boulder. "Hear that?" He smiled and raised his eyebrows. "Music." He pulled her along the path and up the stairs, and they passed by many people entering the hall. The whole castle was filled with music and food, people, fairies, and other races.

Ryan held out his hand. "May I?" Tara smiled, feeling her cheeks grow hot and red. She took his hand as he led her in a dance. They danced to several songs before she told him they should sit down. "I'll go get us a drink," Ryan said and then walked towards a table.

Tara sat down on a bench, just watching everyone. Lou brought over a huge basket that held the sleeping puppies and placed the basket on the floor by her feet. "It seems your sisters have tuckered these wee pups out."

Tara smiled. "Yes, seems they have."

Beira arrived and wrapped an arm around Lou's waist. "They're all yours." Tara looked at them. "All of them?"

Lou laughed. "Well, yes. Father said you can have all of them. Only if you want them?"

"Oh, I do. It's just, were will I put them?" Cian laughed as did Lou, and Beira.

"Okay, well they can't leave Ness until several more weeks, since they aren't weaned yet," Lou told her as she smiled and nodded, understanding now.

Tara reached down to touch one, and its fur was so silky soft. "Okay," she said as Beira announced that they were going to go dance, and she practically dragged Lou out onto the dance floor. She noticed that Ryan was being held up from bringing her drink; he was talking to two very distinguished looking gentlemen.

"Hey," Mark said, sitting down next to her. She looked at him and smiled briefly. "This is where we belong, you know."

"I know, but…"

Anne came walking over to them. Her long, brown hair was curled and she wore a buttery colored dress. She looked lovely, except that nasty bandage on her head. She sat by Tara.

"Oh, Anne," Tara said, embracing her friend. "How is your head?"

Anne shrugged her shoulders. "Better. I still need to rest a lot. Queen Moorigan has a room for me here, and I'll need to go rest soon." Tara nodded, and Anne squealed when she saw the puppies and picked one up. It was a boy, and he grunted as Anne snuggled him in her arms.

"They are darling," she said, kissing his head.

"Yes, they are," Tara said, running her finger down his soft head.

"Have you named them yet?"

Tara looked up into Anne's face. "No. But when I do, you can help me."

Anne smiled. "I need to go back," Tara said, and Anne frowned. "I need to see my uncle Arland and check on the estate." She looked at Mark. "What about your father? If you stay here?"

Mark stood. "I haven't decided what to do. My father wants to see me, but now I have duties here."

"I know it isn't an easy decision Mark, but …"

He sighed. "Yeah, I know."

Lady McMahon waved Anne over to her. Anne gave the puppy back to Tara as she stood. "I have to go rest."

Mark walked over to her. "I'll escort you, Anne." She nodded. He looked back at Tara and mouthed the word bye, and then she lost the sight of them in the crowd. Tara wondered what they thought about Lord McMahon, but she figured that if they all were in on it then they would not be here. Then again, she was not an expert on royal court behavior or politics.

The king saw Tara sitting alone; she had placed the sleeping puppy back into the basket. The king sat down next to Tara. "Enjoying yourself? It's a nice feast, isn't it?" He was smiling, and it reminded Tara of Lir's smile, only the king had longer, strawberry blond hair, and he was taller. He was handsome with bright blue eyes.

Tara shrugged her shoulders. "I guess. I've never been to one before."

"I'm sorry about your mortal parents."

Tara felt a bit awkward. He was, after all, her father. "Yeah, I miss them." She paused. "I need to go back."

He sighed. "I was afraid you would say that."

She looked at him concerned. "Why, can't I go back?"

"Oh yes. It's just we will miss you, and you just got here." Tara realized that they must be dying to get to know her. "You know, when we heard they had found you, well we thought it was rumors. We almost didn't believe it. As soon as I saw you though, in the cave, I knew."

"I wasn't sure it was you and the queen chained to that wall, I wouldn't have done anything differently." The king smiled. Tara saw the queen looking their way, she smiled.

"Take Snowberry. She will guide you, when you are ready to leave."

"I can stay for a while, since there is nothing too pressing that I need to leave for."

He smiled and patted her hand. "Good, good. Glad to hear it." He stood as someone called him over. "Now, I must go." He turned and bent down to look into her face as he placed his hand on hers. "Come back soon when you do leave. My queen, you, and I have some catching up to do." He smiled, patted her hand, and then walked, arms outstretched towards his friends. Or were they family?

"Here." Ryan finally returned to her with her drink. She drank it down without breathing, she was so thirsty. "Do you need more?" Tara smiled. It was a delicious kind of punch. She nodded. Ryan took her mug and went to get more. When he came back, he looked down in the basket as he sat by her. "They are so small. They'll get big though."

"Yeah, they will." Tara set down her glass and turned to face Ryan.

"Ryan, I…" She paused. "I need to go. Home."

Ryan looked up as someone passed by, and he waved and smiled. "I can go with you, ya know."

Tara scooted closer. "You can?"

He smiled then stood. "Sure thing." He looked around. "I just need to tell my Mum ."

"Not now. I promised the king I would stay for a bit longer." Tara saw that Leonard was looking through a window. "Excuse me, Ryan. I need to go talk to Leonard."

"Okay. I will watch the puppies," Ryan said. As Tara got up, one came over to lay by the basket, and Ryan pet her. Tara went outside, where there were kids running around and people playing games. She walked around the castle and spotted Leonard.

He bent down. "Hi, Princess." He smiled, and she smiled back.

"I wanted to thank you for helping me."

Leonard sat down in the shade of the castle and leaned against the wall. He grabbed a big barrel, which looked small in his hands as he opened it and drained the contents. He then threw it in a pile of other barrels. "I will always help you if you need me," he told her as she sat on a low tree branch in the shade.

"Now that the war is over, I would like to see the castles and the bridge up close where you live."

"Okay, let me ask when it would be okay. It might be a few weeks. We still need to let everyone calm down."

"Okay," she said. She enjoyed talking to him and sitting outside in the fresh air and shade. Then, from far away, they heard his name being called.

"I have to go. Bye, Tara," he said, waving as he stood. She watched as the huge giant who had become her friend walked away.

Tara turned when she heard her name being called. "Brin!" Tara exclaimed, greeting her fairy friend. They hugged and Tara motioned for her to follow as they walked towards the castle.

"So, how have you been?" Tara asked her.

"Oh fine. Worried about you, though. Queen Tina would tell us fairies at the castle what was going on, and I feared we would lose you."

Tara chuckled softly. "I am fine," she told Brin.

"Ettrick tells me you are leaving us. Do you know how long you will be gone?"

"I don't," she said as the doors to the great hall burst open and out came several knights, singing and swaying with drinks in their hands. As they passed by, each greeted her with a "Hello Princess," or "Pardon us, Princess."

"Queen Tina gave me permission to visit you there," Brin told her.

"In Connecticut?"

Brin nodded with a smile as big as the widest river.

"I would love to see you there," Tara told her as they hugged again.

"Well I have to go, see you soon Tara," Brin said as she flew away.

"See you," Tara said, waving.

27

Home

Tara was riding on Snowberry's back, and the puppies were in a basket hanging off one side. They were eight weeks old now, old enough to leave Ness. Tara did leave the smallest puppy behind, because she was so little and still liked to suckle. Tara named her Belle. She hadn't thought of names for the others yet, but she wanted to give them all Disney character names. Tara couldn't take her from Ness. Especially when Ness had given her those big, sad, droopy eyes. Tara smiled. Ness and Fenian were great dogs, she knew the pups would grow up to be as well.

Ryan was on another horse that Oren had given him. He was a huge horse, at least nineteen hands high, maybe twenty. Definitely close to seven feet tall. The black stallion was very majestic looking; he was all black except for a small patch of white on the front of his head, and his tail was half black and half white. They led the horses through the mist and down the path. The mist at one point was so thick that Tara could barely see in front of her, but she trusted Snowberry. Before long they were standing and looking at the estate.

"Nice," Ryan said as Tara led the way. The grounds looked the same as they did three months ago, when she had left. Of course, that was Higher Realm time. She guessed here it was only about a week or two. School would be starting soon, and she wasn't sure if Mark was coming back. The last thing he had told her was that he was staying. She had her junior and senior year of high school, and then possibly college. She wasn't sure what she wanted to do, but the king and queen wanted her to go back.

"We can spend a few days here, and then we need to go to my uncle's. He lives in Scotland. He is my guardian now, and my family." Ryan nodded as they came up to the stables. Tara and Ryan secured the horses, giving them fresh water and hay. Ryan grabbed the basket with the puppies that had woken up and were whining. When they got to the front of the mansion, Ryan let the puppies run around on the grass.

A car pulled up the driveway, and Tara's lawyer got out.

"Mr. Patton," Tara said, pleased to see him.

He walked over to her and shook her hand. He wore a brown suit and a light blue tie. He looked good. "Tara, how are you?"

She smiled. "I'm fine, and you?"

He smiled back as Ryan came up to them. "I'm doing well."

"Oh. Mr. Patton, this is Ryan. Ryan, this is my lawyer, Mr. Patton." They shook hands. "I need to talk to him, Ryan. Financial stuff." Some of the puppies had followed them and were running around their feet.

"Yeah, okay. I'll stay out with the puppies a bit longer."

Tara smiled and found the key where Alana told her it was: under the clay potted plant to the right of the front doors. She unlocked the doors, and she and

Mr. Patton stepped inside. It hadn't changed, and it looked as if she hadn't been gone long at all, except she felt as if she had been gone for ages.

"The last time I talked to Alana she mentioned that you got married recently."

He smiled. "Yes, last week."

Mr. Patton set down his briefcase. "To Jenny, Charles's daughter. Charles had been her parent's groundskeeper. He had worked for her parents since she was a small child. He had passed away while she was in the Higher Realms, Alana had told her.

"He will be missed. So, Charles's oldest daughter?"

Mr. Patton laughed. "No, his youngest daughter."

Tara nodded. She remembered that Charles, the groundskeeper, had three daughters, but no sons.

"When Charles passed away, he left the duties of the estate to his youngest daughter Jenny. That's how I met her." He looked around. "It was here one day when I came to check on things after getting a letter from Alana."

"We did not know how long we would be away. Thanks for taking care of things while we were gone."

"Not a problem," he said as he set his briefcase down on the table.

"I'm happy for you," Tara said as they sat down.

Mr. Patton got out some papers. "I have these for you to sign after you read them." Tara nodded, took the papers, and started reading them. She saw that her Uncle Arland had already signed them.

"So where is Mark?"

Tara looked up. "Ah, He is um…" The truth was, Tara wasn't sure what to say. "He's on vacation. Not sure when he'll be back."

Mr. Patton nodded, and he gave Tara a pen. Tara signed the papers and handed them back to him, and he took them and put them into his briefcase. He then stood up and asked, "Will you be attending school here, or in Scotland?"

"I will be moving to Scotland to live with Uncle Arland. I have no guardian here. And Alana is also there with her daughter, who is having a hard time right now."

He nodded. "Well, you will be missed Tara. I will keep in touch."

"Okay." She couldn't tell him that she really wanted to go back to The Higher Realms, that she had training to do with Oren.

Mr. Patton smiled. "Well, until next time I see you. Just don't wait too long before you answer my messages."

Ryan came in with the puppies trailing behind him. "I need to get them some water," he said as Tara stood and showed Mr. Patton to the door. Mr. Patton gave the puppies some room as he backed away towards the door.

"Those are some big puppies," he said nervously.

Tara laughed. She knew he was not a fan of dogs like his parents.

Tara waved as he jogged down the stairs.

"See you later," she said and then turned and closed the door. It was weird seeing cars. She was used to horses and many kinds of carts or carriages. She shook her head.

Ryan came into the entryway. "This place is nice."

Tara turned around and smiled. "Thanks."

"The puppies are sleeping."

"Oh good, they needed a nap."

"I told Ettrick to keep an eye out for them," Ryan said and then held out some heart-shaped tablets. Tara chuckled.

"All these years it was Ettrick who made and left me these, and I never knew."

Tara smiled and took a piece of the buttery sweets. "Good ol' Ettrick," she said, grabbing some and putting it in her mouth. "Let me show you around."

"Will Ettrick stay here and keep an eye on the place, I mean besides your lawyer?" Ryan asked.

"Hmm, yes. He needs to take care of the pups, right? However, he will also go to Scotland when I move in with Uncle Arland."

"Of course," Ryan said as they walked around.

"It's quiet here." He picked up a framed picture off of the fireplace mantle.

"That's me and my parents," Tara told him. "We had gone to Maine that summer."

Ryan smiled. "You looked very happy."

"Yeah," she said, taking the picture and placing it back on the mantle. Her smile faded as she stared at it. She missed them. So much had happened and now she had more family to get to know. Moving to Scotland would be nice, but also hard for her. She would get her father's old room because he had lived with Uncle Arland for a while before coming to the states.

When she opened the French doors to go outside, Ryan gaped at the pool. "You have a pool."

"Yeah, it's heated, and we have that changing shed over there." She pointed and Ryan smiled. "What, you want to go swimming?" She asked. Ryan nodded, with a huge grin on his face.

"Okay, let's finish the tour first."

"Sure," he said taking her hand as they walked back inside.

Ryan was walking slightly behind her as they went up the stairway. A few times she saw him glance out of one of the huge windows that followed them up the stairs, and she would look out as well. She had almost forgotten what it was like here. She briefly went into her parents' room, and it felt lonely. Tara had no idea what to do with the room now that they were gone, or with the estate. She sighed heavily as Ryan came in.

"This was your parents' room, wasn't it?"

Tara turned to look at him, and as he moved closer, she wrapped her arms around his waist. He wrapped his around her back. "I'm sorry Tara, losing someone is never easy."

"Come here." Tara pulled away, taking Ryan's hand. She led him down the hall, into her room, and then over to the window. She pulled aside the sheer curtains, letting in more light. "That's where I saw her. The Banshee." She paused, remembering that awful night. It seemed a lifetime ago. She had wondered were the Banshee had gone but never asked.

Ryan looked in the direction she was pointing. "That must have been scary for you."

Tara opened the window to let in some fresh air. She leaned forward onto the window sill. "She just faded into the trees after –" Her voice cut off. She couldn't relive it.

"That's when my life changed forever."

"Do you wish they had never died? That you never found out who you really are, and never went to the Higher Realms?"

She looked at him as she stood. "What, and miss all the fun? I do wish my parents were alive, I always will. But they aren't, and I have a new family to think about. Also, I have you." She smiled.

"So, are you keeping this Estate?"

"For now, why?"

"Just curious. I mean, with Alana gone, and your uncle in Scotland I just –" she walked away from him.

"There's also coming back. With me. To the Higher Realms."

Tara sighed heavily, causing her back to slump forward. She did not want to sell the estate. It was the last place she and her parents had lived. Although she knew if Uncle Arland could persuade her to sell she probably would. She knew at least for a little while she had to go to Scotland. Besides, her cousin Mary would not stop texting her.

"I will talk to my uncle about it, okay?"

Ryan smiled. "Of course."

"Have you ever been on a plane?"

"No. I haven't."

"Want to come with me?" she asked, raising her eyebrows hopefully.

"First let's go swimming," he said as Tara burst out laughing. She then took a deep breath, smiled and poked her finger into his chest. "Well, young Lord McMahon, you are in for an adventure."

ABOUT THE AUTHOR

Patricia J Ricks lives in Colorado with her family, and loves to eat chocolate while writing.